Spirited Away

Spirited Away

LAST ALLIED POWS ON
CRETE DECEMBER, 1941

―∽―

Anthony W Buirchell

Copyright © 2024

The moral right of the Author of the work has been asserted by them in accordance with the Copyright, Designs and Patents Act 1988. All rights reserved. No part of this book may be used or reproduced by any means, graphic, electronic or mechanical including photocopying, recording, taping or by any information storage retrieval system without the written permission of the publisher except in the case of brief quotations embodied in critical articles and reviews.

The novel is an historical fiction takes place in the past and centres a plot on accurate details of the time in which it takes place. Historical fiction relies on real- life history to propel a novel or story's details and plot. The Authors have used historical fiction to retell a historical event while changing minor details. The fiction often involves traditions and customs of previous periods, and it can include actual historical figures and settings."

A catalogue record for this book is available from the National Library of Australia

A catalogue records is available from the National Library of Australia.

Creator: Anthony William Buirchell

Title: Spirited Away

Target Audience: Youth and adults.

Printed and Channel Distribution

Publishing Consultants "Pickawoowoo Publishing Group"

Publisher

Cric Croc Enterprises, www.criccroc.com.au

For enquiries, write to: rights and permissions via publisher.

Lightning Source/ Ingram Aus.

Artist: Cover designed by Laila Savolainen

ISBN 9780975623015 (paperback)
ISBN 9780975623039 (hardback)
ISBN 9780995424395 (e-book)

Contents

Acknowledgements · 1
Introduction · 13

Chapter 1 · 30
Chapter 2 · 37
Chapter 3 · 47
Chapter 4 · 54
Chapter 5 · 60
Chapter 6 · 66
Chapter 7 · 71
Chapter 8 · 74
Chapter 9 · 82
Chapter 10 · 88
Chapter 11 · 96
Chapter 12 ·105
Chapter 13 ·115
Chapter 14 ·121
Chapter 15 ·130
Chapter 16 ·133
Chapter 17 ·157
Chapter 18 ·184
Chapter 19 · 220

Chapter 20	254
Chapter 21	283
Chapter 22	290
Chapter 23	298
Chapter 24	304
Profiles	307
Notes	383
Bibliography	427
Index	432
Abbreviations	462
About the Author	463

Acknowledgements

When a historical event is discovered eight decades after the fact, the characters involved are likely no longer with us. The writer will keep to the facts as they emerge, but the personal narratives will be his prerogative.

This is a historical fiction that evolves continuously, leaving researchers and writers constantly overriding each other. The facts were placed in chronological order but this didn't fit with the numerous personal stories.[1] The overall story was one of surprise and frustration, from a pair of shorts through to the recruitment activities. Through determination and persistence, the story slowly offered up the men, places and activities.

"Historical fiction takes place in the past and centres a plot on accurate details of the time it took place. Historical fiction relies on real-life events to propel a story's details and plot. Authors commonly use historical fiction to retell an event while changing minor details, like characters' names or the event settings. The fiction often involves traditions and customs of previous periods, and it can include actual historical figures and settings."

New Zealand researcher Andrew Jones (not his real name) chanced upon a pair of shorts in a box stowed in a cupboard. He lived in Christchurch, and the signatures on these opened up a journey.

With persistence, he followed the prisoners of war on Crete and the last ones to Tymbakion, the German guards and the local Cretans of Tympaki, unearthing numerous facts of the period 1939 to 1941. His methodical approach revealed a part of history hidden by time and previously unknown.

The historical events before the Second World War broke out set a tranquil scene, a complete contrast to the events each soldier was confronted with after joining their respective country's armies.

As they carried out their orders, they were flung into mind altering actions. For each of the 151 identified soldiers who ended up at Tymbakion, it was not the physical deeds that shocked them most but rather the mental torment of realising what their actions did to the local population. The Lustre Force's [2] men, without any experience and with limited training were flung into two brutal and bloody battles.

Over the space of five weeks, Lustre Force's men fought heroically in Greece and Crete but were overwhelmed on both occasions. They withdrew from place after place as Germany's well-trained and technologically superior war machine pushed them hundreds of miles.

Then, to add to the shock of war at its most ferocious, they watched, with limited weapons, as thousands of German parachutists descended from the sky.

The final humiliation was being ordered to surrender and knowing they were going behind the wire left a sour taste in everyone's mouth.

To the small group of prisoners of war at Tymbakion Transit Camp V, who grubbed out thousands of olive trees, it didn't automatically trigger thoughts about the owners of these olive groves.

The future shock and feeling of guilt was to find that the Cretan people of Tympaki were having their orchards, houses, families, livelihoods and futures decimated.

This story is eight decades in the making but must be told on behalf of the Tympaki people and the 151 men who toiled, grubbing thousands of olive trees.

The very people who were so considerate and kind to the Allied prisoners were being ruined by the very people they were doing everything they could to keep alive.

Between April 1941 and January 1942 very little had been written in the army records about each individual's life and experiences on Greece and Crete. This period saw the formation of Lustre Force that was put together at the request of the British Prime Minister to defend the northern border of Greece against the German Army.

The men were confronted with the Nazi soldiers and even though they fought fiercely they were overwhelmed. The result was a withdrawal from Greece and an escape to Crete.

The turmoil of the period left little time for individual records to be kept up to date.

It was left to survivors to write diaries, letters and cards to loved ones describing the fighting and the conditions they fought under. They also talked about the years after Crete when most men were incarcerated in German stalags.

There is now insurmountable evidence throughout this book that says that the 151 POWs were the last to leave Crete.

There was a belief that the last prisoners of war were cleared from Crete by the end of September.

There have been three remarkable events that gave the story of what happened to a small group of prisoners of war full credence.

The thorough research and recollections of stories told to others assisted in following the Tymbakion 151 group around Crete and working for the Germans on a secret project on the south side of the island.

Most remarkably was the discovery of copy of Victor Petersen's[3] Diary that enabled the researchers to verify events and people. The information Vic wrote is accurate. His diary covered life on Crete from June 6, 1941, to December 31, 1941, and life at Tymbakion Prisoner of War Camp V.

The researchers also combed the countries of Australia, New Zealand and Great Britain for other relatives to the signatories on the shorts and gather more information. This enabled them to corroborate events in the diary.

The most intriguing occurrence that came to the fore was in 2018, when the Deputy Chancellor of Germany issued an apology to the Tympaki Martyr Villages, but he did not mention the Allied Prisoners of War at Tymbakion. It seemed like he was implying that the destruction of Tympaki and the use of forced local labour happened after February 15, 1942, and thus was not happening at the same time as the presence of the Allied prisoners there.

It became evident, those who left the biggest footprints gave the most depth to the story. The 21 profiles of soldiers investigated mirrored the entire overall movement of the 151 troops. The researchers were able to follow each soldier from home through Greece to the island of Crete.

One may then ask, why is it then we haven't heard about this group of 151 and its remarkable narrative?

Secrecy and isolation would be the two main reasons.

Every man who filled in the Liberated Prisoner of War Questionnaire[4] noted a security or secrecy undertaking that said:

"I fully realise that all information relating to matters covered by questions in Part II are highly secret and official. I had it explained to me and fully understand that under Defence Regulations or U.S.A.R. 380-5, I am forbidden to publish or communicate any information concerning these matters."

The isolation of the area where 151 was held from September 12, 1941, until December 29, 1941, kept everyone hidden from the World. Communication was so minimal that few anywhere ever heard of the place called Tymbakion.

A final thought comes back to record keeping. These men did not have anyone to update their records throughout their experiences from the day they sailed from Alexandria under the code Lustre Force. It was as though they were spirited away never to be seen again.

The story was uncovered after Andrew found the shorts in a box in Christchurch, New Zealand, in 2019. Once he could connect with at least one of the signatory's family, the story began to open up.

No original prisoners remained alive over time, but the diaries and stories shared and left behind were invaluable. These men kept diaries or were interviewed shortly after being discharged from the army. Some shared their recollections with family members.

The discovery of individual's UK (United Kingdom) and Allied Countries, World War II Liberated Prisoner of War Questionnaires, 1945-1946, offered commentary from the grave.

The story can be revealed because these men ended up on Crete during the invasion and the aftermath.

These soldiers, as custodians of the information, have played a crucial role in unveiling the existence and experiences of the missing group.

Never before has there been such extensive reporting of the German covert project at Tymbakion. The soldiers' stories are very similar, with the general trend being joining the army, home training, being shipped to the Middle East, gathering at Alexandria, the Greek War, the invasion of Crete, capitulation, prisoners of war, and being shipped to Salonika before being transported in crowded cattle wagons to a German stalag. Three researchers spent thousands of hours finding relatives of these men and writing comprehensive profiles of each.

As the experiences of each vary, the author accepts the responsibility of adding to what may have been happening. For example, the men were involved in cutting down olive trees. This can be done in numerous ways and with comments from those nearby. Bonnie Buirchell was a local log-chopping champion at home in Australia, and so the author has him showing his prowess to his mates in the olive grove. He may have done this exactly as described or never shown this part of his skills. The author determined that he carried out the activity to invigorate the story.

Special thanks to Vic Petersen and his family, and special commendations to Sue and Grant Petersen for the use of Vic's diary. The information in this diary was the only one that made direct reference to Tymbakion.[5]

From June 6, Vic wrote notes on scraps of paper about his daily activities.

In May 1945, he returned home to Western Australia with over 1400 pieces of paper. His daughter-in-law typed these chronologically so those interested could read about Vic's escapades. Vic's painstaking work in writing and keeping the scraps of paper together and his daughter-in-law's typing of those in an easy-to-read form is acknowledged.

"The other member of the 151 men essential to the story was New Zealander, Private Albert Chamberlain, service number 14242. Albert came up with the idea of making a pair of shorts out of tent canvas.

He persisted in getting as many men as possible to sign the shorts. Albert moved amongst the Tymbakion POWs seeking signatures and collected over 122. He numbered each tent[6] and by visiting one or two every evening he was able to get almost all the men's signatures. He then took charge of the shorts and nursed them in Stalag VIII-B. In this prison, three more signatures were added. The final count was 125 signatures, and the shorts were taken back to New Zealand.

Albert became the custodian of the shorts and it was through the names scribed all over them that Andrew could find the families of signatories and, in some instances, learn more about the person and his wartime experiences.

On the belt of the shorts was a title that read, "Prisoner of War Tymbakion Transit Camp Crete 1st June 1941." The 125 signatures all over the shorts were from British, Australian and New Zealand soldiers. This includes two Greek and one Ceylonese names who were also on the shorts.[7]

These men were eventually found to be in the last group of prisoners to be taken off Crete and sent to Germany. It became evident that they were never recognised as the final group. In fact, many were not acknowledged for their bravery and harsh treatment.

No soldier received any recognition in the wind-swept area of Tymbakion on the southern coast of Crete.

The researchers looked for information about the men whose names were on the shorts. Andrew's main objective was to locate relatives of New Zealand and British soldiers. Once in touch he looked to uncover diaries and other written material.

He sought anyone who left footprints on Crete, especially Tymbakion, between September 12, 1941, and December 29, 1941.

Among the Australians, he found William (Bonnie) Roy Buirchell, WX 2280, from Kojonup, Western Australia. The signalman was one of the forgotten ones. Surprisingly, he left no footprints while on Crete, but he did impact the story of Tymbakion.

Another Australian soldier, Ian Hardie,[8] wrote articles about his war experiences and the conditions the men were fighting under. Many of these were published in local newspapers. These stories informed loved ones back home, bringing comfort in many ways. He also wrote a diary that contained an interesting article about how a deadly incident ended with enemies becoming friends.

8

Andrew discovered Bonnie's son, Anthony, and they became close. An amazing story that needed to be told based on solid evidence emerged. Hearing of the story and Bonnie's dignity and cunning in the face of adversity shocked the family.

His story emerged and followed the infrequent stories he told different members of his family and friends.

Interestingly, few believed his version, but the evidence is clear now that he was 'loose' on Crete for three months before he was incarcerated in Tymbakion Transit Camp V in the autumn of 1941.

The natural leader among the Tymbakion men was an Australian, Captain Walter Holt NX, 12348, a civilian doctor from Sydney. The Germans nominated him as the 'man of confidence' and an unofficial leader at the camp. Other writers presented facts that gave credence to his story.

Private Ray Powell, NX1114, from New South Wales shared his story through his son-in-law and family. Their recall of stories Ray shared with them was invaluable. Ray was one of the few who described the sinking of the *Costa Rica* near Souda Bay in Crete.

Two men's footprints and deeds were far above what was expected of a soldier. Their influence in keeping the captured Allies alive borders on heroism. Neither signed the shorts nor were they at Tymbakion at any time.

Alfred Traub was an Australian soldier, service number WX 858. He was a private in the 2/11th Battalion and fluent in English and Yiddish.

Lieutenant-Colonel Leslie Le Souef, a field doctor whose medical skills saved many injured and sick soldiers, was the second special soldier.

Alf Traub was responsible for standing up to the German commandant on Crete when the latter threatened to execute many Allies in retaliation for the alleged murder of his troops by use of non-military weapons. Alf did not suffer fools when dealing with the enemy or his troops.

Further, he remained behind, looking after the badly wounded while all others dashed for Sfakia and what they hoped was freedom.

Leslie Le Souef was a man larger than life. He wrote his own book, *To War Without a Gun*, which detailed the medical aspect of the war and helped this author write about these areas. He was not a signatory on the shorts but did wonderful work keeping many Allies alive. He is remembered with gratitude by those who crossed his path in prisoner-of-war camps.

A thank you to Kristal Mallon, the step-granddaughter of Private Bernard Mitchell, Service Number 4973574, a British soldier, 1st Sherwood Foresters, Nottinghamshire and Derbyshire, who uncovered all of Bernard's war stories and mementos.[9]

Finally, a recognition of others who kept the researchers and author on the track to Tymbakion. Private William Taylor, AIF, WX 206 [10] kept a personal diary; Wes Olson's book *Battalion into Battle*[11] contained interviews and published stories about soldiers of the 2/11th on Crete. J. J. Donovan, who wrote the newspaper article about sailing from Alexandria across the Mediterranean Sea to Athens and beyond, that was found in Trove,[12] and Molly Watt, writer of the book *The Stunned and the Stymied*, Westralian Publishers, 1996.[13]

The chance to find a diary written by Private Vic Petersen, WX 585 set the course for discovering Tymbakion and a secret project. Tymbakion was to become a life behind the wire for a group of Allies who were the last men to leave Crete.

Other information comes from a search of records from various agencies scattered throughout Australia, New Zealand and Britain.

Red Cross cards in the University of Melbourne digital archive.

AIF casualty cards in digital archives Aust War Memorial.

POW Repatriation Forms in UK National Archives in Kew.

The researchers are in debt to Philip, who was the contact in Britain for information from the National Archives.

The search engines [14] have made researching so much easier.

Virtual War Memorial; see https://vwma.org.au

Forces War Records by Ancestry; www.ancestry.com.au

General Questionnaire for British/American POWs of war;

www.discovery.nationalarchives.gov.uk

Cenotaph found online at www.aucklandmuseum.com

www.powmemorialballarat.com.au

www.awm.gov.au

In researching the Australian Army, the records for every individual are found online at www.naa.gov.au/servicerecords.

The threads of history are multitudinous;
as each is found, they must be followed and
gathered together to find the truth of what happened.

Introduction

A pair of forgotten shorts sitting in a box in a wardrobe.

These shorts became the source of a story about what happened in 1941 on Crete during the Second World War. The last of the incarcerated prisoners of war to remain on Crete numbered a mere 151. It seems the Allies did not know a group of 151 existed on the southern side of Crete from September 12, 1941 to December 29, 1941.

Who were these men? Who chose them and what criteria did they use? Where were the men located? What were they required to do over the three months they were missing? These questions and many others were often asked.

The men were spirited away to an isolated place on the south coast. They came to describe their work party as grubbing out trees as part of a German covert project. They reluctantly became involved in the work, and when the truth was revealed, the men rebelled only to be told to work or be shot.

A pair of shorts, but not an ordinary pair of shorts.

The shorts were made of tent canvas, and the near-perfect stitching showed that a skilful tailor made them.

They were well-preserved and looked as though they had never been worn. The shorts were believed to have been made by Albert Chamberlain,[1] a tailor.

—ϾϾ—

The shorts were found in Christchurch, New Zealand.

Private Albert Edward Chamberlain, a soldier in the New Zealand Expeditionary Force, was also responsible for encouraging others to sign the shorts and he looked after them during his time in Stalag VIII-B and brought them back to New Zealand.

The intriguing thing about the shorts was that there were 125 signatures written on them, front and back. [2]

The finding of a box in which there was a pair of shorts made of canvas with 125 signatures on them became a researcher's treasure trove.

—ϾϾ—

It led to the search to know more about the men who had signed the shorts, allowing information to be divulged that had never before been shared. The 151 men involved had been sworn to secrecy and warned that any leaks would result in the entire group being punished with their lives.

—ϾϾ—

However, the shorts are a partial red herring in that not all men on the shorts were at Tymbakion, and not all men at Tymbakion signed the shorts.

Nonetheless, by attempting to contact the families of the men who signed the shorts, a Tymbakion story has emerged.

A breakthrough came when the family of Vic Petersen shared his POW diary. Vic was at Tymbakion POW camp from its inception to its closing, and to date, provides the only first-hand account of this camp.

The second breakthrough was the family of Richard Lechmere, T/203874, sharing letters he wrote home to his wife and daughter in Britain from the Tymbakion camp. Whilst they paint a rosy picture of life, they also provide some corroboration of information gleaned elsewhere.

The third breakthrough was the family of New Zealander Jimmy Craig, 34623, sharing some information that likely came from an address book belonging to Arthur Lawrence.

After a scary trip from Souda Bay to Iraklion on the ship, Norburg, the final 200 Allied POWs arrived in the vicinity of Heraklion. The German guards considered these men to be the last of the Allied POWs and they were to be sent on to Germany once they completed a vital project on Crete.

At Heraklion, the group was split, with 168 taken south over the mountains and 32 left behind.

Around 5 p.m. on September 12, 1941, the larger group arrived at a compound enclosed by a pre-existing 7-8 foot (2.1m—2.4m) high barbed wire fence. They pitched tents and sourced water from a drain, indicating that there was little other infrastructure.

Vic talks of walking three miles from the camp to work at the Tymbakion airfield site, but the exact location of this camp is still obscured. The Germans insisted that the men's goal was to clear groves of olive trees to prepare the area for planting grape cuttings.

However, it didn't take long for the prisoners to ascertain that the primary objective was to clear olive trees to create a flat runway for an airfield.

The men were well aware and protested that the work they were being made to undertake contravened the Geneva Convention. As Vic wrote on November 15, 1941:

"…. again, working on the airfield, under protest, and threatening to shoot ten men if we refuse to work, and of course, men with rifles prevailed."

Whilst evidence is hard to find, it is likely the British had created a rudimentary runway there prior to the German invasion, but the Germans recognised its strategic importance and dramatically expanded this. Vic talks of planes landing within two weeks of the work starting.

On the belt of the shorts was an enigmatic handwritten label: 'Prisoner of War Tymbakion Camp Crete 1st June 1941'. The mystery slowly unravelled when Andrew [3] chanced upon one name that linked the story to a signatory on the shorts.

By researching all the soldiers on the shorts and their war experiences, Andrew was led to an intriguing story that the Germans wanted kept from prying eyes.

Andrew's diligent search led to Albert Edward Chamberlain, who was a civilian master tailor. Although his signature did not appear on the shorts, Bert (as his mates called him) was a garment maker and his name came up in relation to several of the signatories.

Andrew's observations and thoughts determined that the shorts were handmade by a tailor from tent canvas [4] so it's likely Bert made them himself while at war.

The inscription at the top seemed to place them being made on Crete during the Second World War.

The back and front of the shorts were scattered with the signatures of Australians, British, and New Zealanders. Oddly, two Greek men and one Ceylonese had also signed the shorts.

—⋙—

While awaiting and hoping for a reply from those relatives contacted online, Andrew continued to flesh out other clues about the shorts. An inscription at the top read: "Tymbakion Prisoner of War Camp, Crete 1 June 1941".

He had never heard the name Tymbakion before but found out it was an area in the south of Crete.

Andrew's initial transcription and research garnered information of limited interest. He wrote that most Australians and English on the shorts were assigned POW numbers in the range 45XX, so he thought they were all processed together and that the shorts were signed at this time.[5]

Andrew's theory was that the pair of shorts were made when Albert was a prisoner between Souda Bay and Tymbakion. As a prisoner of war at Stalag VIII-B, he kept the shorts in immaculate condition. After three years of incarceration, he brought them back to New Zealand and placed them in a box at his home. When found, they were still in perfect condition.

Vic Petersen's diary mentions men making canvas clothes at Souda Bay and again at Tymbakion. Either place could be the production centre, but the author chose the latter.

The discovery of the shorts started an Australia-Crete-England-New Zealand research project. This brings the ANZAC connection into play. The shorts had the potential to connect a time and place that might have changed Bert's life, as well as the lives of all the other men.

Andrew began reconciling people from the shorts with their recorded names on the POW list at Stalag VIII-B located in Lamsdorf.[6] He found a few, and the first breakthrough was when the family of Vic Petersen shared his war diary.

The second one for him was the family of James (Jimmy) Craig sharing some information that likely came from Arthur Lawrence's address book. The third one sent chills down his spine. Howard Holmes's recollection (also on the shorts and a New Zealander) talks not just about their capture in Crete but also about Bert Chamberlain. This is the first record Andrew has of Bert at Lamsdorf.

Bert likely participated in the 'Long March' [7] because he arrived in France in May 1945 and returned home to Westport, New Zealand, after the war.

He joined the ex-POW association, the Royal New Zealand Returned and Services Association [8] but was not very welcomed. He never claimed his medals.

Andrew did not want to glorify this time or this war, he was keen to understand this period in history. To Andrew's knowledge, Albert never talked about his war experience. He returned to civic life as a tailor and died in 1973.

After finding the shorts and deciphering most of the names, Andrew attempted to contact the family of a signee whose name was William Roy Buirchell (he went by his nickname Bonnie).

Andrew went searching for a relation on Facebook. He chanced upon Anthony Buirchell, the man's son, who lived in Perth and was an author of Children's books. His patience finally got him a contact from West Australia. He sent a message to Anthony.

"I am Andrew, and my story with the shorts started during 'Covid Lockdown 2020'. There was only so much work I could do from home, so I started delving into the history of Albert Chamberlain, the owner of the shorts I was aware that he had been a prisoner in Stalag VIII-B in the Second World War, but the details were lacking substance. I set out to research his online records, but they were limited.

"A conversation with people in the know, revealed that a box of Bert's things still existed. It took a while to find the box that has moved between houses but never opened, but once found it was full of treasured memorabilia. It contained Albert's paybook, his Kreta [9] POW tags, some papers, and a pair of shorts. The shorts are made from canvas. Bert was a tailor, so he likely made them himself at war."

As perchance, Anthony and his partner, Deborah Johnson, live in Perth, Western Australia. Both are keen researchers and took up the challenge to find out where the shorts would lead them. They undertook research on the Australians, while Andrew searched for the British and New Zealand signatories.[10]

The research team grew to three, and their research found a lot about some of the men and very little about others. The lack of information was caused by the time elapsed since the shorts were made and signed. The passing of all of the men who signed the shorts had taken its toll, and records for the period were scant.

Andrew left the story open, saying, "At this stage, I don't know where the shorts will take me. My intention is to reach out and listen to the stories of each of the men." [11] Andrew's hope was the information unearthed would be formed into a narrative that would tell a story about the men before and after this point in time, the shorts being a focal point. It became a bigger project than imagined and resulted in discovering what had happened to those men who were spirited away to Tymbakion in the period September 12, 1941, and December 29, 1941.

The three researchers were surprised that the men had seemingly been selected to participate in a covert German operation.

The shorts with the 125 signatures are below. The first photograph is the front of the shorts and the second is the back.

On the shorts was William Roy Buirchell's signature and his service number. This signature was the one that reached out to a relative and started the search for all the others.

The research led to further links and eventually to an area in Crete called Tymbakion.

It was here in September 1941 that all 122 men plus 29 others were incarcerated in a prisoner of war transit camp to grub out literally thousands of ancient olive trees in preparation for an airfield.

This huge area that was surrounded by barbed wire was to be turned into a massive German airfield.

One of the earliest identifications was William Roy Buirchell. As the story progressed, the story behind the soldier was revealed.

Soldiers Albert Edward Chamberlain and William Roy Buirchell were ordinary folk but played a major role in the mystery of the shorts and signatures. By following the story of these two and a handful of others the overall mystery came to light.

The other men are from Britain, Australia and New Zealand, and are referred to as the Allies. The snippets of information from these men relate to a story about the last prisoners of war to leave Crete in 1941.

The comparison of life before and after the Second World War reflects the changes that can occur due to trauma and deprivation. Training to be a soldier and the wartime experiences of these,

—⚍—

The Greek and Crete Wars were short and vicious and the area they were fought in was far and wide (from the northern border of Greece, across the archipelago, over the Mediterranean Sea and on the island of Crete through to Sfakia). From the surrender of the Allies, only 52 days transpired. Within that time fierce and bloody action took place in barely 15 days. There were men being moved by the thousands to the battlefields, men retreating in disarray, seeking ships to escape from the ferocity of the onslaught and the airborne invasion of Crete resulting in capitulation at the southern coast of Crete. The entire conflict saw action over a short time, but for the men caught up, it was chaotic and devastating. To describe events and to follow individuals as they fought, retreated and surrendered will be, as the Australians would say, "Like a dog's breakfast".

The uniqueness faced by a small band of men left them mentally and physically scarred. [12] No one acknowledged their sacrifices nor the life they were forced to live, firstly in a chaotic and war-riddled Greece, then Crete. This was followed by incarceration in a POW camp then another four months in isolation where hope was limited and communication with their loved ones almost unknown. [13]

They had no clues as to their end game. They had heard about the shocking German policy of reprisal. It was said that dozens of Cretans were lined up and machine-gunned.

Then maybe they could be taken away to languish for years in a German stalag.

It was the local population who suffered the most. Starting from a reasonably contented life, they ended up being stripped by the Germans of their physical possessions and their families torn apart.

They kept offering to help the Allies and to befriend them, all the while knowing these same people were being forced to decimate their farms and residences.

They steadfastly kept their dignity and their faith in God but the reality was they lost almost everything, especially those living in the township of Tympaki.

It became clear that individual experiences reflected the lives of other prisoners of war of others. The groups' experiences would sometimes mirror those of the whole 151 men. This journey allows the whole story to be told using only the few who took the opportunity to tell their life stories to researchers after the war or who were willing to keep diaries of their wartime experiences.

A viewing of the men's prisoner-of-war records suggested they were all 'processed' together.

The shorts appear to have been signed during the men's stay on Crete. This would place the shorts as being made and signed between June 1941 and December 1941.

Andrew left the story open by saying that at this stage, "I don't know where any of this will lead us but it stirs the researcher in me to want to know who these men were and their life stories. I'm reaching out and listening to stories (mainly from relatives).

"I'm not a writer, so don't know if there is a story here."

The shorts photographed front and back were the brain wave of Private Albert Chamberlain.

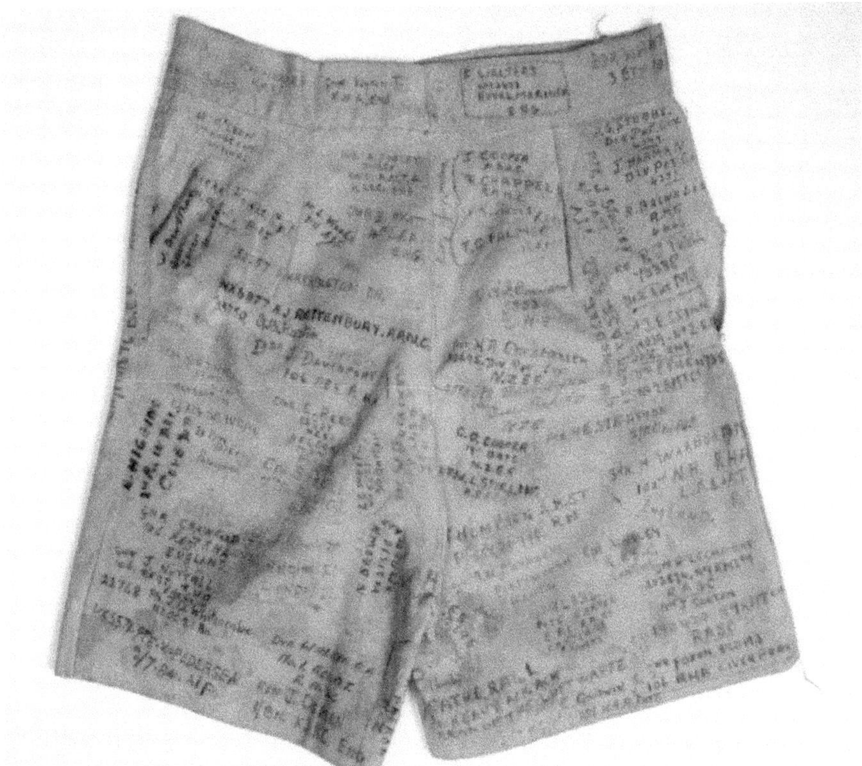

Many men who participated in the Second World War were either toddlers or had not been born when the First World War was fought in Europe. Men from the British Empire volunteered and were shipped to France, Belgium and Turkey. The signing of the Treaty of Versailles ended the state of war on June 28, 1919, between Germany and the Allies.

As the children were born or grew up during the 20s and 30s, they did not hear much about the brutalities of World War I and the atrocious conditions it was fought under.

The returned men remained 'mum', so the deep-seated disgust regarding wars was forgotten. From another angle, these youngsters were given plentiful examples of the returned soldiers as heroes.

The RSL, or Returned Soldiers League, was important to the now retired soldiers and many flocked to the halls and parties that were held by the branches. Even more important was the fact that the mothers and grandmothers looked upon their men as heroes who fought and won peace for the world and freedom for each individual. The returning soldiers were placed literally on a pedestal.

Every year, on April 25th, in Australia and New Zealand, there is a huge local celebration called Anzac Day. The men march along the main roads in every town towards the RSL Honour Board. Here a former officer would read out the names of those who gave the supreme sacrifice. The words, 'We will remember them', echoed from the halls to the outside crowd full of boys and young men. Every youngster would feel the cold but exciting shiver run up their spine. Many a tear was shed for those who did not come home.

Using the same profiling criteria as used for Albert Chamberlain and William Buirchell, it was possible to follow how some of the others in the 151 strong group enjoyed life pre-war.

The Great Depression, 1929 to 1935, decimated countries' economies and left millions seeking jobs. As it came to an end, people were left with few assets and little in savings. However, by the late 1930s, the work horizon had a brighter outlook. Albert, a tailor living in New Zealand, would have been diligent in his business, which kept him busy day and even night.

As a shearer in Australia, Bonnie was also busy rushing with his team from one farm or station to another.

Like most men of the era, Albert and Bonnie were happy with their lives and the people they associated with after the Great War. Their lives were full of freedom and hard work.

They participated in most of the activities offered in their townships.

Bonnie was fully into sports, such as Aussie Rules Football, cricket, and tennis. He had a girl whom he thought likely to marry and went to dances with.

New Zealand is the land of the long white cloud, with the most inspiring scenery in the world. It consists of two main islands, North and South.

The north is mostly warm, and greenery covers the ground. The south is cold and mountainous and can often be snow-bound.

The indigenous people are the Maoris, and up until 1642 lived in isolation unknown to the 'civilised' world. They lived in tribal groups and fought fiercely amongst themselves. Abel Tasman [14] and his crew found the Maoris were an unwelcoming lot who had tattoos all over their bodies and brandished stone-age weapons and made blood-curdling war cries. One of these was called the Haka.[15]

Tasman was not given a welcome when he sailed into Golden Bay. Fearing the unknown, the Maoris put to sea in canoes, and as the boats of Tasman and the Maoris came close, one rammed the other, and four Dutchmen were clubbed to death. The other Dutch sailors opened fire and a musket ball hit a Maori. The place of the incident was named Murderers' Bay.

More than a century later, an English explorer, Captain James Cook arrived on his ship, the Endeavour. He clashed with the Maoris, and one of them was killed. Clashes continued with Cook and his crew while he sailed around the islands. Cook did try to befriend the Maoris but had limited success.

The profiles of New Zealanders Albert Chamberlain and Howard Holmes were compiled by researchers from several sources, including diaries and family members. There was one Maori with a clear profile and a story to tell, and he will be mentioned to show these men's differing experiences. Ponuate Busby from the 28th Maori Battalion had a unique experience.

Only a handful of profiles could be developed to the point that their story was known enough to be placed in the book at the appropriate place.

It is an intriguing true story that will leave you wondering how the people of Crete could be so magnanimous and altruistic while their world collapsed around them. [16] The answer has been lying in a cupboard for eight decades, waiting for heroes to be recognised and shocking experiences exposed.

CHAPTER 1

—ɯ—

Up until September 20, 1941, there was a determined push by the Germans to transport all prisoners still on Crete to the mainland and then onwards to German stalags.[1] The Nazis took anyone who was capable of holding a rifle. The fallback of this was a lack of labourers in the industries these conscripted soldiers had come from. To cover these workers, the Germans wanted to use the POWs who were languishing in prisons throughout Europe and North Africa.

During the month of September 1941, a small group of men were spirited away to a windswept beach on the south coast of Crete. Who they were and why they were sent there is part of the story that will be exposed. What made the Germans select these particular soldiers and what happened to them over a four-month period?[2]

They set up camp at Tymbakion, a low-lying area where the British had built a small runway for their planes some years before the war. The men lived in tents and were pressed into working long hours with little food, hoeing ancient olive trees out of the rock-hard ground.

Towards the end of 1941, Albert Chamberlain, a New Zealander, formed the idea to have all the men sign a pair of canvas shorts so that all those involved would remember their bonding and their odd experiences.[3]

The end result was considered quite a feat, and Bert was rather pleased, so much so he carried the shorts with him for the rest of his life. As a master tailor Bert would have been engaged in numerous situations where he sewed garments of many types. The following gives a peek at what his day-to-day life and work would have been like before the war.

—⁂—

It was nearly Easter, 1939, and Bert was sitting cross-legged on the bench in his workshop. He was a master tailor of considerable talent and skill.

He was totally engrossed in the garment he was sewing. He had been working on it for two days and it had to be ready tomorrow. At this point in time, he could not be interrupted because this job alone would bring in over £50 [4] for his business. After the pitiful income he managed to scrape up during the Great Depression, Bert was desperate because no one had money to spend on luxury items. He badly needed more jobs on the quality of the article he was working on at that moment.

His hands were calloused from the friction between his skin and the metal of the needles. Even taking the caution of using a leather finger cover that he moved from finger to finger he was not able to completely protect the skin. It took strength and accuracy to keep the needle working along hems. Each stitch had to be exactly the same in length and tension.

Bert was pleased to have a client arrive one day at the shop. He heard the small bell on the front door ring and moved quickly. At the counter he met a young lady who introduced herself as Miss Beatrice Johns. The young lady explained she wanted a special dress made for her up and coming betrothal. She also showed her standing in the community by emphasising that money wasn't an issue.

Miss Johns explained she was getting married and wanted her future in-laws to be proud of her when she walked down the aisle to marry their only son.

Bert showed her through the shop and pointed to the samples he had hanging in the wardrobes and those on the floor. The young lady was pleased with what she was seeing but always had a criticism with each article that was displayed for her.

Bert's trained mind was working overtime, and he was swapping and cutting the best examples as they proceeded around the room. He ushered the bride-to-be into his work room at the back of the shop and, taking the first of three dresses he had draped across his right arm, he pointed out the parts she had indicated she liked. "You mentioned the pleated full-length with a thin waist is that correct?"

"Yes, that's the style I like and it needs a train at the bottom. There needs to be a touch of colour to offset the starkness of the white wedding dress."

"Most certainly, madam," agreed Bert. "That is why I have sample two, as it has the train you pointed to plus the full arm-length of lace."

"Yes, they were two things that caught my eye," said Miss Johns. "It's a pity you didn't have everything I want in the one dress."

"Ah, but madam I will have once I draw the pattern and you are pleased with it. I can take this part and add another and so on until we have your magnificent wedding dress."

Bert took a large piece of brown paper and rolled it out on the table. He picked up a thick lead pencil and a tape measure. He began to draw rapidly and little by little the wedding dress as suggested by the young lady stood out on the paper.

Bert measured the lady's waist, forehead, arm lengths and thicknesses. He did exactly the same with her legs and finally the chest.

"There, I think I have included all the parts of each dress that you thought was to your liking. I have all the measurements I need and I have a goodly idea of your personality. The latter is important as I can make the pattern to fit you and make you feel happy and proud. If you can now look at the samples of material and select the pieces you like, then I can start immediately."

After some time searching the material samples that Bert had, Miss Johns came up with a white satin for the dress and a white lace for the sleeves. The veil was a light silk that would trail down her back. Bert suggested that a posy of yellow would set off the dress just beautifully and complement her luxurious blonde hair.

Bert assured her he could make the dress and have it ready for her to try on and have adjustments finished all in good time. Satisfied with the process she had just been through, Miss Johns returned to the shop and paid a deposit, and after receiving a receipt, she walked out smiling broadly. Bert immediately began turning the pattern he had drawn on the brown paper into a wedding gown.

Two days later the door from the shop to the workroom creaked gently and a woman with long brown hair entered. She was carrying a tray on which there was a white china teapot, a plate with ginger nut cookies, a blue china cup and saucer, a small jug of full cream milk and two lumps of sugar on the saucer. A tea towel with pictures of the birds of New Zealand painted on it was folded neatly on one corner of the tray.

"Is it that time already, Diane?" Bert asked without lifting his head.

"Yes dear," said his wife as she placed the afternoon tea on the table, poured a cup and left as quietly as she had entered.

Bert finished the work he was busy doing. He walked to the table and poured some of the milk into the black tea. He drank his tea and ate his favourite biscuits, the ginger nut cookies.

He walked to the telephone that was hanging on the wall, lifted the handpiece, whirled the little handle and waited. "Could you put me through to the Johns' residence please?" he asked the telephonist. A few seconds and he heard a female voice at the other end, "Hello it's Beatrice."

"Your dress is ready, my dear, come along this afternoon and we'll try it on and make sure it's a perfect fit."

Bert looked at the wedding dress and was impressed with the work he had done. He was sure Miss Johns would also be happy with the beautiful dress. As he stood staring, his mind moved to another thought, and he let it grow as it had occupied him for the past week or so.

Bert had thought long and hard about the couple's future when the war broke out in Europe. He had approached the recruiting officer about joining up and to find out what such a job would entail and the wage. He asked numerous questions, but it was the money that he kept coming back to.

He was always truthful and up front with his wife but this time he baulked at bringing up the idea of joining the army. He was sure she wouldn't be too upset as she had mentioned the need for both of them to work to make the money that would secure their future.

He made the decision to find out more about the types of jobs there were in the army. An approach to the recruitment officer got him a long conversation. The sergeant explained the different sections that Bert could join. As he wasn't keen to be shooting at other people anticipated joining up as a non-combat soldier in the medics, or signals. A regular wage would give them both the financial stability they longed for.

As Bert was replacing the telephone, his wife, Diane, came in carrying a yellow envelope, which she handed to him and said, "The wedding dress for Miss Johns looks adorable; you are just so clever."

Bert took the envelope and tore it open. "It's from the Army. They want me to attend the enlistment office next week. I need to talk to you about joining up so as to earn a regular wage for the next four years.[5]

Diane sidled into a chair and listened intently to her husband's plans. She was fearful but so proud of the way he was handling the delicate subject. She could tell he had investigated the possibilities and made up his mind that he wanted to be in the New Zealand Expeditionary Force to help rid the World of the tyrant, Hitler and bring peace to all. She also could see he was looking for the safest position available.

He had explained all the issues about joining up and was now talking about several of his mates who had signed up. They had completed their six weeks basic training and were being sent overseas to the Middle East.

He watched Diane as he talked expecting her to become upset and refuse to listen to such a ridiculous idea. He finished by explaining that he could take a non-combatant role. [6] To his pleasant surprise Diane was onside almost immediately. The money and the period of four years didn't seem to bother her.

A few days later and Bert was standing in a long, meandering line at the recruitment office, ready to sign up and begin his adventure of a lifetime. He looked around but didn't see anyone he knew. Further back in the line was a small group who were talking loudly and bouncing jokes off each other. They were so relaxed and ready to join and sail for foreign lands. One of the chaps was tall and thin. He seemed to be the person of most interest. Bert did not know who he was but in good time they would run into each other.

CHAPTER 2

William Roy Buirchell was a West Australian and was well known in Kojonup where he lived. He was called Bonnie, a name his mother coined when he was a baby.

His grandfather, George, had been a convict who was sentenced to 10 years transportation for stealing a roast leg of lamb from the kitchen of a landlord in England in 1854. He was sent out on a ship to Fremantle in the same year, and so sealed the Buirchell family's future.

There is a poem that most Australians are familiar with. It describes the country of Australia aptly and was titled "My Country." [1]

"I love a sunburnt country. A land of sweeping plains. Of ragged mountain ranges. Of droughts and flooding rains. I love her far horizons. I love her jewel seas."

There are other things that make the country unique. It is an island continent of isolated cities with a small population. The indigenous peoples have inhabited the island for the past 60,000 years. It has the most diverse scenery, flora and fauna in the world.

European voyagers in their tall ships came during the 1600s and took back home specimens of the wildlife and stories of the barren coastline.

The flora and fauna were like nothing seen anywhere else on the Earth. They sailed from places like Holland, France and Britain. It was the British who settled the east coast after Captain James Cook in his ship the *Endeavour* suggested there could be several places worthy of settlement. Joseph Banks, [2] the botanist on the ship, gathered and drew the birds, animals and plants he came across.

The British Government saw it as a penal settlement and in 1788 sent Captain Arthur Phillip with soldiers and convicts to Sydney Cove.

Australia was a tough country in which to build and make a life. The Gallipoli Campaign in 1914 [3] defined the bravery and toughness of the men who fought against the Turkish Army.

Bonnie grew up with a younger brother called Mick and four sisters. Mick and Bonnie were inseparable and were hunter-gatherers. They would go off hunting with a kangaroo dog and a .22 rifle, each.

The produce of their hunting expeditions kept the family fed. They would spend days camping out under the stars. They would often see the Southern Cross [4] and marvel at its place on the Australian flag. They were dinky-di Aussies and loved the freedom they had to roam far and wide.

By the time the Second World War plunged the world into chaos, Bonnie was a shearer and part-time rabbit trapper. He was also a champion country cricket player and an Australian Rules footballer.[5]

There were many farmers and station managers who engaged a shearer of Bonnie's calibre to shear their flocks. He was clean, fast and diligent and worked without complaint.

The job was physically demanding but paid well. It took time and persistence to be a top shearer. He joined a team and travelled around the huge state of Western Australia.

The work inside the wool shed involved many different tasks, and the team had to work as one to achieve the desired result. The following pre-war tale gives a taste of what Bonnie's life would have been like.

William Roy Buirchell stood at the door of the sheep shed allowing the gentle breeze to waft over him. He wore a long pair of khaki-coloured trousers held up at the waist by a piece of binder twine. [6]

Across the yard, he could see the heat shimmering and the mirages this created. The earth was red, hot and dry, packed solid. The vegetation was spinifex, saltbush and low scrub. [7]

The dirty blue flannelette singlet was saturated with perspiration. He took a piece of material from his pocket and wiped the sweat that kept forming and running down his forehead and into his eyes. His wet, curly red hair made it look like he had just finished showering.

The sheep he was shearing loved to roam free across these huge stations in the Australian outback. They foraged as they walked following their well-beaten tracks to the troughs filled with artesian water from bores hundreds of yards below the surface. Suddenly there was a loud "Ahem" from behind him, and a deep, male voice continued, "Lady in the shed, no swearing!"

Through the doors at the other end came the station owner's wife and two beautifully dressed girls aged about 10 and 12 years old. One had long blonde hair, the other a contrast with short dark hair. All three females carried a wicker basket full of scones, patty cakes without icing, sandwiches with an assortment of fillings and chocolate squares.

A tea towel was folded across the goodies to keep away the pesky flies that always swarmed inside the shed attracted by the dung.

All the sheep with long wool caught a lot of the faeces around their bottoms. These clumps were called dags, and although delicious to the flies, they were deadly to the sheep.

The flies would swarm around the sheep daily, materialising at the first sign of the sun peeping over the horizon and laying eggs inside the dags. The farmer had to be vigilant of any such activities or else the sheep become fly blown.

Four enamel mugs were perched on top of the towel of the basket that the Missus had put food inside.

The smile was ear to ear as she greeted each worker by name. In the Missus's other hand, she carried a bucket in which nestled a large vacuum flask, three smaller vacuum flasks of the same size and a tiny China jug. The larger flask held boiling water with three teaspoons of tea leaves soaking in the water. The small China jug was filled with creamy white milk fresh from the cow that lazed in the home paddock.

"Hey Bonnie, come on over and join the boys. From what I've heard you are about to smash the gun shearer [8] of West Acres Station's total. How about that then?"

On hearing his name, Bonnie started to walk towards the group that had settled around the sorting table. This was his nickname from his mother when she saw him as a happy, bonny little boy. The name stuck and anyone who knew him only knew him as Bonnie.

All the baskets were emptied of their contents, and each member of the shearing team selected a cup for a 'cuppa.' [9] As there were eight men in the shed, the plastic tops of the vacuum flasks were inverted and used as cups.

The chit-chat around the table was subdued and pleasant. This was typical, but in contrast to the loud calls and swearing that went on when only the blokes were on the floor.

"By my calculation, you need seventy-two to equal and seventy-three to be the new champ. You must achieve this by five o'clock this afternoon," said Hector, the team's classer. He was the most important man on the team.

The wool classer sorted the fleeces into categories including length, thickness, quality, colour, strength and cleanliness.

Once he had classed the fleece it was folded and placed in a bale with similarly classed wool. As the bale filled it was compressed by a wool press, and when this was full the bale was marked using a tin stencil with the wool grade and the name of the property that had produced the wool. [10]

Hector knew wool, and by simply taking a piece of wool and stretching it between his fingers he knew what grade it belonged to. Wool classing was very scientific and, on this team, only Hector could do the job efficiently and accurately.

The young fellow at the back of the group was the rouseabout who filled the pens with sheep. He took the shorn fleece to the sorting table and threw it like a blanket so the classer and he could skirt the dags. [11]

He would fold it like a blanket and allow the classer to determine what class the wool belonged to. The rouseabout would sweep the floor and keep the wool shed clean.

At breaks he filled up each shearer's pen with the required number of sheep. He also helped with branding the shorn sheep.

The job he took most seriously was counting the number of each shorn sheep in the shearer's pen. This number was pencilled into the boss's finance book so that he would know how much to pay each shearer at the end of each break. Each break is noted and then added for the total once the entire flock has been shorn. The rouseabout would then let the shorn sheep out into the wide, open spaces of the station.

The Missus walked over to William and said, "Bonnie you will be getting a telephone call from Kojonup at six o'clock in town at the hotel. The news came over the radio [12] twenty minutes ago. A woman by the name of Clem Penny will telephone."

Bonnie grunted and pulled at his pants, a nervous habit he had. "Righto Missus, thanks for the message. Well, you lot we'd better gulp this delicious tea down and finish the goodies so we can dive in to these sheep so I can get to the appointment."

Bonnie had smoothly moved the conversation from himself from being a champion shearer to taking a telephone call. This was typical of his personality.

He never liked to be in the limelight and was quick to change conversations away from any achievement he was applauded for.

The Chevrolet truck kicked up the dust as Bonnie and Brian, one of the other shearers, sped into the small town of Marble Bar. Like all thirsty men and women in Marble Bar they headed for the pub.

The town had a reputation for being the hottest place in Australia. Days on end during summer the temperature would top 45 degrees centigrade. The truck pulled up with a screech outside the Marble Bar Hotel. A glance at his pocket watch told Bonnie he was eleven minutes early. Just enough to swig [13] a schooner of ale and then be ready to hear what Clemmie wanted this time.

This dark haired, young woman had an on again off again relationship with Bonnie. He loved her to bits but she could at times be exasperating, demanding and difficult. He had fathered their daughter to her in 1936 but then Clem's mother had become impossible to talk to. She insisted the two girls were to stay on the farm that she and her husband owned.

It was a sprawling oats and sheep farm on the outskirts of Kojonup. The family loved to brush with the upper crust and often threw parties for those in that category. They said Bonnie was not in their league and insisted he stay away from their daughter.

Bonnie was a loner and an easy going type. He was into sport in a big way. He had trophies from playing the vigorous game of Australian football and was an outstanding cricketer. None of this prowess satisfied Clem's parents, the Pennys, so Bonnie followed the money during the week and played sports at weekends.

He kept well away from the Penny property, Glenlossie, as they had made it abundantly clear he was not welcome, nor were his parents and the rest of his family.

He finished the schooner and asked the barman about an incoming call. "Yes, it is booked for six o'clock. Just wait near the telephone, Mr Buirchell, through to the lounge and the telephone is on the wall. When it rings lift the receiver and talk. If there's a problem just call out."

Bonnie had no sooner reached the telephone than it began to ring. He jumped at the uncanny timing and leant forward, picked up the handle and said, "Hello, Clem. Is that you?"

He couldn't hear anyone speaking so he repeated the question. Again, no reply. He was about to call out for the barman when he realised that he was talking into the earpiece. He swapped the position and repeated the question, then murmured, "Third time lucky, maybe?"

"I've come up with a good idea that will put this silly attitude that my parents have about us being together. I want you to come home now, and we'll get married at the registry office in Katanning."

Bonnie was taken aback with the news and too many things to think about. It was Clem at her finest, straight to the point and not willing to hear anything except the word, yes.

"Are you still there? This will force the whole lot of them to accept that we're legally married and that our daughter has a mother and father and she can live with us. Simple solution to what has been going on now for three years. I have been 21 years old since the beginning of last year so I have every right as an adult to determine my own way in life. I can't see you having objections so let's get on with it. I have the Registry Office booked for Friday, 13th December and my sister Ruby can be my bridesmaid. You can drive us across to Katanning and bring us home. We'll stay with your sister until we find a house. I'll see you Friday morning before 9 am. Bye."

She was gone, and Bonnie was flabbergasted.

He stood still for a moment, thinking and remembering the sheer happiness he had felt in the shearing shed that afternoon when he broke the long-standing gun shearer record.

To celebrate, the shearing team was cheering and clapping and dancing with each other. One of the men grabbed a broom and used that as his dancing partner. It was the feeling of bonding, of camaraderie, that pulled all the people in the team into one.

Would he find that when he reached Kojonup on Friday, or would the daggers still be out for him even more fiercely than ever? He knew and always wanted to marry the girl because he was the father of their child. That had to be made right. As for the other problems they could deal with, or would his life, their lives, be bitter forever? Only time will tell.

He called out to Brian and told him he would have to find a ride back to the station because he was wanted urgently in Kojonup in a couple of days. Brian gave Bonnie the thumbs up meaning he understood.

Bonnie would drive through the night for the trip would take at least 12-14 hours. First stop had to be the petrol station where he had to pump a tank full of petrol from the 44-gallon drum and pay the mechanic.

All set, he took off for his appointment with Clem. As he accelerated along the gravel road it suddenly hit him, "My God I'm getting married how much better can life get?"

CHAPTER 3

—m—

When the Second World War broke out in September 1939 in Europe, the governments of New Zealand, Australia and Britain called for volunteers to go overseas to fight against the scourge of Nazism and Hitler, the mastermind behind the idealism. The young wanted to keep the world free of tyranny, so they flocked to recruitment centres to register. The voyages overseas for these men were all happening sometime in the weeks between December 1939 and February 1941. During these months men could end up in North Africa or the Middle East. The British may have been sent into Europe or the Middle East.

All of these soldiers went through a horrid time during their war experiences. There were several major events that kept throwing fear and dread at the men. The campaign in North Africa was a baptism of fire, where fighting against the Italians taught them to keep their heads down. The introduction of the Germans under General Erwin Rommel[1] upped the ante as he was a clever strategist and won more battles than he lost.

The New Zealanders joined the Second New Zealand Expeditionary Force, Australians filled out their forms and the British rushed the recruitment offices. Each would have had a reason for taking such a monumental step. Discussions, arguments and cold shoulders would have resulted in many estrangements with partners and families. There would have been many who were supported and patted on the back for their bravery.

Regardless of their reasons, they would have all travelled to the training camps to learn all the skills they would need. These would have included drills in marching, using weapons of all types and getting fit. They were taught to dismantle a 303 rifle, put it together in rapid time and to clean and oil the gun. They were also shown how to load a rifle, then lock the bolt, use the moveable sights and shoot accurately.

The less savoury of the skills was bayonet practice and hand-to-hand fighting. To fix a bayonet to their guns and run screaming at a scarecrow made of straw before plunging the sharp blade into the figure, withdraw it and plunge again was not for the faint-hearted.

The most difficult part of training was to change the men from pacificists to fighting and killing machines.

This involved brainwashing so that the flight or fight reactions that humans have been moved to the fight mode. This is done by constantly demonising the enemy, and the enemy was out to kill you so you must be first.

On the other hand, it was important to maintain the belief in mateship and camaraderie. Team building was essential to a well-trained battalion.

Throughout the training instructors would have yelled and screamed their instructions. The reaction from the many men listening to such abuse would have varied greatly. The tough types smiled and yelled back, "Yes sir". The timid would have been mortified and broke into tears. Most of the men would have "grinned and bared it". Whatever the reaction, it showed the diversity of the group, and this will be seen in all occasions that groups or individuals are together. Again, the emphasis is on explaining the repetition that will be evident as the men are followed into battle.

When the training was completed, the men graduated as soldiers ready to fight the Germans and become infantry medics, signalmen, or cooks. They were given an Army number and placed in a particular section of a battalion related to their perceived skills. The medic role was popular as you were out of the fighting but being helpful in looking after the sick and wounded.

After a trip by ship from their respective countries, most soldiers were landed in Palestine in 1940.

The New Zealanders did not appreciate the environment they had been sent to.

Therefore, they were given time to acclimatize to the heat, wind, dryness, sandflies and sand.

The soldiers disembarked in the Middle East and set up camp near local towns. Here they were acclimatized to the desert environment.

The Germans, however, were another matter. Their army had, from all accounts, the most war hardened troops and sophisticated weapons. Their commanding officer in North Africa was General Rommel and his tactics were seen as brilliant.

The recruits kissed their loved ones goodbye and clambered up the gangway. Bent over from the weight of their luggage, they turned at the top and waved before disappearing onto the crowded deck.

The early and lucky ones were able to push forward to the railing, and as the ship was nudged away from the wharf by a tug, get one last blown kiss.

Some of the more creative people calling farewell carried rolled-up paper the width of streamers. These were made from any paper that was available, although crepe paper was the most popular because of its colours. They were tossed from shore to deck so that the two people on either end were kept together for as long as possible. Eventually, the streamers would all break.

It was their first time for most of them to have been on a navy vessel or huge ocean liner. [2] It had taken them a week to get their 'sea legs' and feel free of sea sickness. [3] It was also the first time they had crossed the Equator, an adventure many of the men on board thought was a special thing to remember.

After several trips across the Sahara Desert to towns like Bardia, Tobruk, Marsa Matruh and El Alamein, Albert Chamberlain and the New Zealanders were starting to feel they could cope with the Italians who were part of the Axis. [4]

The Allies were just settling in and learning to cope with sudden orders and movements when they were ordered to Alexandria to be part of an army. The top brass used the code system exclusively, which wasn't divulged to the rank and file until necessary. This order made the men feel they were one together, it was the team selection feeling. How they coped with the voyage depended on the individual.

Both Bonnie and Bert would have heard the messages about Greece that came down the wire during March 1941. The Greek government had sent troops to stop the Albanians (who were members of the Axis under Hitler) from crossing their border. They were faring well, but the English Prime Minister Winston Churchill wanted to support the Greek government more.

He was particularly keen to maintain their friendship and was also concerned that the German-Italian Axis was discussing attacking Greece sometime in the near future.

Private Bonnie Buirchell, who had reached North Africa as a signalman in the 2/11th Battalion of the Australian Imperial Force, was putting all his knowledge and experience into his job thereby keeping the field headquarters in touch with each other. He had used the knowledge and skills he had been taught at the Northam Training Centre to run wire by foot and motorcycle to field headquarters and to decipher, read and send Morse Code.

Thousands of Allies came across from their countries and arrived in the Middle East and North Africa. Hundreds from the United Kingdom moved into Europe and the Mediterranean.

Now that Bonnie Buirchell was in North Africa, he was using all his experience to ensure that the Italians were not setting booby traps along the communication wires. He quickly learnt that cut lines could be a trap and that he should move cautiously in these situations.

Then came the sudden order to embark at Alexandria, Egypt to sail to Athens and fight in the Greco-Italian War.

This mission, called Lustre Force, was a bitter and bloody time and the Allies were sent fleeing from the northern border of Greece to Athens. From here they were shipped to Crete. In among the chaos there were captives who were sent off to the stalags in Germany, there were the seriously ill who found themselves in hospitals with German doctors and there were the dead who had to be accounted for and relatives notified.

While all the movements in Greece were happening, the Royal Navy had to line up offshore near Athens to pick up the Allies. The entire scene was one of chaos as groups and individuals rushed here and there trying to fathom what their next moves would be. Knowing they had to keep a rendezvous or miss out on freedom must have been nerve racking.

Within a short time of being shipped to Crete they were in the middle of a war from the air.

The island of Crete was invaded by the Germans using thousands of paratroopers and gliders. The Allied soldiers fought bravely against the largest parachute invasion ever launched. The German invasion was like no other seen before, with paratroopers attacking from the sky.

After the capitulation of Crete on June 1, 1941, and the incarceration of the men as prisoners, the weeks passed slowly.

All their mates and acquaintances had been shipped out, thousands of them. They would be sent through the line to an unknown destination. First, a ship to Salonika, then a train to a stalag in Germany.

The men who remained on Crete were left wondering if their fate was going the same way or if they were to be sacrificial lambs. When the prisoners of war left in Crete got below 500, they began to speculate and think about what they had been involved in that may have caught the eyes of the Germans.

There were others who should have been left on Crete if the Germans were looking for special people to help with planning or assisting the Reich.

Some of these men's stories are included here as they have been narrated or written down as evidence of the trials of the prisoners of war on Crete.

The Germans were intent on keeping a number of men with special skills. They needed these men to carry out a covert project that would swing the war in favour of the Reich.

No one could place their finger on what was in store for the men left behind, nor who the final men would be.

Later in the book, the names of the men who eventually occupied tents at Tymbakion are in alphabetical order. Some also signed the canvas shorts, but not all of them.

Two were not selected and had traits that would have benefitted the entire group. The stories of Private Alf Traub WX858 and Lieutenant-Colonel Leslie Le Souef WX3326 are included as their contribution was important. [5] They kept more people alive than any other individuals between March and the end of 1941.

CHAPTER 4

In late March the New Zealand troops along with the Australians and British were called upon to assist Greece.

The Greeks were fighting the Albanians on their northern border and winning handsomely. The Albanians were pushed back into their own country resulting in a response from the Italian Army. [1]

The Italians were sending reinforcements and this would make the defence of Greece difficult by tipping the balance that would likely see the Greek Army being overrun.

Field Marshall Archibald Wavell was given the task of finding the men who would constitute Lustre Force. Wavell, who was now in charge sent out between 6 and 12 ships daily, all crowded with troops and their equipment.

Adolph Hitler, the German Chancellor, was ambitiously taking over European countries using a strategy which was to be known as blitzkriegs. These were intense military campaigns that were intended to bring about swift military victories. Hitler had already used these blitzes to take over countries such as Belgium, the Netherlands and Luxembourg.

With numerous victories under his belt Hitler turned his guns towards Russia and under the code name of Barbarossa intended to attack that country.

Other generals in Hitler's high command made a case for capturing Greece which, in their opinions, would take no time at all. Then the main bulk of the German troops could go back to the Eastern Front. Hitler agreed and sent his battle-hardened troops to the Greek border ready to move through the mountain passes and push on to Athens.

The Greek government was alarmed at the news and asked the governments of Australia, New Zealand and Britain if they could supply more troops to repel the Germans. Battalions from each of these countries were recalled to Alexandria in Egypt.

They were equipped and readied before being shipped to Greece. Leslie Le Souef explained how Lustre Force [2] was formed in his book *To War Without a Gun*.[3]

Although the resources of the Commonwealth in the Middle East at this time were unfortunately very slender, three divisions were prepared. The Australian 6th and New Zealand 1st and a British armoured brigade were replenished in Alexandria. The Australian division departed for Piraeus between March 19 and 22, supported by the 2/1st Field Ambulance.

On April 1st the 2/7th under Lieutenant Colonel Le Souef and their medical equipment were dispatched.

Bonnie Buirchell, Vic Petersen, Herbert Stratton and Alf Traub were all in the Australian 6th Division, Imperial Force 2/11th Battalion.[4] They were on a different ship from the New Zealanders and headed for Piraeus on a different date.

Another Australian, Ray Powell, who was in the 2/7th, enjoyed the cruise across the Mediterranean. Although they were headed for the battlefields of northern Greece, all the Australians were not fazed.[5]

Ray Powell was born on May 17, 1919 at Devonport, Tasmania. His mother was Noumea Powell and she was his next of kin when he enlisted in the Australian Imperial Force on the November 24, 1939. He was placed in the Australian Infantry with Army number WX1114. On November 30, Ray was posted to Puckapunyal, Victoria, to begin his basic training. On April 15, 1940, he embarked on a ship bound for North Africa, and he and his Battalion, the 2/7th, disembarked at Kantara, Palestine, on May 18, 1940.

Ray Powell was in the Middle East from May 18, 1940 until April 19, 1941, a total of 335 days. Much of this time was spent in desert warfare training in and around Palestine. [6]

The Greek government was successful in convincing the Australian Prime Minister, Robert Menzies, to find spare troops to be sent to the northern border. Ray and his fellow soldiers gathered in Alexandria, Egypt where they were to begin their voyage to Greece. He and his fellow soldiers left the docks at Alexandria on April 1, 1941.

This call for help from Greece would see Ray in his first combat. It would be the first conflict or as many put it, "their baptism of fire," that many of the Allies from the ANZAC countries and United Kingdom took part in.

A few days later, vessels carrying Allied soldiers sailed from Alexandria. It was early April 1941, and they were told they would be embarking on a ship to protect the Greeks from the Germans. They were anticipating a quick victory and a pleasant trip back to their homelands.

Corporal J.J. Donovan, [7] another Australian on board the ship carrying the 6th Division, sat by himself. He desperately wanted time to write a letter home to his parents. Finding a quiet corner on the upper deck, he could see all that was happening around him as the ship slowly moved out of Alexandria Harbour.

The letter contained his thoughts, and with plenty of time, he described in detail what was going on all around him. "As the ship left the Alexandria Harbour the soldiers all marvelled at the scenery. "The busy harbour was a mass of shipping, most on the move. Warships of all types, flying boats, submarines, floating docks and the necessary commercial shipping.

"French warships were inactive as they had fallen out with the British and were considered untrustworthy. There were so many things happening and to see to keep one interested."

His letter continued, "The fact that it was 1st April mattered not, and the scenery resulted in an absence of silliness on April Fools' Day."

On the other hand, Ray Powell was excited and intrigued, as he had never seen a mass of shipping in his life before. He was looking forward to the new adventures that lay ahead. The convoy he was a part of was a formidable one. The weather was sunny and warm, and the Mediterranean was flat and greenish blue. He sat still, absorbing the warmth of the sun and taking in all the sounds, sights, and smells of the harbour.

The trip was uneventful but lifeboat drill was compulsory. Ray would be very thankful for these drills later on in his life.

Ray's first sight of Europe from the Mediterranean Sea was of islands, a few at first, until at the end of the morning lots of sheer, jagged rock formations jutting out of the water. [8]

Ray and his mates were all mesmerised to know they were sailing past the famed Greek Isles.

A continuous shoreline of sheer cliffs made Ray realise he was viewing the mainland of Greece. As the ship moved closer, almost parallel with the shore, he could make out small houses and villages. Later, as they were met by fishing craft, he guessed they must be nearing the port of Piraeus.

They were amazed to see that Athens was a very modern city with all of its historical ruins dotted across the Seven Hills. [9] Ray had heard about the city mainly through studies at school.

These lessons focused on the ancient history of the country and its main city. It was a civilised city with a sense of gracious beauty. Dotted among the Seven Hills were many ancient buildings, like the Acropolis, standing in a state of ruin.

The ship travelled around the back of the city and docked at the wharf. This area was the city's port, Piraeus. It was very busy off-loading people, war machines and goods, all of the essential things that would be required to fight a war with Germany over at least seven days.

J.J. Donovan stopped writing as he now had to disembark and get ready for the next phase in his life. All the men around him stood to attention and listened to the sergeant. He explained to each group what they had to do now that they had reached Piraeus.

They found a convoy of trucks waiting to move them north past Mount Olympus. [10]

He pointed out the army trucks lined up on the wharf and instructed everyone to make for any truck and fill it. In an hour, the convoy would move out and head north; they would not wait for any stragglers or sightseers. There was a general rush for the gangplank, and this was abruptly stopped by the opening that couldn't cope with the large numbers trying to exit all at once.

The sergeant put a stop to the crush and demanded the troops show a bit of common sense. There would be plenty of time later to squeeze into small places on the run. How prophetic these words would be.

CHAPTER 5

Howard John Holmes was born on August 28, 1917, in Gisborne, New Zealand. This small seaside town is on the coast and close to the sweeping waters of Hawke's Bay. This is a beautiful area, and seaside activities would have kept young 'Slim' and his mates occupied all day.

"Be home by sundown," would have been a common call from his mother as he dashed out the door to meet his mates.

As he grew rapidly and tall, he was called 'Slim'. He was very popular and was the typical teenager, come-twenty-year-old of the time.

Adventures kept him out of mischief and built his character. He was aware of the reputation of the Hawke's Bay Regiment[1] that was stationed near his parents' house. It probably crossed his mind to want to join in the future, but for the moment, he enjoyed the freedom of playing wars and counting to one hundred before coming alive.

He had been educated at the primary school and enjoyed keeping up with world news by reading the local newspaper.

He entered the dry-cleaning business but soon changed to learning to be a tailor. He could use patterns to cut and sew garments.

Hunting in the wilderness of the rugged South Island was one of Howard's favoured pastimes.

He would meet up with his mates and go camping for a day or more, hunting for the wild deer that roamed the highlands.

These camping trips were where he learnt all about camaraderie and guns. His shooting accuracy improved with each outing.

His patriotism came to the fore when he heard that Britain had declared war against Germany and that New Zealanders were being encouraged to join the army.

He became a private in the New Zealand Expeditionary Force and was placed in the 19th Infantry Battalion. In no time at all, Howard had a reputation for being a fast sprinter and a deadly shot.

Holmes's story took him to North Africa, Greece and then Crete. This would be a common route for all the soldiers who found themselves still on Crete in the latter half of 1941.

Many New Zealand soldiers were ordered to be packed and on the wharf at Alexandria, where they were to join a fighting group called Lustre Force. They would be moving to northern Greece to fight the Germans, who were about to pass through the mountain passes and invade Greece.

Under Brigadier Hargest, hundreds of soldiers from New Zealand were directed to the Alexandria docks at a given date and time to board a convoy that would sail to the Greek capital.

All members turned up on time and selected a nice warm part on the deck of a ship that was going to take them to Greece.

The New Zealand troops sailed for Greece on April 12, 1941.

Bert Chamberlain was also on the same ship, and like the other New Zealanders, he enjoyed his journey. The Mediterranean Sea was like a millpond, and its deep blue colour was a wonderful sight.

Many New Zealanders sat on deck and soaked up the sun's warmth. They may not have known many of the others, but they were enjoying the cruise. Their journey highlights were similar to Ray Powell's, and they all disembarked at Port Piraeus.

Day after day, Allied troop ships landed at Piraeus and disgorged thousands of soldiers.

The movement of such large numbers and the equipment needed to keep it active for several days were enormous. The convoy carrying Howard Holmes left Alexandria in mid-April 1941, with troops being escorted by Royal Navy battleships.

The distance from Alexandria to Athens was short, but the time would have felt forever. As each group arrived in Athens the ships were directed to Piraeus, from where the men were taken by truck to the outskirts of Athens for a rest.

Crowds gathered at vantage points to see the soldiers disembark. These were the men they believed in to defeat the Germans on Greece's northern border.

They were hoping their actions would make the Germans, who were massing at the border, cease pushing south.

Three hospital ships were in port at that time.[2] There would be no mistaking them from the air or sea.

They were massive, with a white superstructure and large red crosses all over them, and at night, they had all their lights on.

Overhead a flying boat was on patrol.

Thousands of soldiers, under the codename Lustre Force, were to set up a defensive line well forward of the border of Macedonia, Albania and Greece. These bordering countries welcomed the extra troops. Over 50,000 personnel and their equipment were sent from Alexandria during March and into April. The troops involved included British, New Zealanders and Australians.

The Italians were not so pleased and asked the German High Command for help. Hitler [3] decided he would send a larger army to move into the Aliakmon Line and, from there, invade Greece. German forces entered Greece, through Yugoslavia on April 6, 1941. The Allies had dug in by April 6 and organised a defence. They met their first major engagement against the Germans on April 10 near Vevi. After two days of near-continuous fighting with little sleep, the Allies' position had deteriorated. A large number of the 2/28th Battalion had been killed, wounded or taken prisoner.

Lustre Force, made up of Australians, English and New Zealanders moved back and dug in further south and based in Servia.

This was where the Aliakmon Line ran east and west plus the Vermilion-Olympus Line running north and south. The Allies were intending to stop the Germans at the Monastir Pass. [4] Forward scouts reported a strong and mobile German army was headed south through the Monastir Pass and this prompted Brigadier Hargest to withdraw all New Zealand battalions back to the Brallos Pass. [5]

From April, 19 onwards, the Allied forces fought delaying actions at Brallos and the Thermopylae passes. On April 21, 1941 the 2/11th battalion held off the Germans.

For three days at Livadero, the Australian 2/1st fought to ensure the withdrawal of the Allied troops. The action resulted in the battalion suffering the heaviest losses in killed and wounded of any Australian battalion in Greece. The Germans took full advantage here with superior technology and well trained troops. Casualties on both sides grew by the hour.

The Commonwealth troops were hit hard, and it was only a matter of time before they realized the German Army was too well equipped. A withdrawal was urgently called, and the Australian 2/11th was called upon to maintain a rearguard action to allow all other soldiers to reach Athens.

Those withdrawing were tormented from the air by the Stukas. [6] These dive bombers flew over enemy areas searching for targets. Once identified, the pilot attacked by placing the Stuka into a steep dive. As the aircraft dived, its engine made a terrifying, screaming noise. At treetop height, the pilot pulled out of the dive and released the bombs that clung to the undercarriage.

Not only were they able to drop bombs with accuracy, but they also strafed the soldiers who attempted to run or hide. The Allies got to dread the screaming of the Stuka.

The Allies took their heaviest toll in the Greek mountains as the German army brought its war machines to bear. It was becoming obvious that the Allies would need to retreat and at the first opportunity. Field headquarters were busy reviewing a map of the area and seeking to determine the next best place to try to hold the Germans.

CHAPTER 6

—∽—

Near Mount Olympus in Greece, Lieutenant Colonel Leslie Le Souef had his work cut out attending to the wounded and dead at the makeshift 2/7th Field Ambulance. [1]

The advancing Germans broke through the passes and the Allies finished up firing point blank and withdrawing fast to the south. Le Souef had seen the need to pack up his hospital and staff well before the main fighting had finished. He set up further south and continued to treat the casualties with the care and professionalism that he had given in previous situations.

As the last of the troops turned and hurried for Athens, they could see the cigarette smoked by the Germans glowing in the darkness. The closeness was alarming. To allow all the troops a chance to reach Athens and clamber aboard a ship that would take them to Crete, the Australian and New Zealand battalions were given the job of rearguard defence. [2] This entailed holding the enemy for as long as possible before falling back.

After 400 yards they would dig in and keep the Germans under constant fire before falling back and digging in again. By the time Ray Powell and his retreating truck load of mates reached the Port Piraeus they were tired beyond belief. All in the back of the truck jumped out. The first order was to leave the truck.

The second order was to spoil and destroy everything so nothing was of use to the Germans.[3] Thirdly, guns, foodstuffs and excess clothing had to be left behind.

With the food, they punctured the tins, piled them up, poured in curry powder sprinkled heavily with pepper and salt, added condensed milk and threw in dirt in case it still looked appetizing. This was a scorched earth policy [4] used by fleeing warriors in defeat.

The members of the Australian 2/11th Battalion fought in the rearguard before they smashed everything and caught small boats out to the waiting British Navy ships.

Upon reaching Athens, Lieutenant Colonel Le Souef and his entourage had to keep the precious cargo of medicines and medical equipment so he ordered his medics to load as much as they could. Once this was done the 2/7th Field Ambulance personnel were rowed out to the waiting warships.

All the evacuating men made for the dark outlines of the warships and as they drew closer, they could hear the crews shouting instructions and encouragement.

The small boats pulled up beneath the scramble nets and watched as the closest climbed up. Some were so tired and starving that they slid back down. Others helped them up to the deck. A small group was the last, and they were overjoyed when they slumped onto the deck of the ships.

Fate determined the ship that each person caught that night. No one was given a specific ship to board. Most men were just so relieved to find a way out and away from the Germans. It was more joy when the bodies felt the ships, one by one, begin to move, rocking gently as they picked up speed.

On most of the ships, voices came out of the darkness calling for anyone with a Bren gun to go forward. [5] It wasn't long before it became obvious as to why they wanted Bren guns at the bows.

A screaming Stuka swooped overhead and the huge splash from the exploding bomb indicated the ships and their live cargo weren't safe.

Ray Powell reached the northernmost point of the battle before being ordered to withdraw with the 2/7th Australian Battalion. Upon reaching Athens all the men managed to get their tired bodies onto the *Costa Rica*. The ship pulled out of Athens smartly and set sail for Crete. He and his mates were being taken to the safety of Crete.

On April 26, 1941, the day after the evacuation from Greece, *Costa Rica* was attacked by German Stukas.[6] The incident occurred while the convoy was still sailing out in the open of the Mediterranean Sea.

Unfortunately, she was found by the Germans just short of Souda Bay wharf, Crete. *Costa Rica* was attacked by the three German dive bombers around 3 pm, and although not hit, bombs kept being dropped.

They all continued to miss but eventually, a close call from a 1000-pound bomb exploded near the hull. The near miss of that bomb split the *Costa Rica*'s hull and flooded the engine room. The explosion caused severe leaks in the engine room and the call of, "Abandon ship," echoed across the deck.

The *Costa Rica* began to sink rapidly. The ship was just off the shore of Crete. Every one of the personnel on board managed to get off the ship and to be picked up. The swift actions of two of the British ships, the *Hereward* and *Defender* saw all personnel saved. [7]

The *Costa Rica* was taken in tow by HMS *Defender* but sank north-west of Souda Bay. The Australians of the 2/1st Machine Gun Battalion, 2/7th Infantry Battalion, and part of the 2/1st and 2/8th infantry battalions were also rescued.

Ray Powell was on board the *Costa Rica* when the bomb split the hull and the ship began taking water. Ray and his companions were quick to jump ship and were picked up by either the *Hereward* or the *Defender* and offloaded on Crete. They were all thankful for the rescue. All the rescued troops finally reached Souda Bay, on Crete, and settled in to camp on the beaches and in the sand hills.

The 2/11th Australian Battalion disembarked at Souda Bay from the SS *Thurland Castle*. [8]

The first few days of being on Crete was peaceful and the men took time out to recuperate. The Allies had been subjected to their first real encounter with the crack forces of the Nazis. They realised that war was not just pointing a gun and pulling a trigger. What they had been through was brutal and savage. Their whole world was upside down as they tried to take in what had happened in the space of a few days.

Many of the men were keen to tell their stories to the others. Their stories started near Mount Olympus, where they dug defensive foxholes and settled in. The weather was the most deplorable they could have ever imagined with heavy snow and freezing temperatures.

The terrain around Mount Olympus saved many lives. It made it difficult for the German tanks and their other mechanised forces to move.

How quickly things change. Now, 48 hours later, they were on a sunny beach in Crete without the feeling of a deadly threat hanging over them. This small amount of time played on all the men's minds as they walked around the beaches on Crete.

If this was war, then no one wanted a bar of it. Their minds were in turmoil, and as the days continued to pass it was becoming obvious that worse was to come.

The rumours were coming in thick and fast with the belief the Germans were likely to send a seaward invasion group to capture the Allies and the island of Crete. [9]

With the knowledge from ULTRA Intelligence, a German code, the Allies learnt that Germany was going to continue to chase the Allies onto Crete. The Allies had to develop a plan to stop them and this was left to General Bernard Freyberg, to organize.

The decision to destroy all arms and equipment and to make food inedible was made in haste. With thought and long-term planning, it would have been sensible to prioritise what was to be kept and what was to be destroyed. By maintaining their arms, the men would have been armed against the pursuing enemy. Now, it would appear this enemy was likely to be fully armed and swarming all over Crete within the next month or two.

The shortfall of arms left the remains of Lustre Force vulnerable. This was the major problem General Freyberg faced when he and his team sat down to plan a defence of the island.

CHAPTER 7

The *HMS Glengyle* was among the rescue ships in Athens, and on board was the 28th New Zealand Battalion,[1] made up of Maoris. These indigenous New Zealanders were fearless soldiers, and they would soon be involved in several heroic clashes with the Germans. At this point, they just wanted to disembark, have a long rest, and find some food to alleviate their hunger and water to quench their thirst.

One of their members was Ponuate Busby, who would find that he was one of the last Allies to leave Crete. He was unaware of what was going to happen in the next eight months but he was going to witness the extraordinary invasion of Crete by German paratroopers.

He would also survive the bayonet charge that saw the Germans falter and turn tail on 42nd Street. And he was going to spend day after day grubbing out hundreds of mature olive trees.

Ian Alexander Hardie,[2] was to become one of the selected ones who ended up at Tymbakion in September 1941. Ian was born on March 11, 1918, in Peak Hill, Western Australia. His father was a gold miner. Ian, or Jock as he preferred, joined the Australian Army and trained at the Northam Camp.

He joined the 2/11th Battalion with the number WX2371. After embarking from Perth, he spent time in the Middle East before being sent to Greece as part of Lustre Force.

As he grew up Jock took to writing articles for the local papers. Some of his articles were published in *The Yalgoo Observer and Murchison Chronicle*. [3]

He was in Alexandria, Egypt, when he wrote to his fiancée: "At present, I am writing this from Egypt and believe me, this place isn't as green as it's painted. The game is just as hard here, conditions too, but we still take it for we're in the army now."

He was happy to tell his news through the *Murchison Chronicle* and they published his articles for the locals to read. One of his published pieces reminisced about home. "And believe me folks; there's many a time I've wished for the old place again, but still. I guess the only way out is to see it through, that's with plenty of luck, which we'll all want, and it won't be long now, well folks, there's nothing much to write home about from this place.

"Before closing, allow me the liberty to tender many thanks for all the parcels and funds that most of us have received. [4] It gives us a lot of heart to carry on, and even if some of us do have bad luck, those happy days we all enjoyed, especially myself, will never be regretted. So now, friends of Meeka (Meekatharra), remember we're as yet still on deck and not afraid of anything we've hit yet, so remember us, and we'll remember you. Au revoir, keep those chins up. Sincerely yours on behalf of the boys, Ian Alexander Hardie."

On April 1, 1941, Ian found himself on a ship sailing out of Alexandria bound for Athens in Greece. He was one of the many Australians to make up a fighting group going to Greece to bolster that country's defence.

After escaping from Greece, Jock Hardie and his fellow AIF soldiers were evacuated to Crete. [5] Here they settled into a happy and busy life with the locals welcoming them with open arms. Ahead of them was a German invasion fronted by paratroopers.

Alexander Ian Hardie had his name listed under the heading, "600 in WA Casualty List", Daily News, *Trove* article dated July 12, 1941. The Melbourne University lists from the Red Cross had Jock missing on June 20, 1941. [6] His fiancée, Miss D. Wakefield, advised the army that she had received cards from Jock on December 31, 1941, noting he was a prisoner on Crete.

On January 30, 1942, his brother Adrian notified the 2nd Echelon that he had received letters from Jock on August 20, 1941, and September 21, 1941, indicating he was a POW on Crete.

These dates placed Jock on the island but not necessarily Tymbakion. The September letter may have been sent prior to the group moving from Souda Bay. Nevertheless, the evidence strongly places him in the 151 at Tymbakion [7] from September 12, 1941, until December 29, 1941.

Like so many others, Ian's communication line relied on the Germans, who were not all that keen to send or receive letters and cards from outside. Ian was definitely at Tymbakion from September 12, 1941, to December 29, 1941. The German records have been located and verified by the author and the researcher.

CHAPTER 8

—⟆—

Bernard Mitchell, a British soldier, Army number 4973574, was a signatory on the canvas shorts. He was born on October 11, 1914, in Grimsby, England. During his working years, he became a tailor.

When Bernard Mitchell joined the British Army, he completed his basic training and then was sent to Palestine to learn about desert warfare before encountering the Italians in North Africa.

In late March 1941, he and his battalion, the 1st Sherwood Foresters, Nottinghamshire & Derbyshire Regiments were called to Alexandria. The British battalion was to join other Allies to form a fighting group under the code Lustre Force. The goal was to stop the Germans from entering and capturing Greece. The best place to put up a defence was considered to be Monastir Gap.

The Italians under Benito Mussolini had formed an Axis with the Germans to wage war against the British and other countries that had been brought together to form an Alliance. North Africa, the Suez Canal and Iran were considered strategically important and were on the Axis list to be conquered.

The North African cities would allow a direct assault line on Alexandria the headquarters of the Alliance. The Suez Canal would provide a shortcut to

Australia, New Zealand, and India, and prevent them from assisting Britain in Europe. Iran was oil rich, and this oil was essential in keeping the war effort moving. [1]

The British government had no sooner declared war on Germany than the recruitment offices opened, and thousands flocked to sign up. Bernard Mitchell was in an early batch. His records show he was in a 1939 intake.

Tens of thousands of soldiers from the United Kingdom, united by a common goal, moved into Europe and the Mediterranean. They formed a formidable army, each soldier contributing their unique skills and strengths, but all working together as a team to realise the goals they were all seeking.

On April 1, 1941, Private Mitchell's regiment embarked for Greece from Alexandria. He would have seen the same scenery in the port as described by Corporal J.J. Donovan. Bernard's trip across the Mediterranean was peaceful and restful. The only news that was churning in the stomachs of the English soldiers was that German forces had massed in readiness for a push into northern Greece and threatened to overrun the country.

Bernard had seen several female nurses board the ship he was on.[2] When the ship docked at Piraeus these nurses were off first and stepped into a waiting coach. He thought of the care and kindness these young ladies would offer to those who would be maimed in the forthcoming fighting. How brave and concerned they would be, and their care was legendary among the soldiers.

It was very unusual to see the female groups assisting the soldiers during wartime. Many were there but hidden from clear sight.

At home the women were busy taking over the responsibilities when the men departed. They were learning new skills that would keep their economies functioning and their men folk equipped to fight in the forthcoming battles. Bernard carried his gear to the military trucks that were waiting in a convoy to take him and his mates north to a camp near Mount Olympus.

The convoy of trucks and their drivers waited patiently at the wharf. Mitchell and his many other fighting men were directed to a truck with a canvas canopy. He threw his rucksack onto the tray before climbing aboard.

As they left the port area, they were besieged by boys and girls and a few grown-ups wanting to buy bully beef. Like all the soldiers who had already passed through Piraeus, they gave away a few tins only to find that selling or accepting goods such as meat was a crime.

The trucks stopped just outside the sprawling city of Athens, and the men were told they would camp overnight. The officers, in their wisdom, allowed a furlough, [3] which was to be tomorrow. This was a way of achieving two important goals. First, it allowed the men to look at the sights of a famous city that most only knew by name, and second, it rested the troops as they were going to be in for a hard time.

Bernard and his mates enjoyed their day off but did not realise what they were walking into until they confronted the German Army near Mount Olympus.

Ray Powell was sitting near his partially made up tent camped just outside Athens. His battalion the 2/1st AIF had also been ordered to help the Greeks stop the Germans. His descriptions of the countryside would have been the same as those of J.J. Donovan, who wrote about Greece in a letter to his parents.

Ray, on his first day on Greek soil, rested up. He was munching on a packet of biscuits and they were delicious. He had offered them to his mates but they called, "No thanks, mate," as they ran after a truck that was picking up those wanting to go on a sightseeing drive.

They had made their intentions for the furlough day well known. They were going to spend a full day wandering around Athens tomorrow and buy a little something for the missus or girlfriend. This would be posted before they left for the battlegrounds.

While everyone was rushing off to catch a truck the next day, Ray felt tired, so he wandered up a hill and dreamed away the day.

To Ray this was spring, a time when nature sprouted a fresh awakening. There was the greenness of everything fertile soil, healthy cattle, bees, flowers and nature in full swing in. [4]

Fond memories of home flooded back.

All around Ray were mountain ranges of tremendous size, some out of sight due to cloud cover. Above the halfway mark most of these mountains were covered in snow an ideal place to visit and ski all day long. He knew that was wishful thinking because he was being driven into hostile territory.

The following day, the men received orders for an early move. They were told to drive north for 300 miles, which they would cover in three days, in three stages, in a 70 mile long convoy. They set off at a merry pace.

Ray was sitting in the front of a truck reading some air mail letters that had arrived. [5] The driver somehow lost the convoy and ended up giving his passengers a tour of the city.

Athens was very modern, with elegant, well ordered people in the streets. The men in the truck saw the Acropolis in the distance.

The driver caught up with the convoy on the other side of the city and fell back in his right position.

The Greek people who lined the streets of their small towns were real country folk. They were happy at the thought that the soldiers driving by were going to relieve their men in Albania.

Every town gave a raucous welcome as the trucks drove north. The further they travelled, the more the country and people changed. There were no longer the city types but more the agricultural, farming people.

Each village grew more ancient, with storks nesting on nearly every chimney stack. Children threw beautiful, colourful flowers and blossoms at the trucks all along the road.

The trip took the trucks and men uphill and down dale, and the scenery was breathtaking. Along the way, older women threw water on the road to keep the dust down.

The destination was eventually reached and the men set about digging trenches and foxholes in readiness to defend the land belonging to Greece.

On April 6, 1941, German troops invaded Greece and Yugoslavia and outflanked the Aliakmon Line causing the Allies to begin to retreat south towards Athens.

On April 11, the German troops seized the town of Vevi but were stopped by a mixed Commonwealth and Greek formation known as M (Mackay) [6] Force at Klidi Pass. The fighting was fierce and desperate before the Allies withdrew towards Mount Olympus.

The 2/7th Infantry was digging in on Mount Olympus. They dug with their overcoats on as it was so cold with continuous drizzly rain. When that let up, it snowed. Once prepared they could only wait for the casualties to begin to arrive.

By April 14 , the German spearhead had reached Kozani. In the meantime, more German troops broke through the Monastir Gap. The Allies moved places a few times and dug in. Eventually, they reached Larissa and formed an Anzac Line at the village of Bralos [7] beyond Lamia.

When the New Zealanders reached the battlefield, they were plunged into a deadly nightmare. The fighting was hard and the casualties were the heaviest of the Greek campaign. They were constantly harassed by the screaming Stukas. They would dive directly at the first sight of the enemy. The pilot would line up on the bigger objects of the enemy such as trucks.

It was soon discovered that if a soldier was in a vehicle and he heard the Stuka scream, the drill was to abandon the truck and dive for the roadside gutters. It was not wise to hesitate.

A major weakness of the Greek and Allied armies was the lack of aircraft. The Luftwaffe ruled the air which gave their ground troops a distinct advantage.

The Allies, led by Australian and New Zealanders, stalled the Germans for three days. The New Zealanders put up the most resistance but even they ultimately had to withdraw from Servia. They used a leapfrogging withdrawal to Thermopylae.[8] The Germans continued south relentlessly.

The Allies were finally ordered to withdraw and make haste to Athens, boarding the ships that waited in the harbour or just offshore. The overall organisation for the Allies to carry out the instructions and flee the fighting shows how chaotic the situation was.

The New Zealanders were given the responsibility to slow the Germans' southward push. They had to work as a total unit to do this effectively. Once at the seaside near Athens they had to make haste to destroy any equipment or food stuff. In the meantime, the locals were rounding up small boats to ferry the New Zealanders out to the waiting Royal Navy ships. Once the men met a ship and got on board the ship it could sail away to Crete. All these movements had to be carried out clinically or else the situation would fall into chaos and many lives would have been lost.

The entire operation was in the hands of the total group, as well as each individual. The writing of each soldiers' part would be impossible and this shows the difficulty of reporting what happened in the Greek War arena.

The Greek Campaign proved the Germans were ahead in the sophistication of their armour and planning.

As they ran for safety, the Allies destroyed anything that was seen to be valuable to the Germans, including fuel, oil, foodstuffs, armour, and transport vehicles. This list does not cover all the things that were destroyed because it was not possible to identify every person and determine what they individually destroyed.

They were to carry as light a load as possible. This order left the Allies with few rifles and next to no heavy calibre guns, such as machine guns and Bren guns.

During the run down the Greek Archipelago, to Crete New Zealanders and Australians had slowed the Germans with a rearguard fallback. This gave all the other troops a chance to find and board the Royal Navy vessels waiting along the shores of Athens.

Like the other battalions before them, the end result was the Allies evacuated Greece and found shelter on the island of Crete.

The Germans who eventually followed the Allies into Crete had a distinct advantage due to this decision to destroy all equipment.

CHAPTER 9

Germany made overtures to invade Greece, so the government sent urgent messages to the Allies for help. Winston Churchill [1] took up the request, seeing the need to keep the Greeks free and on the Allies' side. He convinced the Anzacs [2] to send troops and added British soldiers to bolster the numbers.

The movement of these troops began from Alexandria in March 1941 under the code name Operation Lustre.

The individual soldiers were involved in a wide range of activities at the same time. There are several soldiers who can be presented because of the information collected.

Alf Traub was in North Africa when the order came for his battalion to return to Alexandria in Egypt. The battalion that Traub was assigned to, the 2/11th, was involved in operations against the Italians in and around Bardia and Tobruk. [3] He would have been fighting in North Africa when news came through that the 2/11th was to be shipped to Greece.

The newly formed group was to help the Greeks defend the northern border of Greece against the Germans.

In readiness for the confrontation with the German troops the British ships moved 58,364 troops, 8588 motor transport vehicles, guns, tanks, stores and other equipment to Greece. All the ships used to move troops from Alexandria to Athens were British.

One ship, however, was an exception: the Australian ship HMAS *Perth*. She joined the armada carrying troops.

The Albanians had set up a defensive line against the Greeks and had called in extra Italians.

Private Alf Traub WX858 had been trained at Northam, Western Australia before moving overseas to North Africa. He was bilingual, speaking fluent English and Yiddish which gave him an understanding of the German language.[4] A more valuable soldier for the rank and file as well as officers, one could not find.

Alf Traub's Army records, like so many others who managed to make it to Crete from Greece, were non-existent. The officers who filled out the records had been too busy fighting the enemy and fleeing from one place to another to find time to write what each individual had been involved in. Battalion records continued to be kept up to date which gave valuable information about their movements.

On April 10, 1941, Alf, along with members of the 2/11th disembarked from Alexandria for service in Greece. The 2/11th was sent to Athens and, from there, trucked north to Mount Olympus. All of the soldiers were taken to the defensive line and dug in. Alf Traub and others of the 2/11th Battalion spent a day digging defensive trenches on and around the passes. It was very cold and drizzling when they began.

During the fighting north of Mount Olympus, signalman Bonnie Buirchell ran through sleet, rain, and freezing conditions to keep the lines open.

He heard the messages and knew the Australians and New Zealanders were being hit hard up near the passes. He was in action getting word to the troops to fall back to Bralos.

The 2/11th found out later that it was at Bralos that the deadliest firefights occurred with hundreds of Allies wounded or killed in the action. [5] The next retreat order came and a new defensive line set up at Mount Olympus.

—✼—

The next morning the defenders were strafed and bombed by Stukas. The diving stukas continued to be fearsome. [6] The 2/11th stood its ground but the tally of wounded and killed rose steadily. All of the soldiers and the wounded were ordered to withdraw back to Athens. This immediately took effect with all soldiers packing up.

The Australians and New Zealanders set up rearguard actions to give the main body of Lustre Force a chance to escape through to Athens. Further retreats found the Anzacs in an all out race to Athens and to find a ship that would take them off Greece.

On April 25, 1941, at 10pm the destroyers HMAS *Vendetta* and HMAS *Waterhen* were approaching Megara Beach in southern Greece. Already waiting were the SS *Thurland Castle*, HMS *Coventry*, HMS *Glengyle*, HMS *Hasty*, HMS *Ajax*, HMS *Kimberley*, SS *Costa Rica* and HMS *Wryneck*. [7]

Their sole intention was to rescue as many of the Commonwealth troops as they could from mainland Greece and drop them off in the safe haven.

The troops were also aware of the haste with which they needed to board the waiting ships.

When the troops from New Zealand, Australia, and England reached the beaches around Athens, they were ordered to break, smash, and ruin anything that might be useful to the Germans.

Even though they were totally exhausted after a full day and night without sleep, they carried out the order as required.

They began contacting the small local boats that were waiting in the gloom to transfer them to the British Navy vessels. While the contact was being made others in the groups carried out the order to destroy everything.

The order to destroy anything that might seem useful to the Germans was later seen to be a poor decision, as the troops defending Crete did not have the equipment, weapons, ammunition and food that was necessary to defeat an invading army. [8]

The troops were rowed out to the ships, and with encouragement from the crews, the exhausted soldiers boarded whichever ship they found. They collapsed on the deck or in the cabins below decks.

In haste to leave Greece by ship Alf Traub was having difficulty as he tried to drag the Boys anti-tank rifle which he had carried with great tenacity all through the campaigns. He refused to let anyone else have it.

A mate of his, Lou Williams, said, "Give it to me, Trauby," and unthinkingly, he handed it up to Lou, who promptly diced it into the sea. Traub was gibbering with rage when he finally got on board the British destroyer HMS *Hasty*. [9]

Even as the flotilla began its urgent trip to Crete several Stukas and bombers used the lights of the city to bomb and strafe the ships. Amongst all the action on the *Thurland Castle* were several other 2/11th Battalion soldiers. namely Bonnie Buirchell, William Taylor, William Pauley and Vic Petersen. [10]

The captain of the *Hasty* took several of the 2/11th men, as well as New Zealanders, before pulling away. There was no time to pick a particular ship it was board whichever one you could. All the rescue ships had to be in Souda Bay, Crete, well before sunrise, or the Luftwaffe would find them.

Many a ship had met its fate in the waters of the Mediterranean as the Luftwaffe ruled the skies.

After a short, uneventful cruise; the men reached the island of Crete. With little in the way of weaponry, Alf and his mates disembarked from their ship.

The island of Crete was a paradise and a welcoming place. After three days of fighting, lack of sleep and constant vigilance, this rest was one the men needed.

After a day or two laying around on the beach and under the grapevines Alf and 5 others were organised to begin setting up defence lines. The rumour that was being passed around was that the Germans would be sending troops to invade the island. From all accounts, it was seen as a seaward invasion. There was a whisper that the Germans might send in paratroopers and invade from the sky. [11]

All that the war-weary Allied troops could do was wait to see what transpired. The population of Crete welcomed the Allies and was always ready to help and offer any victuals. They knew all too well what being invaded meant, as their tiny Mediterranean island had been a target for marauders over the centuries.

CHAPTER 10

The majority of Allied troops evacuated from Greece were shipped to Crete. By the end of April, more than 42,000 British, Commonwealth, and Greek soldiers were on Crete. Some of the wounded and ill were deemed necessary to be moved directly to Alexandria, where hospital treatment was available.

On April 30, the command of 'Creforce' the designation for the Allied troops on the island was entrusted to General Bernard Freyberg. He faced a daunting task.

The main issue for Freyberg was the lack of weapons and ammunition. All he could muster were small calibre rifles and bayonets. Ammunition and stores were in short supply. Soldiers had to use their initiative to dig defensive positions with steel helmets. Heavy weapons such as tanks and artillery were few and far between. Air support was also scarce.

The geography of Crete made defending it difficult. Running through the centre of the island in an east-west direction were three mountain ranges: the Dikti Range in Lassithi, the Ida Range in central Crete, and the White Mountains in Chania.

The White Mountains [1] are the most spectacular, rising to 6,000 feet. During winter, the Crete mountains have snow on the upper reaches. This spine consists of mountains up to 7,500 feet.

The key points on the island were the airfields at Maleme, Rethymno and Heraklion, and the port at Souda Bay. All were located on the northern coast and faced German-occupied Greece.

The loss of any of these positions would make the defence of the island virtually impossible, allowing the Germans to deliver men and supplies from bases on the mainland.

The British had one advantage: they had German codes, dubbed Ultra Intelligence. [2] By deciphering these codes, the British knew in detail what the Germans were planning. They were also aware of the invasion date and the comparative strengths of German sea and airborne forces. Armed with this knowledge, British Prime Minister Winston Churchill was convinced the defenders of Crete stood a good chance of repelling the invasion and achieving a morale-boosting victory over the Germans.

The British expected the Germans to launch their attack on the island in mid-May 1941. The Germans planned to begin the invasion on the 15th, but supply problems in Greece delayed the assault by a week. Informed through Ultra sources of these changes, General Freyberg was confident he had done all that was possible to meet an attack with the limited resources and time available.

Time on Crete was welcome as the men were totally exhausted. They had had little to eat and missed a full night's sleep. They soon made up for all the things they lacked. Swimming in Souda Bay was a welcome daily ritual. The water was a magnet for swimming and fun. A small group formed and was soon found enjoying each other's friendship. The men in question were Les Armstrong, Charles Aitken, Bill Aldersley, Mal Beaton, John Crawford and Ted Rees.

On the second day, John Crawford was observant to see two young soldiers bargaining with someone at the wharf and ended up with a box of grenades.

He watched them rowing out into the bay and guessed that they were on a fishing expedition. Crawford called to his fellow swimmers, "Be careful and stay clear of the boat with the two men rowing out into the bay. I overheard those two men requisitioning a box of grenades to go fishing. I believe they are going to toss the grenades in to stun the fish, then pick them up."

"Who are they? asked Mal.

"Don't know them for sure, but from here, it looks like Alan Bunn and Ernie Pyatt."

Suddenly, the group heard an explosion, and sure enough, it was near where the boat was anchored. Another grenade followed, and the two 'would be' fishermen pulled up the anchor. One proceeded to row around while his companion leant out and began picking up the silver-coloured fish.

"That's an ingenious way to get a feed," said Ted Rees.

"I agree with you, Ted, but not for the faint-hearted," said Les Armstrong before diving under.

Another way to get fit was to participate in daily marches. The officers insisted the men train every day. The men would form up in threes and march fifty to one hundred yards before making an about turn and marching back again.

After sleeping on the beach for a few nights, the troops were moved to the hills to settle under the olive trees and vineyards. These trees and vines protected the soldiers from the prying eyes above.

Every day the daily German reconnaissance plane flew across the populated area of the island.

It had been obvious that sleeping out on the beaches was too easy for the Germans to know where the battalions were dug in.

—⚋—

The Mediterranean Sea was controlled by the British navy which gave the Allied troops on the island a comfort that a seaward invasion would be dealt with by the Royal Navy. Daily bombing raids went practically unchallenged because the Allies' air force was almost non-existent. The Luftwaffe was in control of the skies and was able to know much of what was happening on the island.

The troops were mainly placed around the strategic airfields at Maleme, Heraklion, and Rethymno.

—⚋—

The New Zealanders who had been formed in Alexandria and whisked into the northern border of Greece had enjoyed their trip. On the journey across the Mediterranean, they were in a playful mood. By the time they passed Mount Olympus, fatigue had slowed many down and the anticipation of battle was playing mind games.

One of these men was a tall, thin soldier named Howard Holmes, who preferred his school-acquired nickname of Slim.

Slim and his mates had followed the trail like all the other Allies. After reaching Athens, Slim's group had been whisked away from Piraeus to the Aliakmon Line, a naturally strong but ill-prepared defensive system between the Gulf of Salonika and the Yugoslav border.

The Germans' might and efficiency shocked Slim and all the other Allies who were sent to northern Greece. It became quickly evident as it had for the other Allies who had reached the northern border of Greece that the strength of the Germans was over powering. They were moved back and began a withdrawal towards Athens.

German forces had pushed into Greece and came through the mountain passes. They outflanked the Greek defences, and the Allied forces deployed to help were overwhelmed.

Like all the other battalions, the New Zealand 19th Battalion, along with Private Holmes, was forced to conduct a fighting withdrawal south to Athens.

Howard found the Stuka bombers set his nerves on edge as they constantly flew over and then dived almost vertically at the trucks and other equipment.

With full throttle and diving the Stuka screamed a most frightening sound. At the tree tops, the pilot would level out and drop his payload. Each Stuka carried an 1100-pound bomb under its fuselage and two smaller bombs of 110 pounds under each wing.

The bombing was so accurate that the ones under attack knew they had to pile out of their vehicles and dive into the roadside gutters. They lay in a crumpled heap while their trucks took direct hits.

Slim and his mates had received the same orders as the other Allies. They were to destroy all food and equipment and withdraw towards Athens. All weapons were to be smashed, and rifle bolts ditched. Ammunition was fired or buried; motorised vehicles were smashed; petrol was spoilt with sand, and foodstuff was left uneatable.

—∭—

Howard and his New Zealand mates had spent the night racing back to Athens, knowing that the Germans were close behind. He and his fellow soldiers made it to the shore, where fishermen were waiting. Local rowing boats and fishing vessels took the New Zealanders to the British warships lying at anchor.

Howard scrambled up the nets hanging down from the railing and collapsed on the deck with fatigue. He felt the ship moving and was pleased when the HMS *Kimberley* hightailed it away from Greece.

After two hours, the sunrise was spectacular on the eastern horizon. This was a dangerous time because the Luftwaffe ruled the skies across the Mediterranean Sea and would not hesitate to strafe or bomb an Allied ship with crowded decks.

The New Zealanders on board the HMS *Kimberley* disembarked at Souda Bay and marched off with their mates to Maleme Airfield .

—∭—

When the Australian 2/11th Battalion landed on Crete, Major-General Eric Culpeper Weston of the Royal Marines was in charge. Twelve days later, the job was handed to the British General, Henry Maitland Wilson. Further shuffling, General Freyberg was given the task of setting up a defence that would not only halt an invasion but also disperse the Germans back across the Mediterranean Sea.

Freyberg was convinced the Germans would attack by sea and land on the north coast of the island. This was based on intelligence that said the Luftwaffe ruled the skies and the Germans had begun calling up hundreds of ships of all sorts and sizes to carry soldiers across the Mediterranean from Europe to Crete.

The Commonwealth forces dug in, waiting for the expected German invasion from the sea. General Freyberg was informed that the enemy would most likely come from the sea, but an airborne invasion could also occur.

A count by Freyberg's headquarters on May 17, 1941, found there were 15,000 Britons, 7,750 New Zealanders, and 6,500 Australians from the Greek War on the island. Locally there were 10,200 Greeks and 2,800 other troops at Freyberg's disposal. This made a grand total of 42,250 men.

—⚜—

On the morning of May 19, 1941, in the dawn gloom, 700 men were transported from Alexandria to Tympaki.

These men were from the Argyll and Sutherland Highlanders and were sent to augment the current numbers. These troops were landed on the south coast and sent over the mountains to Heraklion. After a day the soldiers were withdrawn back to the ship HMS *Glengyle*. Unfortunately, the Luftwaffe found them in the gorges and attacked. Many were killed, and in their haste to seek the protection of their ship, they had to abandon several MLCs.[3]

The boats would be seen as a godsend later when some of the men searched for a way to escape from the island.

The problem confronting General Freyberg was simple but extremely frustrating. These men did not have the necessary equipment to fight an enemy as strong as Germany.[4] The weakness in all of this was there was a majority of artillery men without guns, drivers without vehicles, and base and service troops without rifles.

With due consideration, Freyberg set up four defence sectors at Maleme, Heraklion, Retimo and Souda Bay. These were the likely targets for the Germans whether by sea or air.[5]

The locations of units and the time did not remain static, so moves were made every few days, taking in the latest intelligence. On May 6, the news indicated the Germans were planning to attack by air on May 17. The three main airstrips were the likely targets.

On the northern strip, four hills ran parallel to the sea. These were named A, B, C, and D. They gave a sweeping view of the road between the villages of Stavromenos and Perivolia. The former had an olive oil factory with a huge chimney, and the latter had a stream called the Perivolia River, which was dry during summer.

CHAPTER 11

The plan and the positioning of manpower was well-considered. However, the strength of the German Army had been overwhelming in the north of Greece. The losses to the Germans were minimal and so the commanders of the Allied battalions knew they were going to be short in numbers.

Brigadier Edward Puttick, in command of the New Zealand contingent, had only two of its three brigades and its divisional personnel.[1] The Australian troops under Vasey were a conglomeration of soldiers from a number of units. The British detachment consisted of the 14th Brigade and improvised battalions from Rangers, Northumberland Hussars, 7th Medium Regiment, 106th Royal Horse Artillery, and various coastal artillery, anti-aircraft and base units.[2]

The Greeks had a number of troops consisting of three garrison battalions deployed at Rethymno and Heraklion plus eight recruit battalions. These latter troops were poorly equipped and had little in the way of weapons and ammunition.[3]

General Freyberg set about placing his troops in the expectation of an invasion by air or sea. He clearly thought the invasion would come from the sea. Freyberg amassed his main battalions along the northern shore and in the hills.

Brune, Peter. *We Band of Brothers*, Allen and Unwin, 9 Atchison Street, St Leonards, NSW, 2000 page 88 noted, "General Freyberg worked on a four-sector system starting at Chania.

"In the first sector, he placed the New Zealanders. They were situated west of, and adjacent to, the main town.[4]

"The British were responsible for Souda Bay and Chania. This included the central and east end of Maleme Airfield.

"Australians under Vasey were to hold the third sector consisting of an area that arced from Georgioupoli to Rethymno. The Rethymno airfield was to be held by the 2/1st and 2/11th with added firepower from the 4th and 5th Greek battalions.[5]

"The British 14th Brigade around Heraklion covered the fourth sector, Australian 2/4th Battalion, and 7th Medium Regiment and the two Greek battalions."[6]

General Freyberg knew his weaknesses included a multinational force whose components varied greatly in terms of training, equipment and lack of basic stores.

The Royal Air Force had been decimated and that left Freyberg with a total lack of air power. The Luftwaffe enjoyed total domination of the skies over Crete.

On one occasion General Freyberg thought it important to rally his troops by visiting the sections. His intention was to boost the morale and fighting prowess of each man in readiness for an inevitable invasion of Crete by Germany. He set off and, accompanied by Brigadier Vasey, addressed the troops near Neo Chorio. In it, he gave an inspiring speech, according to Lieutenant-Colonel Leslie Le Souef. [7]

"His address as a man to man, caused a great impression, and the men were more than ever resolved to follow the policy he laid down." From Leslie Le Souef to *War Without a Gun*, Artlook, 1980, page 116.

The British had made good use of their one advantage in the deciphered German codes. Using these Ultra codes, they now knew the enemy details relating to their future plans.

The British discovered the Germans had supply problems in Greece, which would delay the assault by a week. Informed by Ultra sources of these changes, Freyberg was confident he had done all that was possible to meet the Germans with the limited resources and time available.

Later information concerned the British expecting the Germans to launch their attack on the island in mid-May 1941. The Germans planned to begin the invasion on the May 15th.

The Ultra code provided vital defence details, including the invasion date and the comparative strengths of German sea and airborne forces. Armed with this knowledge and Churchill's words ringing in his ears, Freyberg finished his speech by saying, "I am convinced that we stand a good chance of repelling the invaders and achieving a morale-boosting victory over the Germans."

The Germans were developing two plans to implement: seizing Crete and then setting in motion Operation Barbarossa, better known as the invasion of Russia. [8] After being assured that it would not seriously disrupt his plans in Eastern Europe, Adolf Hitler agreed to the invasion of Crete, known as Operation Mercury.

The Germans' plans would result in world domination for the Third Reich. Plan Merkur (Mercury) was to seize Crete using *Fallschirmjager* paratroopers. [9] The Germans under General Kurt Student had planned a three-pronged attack for the invasion. They settled on an airborne attack using gliders and paratroopers.

To support this initial attack, they would use two different timed assaults.

The first is in the morning on Souda Bay and Maleme, and the other is at Heraklion then Rethymno at 3:30 p.m. in the afternoon.

After the initial airborne attacks, the Germans intended to land a battalion and various heavy weapons and supplies by merchant ships at Souda Bay. This convoy was to wait just south of Greece until given the all-clear to attack Crete.

The Germans intended to mass an invasion force containing the following German manpower: The airborne invasion was to consist of 750 men riding in gliders and 10,000 in parachutes. These soldiers were to float into planned areas, build bridgeheads, and, when the numbers were right, attack the Allies.

Once the ground soldiers were in control, 5000 more would be landed by aircraft and 7000 from ships. To carry out the initial part of the plan, 70 to 80 gliders, 600 to 750 Junkers, and 52 Ju-52 transports were needed.

The main objectives were to capture the airports of Maleme, Rethymno, and Heraklion, along with the port at Souda.

On waking on the morning of May 20, 1941, the Allies went about their normal routines. The airborne invasion prediction for May 17 had not materialised; many, therefore, convinced themselves it would not take place at all. [10]

After a breakfast of bully beef, the men cleaned their rifles and swept tracks and footprints off the ground so that nothing could be seen from the air. This was what the Allies had done each day as the German spotter aeroplane that flew over each morning was taking photographs.

When analysed even the footprint of an army boot could be seen. Any information like that could alert the Germans to where the Allies were hidden and the numbers.

After eating a hearty breakfast on May 20, 1941, Sergeant George Flannagan, an Australian with the 2/7th Platoon of the Volunteer Defence Corps was sent out to patrol the beach. It was a few minutes to 8 am when he called for volunteers. There were plenty of takers mainly because those in the patrol got to go swimming immediately after the examination of the bay for any signs of enemy action or weapons washed up.

"Count me in sir," yelled a young private with great enthusiasm. He was an Australian serving in the 2/3rd Battalion, 16th Brigade.

"I'm in too, sir," called another Australian one of those types who always volunteered. "I'll grab my bathers."

With that comment hanging in the air, he ran for his tent.

Three New Zealanders who were always knocking around together raised their hands and said in unison, "We'll go with you."

The three inseparable soldiers were originally in three different battalions but since the Greek Campaign they had been recorded as missing and placed in X Battalion. [11]

Once the Army found them again, they would be returned to their original battalions. These moves would strengthen each of the 2nd New Zealand Division Platoon, 21st New Zealand Battalion, and 29th New Zealand Battalion.

"Right, looks like there are too many hands in the air so I'll do the selecting." He pointed at two nearby New Zealanders, one from the 20th New Zealand Battalion and the other from the 1st New Zealand Supply Company.

Flannigan needed two more, so he scanned the group and settled on a sapper from the Royal Engineers and the lucky last, a corporal from the 18th New Zealand Battalion.

"Right, on the double and no fooling around."

―∽―

The patrol set off at a merry rate as it was turning into a beautiful and sunny day. There wasn't a cloud in the sky as far as they could see.

Those who were up and on the move couldn't have asked for a more delightful summer's day. For late risers, breakfast was served, and this was a meal to remember.

Over the last couple of days, the eight o'clock routine visit of the 'shufti plane' the reconnaissance Dornier known as the 'flying pencil' because of its long thin fuselage, had been followed by intense waves of air attack. [12]

No one expected anything except the same as yesterday and the day before that. The reconnaissance aeroplane used by the Germans to obtain photographs of troop movements droned across the sky.

The film would be transferred to the brain trust at German headquarters, and they would magnify it dozens of times until they could see prints of army boots on the sand. This flyover was so regular that you could set your watch by its visit, that is, if you had a pocket watch.

The Luftwaffe would fly over around 0800 hours and drop a few bombs to scare everyone. Then, the rest of the day was fun, and you could frolic with your mates.

—ɯ—

May 20, 1941, looked like every other day since the men had landed in Souda Bay and gazed upon an idyllic island in the middle of the Mediterranean Sea. Their escape from Greece was still fresh in their memories, and they still wondered about the fate of the tens of thousands who didn't make it.

The odd but distant humming noise had not registered other than being a part of the island's background noise. You hear things around you but nothing materialises. The croaking of frogs, the incessant sawing of crickets' legs or the rustle of wind through the trees.

Everyone just continued their normal routines. They would soon find out what was going on. Apart from the usual noises there was, however, a more potent menace, and it was just over the horizon.

—⚊—

Then they heard what every other person on the island reported hearing. It was a low, almost inconceivable, humming far to the north and above the Mediterranean Sea. General Student, the German in command, was about to surprise and shock the Allies.

He had been training the 5th Gebirgs Division [13] on an airfield in Greece for several days along with other German soldiers. They had all learnt to jump from the aircraft and felt the ripcord being automatically wrenched. They felt the tugging on the backpack as they fell from the aeroplane.

They had learnt to absorb the shock as the legs touched the earth then how to roll and begin unfastening their harnesses.

All were involved in simulation parachute jumping. The men practised over and over until they felt that it was easy and smooth. Unfortunately, it didn't turn out so easy on the day and from a height of 900 to 1500 feet.

General Student [14] had planned an attack using thousands of planes, gliders and paratroopers. He had been training the Austrian elite paratroopers for a blitz on Crete from the sky.

The men were up bright and early, checking and folding their parachutes and checking that the pistol they carried was fully loaded. The leader of each group and the aeroplane made sure they had the coloured parachutes and the canisters they would throw out of the plane once the men had jumped. These coloured parachutes contained the supplies the men would need once they landed.

The colours indicated medical supplies, ammunition, guns, grenades, tents, and food, everything they would need to capture the enemy.

Before General Student sent his paratroopers onto the planes, he ordered the bombers to continuously bomb Crete to soften up the troops hiding on the island.

The sight of watching thousands of paratroopers loaded into hundreds of aeroplanes and gliders would have had General Student smiling widely. The formation of aircraft began taxiing onto the main tarmac, and hundreds of Junkers, Dorniers, Heinkels, gliders and Stukas roared into the cloudless sky, linked into formation and headed for Crete.

Inside each German aeroplane, the dispatcher opened the door in the side of the fuselage, and the roaring throb of the engines, both hypnotic and disturbing, was altered by the rush of wind. The parachutists were alerted, it was time to go.

The call to get ready, and all the paratroopers stood lining up one behind the other. the pushing of each man out the door at the signal told everyone that the enemy was below. Parachutists were specially trained to know the routine from, 'Ready, to landing'.

CHAPTER 12

—☓—

The invasion of Crete was like watching a kaleidoscope, except instead of changing colour patterns, there was a whirl of aircraft, parachutes, men, soldiers and weapons. Every man had a different description of what they saw and what they did. It was chaos at boiling point.

Starting just after 1030 hours, the Luftwaffe sent in their Stukas, Junkers, Doniers, Heinkels and Messerschmitts to bomb and strafe the airfields, towns, roads and beaches along the north coast. [1]

Bomber raids softened up the entire area of northern Crete. This had become a normal expectation but it became obvious that May 20 was stronger and longer as the Germans pounded and strafed Crete from Retimo to Stavromenos.

The German invasion of Crete caught the Allies unawares even though they knew through Ultra that it was going to happen mid May. 'The longer you wait, the more unlikely things will not happen,' seemed to be the attitude.

An airborne invasion the size of which the Germans had amassed was certainly a shock to all who witnessed it. By keeping their heads down, the Allies were safe for the moment. [2]

Lieutenant Gerry Wild was returning to Hill B, where his Battalion, the 2/11th, was camped when he saw one of the most amazing sights ever. "Coming in across the sea towards the island was a tremendous column of low-flying aircraft as far as the eye could see. Wild commented later, "Before I reached my headquarters, the first of them had arrived. They swept from the sea over the airfield and then flew parallel to the coast, moving west."

It became evident that the Germans had not found where the Allies were hiding, as their attack was indiscriminate. The battalion being hit hardest was the 2/1st.

Lieutenant Wild and the patrol he was in charge had to take urgent action. They hid as best they could and were, by some miracle, unharmed. They remained quiet and still throughout the bombing. As the minutes ticked by, a small black cloud developed again to the north, but no one seemed to be aware of this.

The noise gave the clue that something far out to sea was on the move. Those who were always alert heard the humming at first, and then a while later, this turned to a throbbing of engines, aircraft engines.

"All eyes turned seaward, and another large number of aircraft could be seen coming from the north," Wes Olson *Battalion into Battle*" page 155. [3]

Major Raymond Sandover, in charge of the 2/11th Battalion, called all his men to battle stations and added that no one was to open fire until ordered. He reasoned that by remaining quiet, the Germans would not be able to find a target for their strafing and bombing. They watched as the gliders being towed came overhead. Following behind came the rumbling of the approaching air armada.

The first planes turned west as they crossed the coast away from Rethymno. A second wave appeared with some of the Junkers 52s also towing gliders.

From then on, larger formations flew towards Chania every 15 minutes. The blitz to take control of Crete and dislodge the Allies from the island had begun in earnest. Hundreds of planes lumbered through the sky, dropping German paratroopers into the area around Maleme and the township of Chania.

The Allies stood still, watching, and not yet realising they needed to retaliate. They had been told not to engage the enemy until given the order. Suddenly, Major Sandover's loud shout broke the air. "Fire!" he called.

Another cry went up from within the ranks and this was echoed across the areas where soldiers waited. Every man obliged, and aiming their rifles and Bren guns into the mass of parachutes descending so gently, they opened fire. The men of Creforce started to make out gliders being towed by the larger Junkers 52 planes.

As soon as the men were jerked into action, a 'duck shoot' began. The paratroopers who cleared the aeroplanes floated ever so slowly down. In addition to the ones the soldiers wore, there was an assortment of coloured parachutes. The other coloured parachutes carried canisters to the ground. The Germans would hunt down these canisters as they carried vital equipment needed by the troops to operate.

The paratroopers twisted and spun, and their legs jerked. When they went still the Allies knew that they had been killed.

No sooner had the first wave passed when another 20 aeroplanes came out of the northern sky. Mortar bombs soon rained down on the Hawke's Bay Battalion positions, indicating a German group had reached the ground. The Taranaki Company was sent to deal with the mortar. This was quickly done.

The 3rd German Parachute Regiment had established a foothold near Maleme and began to make its way across the island.

More aeroplanes, Junkers 52s, came in from the north. They were flying at 1000 feet, and doors were seen from the ground to be open. Paratroopers were jumping out every second. The air invasion of Crete was well underway. Another 20 planes came out of the northern sky. The New Zealanders got to work again, as did the Australians up on Hill 107.

Through sheer numbers, it was getting to the point where some Germans were getting through and joining up into fighting groups. Some tried to retrieve the canisters but were picked off by snipers. The airborne invasion and the one to come via the sea were both going badly for the Germans. [4]

At another position, 10 groups of 500 soldiers had landed safely, and they began to set themselves up by grabbing their guns and ammunition from the canisters. [5]

The Royal Navy had been busy at sea and dealt with and sunk part of the German invasion fleet, which had been mustered off the coast of southern Greece. This convoy of ships was waiting for the paratroopers to indicate they had captured the port at Souda Bay and the Maleme Airfield. On board were thousands of German soldiers waiting to assist the paratroopers.

Due to the Ultra code, the Allies were aware of this armada and contacted the British navy to seek out and destroy the shipping before it could reach Crete. The Royal Navy accepted this, which lifted a huge weight off those on the island.

The Junkers 52s reached land and disgorged their cargo of hundreds of paratroopers. Each plane was also towing three gliders, which were full of parachutists. So much was happening that William Taylor and his mates had difficulty describing the scene.

Some planes crashed, some flew lower than others and tangled parachutists in their propellers and wings. The continuous firing from the ground killed hundreds.

William Taylor's Diary described the parachutes as they drifted earthwards. "There were different colours to mark the ones carrying in the canister medical supplies, food and ammunition. Then there were ones supporting motorcycles, four-inch mortars and other heavy guns."

All the while, the Bren and machine guns of the Allies kept up a steady firing.

What was planned to be a parachute invasion that would have the Allies surrender within the day became utter chaos.

The taking of prisoners became a problem. Able-bodied infantry had to be taken away from the fight to supervise them. German casualties mounted quickly. Many paratroopers died before they could reach the ground, others were mown down after landing as they struggled to release themselves from their harnesses.

Despite heavy losses, enough troops landed safely to secure tenuous footholds. One such area was west of Maleme, which General Freyberg mistakenly left unguarded. Another, along the Prison Valley Road, was established southwest of Chania.

The paratroopers who cleared the planes floated ever so slowly down. The men looked like "Macabre puppets on a string", the white parachutes billowing above them.

The shooters watched as the jerking figures ceased moving. They moved their gun sights to the next figure and pumped more lead into the sky.

During the fighting, many German prisoners were taken. One of these was the German force commander, Colonel Alfred Sturm.

Eventually, the Germans did get a foothold in several areas, but the Allies never gave up.

—⚇—

Five West Australians lay low on Hill A, watching the incredible scene unfold and waiting for further orders. Bonnie Buirchell, Vic Petersen, Herbert Stratton, William Taylor and Alf Traub stood fascinated but shocked at what was unfolding.

They had never observed such an amazing spectacle and were unlikely to ever see one like this again in their lifetimes.

Each of the men stood still, taking in what appeared to be an imaginary scene on an artist's canvas: hundreds of aeroplanes, thousands of parachutes of differing colours, and thousands of parachutists hanging from their parachutes. The latter floated like dummies in a surreal scene above the heads of the Allies.

The German paratroopers tussled with their parachutes and their landing places; others got pulled into the aeroplane they had jumped from, and others were blown off course. It was a chaotic scene that captivated the Allies. These men were so shocked that in the future, they would push these scenes to the back of their minds and rarely speak about them.

There were reports from sections of the field of a Junkers Ju52 crashing and killing many of the passengers and crew. The highly trained German *Fallschirmjagers* would find that by the time their group landed, so many had died that they couldn't gather together all the soldiers and weapons they needed.

One Junker crashed near Major Sandover's headquarters and another four near Perivolia. Private Edgar Randolph of the 2/7th Field Ambulance had an exact view of a Junker that was machine gunned.[6]

In an interview with author Olson, Wes. *Battalion into Battle: The History of the 2/11th Australian Infantry Battalion 1939 – 1945*. Quality Press, 2011, Randolph was reported as saying, "The front engine caught alight, the fire spread backwards in seconds, and the plane nosed down. Four men got out, but their chutes had no time to spread out and went in hard. The plane just ploughed on into the olives and smashed along about half a mile, a total wreck with no survivors."

Another oral report to Sandover spoke about six parachutists jumping from a low altitude and three luckily got their chutes open. Still, the other three missed the opening of parachutes and went in too hard. For those Germans who could parachute safely, the next challenge was recouping the canisters and the items stowed inside. Until they had unpacked enough of these canisters, they would continue to be at a complete disadvantage. [7]

They were only permitted to carry a pistol as a side arm and some small egg grenades while parachuting. They had to get to the canisters carrying the heavier weapons with larger calibres.

By the close of the first day, the Germans had suffered terrible defeats in all the sectors the Allies were defending.

In the Retimo Sector, the estimate of the number of captured, wounded and dead was half of the entire 1550 parachutists.

By the end of May 20, German forces around Maleme, Rethymno, and Heraklion had failed to secure any of their objectives. The commanders and planners of the operation in Athens were dismayed that the carefully laid-out plan was a failure. The prospect of a humiliating German defeat loomed. It was decided to throw all available resources into an attack on Maleme.

The calculated risk was extremely high, but the commanders had to try to salvage something from the disastrous situation.

Securing the airfield was the key to the invasion's success; reinforcements could not be sent in without it.

The German commanders' idea was to send an aeroplane full of Austrian trained commandos into the pitch black of a moonless night.

They would be under orders to take the Maleme Airfield and hold it until other forces could be sent in. The danger here was the landing of an aeroplane in the dead of night on a runway that was in disarray from bomb craters and wreckage of all sorts.

The pilot was specially selected, told of the dangers, and assured he would be a hero by turning the war in favour of the Germans.

Through skill and determination, the selected pilot landed the aircraft, and the commandos were able to set up a base in and around Maleme airfield. This daring manoeuvre became the defining point of the war and switched the advantage to the Germans.

—⚍—

Charles Amos George Victor Petersen, WX 571, preferred to be called Vic, and most of his mates were happy to call him by that shorter version.

Vic was born on August 27, 1913, in Bridgetown, Western Australia. He was one of many who volunteered for service during World War II's outbreak. He enlisted in November 1939 and trained at the Northam Army Camp, about 95km east of Perth, the capital of Western Australia.

Being a West Australian, he was placed in the 2/11th Battalion, often called the Perth Battalion. The 2/11th Battalion was part of the 6th Division under Lieutenant General Sir Thomas Blamey.

Blamey chose Brigadier Arthur Allen, Brigadier Stanley Savige, Sir Lesley Morshead, and Lieutenant Colonel Duncan Maxwell as Brigade leaders. These men would lead the 16th, 17th, 18th, and 19th Brigade in the early 40s.

—⚍—

Three weeks after the newly formed 2/11th Battalion began its basic training, the whole unit was transferred to Rutherford, New South Wales and moved by road to Greta, New South Wales, to continue army training. During Vic's time spent in eastern Australia, he had the fortune to meet and befriend a farming family called the Walkers. One of the daughters caught Vic's eye; there was more to tell later in his life.

In March 1940, the Battalion returned to Perth for pre-embarkation leave. That was the last opportunity for the soldiers to visit their families and friends.

Private Petersen was a robust man who stood up for what he believed in. He was always ready to help his fellow mates and readily volunteered if an important or dangerous mission was put forward.

After a farewell march through the streets of Perth, the Battalion departed for the Middle East on April 20, 1940.

The entire Perth Battalion was on board the troopship HMHS *Nevasa*. One of the escort ships was the Royal Sovereign-class battleship HMS *Ramillies*.

CHAPTER 13

Arriving in Egypt via the Suez Canal, the 2/11th Battalion continued training and acclimatising [1] to desert conditions in Gaza and Egypt.

Vic was involved in manoeuvres throughout North Africa and Palestine before being recalled to Alexandria, where he was re-assigned to assist the Greeks in stopping the Germans from invading their country. As a member of the 2/11th Battalion he was ordered to muster at Alexandria. The ship sailed to Athens, and from there, a convoy of trucks set out for Mount Olympus.

The soldiers in the truck that Vic was with were excitedly talking about their 'Greek Tour". It seemed surreal to them all to be cruising the Mediterranean Sea for free and viewing all the sites they had only seen on tourist pamphlets. Having sailed through the famous Greek Isles, they were presently being driven through the ancient ruins of Athens. The Acropolis stirred the thrill of seeing such buildings that still stood after thousands of years.

Mount Olympus was the main topic of conversation as the lorry sped along after the many ahead of it. By the time the Battalion reached the passes through the mountains, it was drizzling and snowing.

The Yugoslav and Greek armies, which had held off Italian Army attacks, collapsed against an intense German attack. The Germans then provided direct support to the Italians.

The Germans were beginning to break through, and the Allies' forward scouts brought back ominous observations about their strength and mobilisation.

It was recommended the Allies retreat to Mount Olympus. The retreat order was to become all too familiar for Vic and his mates. More was to come in his direction in a way very few would have expected.

In northern Greece, the Australian, New Zealand and British were continuously attacked by German Stuka dive bombers. The screaming bombers were scary and lethal.

The next action for the 2/11th Battalion was against the German Army in northern Greece.

There were Panzer tanks and battle hardened SS troops from the elite *Leibstandarte* Adolph Hitler Division. The Allies were completely overrun and had to fall back, resulting in a retreat to southern Greece. Vic Petersen and his mates were evacuated to southern Greece. They found themselves in a rolling retreat, which took three days, constantly defending and then retreating. They were trying desperately to give the thousands of Allies time to reach Athens, find a British warship, and sail to safety.

Once the troops reached the southern shores, they found several British warships waiting to take them away.

They were all too aware of the danger that lurked [2] only a few miles to the north and moving fast.

Many of the soldiers of the 2/11th were rowed to British ships which were waiting to sail to Crete.[3]

Vic and his mates were already on board and were pleased to see so many of the Battalion climbing the scramble ropes.

On April 26, 1941, a nighttime embarkation from the Greek ports of Nauflion and Kalamata was made, thus allowing the bulk of Commonwealth forces to escape to Crete. This daring evacuation of 40,000 Commonwealth forces from Greece is recorded as a major achievement of WWII. The Royal Navy [4] did a brilliant job taking so many off Greece and landing them on Crete.

The Greek Army had no option but to negotiate an armistice with Germany. They refused to surrender to the Italian forces.

—⚡—

The Allies who landed on Crete were thankful for the rest and food that was on offer. The local inhabitants were pleased to welcome them as they feared they would also become a target of the Germans in a few weeks.

The two groups got along and helped each other set up defence systems as ordered by General Freyberg, the officer in charge of the army on Crete. The General was helpful in setting up the defence around Hill 107 [5] and Maleme Airfield in the days leading up to May 20, or Blitzkrieg Day.

It was a major concern and a talking point that the soldiers did not have enough weapons and ammunition. As requested, the men had been ordered to destroy all the gear they carried or might be useful to the Germans.

The Australians were joined by the other countries comprising the Lustre Force, including Britain and New Zealand. The defence system was designed to keep the men of each battalion and country together and to defend the four hills beyond Souda Bay. In addition, they had to defend the airfields, as an invading country would use them as a landing and gathering point. The airfields included Maleme, Retimo, and Heraklion.

The Australian 2/7th and 2/8th battalions joined the New Zealanders in trying to keep the German commandos and others from capturing the Maleme Airfield and surrounding areas.

On May 27 the 28th New Zealand Battalion, which was defending the Maleme Airfield, was attacked by a small group of Germans. A signalman was sent for reinforcements, and the Australian 23rd Battalion and 28th New Zealand Battalion obliged, sending a company from each.

The extra numbers helped to decide to attack the Germans. They lined up with the New Zealand Maoris in front, Australians next, and a group of locals armed with kitchen and agricultural equipment (to be used as weapons). They were looking down a line running south from Souda Bay to the foothills of the Malaxa escarpment. The line followed 42nd Street.

The action fought on this sunken road was crucial in delaying advancing German troops moving east from the Maleme airfield. That road ran southeast from Chania to the giant naval port of Souda Bay, vital for incoming supplies delivered by sea.

It was known as 42nd Street and would become the last hoorah for the defenders of Souda Bay, mainly New Zealanders and some Australian troops who would undertake most of the hand-to-hand fighting on Crete. [6]

As the two antagonists moved towards each other, Maori soldiers reverted to traditional methods with their war cry known as the Haka. One of the young soldiers began to yell out, "Let your valour rise! Let your valour rage!" [7]

Hardly had the first line been called when all the New Zealand soldiers fixed bayonets. Ponaute Busby was directly behind the leader, shouting loudly and brandishing his rifle, the bayonet catching the light as it was waved around. He was a young Maori and one of the soldiers who remained on the island beyond early September 1941.

Behind Ponaute [8] and his mates, the Australians followed suit and began their war cry. The group further back were the locals carrying various tools such as axes, knives, and scythes. They were proud Cretans prepared to defend their country by any means possible. Within the crowd there were family groups, old people and young, married couples and even children. Their adrenaline built up as they raced after the Australians and New Zealanders intent on engaging the enemy.

The Germans hesitated for a split second, some to loosen off a round or two before they broke ranks and tried to outrun the screaming horde. For most, it was too late, and they were killed. More than 80 German troops died in the action. However, there would be repercussions for this Allied success in more ways than one.

The victory on 42nd Street was morale boosting but it came too late for the Allies on Crete. The spread of the Germans across the northern beaches was such that General Freyberg determined that the Allies were losing too many men and too much ground. He believed only an evacuation could save most of the remaining men.

CHAPTER 14

—m—

Only four lines in his records describe what happened to Alf Traub from when he left Alexandria until he arrived at Stalag VIII-B.

These showed that on April 10, 1941, Alf embarked for Greece; on June 4, he was missing; by June 8, he was believed to be a POW, but no location was given; December 15, 1941, he was officially recorded as POW incarcerated in Stalag VIII-B.

Traub was one of those men who showed a determination to do his best at all times and to use his initiative as shown.

The following story is from Alf Traub's interview with Wes Olson, author of *Battalion into Battle*.[1]

Alf Traub liked to help out in the hospital and did so at every opportunity. He found he could converse with the patients as he spoke Yiddish. One particular German officer was in a bad way and it was Alf's kindness and chatting that he befriended Alf. They were able to talk about how to alleviate the suffering of the officer. He recuperated quickly and was so impressed he told Alf that he would return the favour if he ever wanted one.

A few days later Traub, was deputised by Colonel Campbell to speak for the other ranks and ask to see the German officer-in-charge of the Retimo Sector so that he might arrange food and water for the men. The officer duly met with Traub, but said there was no food and as for water, 'you will have to look for that yourself'. In the meantime, he informed Alf that, owing to the finding of the mutilated corpses of German soldiers after what he called the 42nd Street Incident, he was taking steps to execute 10 percent of Allies and Greeks as a retaliatory measure. Alf was then dismissed.

Traub related that at that time he was furious and that things looked very grim but then a miracle appeared. It was the paratrooper officer whom Traub had administered first aid to when the German was a prisoner of the Australians. The officer recognised him and asked if there was anything he could do.

"Yes," Traub said, "Plenty."

Traub explained his predicament and asked the German if he could arrange a meeting with his commanding officer and the senior Australian officer, Colonel Campbell.

The German immediately made contact with his headquarters, told Traub that a guard would be calling for them in the afternoon, and arranged for an issue of water before departing.

Colonel Ian Campbell, Major Ian Bessell-Browne and Private Traub were duly collected and taken to German headquarters where they were confronted by the general commanding the Retimo sector. With the help of three German paratroopers, they convinced the general that the Allied troops were innocent of the charges. It was Traub's tenacity and his strong belief in justice that had saved the lives of dozens of soldiers.

One issue Alf was never able to resolve, according to military rules, was his status in the Army. When he joined the army, he was a private, as were most volunteers or conscripts, but his willingness to accept extra duties and to use his initiative should have led to promotions.

He rose to corporal and then, during his time on Crete, showed such commonsense and gallantry that his senior officer verbally told him he had the skills and ability to be a sergeant. The role of interpreter is seen as equal to that of a sergeant. Therefore, as he was acting as an official interpreter, he should have automatically been given the rank of sergeant. This promotion was never confirmed, even though exhaustive inquiries were made.

What Alf did on Crete was way beyond the call of duty, and the effectiveness of his decisions marked him as a sergeant.

The Cretans were hell bent on defending their land, heritage, and freedom. They saw nothing wrong with attacking the invading troops of Germany and using whatever weapons they could find. [2]

The first incident involving the local Cretans in fighting the Germans occurred near the village of Perivolia. On May 20, 1941, the German paratroopers had found their descent near the area of the village relatively easy and the landing uneventful. Unfortunately, those who dropped into and near the village of Perivolia were quickly set upon by the civilians and dispatched. [3]

On Invasion Day, a team of German paratroopers from the 3rd Battalion of the 1st Air Landing Assault Regiment was dropped near Maleme. The landing sites included the villages of Platanias and Kondomari.

One of the first examples of spontaneous mobilisation [4]

was an attack on the rear of the Parachute Engineer Battalion, which had landed around Lake Ayi. Cretan irregulars advanced from their large village of Alikianos. They meant business and were readily searching for Germans.

The village of Alikianos is situated on a plain on the northern side of Crete. It is 12km from Chania and is surrounded by several small villages Skines, Fournes, Vatolakos, Prases, Karanos, Lakkoi, Orthouni, Hosti and Nea Roumata.

The Third *Fallschirmjager* Regiment was to land on the plateau and advance towards Maleme Airfield. Covering the rear of these parachutists was the 7th Engineer Battalion between the village of Alikianos and the dry river bed of the Keritis River.

The 7th Engineers were stopped by the 8th Greek Regiment, an assortment of locals with primitive weapons who attacked the Germans, killing many of them.

The fighting around Alikianos lasted for seven days, and fighting broke out daily between the village and what was to become Prison Valley.

The Germans were incensed by the attacks carried out by non military personnel.

There was never any doubt that the Cretans would defend their land tenaciously, as they had done for millennia. The history of Crete has been one of almost constant invasion, as the island was in a strategic position in the Mediterranean Sea.

Boys, girls, men, women, and the elderly displayed breathtaking bravery in facing the German invaders.

Priests and monks led their parishioners into battle. Father Stylianos Frantzeskakis [5] rushed to his church to sound the bell upon learning of the airborne invasion.

Taking a rifle, he marched his volunteers north from Paleokhoria and later fought German motorcycle detachments when they reached the village of Kandanos.

On May 24, 1941, while the battle on Crete raged, a German patrol arrested six locals in Alikianos after finding the body of a German parachutist. As a reprisal, the patrol killed the civilians by firing squad.

However, on June 1, 1941, the Germans began a planned reprisal campaign. They would send out patrols to round up local Cretans in towns. The men and boys would be separated and taken away to be shot by firing squad.

To add to the terror and to emphasise that what they were doing was a payback for the deaths of their comrades, they would take torches and raze the town. The women and girls would be left with nothing except the sorrow of the death of their husbands and sons. The reprisals [6] had begun, and the Germans were extremely brutal in the way they carried these out.

The Allies became aware of these indiscriminate killings without judicial proceedings.

Although they could do very little as they were too busy fleeing either to Sfakia or into the hills, they verbally protested whenever they found the chance.

The people of Crete continued to use primitive weapons such as axes, scythes, and spades to attack and harry the invaders.

During the airborne blitz on May 20, 1941, the parachutists found that removing the parachute was cumbersome and took too long. The people of Perivolia used this to their advantage and would move swiftly and determinedly. They managed to kill more than 400 Germans. The New Zealand 26th and 28th battalions were also involved but stuck to the rules of the Geneva Convention.

There were other skirmishes where the Cretans took up arms and chased down the Germans. Rumours and exaggerated stories abounded among the German paratroopers. The Allies were being blamed for attacking and mutilating German soldiers.

The German General Julius Ringel, [7] commander of the 5th Mountain Division, was incensed.

Ringel reported that the Cretan civilians were picking off paratroopers or attacking them with knives, axes and scythes. Ringel was particularly infuriated and argued that this was against the Prussian sense of military order, which stated that no one except professional warriors should be allowed to fight.

Rumours across the island suggested that these attacks were causing high causalities to the German paratroopers. General Ringel reported his observations and rumours to General Student and demanded retribution. Student sent a message to Berlin declaring that some of the German soldiers had been found mutilated.

He demanded that the people responsible for using non-military weapons be executed.

The Nazi high command, through General Hermann Goering, gave approval for reprisals against the people of Crete. [8] General Kurt Student immediately arranged to have reprisal units target the Cretans. He sent patrols to villages to interrogate the locals and to then execute the men and youths. His favoured method was firing squad. In some more brutal attacks, the Germans were ordered to torch the entire village.

The local Cretan people had a ferocious desire to keep their land free from invaders and to live a peaceful life. Family was important, and the older generation believed in doing everything possible for the younger generations.

―⁂―

After 10 days of brutal fighting and heavy losses on both sides, General Freyberg was becoming concerned that his troops were being overrun. He contacted headquarters in Alexandria to arrange for as many ships as possible to pick up his troops from Sfakia, a small fishing village on the south side of Crete.

After a week of fighting, General Freyberg ordered the Allies to flee south to Sfakia. This village was on the south coast, and British warships were arranged to take the soldiers back to Alexandria. The men were to make their way to Sfakia while commandos comprised of Australians and New Zealanders would hold the Germans by rearguard action.

On May 29, 1941, tens of thousands of soldiers begrudgingly set off to cross the mountains for Sfakia. The Alexandria Headquarters was able to organise several Royal Navy ships to sail under darkness to Sfakia and pick up as many Allies as possible. They were then to return under darkness to Alexandria.

It was imperative to sail only at night, as the Luftwaffe controlled the skies and would be ready at light each day to hunt down Allied ships still at sea.

In the meantime, the Allied soldiers had to move quickly to catch the British ships waiting off the coast of Sfakia.

They were given three days from May 29 to be on the beach at Sfakia. The ships were going to be available for three nights only.

The going was tough as the days were hot and water was scarce. Those who tried to carry much equipment soon found it too difficult. They had to rest during the day in caves and under shade and travel carefully at night, avoiding the terrain's dangers.

Between the Allied troops and Sfakia was a range of mountains called the White Mountains, which proved difficult to negotiate and a tough climb for many.

In an effort to give the fleeing soldiers a chance to reach Sfakia in time without being hassled by the Germans, the New Zealand commandos and the Australian 2/11th slowed the Germans through rearguard actions.

The men were told to make for Sfakia, where they would find British warships waiting to take them off Crete and back to Alexandria, Egypt.

Some of the field officers decided to offer their troops a chance to escape into the hills. Many men accepted this idea, going off in groups to hide in the mountains until they could be rescued or find ways to get off the island through their own ingenuity.

While the Allied soldiers made haste for Sfakia, they left the locals vulnerable. The Cretan population was left to the mercy of the Germans.

The next message from General Freyberg shocked many of the soldiers on Crete as he ordered them to capitulate on June 1, 1941. [9]

This meant they would surrender, an idea none of the Allies had ever contemplated.

The day after the Allies surrendered, the Germans turned ferociously on the people of Crete.

There were four lorries loaded with Germans sent to the village of Kondomari. The town was quickly surrounded by the populace, who paraded in the town square. While the women and children were separated from the men, the Germans moved the adult males in groups over to the churchyard. Here they were shot in front of their relatives.

On the same day, in two villages, 12 males were shot in Agia, and another 25 civilians were shot by the firing squad in Kyrtomados. On June 3, 1941, Kandanos was razed to the ground as reprisal for what was later found to be exaggerated stories about the killing of German soldiers by locals. Nearby towns such as Floria and Kakopetria met similar fates. During the weeks of the reprisals, 160 men were shot, livestock was slaughtered, and houses torched.

CHAPTER 15

—◊—

Alf Traub set the example for the severely wounded who would have died given the journey over the mountains. Considering the terrain, lack of food and water, and the makeshift way they would have been moved, they would certainly have suffered excruciatingly. He volunteered to stay behind and look after the patients. [1]

The Germans discovered what the Allies were planning, so they followed the trail over the mountains, intending to catch and turn the fleeing soldiers around.

The Germans were more mobile and moved quickly into the mountains. Because of the great work done in a similar situation in Greece by the New Zealand commandos of the 5th Infantry Battalion, they were selected to do the job. The New Zealanders had to slow the Germans and not allow themselves to become outflanked. The two Australian Battalions, the 2/7th and 2/11th, were called to help by manning up on the outside flanks. [2]

The action by the Anzac troops resulted in vital minutes for those fleeing to get through difficult terrain and reach Sfakia. Time was also needed to load the evacuees onto the British naval vessels.

Day after day, the Anzacs held the Germans at bay, falling back and attacking repeatedly. The New Zealanders and Australians were pleased that night fell so the enemy couldn't see them. The rearguard effort left the men exhausted and thirsty, but it was successful.

Headquarters was concerned that the Maleme garrison needed to be evacuated. General Freyberg sent a signalman with a message that basically said all Allies were to pull out and begin a withdrawal towards the town of Sfakia.

Thousands of men climbed the hills and mountains on their way to Sfakia during the three nights from May 29 to May 31. [3] They fought off fatigue and thirst to make the rendezvous. The rearguard soldiers kept the Germans out of range until they rounded the corner at Sfakia. They were shocked to see there were still thousands to be evacuated.

They waited for the morning only to find that the ships had not returned. Rumour had it that the Allies were ordered to surrender in the morning.

Upon hearing that the Allies had surrendered, Traub, who had not fled but remained at Rethymno, was one who was 'rage fluttering' [4] because the men had been left to fend for themselves.

It was still dark when General Freyberg was driven to Sfakia with selected officers. This group made its way through the throngs of soldiers who waited patiently for their turn to embark on one of the three ships they could see the outline of the ships out to sea. General Freyberg and his leadership group found the men parting away as he progressed towards the water's edge. Several lower-ranked officers greeted them, ushered them into a small boat, and rowed them out to a flying boat specially sent from Alexandria to assist their escape.

Not one of the officers in the flying boat turned to look towards the shore even though they were fully aware they had jumped the queue and that the lines of men had come to a final stop and no one else would make it to the ships. Like many of the soldiers on Crete that day, Alf's opinion [5] of the officers took a nosedive.

CHAPTER 16

—m—

Another member of the Allies who went way beyond his call of duty was Colonel Leslie Le Souef.[1]

It was near Sfakia on the south coast of the island of Crete on June 1, 1941, that the Colonel was trying to wake up but struggled to do so.

"Through the haze of almost conscious sleep, a voice intruded, carrying a sordid message that the navy could not come anymore. General Freyberg had left an order that all members of the Allied fighting battalions must capitulate. Leslie Le Souef, *To War Without a Gun*, Artlook,1980. The importance of what filtered into Colonel Le Souef's brain suddenly welled into his consciousness. Now alert, he instantly sat up and found himself thinking and repeating: It cannot be happening, not to me! Surrender!" [2]

Le Souef never contemplated becoming a prisoner of war, but Major-General Eric Culpeper Weston, commander of the remaining forces in Crete, apparently ordered him to surrender to the enemy. The last ship had sailed, so it was deemed necessary to surrender. [3]

"Le Souef awoke to find white clothes and rage fluttering everywhere. On enquiring of W. W. (Bill) Gunther what was up, he was set right back to be told HQ had gone during the night, leaving orders to surrender and that the Germans would arrive in a few hours." Molly Watt in *The Stunned and the Stymied*, Westralian Publishers, 1996. [4]

Leslie Le Souef rubbed his eyes with his fists and tried to get his head around the message. He threw the blanket off and jumped to his feet.

Two steps and he was looking at a world gone mad. In the entire area, from the caves high up on the hills overlooking Sfakia to the edge of the Mediterranean Sea, men were smashing their weapons and shouting obscenities.

One of Le Souef's officers, W. W. (Bill) Gunther, [5] was the messenger that Le Souef heard in his waking daze. The men were running around aimlessly, trying to understand what was senseless. No one could get their heads around the fact that the Australians, New Zealanders, and British soldiers had to surrender. Not one of them, in their wildest dreams, had anticipated such an outcome. They had considered themselves invincible.

These men had been through hell and back. They did not select the time or place for this to be part of their lives forever. The thoughts to connect the time and place together would leave them all changed men. [6]

Even more daunting was the behaviour of those on the edge, having endured 10 days of fighting a formidable enemy.

They had been in the thick of fighting in Greece, the parachute blitz on Crete followed by 10 days of combat. To top it all off, there were three days of exhaustion while making a desperate run for Sfakia. After all of these frenetic efforts, they were made to surrender and then marched back over the mountains, without food or water, into captivity.

Every man's mind had been altered, and now, as stories filtered in about the Germans' treatment of the local population, deep sorrow for the Cretan people enveloped many of them. To think that the Cretan people were watching their lives implode was the last thing the Allies wanted to hear.

At Sfakia, before the march back, one of the soldiers took his pistol out of its holster and ended the mayhem right where he stood. [7] Another was so shocked he voided and then, facing disgrace, ran into the Mediterranean Sea to wash himself. [8] Others were swearing and smashing their weapons to pieces. Yet others stood stock still as though their life had been sucked out of their physical selves.

What now was in store for the Allies? Could they contemplate that it would involve capture, thirst, incarceration in a prison and a trip on a ship to the notorious Salonika Prison? From Salonika would come a train ride in cattle trucks during a freezing winter and a final stop at a stalag in Germany where they would be used as slave labour to keep the German war machine advancing across the world.

—m—

Gunther was standing some distance from the tent from which Leslie had emerged. He called out further parts of the message, which indicated that several colonels were meeting on the beach to study a hand-written order from General Freyberg. [9]

Leslie set off to see if he could add anything further to the discussion. As he approached, he could make out three officers, and they were examining the contents of a piece of paper.

Perhaps there could not have been a more beautiful and peaceful morning. Not a ripple stirred the top of the water to vary the light effects on the visible sandy bottom. This was a beach barely twenty yards long, over which thousands of men had already passed to be ferried by landing barges to the waiting ships during the preceding few nights.

Near the beach's waterline, three officers were earnestly debating how to continue. They sang the praises of the men in the rearguard for the past 30 hours.

One officer in the group was heard to say, "Terrific job the boys did in slowing the Germans down."

Another replied, "I would have liked to have been a fly on the wall to see that action. It was bloody amazing.

"Those New Zealanders, the ones they call Maoris, routed the Germans at least twice with fixed bayonets and blood curdling chanting. It really must have been sensational to watch and hear."

Now, the officers had to determine how to negotiate a formal surrender situation. They knew they had to wait for Lieutenant Colonel Theodore Gordon Walker [10] to arrive and work out who was the most senior officer at the beach.

As Le Souef approached the group, one raised his hand and pointed inland. "Here comes Lieutenant Colonel Walker now." They all snapped to attention and saluted the officer arriving in haste. He returned the respect and asked, "I assume you have all had time to digest the situation and the steps left?"

The group nodded, and he continued. "We must appoint a senior officer to negotiate a surrender with the Germans immediately. We have no options but to seek a surrender on their conditions, and that will make it hard for every one of our men."

It took less than a minute for the group to agree that Lieutenant Colonel Walker was the most senior officer at Sfakia. He had to determine what would happen and who would accompany him to the German headquarters. Walker chose Captain Archie Cochrane to negotiate a formal truce.

Every one of the officers standing around the original three nodded in agreement.

As the message and the line of command were dealt with, Colonel Walker and Captain Cochrane, the regimental medical officer of the commandos who spoke fluent German, set out to contact the Germans. They set off for Komitades, where the Germans had set up their headquarters. It was a rocky outcrop with three spacious caves. Walker carried a white flag of truce.

After being fired upon by a machine gun, the two officers were allowed to proceed and found an Austrian officer who accepted a formal surrender. Walker and Cochrane returned to the beach in Sfakia to tell the Allies' officers what the next move would be. The group on the beach broke up, and the officers sought their men.

The general message centred on everyone surrendering. Some would be offered the chance to "Run for the hills". [11]

Many of the men, upon hearing the decision to surrender and then the instructions to prepare to capitulate, felt they were still in Greece. Those surrendering were told to destroy all weapons and discard all ammunition.

This was best done by breaking the butt from the barrel and removing the bolt. All pieces should be thrown away to separate parts of the rough terrain or into the sea.

No doubt, the Germans would interrogate each prisoner, so the officers told them only to tell their name, rank and service number and nothing else. Each man was then told to seek out any white material that could be held up or waved as a sign of surrender.

It became evident that the message was getting through when white clothing and materials from various places were carried or tied to sticks the sign of surrender.

"There was a certain resignation mixed with consternation and incredulity on every face," observed Le Souef. [12]

The Luftwaffe arrived just after capitulation and strafed the beach and higher areas where men were brandishing white material as a sign of surrender.

Eventually, the German foot soldiers arrived and began to line up their captives in groups of 500. These groups were then marched back the way they had come. This time they were under strict supervision and refused both food and water. The lack of essentials was a means of keeping the prisoners weak and suffering. In this state, they were less likely to escape. All pinned their hope on a drink and a bite to eat at the journey's end.

The taxing journey back over the mountains was more difficult than the one to Sfakia. The worst part was that the men were refused the essentials of life. On the way to where they had started, some were lucky enough to pass locals who readily offered them food. The guards were angry with the giver and taker and made diabolical threats.

Throughout the Allies' stay on the island of Crete, the local population did its utmost to help, whether by providing food and water, guiding people across the alien landscape, offering shelter, or offering to be lookouts.

The end of the trek down the mountains from south to north was at a dry and dusty area near the village of Skines.

Back at Sfakia, Captain Holt of the 2/5th General Hospital went to Konledes to deal with the wounded and other casualties. He imagined his medics and the patients would be in for a torrid time getting everyone back on the track they had just negotiated.

Le Souef gathered his medical staff to warn them what information to divulge to the enemy. He told them only to tell their name, number and rank. [13] He concluded his talk by saying, "As you pass into captivity, always remember one thing never forget your pride in race! Goodbye and good luck."

The Germans remained quietly out of view while demands were sent through Captain Holt. After a while, the mood changed, and the Germans started demanding that the wounded be sent back to Chania as soon as possible.

This was easier said than done, as many medics were weak and tired. To climb back down from Sfakia to Chania meant reversing the trip. Navigating the steep slopes and ravines carrying a stretcher, and on top of this without food and water, would prove diabolical. The ones who suffered most were those wounded or ill who had already put up with sheer agony.

When he reached the flatter parts of the island, Le Souef picked up a truck. This enabled him to reach Maleme faster and help supervise the placement of the wounded into four categories. Once placed, they were prioritised, with the more serious wounded loaded onto waiting Junkers 52 to be flown to Athens.

The criteria used were walking (wounded), lying (on a stretcher), dysentery and exhaustion.

The worst cases were processed and then taken directly to Maleme airfield where they were placed in a Junkers 52.

Once in Athens they would receive the medical help that would see many of the patients make a reasonable recovery.

The airfield at Maleme was a mess of smashed and burnt-out vehicles and weapons, plus dead bodies. The pilots of the Junkers 52s skillfully negotiated through the latter to get airborne. This exodus of Allies to the mainland had begun and would continue across June and July. [14]

The movement of the badly wounded from Chania to Greece was to become a daily routine. Hundreds of wounded and sick were moved, and slowly, the number of prisoners of war was reduced.

This made managing those left behind much easier. However, it did raise a question that lingered into August.

The able-bodied left on Crete were set up in working parties and made to toil in jobs like burying the dead, filling up sandbags for gun emplacements, and loading equipment and essentials from ships. Much of the work they were forced to do was contrary to the Geneva Convention.

These men needed rest and food to recuperate, so the locals' charity was crucial in nourishing the dangerously ill.

This prolonged lack of nourishment caused the men to develop pot bellies, gastrointestinal disturbances and laxity of joints. Le Souef was concerned that all the men had lost weight and showed signs of vitamin and protein deficiencies. [15]

The people of Crete proved marvellously loyal and courageous, suffering heavy reprisals for their assistance to the Allies. They often left food at the gates of the transit prisons, which was frowned upon by the German guards, but the Cretans continued to try to help out.

At Kalyves village, [16] people gave the patients food despite German disapproval. Over at Chania, the food was left at the main gates.

Within a few days of the transport of the sick and wounded by the Junkers 52s, Le Souef was ordered to remove all patients who were still mobile from the hospital to Souda Bay. Here they were to be placed aboard the ship the *Arcadia*. These men were the walking wounded and, therefore, considered to be able to suffer a voyage by ship to Greece. The ship was to sail to Athens, where the sick and wounded would be looked after at one of the hospitals, and the staff would remain with them.

After nearly three days of fighting and a rearguard action in Crete, the New Zealand and Australian commandos were congratulated for successfully carrying out their mission.

Many recounted their stories. They all ended up reaching Sfakia on the night of May 31. They could see the ships offshore, which was a welcome sight. As the commandos meandered through the crowd, some became aware of the silence among the hundreds of men looking out to sea. It was odd for those next in line not to be boarding one of the ships.

One may have thought the atmosphere would have been full of excitement, and they would have been loud in their restlessness to move along.

But alas, they were not in a happy frame of mind, in fact, they could have all been statues. What was wrong? The question spread fast, and an answer that no commando wanted to hear. "Those are the last ships to sail, mate," said one of the soldiers. "Like the rest of us, you've missed the boat."

The dread of being left behind was barely acceptable, but expected to surrender was more distasteful, to say the least. What really struck these men was becoming prisoners of war behind the wire.

Other commandos learned about the situation through some officers waiting their turn. The partially filled ships were to be the last to sail from Sfakia. The whole plan to evacuate the Allies from Crete to Alexandria had been a disaster.[17]

An hour or two later, the warships began to move off and disappeared into the night. They had to be well on their way when the sun crossed the horizon to welcome a new day. The Luftwaffe would search for any ship sailing on the vast Mediterranean Sea.

Many of the crowd had remained awake all night, tossing and turning the thoughts of their future in their minds. There was talk of surrender, forming gangs to fight, and escaping into the hills. All and none of these were palatable.

High up on a rock ledge near Sfakia someone was calling to those who didn't want to obey the surrender order to join him and take off into the hills.

One strapping lad ran forward and, looking up, shouted, "We're with you, mate, lead the way. I'm not for spending my life behind the wire."

Other men gritted their teeth and moved forward in the direction being pointed to by the agitator on the rocky ledge. They knew the time was limited, and they had to be well away from Sfakia before the Germans got the message that some had escaped into the hills.

The group Vic Petersen was with was well away from Sfakia. Its leaders were Major Ray Sandover [18] and Major Ralph Honner. The group hid under the grapevines, watching the Germans get ready to chase after the Allies on the track to Sfakia.

These officers had offered their men the chance to run away and hide in the hills. This gave a possible two or three days to move well to the east while the Germans tried to catch up with the main body of Allied troops. The total number had grown to about twenty. The two officers whispered together and then set out to the east.

The first several miles walking had been a struggle, as it was summer, and the heat was exhausting. They initially carried too much equipment and personal gear.

After a short discussion, the men and Ray headed southeast into the hills. Ray had heard that there might be some boats along the south coast they could commandeer.

They set off only to find they were still carrying too much gear. Subsequently, most of the equipment was abandoned as they moved along. Lightening their load made moving easier. There was a total lack of water as the streams had dried up, and the few wells were down to a muddy bottom.

Sandover wanted them to walk to the beach further east of Heraklion and find a boat or motorised landing craft (MLC) to get off the island. The MLCs were abandoned after a British mission was trapped in the mountains by the Luftwaffe on the eve of the Blitz.

The group comprised British troops from the Black Watch, Argylls, Yorks, and Lancs. They had been sent from Alexandria to assist the Heraklion area in setting up a defence around the airfield. MLCs initially dropped them off at Massara Bay and then marched over the mountains to Heraklion.

After accomplishing their mission at Heraklion, they retreated towards the south coast. Unfortunately, the Luftwaffe found them and attacked with ferocity. Bombing and strafing reduced the numbers and held up the troops. The main body returned to the coast and was evacuated by the Royal Navy.

Several MLCs were left on the beach because they were either holed with bullets or abandoned because there were not enough people to fill them. Numerous stories from Crete are either well-known or literally unknown, and the MLCs were the subject of several such stories.

Several escapers kept diaries or wrote one after returning to their homeland. Historians turn to these men to learn the movements and thoughts of those on Crete from April 1941 to the end of 1941.

Vic Petersen kept a diary [19] of his experiences from June 6, 1941, until May 1945. The diary gives an insight into his short stay on Crete and later in a working party based in Stalag VIII-B.

This is the only diary written by a Crete veteran and has been proven many times to hold the truth. It is the work the author turned to tell the story of Tymbakion and the signed shorts. All quotes across the pages from here are from Vic Petersen, *Memoirs Prisoner of War Days, World War II*, Petersen Diary, 1941, pages 1-16. It shows how one man can offer friendship and comfort to his workmates, the local civilians and even the enemy, making everyone's life easier and less stressful. He was constantly hungry and missed his family daily.

It was William Taylor WX 2061 who wrote about the days of fleeing in the hills from the Germans. "A runner then came and said every man for himself, so our group hid in the vineyard until the tanks went by on the road, then we made a dash up a deep creek into a wadi area and finally made it into a safe spot in the hills totally exhausted and hungry." William Taylor *Diary, June 6th, 1941, pages 1 - 21, short version only,* page 18.

Vic did not note the day his group escaped to the hills, but he did recall that all who volunteered to run for the hills set off to the east. Major Sandover became concerned that the size of the group made it too conspicuous and suggested they split in two. Captain Honner took one group and headed for the mountains.

Major Sandover's group was about 10 strong and included Lieutenant Art McRobbie, Major McNab, Vic Petersen, Bonnie Buirchell, Bill Pauley, Bill Taylor, and Captain 'Killer' Ryan (a doctor). [20] This group walked all day and finally reached the small town of Imballion.

For Ray's party, the rocky pathway was difficult to negotiate, and the men who had not slept or eaten for several days kept losing their footing. So far, they were lucky not to cause major damage to an ankle, arm or head.

On the way, they came across a Cretan with a donkey. He offered the men some of his cherries in a small basket. He was rewarded when the men produced some loose Greek coin [21] as payment.

After travelling until sunset, Major Ray Sandover, came to a halt and signalled to his small band to squat down.

Necks strained, and eyes peered forward as the men tried to determine whether a friend or foe was ahead.

Ray beckoned to two of his men and whispered his message.

"Private Pauley and Private Petersen, I want you to move forward and do some scouting. There's a hut about a hundred yards ahead. I want you to reconnoitre the area and see if anyone lives there. We desperately need food, water and shelter, so hightail it and report back."

The men had reached the small village of Imballion and could make out one of the houses on the outskirts.

During the 40km walk since meeting the cherry man, they encountered a group of Cretan farmers gathering grain. They happily shared some of their lunch which consisted of olive oil and half a cup of wine. They were also offered some bread to dip in the concoction. As Bill Taylor WX2061, *Battleofcrete.org.au,* wrote in his diary, page 17. "It tasted good to us."

William Pauley and Vic Petersen split off and doubled over, ran through the olive trees and prickle bushes toward the old house, seeking help and direction.

Bill Pauley, a soldier of the 2/11th Battalion and a fast runner, wasted no time reaching the hut and peering in the window. He could see that there was the usual household furniture and family memorabilia. What took Bill's attention was the bottle of red wine and a half loaf of bread sitting on the table.

He turned to signal to Ray when a young voice said, "Are you hungry and thirsty, mister?" The voice was from a young teenage Cretan. [22] He stood no more than five yards from Bill, dressed in work clothing and high leather boots that had seen better days.

On his head was a hand-me-down hat, probably from his father. It was black and had a brim running all the way around. Bill was taken aback he considered himself a pretty good scout, but this kid materialised out of nowhere.

He was pleased to hear the boy speak in English, as this would make their communication easier. "My friends and I are trying to get to the beach to find a boat to get off Crete. We have been moving all day and need food, water, and rest."

"Come," said the boy, "I will help you, but we must be quiet because some Germans are down by the beach. They have already shot some of my friends for helping escapers. If they see me helping, I might get shot, as well as my family."

Bill was amazed at the boy's confidence and friendliness and hesitated to ask, "What's your name, son?"

The youngster readily said, "I am Elias, the son of Jonas. I live with my family in the nearby town of Imballion."

Elias beckoned the two scouts and walked to the house's front door together. The boy lifted the mat at the front door, picked up a key, and opened the door. "You may eat and drink whatever you can find. Please share with your other comrades. I must return to my father."

Bill and Vic alerted Ray to the situation, and he moved the other men inside the house.

He sent scouts to watch while the resting group grabbed a bite to eat and a drink before being sent to snuggle under the grapevine. The bottle of wine that first attracted Bill was shared equally and greatly enjoyed. "These people sure know how to turn grapes into wine," said Bill Taylor.

At midnight Ray swapped the two sentries. The boy had disappeared into the night.

The next morning, as the sun peeped from the Mediterranean Sea, there was a commotion outside.

Ray had set up two of his men as lookouts. He raced towards the sound, drawing his pistol as he ran. He could make out in the gloom five men and the young boy, Elias, with their hands up, the two lookouts menacing them.

Ray called out. "Friends, that's young Elias, the youngster who helped us last night. The others must be his family. Bonnie Buirchell and Herbert Stratton, stand down."

Sheepishly, the lookouts lowered their rifles and stood still, waiting for Ray's next move. It became clear what had happened. The boy had gone off to tell his family about the men waiting at the old house. The family agreed to help the soldiers by supplying water and food for the escapers. The women spent the night baking bread and cooking rabbit stew.

They had carefully loaded these into wicker baskets for the men to take to the soldiers. [23] Major Sandover welcomed the men and walked them back to the house where all the others had gathered, awaiting the outcome of the challenge made by the lookouts.

Major Sandover was amazed that these men and women were so kind to people they did not even know.

The soldiers, overwhelmed with gratitude, thanked the men profusely and even managed to find more Greek money to pay them.

The oldest man wore boots up to the knee, a black shirt, and a black fishnet weave headdress. The headdress was wrapped around his head and draped over his shoulders.

The clothing gave the impression he was out on an important village visit; however, his choice was the traditional Cretan dress worn in everyday life. To top off his distinguished look, he had a grand moustache, which, to the Cretans, was a mark of masculinity.

As they talked, the older Cretan spoke Greek, and Elias interpreted. "My son tells me you have others in the hills who might need our help. If you can give us a guide, we will take food and water to them, too."

"You are so kind to volunteer to help us. We thank you and take up your offer," said Major Sandover. Again, Ray could barely hold back tears of gratitude. These people were not just offering food and water but their lives. One loose tongue about this family helping the Allies, and they all would be lined up against a wall and machine-gunned. Their bravery was a beacon of hope in these dark times.

They were probably related to others who had already met this fate. The other men had heard about the German reprisals, which they regarded as a cowardly reaction and lawless in the extreme.

The locals seemed unperturbed by the threat, all they wanted to do was to be there for the men who were striving for peace.

Two men were selected to show the Cretans where the Honner group went and to let them know they were friendly. [24]

The rest of the group of eight, under the command of Major McNab, said their goodbyes to Sandover and four others. They waited for the Cretans and their mates to melt into the distance before setting out for the beach.

As they moved, they meticulously worked out a plan which they desperately hoped would result in their escape from the island. The idea was to split up with two searching the beach to the east and another two to the west, their every move calculated to ensure their safety.

The men started walking towards the beach, with Major McNab now in charge.

—m—

Seeing the beautiful calm waters after three days in Crete's barren, rocky interior was a grand sight. The four selected to search the shoreline were looking for any seaworthy boat the group could use to escape from Crete. Alexandria was the destination long way south, so the boat had to be reasonably sturdy.

McNab and the other three soldiers thought it prudent to keep hidden until they saw a signal that a boat had been found, as they were threatened with being picked up by a German patrol.

The four men heading for the beach moved in pairs across the sandhills and rocks strewn here and there in the storms that lashed this coast in winter. They reached the final line of sandhills and were pleased to see no signs of life.

More importantly, they could make out several boats that might be seaworthy. Two were small rowing boats.

Upon close examination, it was found that the flooring boards were split and some were missing. Two other boats were MLCs that lay in the gentle wash on the shore. [25]

This constant movement had worn the bottom of one boat badly, and over a foot of water was awash.

The two of the group heading east, went in search of a small yacht. Without telling the others, they used the yacht to head to an island, some 40 miles away. They made it but were later captured.

The other two heading west found an old rowing boat in better state of repair, although plenty of water was in the bottom. The two men scouted around and found a bucket shaped object that they used to scoop out the water. It became evident that water was leaking into the boat, so they would need to bail frantically and for a long time to stay afloat.

The two men on the beach signalled to the four hiding in the sand hills.

Once all together, they came up with an idea and hoped it would work. Their first two efforts to launch the boat were reasonable and offered possible success if they could get the bailing up to a higher speed. Two of the men had found some rope tied to the boat's front. They tied this over their shoulders and swam out. The other four pushed the boat into the water.

When they were waist deep, they began swimming while those in the boat and all began furiously bailing.

They were moving well and 100 yards offshore when a German fighter flew over and sprayed them with bullets. No one was hurt, but when the plane banked and came in for a second strafing, the men lost their nerve and headed back to shore. Within 50 yards of the beach, the boat sank.

Half an hour later, a commotion to the east and near the water's edge caught their attention, and then shouts in German and the revving of a motor-cycle. "Damn!" said Blue Pauley aloud. "The Germans have found us."

All at once, the beach scene changed as over half a dozen Germans on motorcycles and sidecars roared towards them, stopped and began harassing the men. The Germans took Major McNab and tied his hands behind his back. He was being used as a hostage. The Germans indicated they would be back the next day to either take the others as prisoners or to shoot it out to the death.

The Major was marched off in a westerly direction by two Germans. The other Germans mounted the motorbikes and sidecars and roared off in search of more stragglers.

The men sat on the sand and talked about their lives back home and how McNab was being treated. For lunch, they ate a bit of meat, a tin of bully, fried onions, and potatoes, most of which they had received from the Cretans.

At 1800 hours, the German soldiers reappeared on the scene, evidently doubting the willingness of the Allies to surrender, and thus, they became prisoners of war. "You all prisoners now. You go behind the wire," said one of the Germans.

Vic Petersen and others surrendered on the evening of June 6. This started Vic's incarceration as a prisoner of war. The reality of the situation did not immediately sink in. He was too busy working out how to survive the trek back over the mountains. The height of the monolith that they could see in the distance left a daunting feeling.

Vic and his mates were aware they would now be marched back over the mountains to Heraklion.

From there, they were to turn west towards Retimo. Under the guard of two of the Germans, they turned inland and set out for the mountains. It became a long night as the group, under guard, was pushed and shoved along.

Their trek took them along the winding mountainous tracks. They rested at midnight but were refused water and food. [26]

As the sun rose, they were shaken awake and pushed along to start the next leg of their trek. At some point, they were joined by others who had been trying to find a way off the island. The group slipped and slid down steep rock faces for nearly 12 hours without stopping for a rest, food or water.

—⚞—

So began the next chapter of these soldiers' lives. They had no idea of what was ahead of them or for how long. Surrender was a concept none of these men had contemplated, nor were they aware of what the enemy would do to them. They were in complete shock, and all sorts of demons would flash into their minds, day in and day out.

That night, the Germans kept them on the march until midnight before resting at a place called Idecca. [27] Here, they camped for the night. As the night was dark and the terrain was very hilly with boulders and trees all around, one could have slipped and broken a leg or arm. There was also the possibility of sneaking off into the darkness.

Vic thought of his parents and wondered what they were up to and whether they were thinking of him.

On Saturday, June 7, 1941, the sun was hardly above the horizon when the German guards roused everyone. The Germans demanded everyone march all day without a break, food, or water. The much-needed rest came at 2300 hours. The entire contingent was very footsore, and most had blisters. They all sat down and no sooner rested their heads than they fell asleep.

In the morning, they were rudely awakened and set off down the slippery slope of the mountain.

The group limped past many Cretans who were working in their fields. When they saw the ragged group, they tried to offer drinks and food.

There was a bit of bread when they met Cretans on the track and, another time, a few cherries. The Germans would threaten the prisoners and aim their rifles at approaching farmers. To their credit, these brave men and boys would push the food into the prisoner and then run away.

The ragtag army reached Heraklion on Sunday, June 8, 1941, and the local inhabitants gave each soldier bread and plenty of raisins.

At 1300 hours, they were moved to the barracks and at 1500 hours, the Germans gave them their first meal, which consisted of two biscuits, some cheese, and a hot drink. The drink was herbal tea, tasting like the herbs that grew in the hills nearby. At 1800 hours, a couple of the men made boiled rice and raisins.

On Monday, June 9, 1941, Vic began to write in his diary. Why he chose to write a note [28] about each day is anyone's guess. The uniqueness of his choices was why he decided to write on scrap paper when most would have sought out a blank book.

His first entry in his diary appears to be, "At Heraklion and up at 0530 hours to a meal of raisins and mint tea and on the march again. The Germans pushed us to cover about twenty miles for the day."

By the time Vic had been through all that the war could throw his way, he would have written about 1440 entries on paper.

The German guards began to be less demanding, allowing a rest at 1300 hours. The men were given bread and raisins. Later, at sunset, the group stopped for the night at 1730 hours. They were offered no rations and told to go to bed and rest for tomorrow's march.

They lay on their backs and stared at the bright, twinkling stars in the heavens above. Some of them knew the names of constellations and took great pride in pointing these out.

No one could find the Southern Cross, which mystified them all as it was one of the brightest constellations back home in Australia and New Zealand.

Vic, in his best school teacher manner, tried to explain this phenomenon. "The Northern and Southern hemispheres of the world had been a mystery to mankind since the first explorers crossed the Equator. The trickery of reversing the activities in these hemispheres also confused many exploration groups and settlers in new lands. The seasons being back to front would see crops planted in summer by those from the Northern Hemisphere who had settled in a country in the Southern Hemisphere. Of course, the crops failed, and the people perished."

Some drifted off to sleep and soon the entire camp was silent.

CHAPTER 17

—m—

The next day, after another exhausting march, the group halted at 1200 hours. They reckoned they were halfway between Iraklion and Retimo. Each was issued a loaf of bread for the last three days. The afternoon march brought them within reach of Retimo.

That night they slept amongst grapevines not far from the town. The harrowing experience of marching as captives from the South to the North was experienced by all the captured Allies. Vic Petersen's diary description is poignant and highlights what these men endured in the days after capitulation. [1]

The final march placed the prisoners just outside of Retimo, the town where the men from the 2/11th Perth Battalion fired their guns in anger at the Germans during the Battle of Crete.

Most of the group fell into an exhausted sleep. They were grateful for the rest, even though the ground was hard and rocky.

The group had marched 150 miles in six days over steep inclines and rugged ravines without food or water. Vic nearly died on the return march to Souda Bay. On the evening of June 10, the column he was in went to sleep under grapevines near Retimo airstrip.

Vic Petersen had been asleep for some time and suddenly awoke from a sharp pain on the back of his neck. It was around 2230 hours when he startled the others awake. The pain was so severe that he was screaming and holding his neck, but he could not explain to the others what was causing him to scream.

All he knew was that the back of his neck was painful as if someone had poked it with a red hot branding iron. No one knew what to do so they called the guards who promptly attended. They were somewhat cynical and told Vic to shut up and go back to sleep. As they made their point, Vic became paralysed and collapsed right in front of the two shocked guards. He had been calling out that he could not feel his arms and legs.

Such a sudden collapse shocked the guards, who quickly changed their minds. They realised something was drastically wrong and frantically called others to help. A truck driver soon arrived in his lorry. Vic was loaded in the back, with one of the guards staying with him. He was taken by truck to the nearby Retimo Hospital, where a German doctor froze and lanced the area where the pain and a red swelling could be seen.

Later an orderly stated, "Your life was saved but it was very difficult." Vic had great respect for German doctors and orderlies after this experience.

The German doctor told Vic a snake had bitten him during his rounds the next morning. The Doctor said another three minutes, and they could have done nothing for him.

The doctor explained that he had given needles and oxygen to keep Vic's heart going. No wonder Vic thought he was on death's bed. How ironic, he thought, that Australia had so many poisonous snakes, yet he had rarely seen one.[2] He had to venture all these miles to this part of the world to get bitten.

—⋙—

It was 2200 hours on the 10th June a day to remember forever or so Bonnie Buirchell thought and he hadn't met tomorrow as yet.

The men who had been captured with Vic and made to walk from Tymbakion to Retimo were awakened by the screaming of their mate when a snake bit him.

They had rushed to Vic's side but could do little to help.

It was clear that he could not communicate due to the screaming and then the paralysis.

They were thankful that the lorry driver had come to the rescue and taken Vic to the Retimo Hospital.

The guards turned back to William Taylor, William Pauley, Walter Pedersen, Bonnie Buirchell, Robbie McNab and Herb Stratton and demanded they get back to sleep.

The next morning the group plus a number of other men who had been captured in other parts of the island were paraded in front of the Commandant who then addressed them all. He told them they must not try to escape as the guards have orders to shoot anyone attempting such a mission. He further told them they were being placed in work parties and must complete the job allocated before being fed.

The fifteen men in the parade lined up near a lorry and were told to get on board. The driver set off around Retimo, stopping here and there. At each stop, one of the guards would call out the job to be completed at that place and then point to the number of men issued to complete the task.

The first stop was for four men to clear all the rubbish and smashed aeroplanes along a road and move the pile to the side

Stop two for 8 men was filling in holes along the Maleme Airstrip.

The final two men in the back of the lorry were Bonnie Buirchell and Bill Taylor, they were handed a spade each and told they were to bury the dead who lay in a field 50 yards from where the truck pulled up.

Bonnie looked at Bill and their silent communication was one of shock and revulsion. They jumped down and trudged across the open grassy paddock and began digging the first grave.

They knew the grave was to be at least three feet deep. The digging part was difficult because of the hard and stoney soil. The moving of the body was not only difficult but revolting. To describe some of the mishaps and the distinctive smell emanating from the bodies was too horrendous to put into words. The two men learnt what was meant by 'grin and bear it' from each body that would turn others off. In other words, accept something bad without complaining.

At the same time, the guards called them and gave them a mug of water, a slice of bread, and a handful of sultanas. It was difficult to eat using a hand that had been dragging bodies.

Bonnie stood up and counted the little white crosses that signalled the German dead. "Fourteen done and about the same again," he said to Bill.

By 1730 hours, the two men had banged in the last cross and walked back to the truck. They were both exhausted, and every muscle ached. The final cross brought the body count to 30. Looking at the crosses as they moved past them, they could count 29 Germans and one New Zealander.

On returning to the POW Camp at Retimo, the truck picked up the other prisoners. Everyone commented on the smell wafting from Bonnie and Bill. The two were ostracised to the back of the truck and rode with their legs hanging over the edge.

As they jumped down a guard pointed to them and said in broken English, "More for tomorrow and for some weeks to come. You did a good job today."

Once around the corner and headed for the ablution room Bonnie said to Bill, "I'm not burying one more body, now or ever. What about we take off into the hills tonight?"

Bill didn't hesitate and replied, "I'm with you. I can't do that job again."

Whispering as they scrubbed in the little water, they could get out of the rusting taps, they made their plan to take off after midnight and to keep going into the highest mountains to the east.

They returned to their sleeping area and fell into an exhausted sleep.

Bonnie was awakened by the sound of someone dry retching and vomiting. He looked over to where Bill was sleeping, only to see an empty rug. He stood up and followed the sound outside, and Bill threw up. In between vomiting and moaning, Bill tells Bonnie he is too sick to run back into the hills. Bonnie agreed and said he would abandon the idea and stay with and help Bill.

Bonnie assisted Bill back to his bed area and watched him go to sleep. He could not keep his promise, as the experience he suffered today was still like a bitter taste. He had to get out and stay free.

He grabbed his few possessions and, with bare feet, snuck quietly out to the main gateway. His boots he tied the laces together and hung them around his neck. He watched the guards and worked out their duty pattern. The two he was watching walked across the gate and away about thirty yards before turning back again. They did not look back once passing the gate. To make things really easy, the gate was over two feet high off the concrete. All Bonnie had to do was wait for the crossover, count to twenty and lay at the gate, roll under and run into the night.

The next day, Bonnie felt exhausted under a rocky hangover a couple of thousand feet up White Mountain. He had kept up a half-pace all night and up to midday, not once looking back. Now, he was by himself and in his element. His intention was to climb even higher and move to the east, which was remote.

June 12, 1941. He had felt guilty leaving his best mate, William Taylor, behind but he had no choice. His day burying bodies was so ugly he couldn't face that type of activity again.

Bonnie's story was his own; only he knew what had happened.

After wandering the hills and mountains, he found a refuge that contained a waterfall, a cave, and plenty of wildlife.

After his escape, he wandered the mountains, where he felt safe and comfortable until he could find a way off the island. Bonnie's background was hunting and gathering. From Kojonup, Western Australia, he was exceptionally sharp at tracking, hiding and using camouflage. His skills enabled him to live happily alone and be well fed for months on end.

Of course, there were the odd scares that nearly saw him caught by the many German patrols that hunted the escapees daily.

Later, when Vic recuperated, he met up with some of the boys of the 2/11th who were there, and they told him they could hear him screaming from three miles away.

Due to overcrowding, Vic was selected to be moved but the doctor attending him overruled this decision so he remained at Retimo Hospital. Here there were a few Allied troops but the majority were Greeks and Cretans.

Vic's piece of paper entry for Tuesday, June 24, 1941, indicates he was at Retimo and being given painkillers which offered him some relief from the searing pain across his back. The pieces of paper would eventually develop into his diary. Vic began to find he was suffering different symptoms each day, and his recuperation was so much slower than he and the medical staff had reckoned upon.

Ten days after the bite, Vic was still experiencing pain. Painkillers were helping him tolerate the aching, and as there was little else the doctors could do, he had to accept things as they were.

Another note tells how he was coping with the meagre food that was somewhat foreign to his normal Australian diet. "Not much to eat, rice or beans done with olive oil which takes a bit of getting down. He asked the cookhouse to leave out the olive oil and only serve him rice and beans. The cooks were at least understanding and obliged his request.

This enabled him to feel far better than he had been over the last fortnight. He hoped he was finally on the mend.

He was a prisoner of war in a compound with many Greeks and Cretans and about nine Allies. These nine proved to be good companions while they were together. At this time, these men had no idea they would, in the future, be signing their names on a pair of canvas shorts.

They would be prisoners of war in a very isolated situation. They introduced themselves individually to Vic, who made a list on a piece of paper so he could recall their names later.

> William Barrow 14244 Greymouth, New Zealand
> Kenneth Bowden 30242 Wellington, New Zealand
> Ronald Chappell 7347150
> Hans Cooper 7347238 England
> Colin Heenan 8571 New Zealand
> Alexander McLean 7902927 England
> John Magee 32086, New Zealand
> James Kirk, 30071 New Zealand
> Laurience Woods WX443 Perth, Australia. [3]

Two Greeks befriended the group, and the 12 had fun communicating with each other. These two became integral members of the group. Their names were, Anastasios Kollias and Ionnis Petrou.

On Saturday, June 28, 1941, Vic woke with pains in his chest and legs and felt pretty weak from the waist down. His biggest fear was that he was going to become paralysed and lose mobility in his legs.

Boredom was his worst enemy, and that gave rise to the feeling that the day was terribly long. Over the following two days he had bad pains in his stomach on several occasions.

The food was still nothing much. At times he felt like wandering into the kitchen and offering to be chief cook and bottle washer. He would cook up a real storm for the boys.

A couple of days proved to be interesting as he found some new friends who he would meet at a different location in the near future.

On Saturday, July 19, 1941, four Australians and one Englishman came into camp. They shook hands and introduced themselves. The names and places of residences were written down for future reference:

Robert Johnstone VX8887 Victoria, Australia
Douglas Rainford NX1497 NSW, Australia
John Stuckey NX11243 NSW, Australia
James Thompson P/SSX20790 England
Edward Face NX11441 NSW, Australia [4]

A major panic arose on July 20 and 21 when the Germans discovered several men were missing. They had a roll call and discovered the 'missing' men had been sent to the medical room overnight. They had a bout of severe diarrhea that caused the medics to be run off their feet, treating the men and moving them around. There was little time to report the situation and the men involved. Vic wrote their names into his diary sheets because he felt they were likely to be important later in life.

> Thomas Armitage 33221 New Zealand
> Harry Barnes NX32898 Australia
> Charles Giles 3964606 Wales
> Arthur Todd 7272 New Zealand
> George A. Roberts 132569 England
> John Skinner 218039 England
> Clive Whatling 902385 England
> William Topia 22724 New Zealand
> Harold Warburton 1058195 England
> Andrew Collins 24196 New Zealand [5]

Vic read books to fill in the time. Reading was the most enjoyable of his pastimes.

Others often wondered where he got all the books from. They seemed to materialise out of thin air. The reading gave credence to Vic's vast general knowledge. The more intriguing part of the Petersen library was the number of non-fiction books he could get his hands on. It didn't take long for other prisoners to seek out Vic to borrow his latest book. He was always obliging.

On Tuesday, July 22, and Wednesday, July 23, Vic was prepared to go to Chania but only got 300 yards and had to be returned. He was sometimes weak and would break out in a dizzy spell. The German doctor who had treated him after the snake bite warned him of such episodes and to always have a friend nearby in case, he collapsed.

Interesting news was filtering in from other camps on the island. At one of the prison transit camps [6] the inmates revolted. This sort of news made the guards jumpy. What it told the present group was that they were not the only ones left on Crete. It also suggested there may be others in those prisons who were yet to join the team. Just what were the Germans playing at and when would the group find out with certainty?

Meanwhile, the Germans were keen to start a work party system, which would be better organised than the system used so far across the island.

The German commandant gathered the prisoners and the guards and put it to them about forming work parties.

He outlined a number of jobs that would benefit the Germans and the prisoners. Some ideas included agriculture work and helping the local farmers pick their fruit, vegetables, and cereal crops. He emphasised that the work would not be arduous but they would be rewarded by receiving free food.

It didn't matter much in the end because the Germans picked a group and took them out. The returning men thought it was a better way to spend the day than the pure boredom of lazing around camp day after day.

Vic Petersen added another piece of paper to his growing lot and wrote, "Thursday 24th July 1941, our move to Chania finally was real. The working party was cancelled because of a revolt in one of the prison transit camps. [7] At roll call, two men were missing, but we were told, matter of factly, not to worry as they had been captured and would be shot." [8]

It was important for Vic to keep his prisoner mates well-behaved. The more he thought about it, the more he believed he remained on the island because there was a crucial role he and others still had to play. During this incarceration, it was like a premonition or just silly thinking of being a hero.

At this moment his life was ebbing away quickly, but he still had much he wanted to achieve.

"Saturday 26th July, 1941, at Retimo on Crete Island as a prisoner of war, we left here by truck to a camp at Souda Bay, arriving at about 0830 hours. Sixteen men were incarcerated in the Souda Bay prison, and the way they were bedded down gave Vic the impression that they would be there a while."[9]

Vic was not too keen on the Souda Bay camp and said so. "The new camp was small and dirty, and the Greeks were very filthy. However, because the camp joined the bay, they could all go swimming to get clean." [10]

Vic knew half the men in the prison, so he set out to introduce himself to the other eight. Of course, he tried to talk to the Greeks who were also there, but it was too difficult, so a wave or gesture had to suffice.

The eight men were Edward East, Zamoni Foley, Louis Gusscott, Edward Carter, Joseph Davenport, Geoffrey Harman, Thomas Foxon and Cyril Grimsey. [11]

On Sunday, July 27, 1941, Vic and his mates got a dixie [12] of meat and vermicelli. They were excited as it was the first meat the cook had offered them in ages.

There was a scare through the camp when a Greek was dragged howling outside into the quadrangle and tied to a post.

It was a stinking hot afternoon, and the sun burnt deep into his skin. He suffered for the whole afternoon, and no one knew what the circumstances were. It certainly put the wind up all the others to see how brutal the Germans could be in the name of discipline. [13]

The work party system finally got off the ground, and Vic and his mates were scheduled to unload a ship at the wharf in the morning. The next day he was offered a more difficult job, handling British ammunition. It wasn't so much the possible danger but the heaviness of the crates. For weeks the men had been on a diet that just sustained them. Everyone had lost a lot of weight, and their muscle power was poor. So lugging crates full of ammunition was tough and tiring.

The next camp Vic was moved to was on the other side of Chania. This camp was very dusty and windy. Ray Blechynden, a 2/11th soldier, [14] was in this camp. The inmates were given buckets of grapes and pears by the civilians.

Vic liked the new camp as it was near "Chania, very handy to the beach and some showers. The inmates had porridge for breakfast, bread and drink of tea for dinner and mixed stew at night with some grapes. Have to watch the figure or will be putting on weight."[15]

On Friday, August 1, 1941, Vic was in Chania, where he and the others lived in tents. British planes bombed and strafed Maleme airfield. Some planes were hit as the Germans retaliated.

A bridge was wrecked, and three Germans were wounded. This was a good indication the war was still happening.

Nothing much changed from Saturday, August 2, to August 3, 1941.

Although there was no work for most, a small group helped the Germans take searchlights and ack-ack guns up to Maleme airfield.

Monday, August 4, 1941, the only excitement over the last three days was an Australian and English cricket match. The Australians won by six runs.

Between August 7 and 9, no working parties were allowed out on account of an outbreak of infantile paralysis. This was known as poliomyelitis and caused by a virus [16] which attacks the brain and spinal cord resulting in paralysis or even death. It was easily spread from person to person.

Over the fortnight, August 10 to 25, 1941, everything was rather quiet, with very little to do. Vic found that if you could get a little work in the German cookhouse, you could always look forward to a handout.

Another week idled by, and all days were quiet and boring. Vic wrote another note for his diary, "The camp is using German food which is tasteless, especially that using sugar." [17]

Wednesday, August 27, was Vic's birthday. His diary scribblings found him somewhat indignant that he had to spend it as a POW on the island of Crete. To add to his annoyance, he was not feeling the best, having a spell of giddy turns.

Some boys were filling in time making hats and trousers out of tent canvas as their clothes were wearing out. Making clothes from tent canvas could be done in any spare time. [18]

There were a number of men who had indicated that in their pre-war years, they had trained as tailors.

The diary entry had significance for a future time and place. At this point, it was merely an observation like a note that says, "Watch this space!"

There was a roll call on the morning of August 27. A dozen men appeared to have escaped.

There were a lot of concerned guards after it was found they were not on parade and apparently not in the prison. The guards were rushing here and there in an effort to find the missing and to keep the escape from the ears of the commandant.

The men on parade were left standing on the parade ground. This punishment caused great angst, as men would faint if expected to maintain that position for a long time.

They had done nothing wrong, so it seemed unfair, and many began to mumble in their protest.

This grew to an all out yelling, and the guards became savage, with rifle butts being used and threats of shooting. Quite suddenly, the frantic searching ceased, and the guard's spokesperson exclaimed that the men had been found. With that, he dismissed the prisoners. Those who turned up later after a day's work on the work party were Arthur Hewett, Fred McKain, Richard Lechmere, Aubrey Leviston, Sydney Pearce, John Ainsley, Avery Bennison and Clifford Freeman.[19]

The next day, the men went through a similar panic, except this time, the commandant turned up and read out the names of seven who were taken to the hospital overnight.

He was visibly shaking, and perspiration formed across his brow as he yelled in broken German mixed with English, This must stop, or I will execute anyone who escapes. You are well fed and looked after."

The names on the list he read out were John Moss, Jack Singleton, Ralph Veevers, David Walker, Leonard West, John Whitcombe and Eric Tyrer. [20]

Vic heard the names of men he had never seen or met before. It was like an omen that these people had to be kept alive for a predetermined reason.

A fair amount of enemy air activity, from Thursday to Saturday, August 29-30, 1941, excited the men across the three days. The Luftwaffe was tangling with the Royal Air Force. The smoke trails behind each hit fighter were cheered, but the men couldn't tell whether the plunging aircraft was a friend or foe due to the distance away. The consensus determined that any plane hurtling towards the sea and with a smoke trail behind had to be German.

Later on, in the week, the men all cheered when the official news arrived telling them that our fighters brought down four Stukas. However, it seemed the observer wasn't too good at counting, as all the prisoners agreed they had seen no fewer than a dozen enemy fighters bite the dust. [21]

The 15 soldiers who missed the two roll calls did not know if they were in the group of 151, but considering the number of Allied prisoners of war that were left in Crete, it is likely they were going to be in that special group.

Could this be the news that Vic and many others have been anticipating? "Sunday 31st August 1941, heard that some of us were moving this coming week to Iraklion."

This is the clearest hint that many of the men still on Crete must be the ones in the 151; time will tell. [22]

Vic's notes gave a clue as to how the prisoners were keeping themselves occupied and busy. New Zealand and Australia played cricket, New Zealand winning by two runs.

Vic Petersen and his new mate, John Rattenbury NX6877 from Leichhardt, New South Wales, enjoyed watching the game. The two could not help ribbing each other about the game's outcome as it slowly wandered to its conclusion.

Both men were particularly concerned about sailing in the old ship, the *Norburg*, [23] which they knew was sitting in the dock at Souda Bay. It was an ageing coastal freighter designed to move cargo from town to town along the Mediterranean Sea coastline. Stevedores stacked its spacious holds with merchandise before sailing to the next port. It was not made to move people, as the holds were windowless and pitch dark.

On September 3, Vic Petersen was reminiscing about the past few years when he realized it had been two years since Australia entered the war against Germany.

The men were ordered to pull down the tents and prepare to move. The tents were packed away in the *Norburg*, but the men did not start embarking straight away. Over the next two days, the group was given half an hour's notice to move, but nothing happened.

What began as another normal day became hectic later. Vic outlined the happenings across Friday, September 5. They were roused at 0550 hours, and a roll call found everyone present. They were served breakfast at 0630 hours. They were paraded at 0715 hours and on trucks at about 0800 hours.

The group was moved from Chania to Souda Bay, where they boarded the *Norburg* at 1200 hours. [24]

Dinner and tea comprised half a packet of biscuits and a quarter tin of bully beef. Many of the soldiers pleaded with the guards to let them remain on the deck in the fresh air so they could see what was happening around them. The guards allowed this but gave a stern warning that once the ship sailed, everyone would be moved to the ship's holds. Overnight, with lots of arguing and refusal to go below, the group was finally forced to go below the hold to bed down.

The next day, September 6, 1941, they waited patiently to be shipped to an unknown destination.

The men kept up a constant stream of whispered thoughts about what would happen to the small contingent. The scaremongers came up with some wild ideas while the level-headed wagered on a work party to build defences that would keep the Germans in control of the island.

Bert Chamberlain, Vic Petersen, John Rattenbury and Captain Wally Holt were more realistic and very concerned. They had heard of the reprisals against the Cretans, so lining an enemy up and machine gunning them was not beyond the Germans. They thought this might be the last hurrah given that as far as they could tell every prisoner except their group had been taken out of Crete.

Another of their thoughts was being involved in some secret project on some isolated part of Crete.

It was Wally Holt who offered the latter idea and he put forward some proof of his thinking.

"If you look around and see what each man's strength offers, you will be very surprised to find many engineers and mechanics. These blokes got into these trades either pre-war or during training. Others are lorry drivers; many have medical qualifications, and lots are big, strong men. We are like a specialist group ready to take on a project of importance. Well, we'll have to wait and see whose guess is the right one."

Nothing happened during the next three days, and thankfully, the rumour-mongering ceased. The men disembarked to work on the wharf. [25] At one time, three cargo boats and two escorts docked, and the men were sent aboard to unload the merchandise. The cargo amount and weight kept the group busy for over two days. There was a fair amount of complaining, but eventually, the job was done.

That evening they were placed back on the *Norburg* to sleep as normal. The next morning the men were kept on the *Norburg* and did not work on the wharf as previous. Was this a sign that the men were no longer useful to the Germans. Could that be leaning towards a firing squad or would the *Norburg* head for Salonika. If the latter, they would soon find that they would be in a stalag in Germany.

The excitement that had built because of the flurry of activity of the crew aboard the *Norburg* turned to fear when the ship moved quietly and slowly out of Souda Bay.

Most of the men stayed on the deck, pleading with the guards to allow this. They were told that in an emergency, they would have to go down to the hold; no arguments were allowed. Vic and Wally Holt asked one of the guards what was happening, and he obliged by telling them they were sailing for Iraklion to begin with.

As prisoners of war, the men aboard the *Norburg* sailed for Iraklion at 0600 hours. At 0800 hours, terror struck at the hearts of all as a general broadcast raced through the ship.

A British submarine was lurking off their port bow. The likelihood of it firing torpedoes was considered high.

The prisoners were crowded into the pitch-black hold. They were scared witless, knowing that a British submarine was stalking the ship. The whispers were that it was preparing to fire torpedoes. The submarine crew did not know that Allied troops were on board. This situation was too much for many of the men.

Vic was frightened because the ship was about to be torpedoed by a submarine that was friendly but seemed to be unaware that there were a couple of hundred Allied prisoners of war in the hold. Not only did he curse his own navy, but also himself because he never learnt to swim. [26]

A long, agonising time kept the men on tenterhooks. Some were at the panic stage, and the guards added to that problem by battening down all the hatches. As far as the guards were concerned, if there was going to be a riot, then it could be sorted out without their intervention.

Then the worst possible thing happened. The British submarine fired a torpedo at the *Norburg* and the captain began weaving the boat. The ship stopped weaving as the torpedo [27] narrowly missed. By chance, the *Norburg* got protection from a German sub-chaser.

After the British submarine fired the torpedo and missed, the subchaser saw the submarine's location and attempted to sink it. The men listened as the subchaser dropped depth charges.

A roll was immediately called, and one man was found to be missing from the 2/11th Battalion. He apparently got off the boat in Souda Bay the night before. The Germans reckoned he was a spy and had alerted the submarine that the *Norburg* was going out.

The ship was now under full power and carrying its load of 200 allied prisoners of war to Iraklion. The ship and its passengers arrived at Iraklion at 1330 hours. There was discussion about leaving the prisoners aboard for the night. Many of the men were still terrified by the submarine experience and pleaded with the guards to change their minds. They agreed and marched the prisoners about 20 minutes to the local prison barracks, which Vic had been in about 13 weeks previously.

Not long after settling into the barracks, there was a loud explosion in the direction of the harbour.

It was some time before a German officer arrived at the barracks to inform the prisoners and their guards that they had been lucky. The submarine had fired a torpedo at the Iraklion port and caused an explosion. The *Norburg* was damaged and would need work below the waterline before it would sail again.

This news spread through the crowded barracks and many were shaking from the news.

The barrack they were in was practically standing room only, and they were not allowed outside to the toilet. Some guards were drunk from drinking wine, so it was a pretty exhausting night for everyone.

Looking out the window, Vic saw that there were plenty of Germans around Iraklion. The prisoners of war held in a barrack at Iraklion were being treated harshly to the point they were only allowed outside under guard for a wash.

One of the German guards told Vic that the explosion of the previous evening had been aimed directly at the torpedoing of the boat, the *Norburg*.

This information was confirmed by direct evidence from some of the boys sent to work on the boats the next day. They were supervised by an officer of the guard who was a little worse for wear after his binge drinking last evening. It turned out that the submarine the Germans said had been sunk, had evidently followed the *Norburg* to the harbour and torpedoed it at the wharf. [28] The alarming part was that where the torpedo hit was the hatch that Vic and John Rattenbury had been standing near. How lucky was that?

Finally, Vic was told some news that directed the group's movement.

In his diary, he wrote, "The group was notified that it would leave Iraklion for a new campsite by truck at 1330 hours today, 12th September." [29]

More than 62 of the prisoners were to be offloaded at Iraklion while the rest of the men would be moved by truck over the mountains to a new prison.

While the entire group was together in the barracks waiting for the trucks Bernard Mitchell and Wally Holt caught up with Ray Blechynden and wanted to know why the group was being split?

"To tell you the truth," said Ray, "I don't know, but I'll find out. I've a German officer who is indebted to me.

"About time he can repay that in kind."

With that he abruptly turned and pushed his way through the throng. Ten minutes later, Ray returned with a grin sweeping across his face. "Apparently, your crowd is off to set up a vineyard, and we are here to clear up the airfield and fill in the bomb craters.

"At certain stages, you will need extra help doing the job. For instance, a bridge needs to be built, and extra hands will be required. When the grapevine cuttings are first struck, the plants need to be watered twice a day. The Germans developed a special liquid fertiliser to boost the vines' growth. After it is poured around the plant, it must be soaked in water, and so on. It is very labour intensive but apparently vital to the project's success.

"At these times, some or all of us from Iraklion will be trucked down and live with you all. There are extra tents and equipment already at your site to accommodate us. As an aside, it might pay you to number your tents for ease of distribution of personnel."

At precisely 1330 hours trucks arrived in convoy outside the barracks. 10 trucks were waiting with drivers for the prisoners to clamber on board. The canvas cover had been pulled back on either side to make loading easy.

A command by a German guard set the men in motion. They shuffled forward and pulled themselves up into the back of the first truck. On either side was a bench, so the first man sat on the bench and bounced his backside towards the cabin. The following man did the same, pressing up close to the mate ahead of him. All the shouting made it clear that the Germans would pack each truck tightly.

Once one side was filled the other side soon had men pushing up along it. As the quota for truck one was reached, the men standing on the ground in line were prodded with rifle butts and barrels to move to truck two. The process continued until the last truck was filled.

Captain Walter Holt climbed into the last truck. There were fewer in the last two vehicles so plenty of room.

A fellow companion sat beside Wally and said, "Name's Ian Hardie, [30.] I come from a small mining town, Peak Hill, in Western Australia." He shook hands with Wally. Wally returned the compliment and introduced himself. "Captain Wally Holt, a medical officer from Sydney."

They were in the final truck and Wally said, "Did you get a count. There were twelve 'bums on seats' for each of the first nine trucks. The last three trucks had the leftovers with ten in each. Total is 138 [31] he whispered.

Ian said, "That's my number too, Captain.

"We arrived with 200, and now 138 are being sent to an unknown place that, by my reckoning, is in a southerly direction. We have been travelling for over twenty minutes in pretty much a direct line. What were the 62 going to be doing back at Iraklion?"

Ian Hardie shrugged his shoulders and replied, "I'm more concerned about what the 138 onboard these trucks are going to be doing and where the place is that we are going to stop at. I feel disturbed that we are being spirited away to the Land of Nod. Sure, hope we get better treatment than Cain [32] got after he murdered his brother."

The lead truck moved fast along a straight road full of ruts and potholes.

They travelled a fair way from Iraklion before they came to a meandering road through hills. Plenty of grapes were growing, and the local population was waving.

The Germans were not going to let out any secret destination. The guard pointed his gun towards Walter and Ian and told them to shut up and no talking.

Listening to the engine and feeling the truck's lurching, they believed they were climbing rather steeply. They were constantly cornering right and then left. They were on many switchbacks, which made it easier for them to negotiate high, steep hills or mountains.

The drive was long, and the afternoon sun was dipping over the distant mountains when the first truck finally came to a halt.

The canvas covers, which had afforded some protection from the wind, freezing temperature, and rain were pulled open to let each man jump off the back of the truck.

With lots of shouting from the German guards, the prisoners were lined up in fives and marched across a rocky slope towards a small building. They passed through an open gate, and on either side was a barbed wire fence.

The prison was oddly set out with several tents and an old house as headquarters set up in one remote corner. It was demarcated by a huge barbed wire fence that disappeared into the olive groves on the other two sides

Vic had caught up with Wally and Ian and whispered his concern about the barbed wire fence.

The others nodded in agreement and Captain Holt said, "This does not augur well for our future. It must be six to eight feet [33] high and stretches well into the distance. What the hell are we doing in a place like this?"

Albert Chamberlain cleared his throat and said, "I have no idea but the way we are being herded through the gate we are about to find out."

One of the German guards halted the group and all 138 men came to attention.

"Old army skills and marching drills are so ingrained you never forget them," mused Wally.

A rather stern-looking German officer came on the double from the building. He was followed by a Cretan youth carrying a stool. The stool was placed on the ground, and the officer stepped up to address the large gathering.

In almost perfect English, he said, "Welcome to my camp. I am your commandant. I will stand no nonsense. I will reward those who co-operate. My camp is secure and guarded. It is pointless to try to escape because you are many miles from other people who might foolishly offer you help. If you are silly, you will be shot, and so will anyone who wants to offer you food or assistance.

"Your job will be to dig out hundreds of olive trees so that our horticulturist [34] and his team can grow grapevines.

"The grapes will be sent for processing into wine. Now you will pitch your tents in the area behind you and settle in until called for breakfast. Guards take over."

Vic Petersen wrote in his diary on September 12, "Arrived at the new campsite about 1700 hours and put up a tent for the night."

Many of the men were exhausted and some complained of nausea caused by the trucks' movements. They described their affliction as car sickness.

CHAPTER 18

Half a dozen camp stretchers were found amongst the canvas tents stacked in the open space, pointed out by the commandant. Captain Holt, who was in charge of the medical team, organised for each unwell prisoner to lie down on a stretcher until their giddiness abated.

In the meantime, he started to get the men into groups of 10 and issued tents and tent pegs.

Soon, tents dotted the grounds, and many of the men had gone inside to rest. There was much speculation as to where their location was and what the work of chopping down olive trees entailed.

The men were roused early the next day to have breakfast, to orient themselves and to settle in.

Last evening, due to their late arrival, the prisoners were offered a snack of one loaf of bread per six and half a cup of olive oil. This was washed down with a muddy tasting cup of water. After that, they slept where they fell. Sheer exhaustion and constant swaying in the trucks had left most unwell.

During the day the men were allowed to wander around the area. They soon discovered that they were inside a fenced area with plenty of barbed wire about six or eight feet high.

Wally called Vic and Bernie in the afternoon to catch up with a few volunteers to erect another six tents, explaining that there would be visitors from Iraklion every so often to bolster the workforce.

Bernard (as he preferred) Mitchell was from England and had been in the 1st Sherwood Foresters, Nottinghamshire & Derbyshire Regiment. There were quite a few men from Britain, and he had made mates among them.

Wally came along to check on the layout and numbers. He also pointed out that a medic tent needed to be erected and furnished in case of sickness or injuries. He made it known that as a qualified doctor, he would take charge of this tent.

As the men walked between the tents, Ian (Jock) Hardie wandered past and, in his usual dry humour, suggested, "You need to paint a number on each tent so no one gets lost after the bar is closed."

He then produced a four pint tin of black paint and two small paintbrushes. "Compliments of the commandant and now a couple of volunteers to paint a number on each of the tents."

After further wandering, the group came upon the camp's water supply. It was from a drain, or maybe it was a creek. This waterway ran just inside the camp fence. Well to the south, beyond grove upon grove of olive trees, they could glimpse the Mediterranean Sea.

Vic Petersen wandered over to the barbed wire fence. Looking up the slope he could make out the foothills and mountains. When he turned around, he could see a vast amount of water. He turned back to the hills where the sun was just above the horizon.

That was east. He nodded and said to himself, "We are on the southern side of Crete and it reminds me of where I was picked up by the German patrol last June.

It certainly wasn't a pleasant place to pitch a tent and start grubbing out olive trees. The memories of the day in June, when the boys reached this beach after taking to the hills, were filled with mixed emotions. They were very keen and happy to have reached the water and seen several boats and the two MLCs. They had a renewed hope that one seaworthy boat would be found and used to get them off the island and back to Alexandria.

Unfortunately, only one of the boats was worth a go, and even that one gave in. Then the shock and disappointment of being caught by the Germans put an end to any hope of getting away scot-free.

The biggest downer was watching Major McNab being tied up and taken away. The small group spent much time guessing what might be happening to the Major. When he was finally released, they were jubilant, although that lasted less than a couple of minutes as the next order was to start walking back over the mountains.

The small group set off without food or water, walking for three days before reaching the prison on the northern side of Crete.

Now Vic was back, and so were some of the others who had been with him. He searched his memory for the name of the place. As he tried to recall, there was a flash of a Greek name used by the Germans something to do with Tim and odd letters after that. Then it became clear, they called it Tymbakion.

Vic Petersen wrote in his diary, [1] "In Tymbakion camp as a POW, Saturday 13th September, 1941." [2]

Vic wandered back towards Tent City, noting that almost every group had finished putting up their tents and were tightening the guy ropes. There were 138 prisoners of war to be accommodated, so 15 tents had been erected. Nine men were to be in 12 tents. The other 30 were split up into three lots of 10. This was seen as a comfortable arrangement, as on occasions Vic could recall over 20 men packed like sardines in one tent.

He saw Captain Holt and beckoned to him, "Hi Wally, I've figured out our location, but I won't buy the bulldust about pulling out olive trees to plant grapevines. This is far more of a set-up with an inkling of secrecy.

"Keep your ears and eyes open and no doubt we'll figure out what the Germans are up to. You don't fence in a huge area with barbed wire six to eight feet high to keep the wild donkeys from eating the grapevine leaves."

It had been a long and tiring day, so Vic was aching to find his way into a bed. He chuckled when he realised what he had just said to himself. A bed in a prisoner of war camp is not a bed in the word's true definition.

He walked along the rows of tents until he could hear the voice of Edward Rees, a New Zealander. He had a loud voice in normal conversations, so all around him could hear clearly what he was saying. At that moment, he was telling a joke that was a joke for all the mates to hear.

"You fellows have got to wait for the line, and then you either laugh or add to the joke. It annoys me when you tell a joke and you get constant interjections, so when the punchline arrives, and everyone is more interested in the other idiot's ideas about the ending. Now, where was I?"

Ted Rees was offered no end of ends for his joke.

Vic pushed aside the tent's flap and entered, like a leading man in a play, "The Germans want us to clear the olive trees and plant grapes. That's got to be the joke of the year."

The entire men in the tent, including Ted Rees, all burst out laughing, some at Vic's timing and others because it sounded like Vic's wisecrack associated with the punchline.

The next morning, after a sleep, Vic woke Wally, and they set out to find the men who had been captured at Tymbakion.

He had been with them when they first ran and hid in the hills. He wanted to get their opinions as to whether this was the same place.

Private Walter Pedersen from Melbourne, Victoria, was sitting on his stretcher inside a tent when Vic caught up with him. "Hi, Wal, got a question for you to contemplate. This place looks mighty like the one we got rounded up by the German patrol back on 6th June. What're your thoughts?"

"Could be, but then again, the terrain is much of a muchness wherever you stand. If you find that signpost [3] with the name on it, that might help."

"So, you remember that landmark as well?" queried Vic.

Pedersen said, "I do recall seeing the signpost on the slope above the sandhills. It was about 6 feet tall, and a sign was attached at the top giving the area's name. Although it looks like the Germans have been doing much work down here so it may have been knocked over. Have you seen the barbed wire fence that runs for miles from here to the beach and across the foothills to the west? What the hell are they trying to hide from prying eyes?

"Let's catch up with Ray Powell and Ian Hardie and see what they think. Fancy a walk towards the beach?"

"Sure," came the other's quick reply.

They found the two men, walked together for an hour through olive trees, and came out onto a rocky desert like area before coming across an upright post about three feet high. It was easy to spot in the terrain because it was the only object with height.

The top was splintered and jagged edges stuck upwards. About ten feet away was a similar object lying in the rocks.

"You know what this is?" asked Vic turning to his companions.

"Looks like someone had some fun with a rifle or Bren gun and shot up the post for fun," said Ray Powell.

"Looks more like those Tommy guns that the Germans are so proud to sling over their shoulders. They would smash up and splinter the wood like this," said Wally Holt.

Ian Hardie joined in with an Australian explanation. "We were always doing that back home. You're out with your mates in the ute[4,] and you see a signpost, skid to a halt, grab the twenty-two or whatever pump a few rounds into the nominated parts, hand the gun on and watch your mate's aim. Lots of fun but really stupid, especially when some poor farmer tries to use such a signpost to direct visitors to his place. If the cops catch you, you're gone and ditto the rifle."

"And what of your old man?" asked Wally.

"Good kick up the Khyber,[5] and a demand to report to the Roads Board and drop off a donation. Soon teaches you to behave," said Ian.

"My, my, my, look what I have found." Ray had just kicked a piece of flat wood and it flipped upside down. He gathered it up and walked over to the others. He held it up like it was a trophy given to a sportsman for being the fairest and best competitor.

On the side facing the men, in fading white paint, were the letters YMBAKIO. The T and N at either end had been shot off by shooters.

"Proof positive," said Vic. "We are at Tymbakion, just like I thought. The same place where we were captured by a German patrol in June. This can only be fate working its mean magic against me.

"So, I can say I'm a prisoner of war on the Island of Crete at our new campsite, which is near Tymbakion. In future, when I write in my diary, I won't need to repeat that part."

Wally picked up the shattered piece of wood with the letters painted on it and carried it all the way back to the front gate. Here, he pushed his arm through the wire, being careful of the barbs, and managed to get the sign to hang on the wire of the gate. Now they had a real name for their prison, Tymbakion Prisoner of War Camp. [6]

On the upward slope, a Royal Air Force group had erected their tents. The wandering prisoners noticed there were two tents with an assortment of men hanging around. They all wore the Royal Air Force [7] badge on their blue-grey uniforms. "Looks like the flyboys have been separated from the rest of us. Probably something to do with privileges because they are Air Force," said Wally Holt. "Wonder how many there are and if they are part of the work party?[8]

"A more interesting question would be to ask if they were the ones who erected the barbed wire fence. To do that it would have taken a working party a couple of months to get it established. My feeling is that the Air Force had been here for some weeks and was used to build this humongous fence.

Clearly it is to keep us in and the locals out. The area inside looks like the secret that we may soon be part of." [9]

Bernard Mitchell was settling in to the new camp site on the second evening and recalled standing on the wharf at Souda Bay a few days ago, along with some 200 others.

—⚎—

He remained puzzled as to why he was in a group that contained the last prisoners on the island and more so, why he was selected to go on the trip over the mountains with these other men. He observed the others and listened to their chatting in an effort to get an answer but nothing came of his thoughts.

He met several of the other inmates and the question was asked many times but the answers were never definitive. He questioned them as to what employment they had prior to the war, what section of the army they were in and their interests.

The replies were varied and offered no clear characteristic that defined the group. It would be a few days hence that the question was finally answered.

Bernard Mitchell heard about some of the prominent members of the group and was keen to meet them. Bernard set off to find and talk to Captain Holt and Bert Chamberlain.

Both men could not shine a light on the reason why they and all the others were still on the island nor why they were chosen to be in this particular work party. Their guess was that the Germans needed a group of labourers and it was by bad luck that they were the ones selected.

The likes of Alf Traub and Leslie Le Souef had better credentials but they were sent on to Salonika.

The men who were here in this prison were of a similar ilk but with different experiences. There would appear to have been a German selection going on over the past months.

Captain Walter Holt felt it was his mission to find out why these men were chosen to be at Tymbakion for the latter part of 1941 and beyond. He decided to visit the commandant and ask directly and see what information was forthcoming.

The commandant looked at Wally and smiled before saying, "You are all here to chop down the thousands of olive trees growing on the slopes below camp. I have been told to get the area readied by spring next year."

"What are you planting in the vacant area?" asked Walter innocently.

"I am directed to plant special types of grapevine cuttings. This job will take men of strength and persistence. That is all I know but I do have a record for each man that you are welcome to view."

Wally was very quick to accept the commandant's invitation, and a date and time were set. In two days, Wally was to go to the main office at 1900 hours.

The commandant also asked Wally if there were anything specific he would need to view so that he could make it available. Wally was content to see the roll of all the prisoners at the Tymbakion prisoner of war camp. He believed this document would be set out in columns for ease of reference, and if that was the case, it should show the prisoners' strengths.

Wally thanked the commandant and left the office in a happy mood. He would find out a great deal about the men who presently inhabited the transit camp.

The next morning, during breakfast, Vic Petersen and Walter Pedersen approached Wally Holt and asked about the RAF [10] boys.

Walter Holt explained that, according to the commandant, there were 12 Royal Air Force officers, [11] ranging from pilots, squadron leaders, flying officers, and flight lieutenants.

Under the Geneva Convention, these men were not allowed to do any work for the enemy. They were separated from other prisoners until the High Command in Berlin (Hitler and henchmen) decided what to do with them. They certainly didn't want them back in the air, causing destruction. Every other prisoner of war on the site was ordered to stay away from them.

Wally and Bernard heard the call for all prisoners to attend a parade. The two mates walked swiftly towards the area used as a parade ground. They stood lightly clothed and shivered in the freezing wind that whipped off the snow covered mountains to the north.

The commandant marched from his building and stood at attention, surveying the motley crew.

He waved to the guards, who promptly rushed into the men, pushing, pointing and shoving them into lines. They walked down each row and stopped at the end.

The commandant called something in German, and each guard responded. He addressed the lined-up soldiers. "*Gut*, one hundred and thirty-eight souls, exactly as I was told to expect. Today and forever days, you will be working digging up the olive trees [12] you can see stretching away towards the beach. You work hard, you get to eat; you slack, then the cook will be slack. Time of work 0730 hours to 1700 hours. Very important work must be finished quickly.

"I will need help with sick people, cooking and shopping, so please step forward and volunteer. I will ask you to call your name, number and country."

There was a hesitation as the men looked around to see if their volunteering was going to cause a problem. In the front, one of the men lifted his foot and was about to step forward when the man behind grabbed his shirt and pulled him backwards.

Captain Holt called out, "You heard the man? Are there any volunteers? This is usually considered a privileged job with plenty of time on your hands. If there are no volunteers, I will call you out in one minute?"

There was a lot of murmuring and sideways looks, but everyone stood steadfast. Holt was getting concerned, as he wanted his men to act responsibly and on their own volition. Just as he was going to start calling names one by one, eight men stepped forward and called their names. The first volunteer who tried to step forward kept his nerve, and others followed.

R Bristol VX 26839 Melbourne Australia A I F
W.A. Beacham 23275 New Zealand
R.G. Bentley NX 13532 Canowindra Australia
Robert Brownlie 5409 New Zealand
H. Arroll 2086 Auckland New Zealand
J.T. Burne 35322 Wellington New Zealand N Z E F
George Howes NX2918 Paddington Sydney Aust A I F
G Coombs 22262 Hamilton Waikato New Zealand N Z E F

The commandant pointed to the building behind him. To the rest of the men, still at attention, he said, "You will find your hoes, axes and shovels on the way to the olive grove. Guards march out."

At that command, a German wearing three stripes marched to the back of the assembly and yelled in German, "About turn and form into fives. March on the command. No singing allowed."

Today was the first day of work on a new job, and they had to march about three miles first.

The job was chopping down olive trees and grubbing out the long, entangled roots. This was to make way for land to grow grapevines. There was total disbelief among the prisoners that grapes were to be planted in the area.

The labourers followed the Unteroffizier, and after about 200 yards, they were halted.

The Unteroffizier gestured to his fellow Germans to distribute the tools. Three piles of shiny axes, spades, picks, and mattocks were present. Everyone was allocated at least one tool per person, although some took more before the group marched towards the beach.

After nearly two miles, they were halted, and the guards began to pair the men up and allocate an olive tree to each couple. They pointed out the olive tree that was to be tackled. Reluctantly, the men picked up their tools and set to grubbing out the weirdly twisted trunk of an ancient olive tree.

Vic was paired with a New Zealander who introduced himself as Eric Gaudion. [13] Vic had selected an axe, and Eric had taken a spade. They had been coupled up and sent to a large, gnarled olive tree estimated by Vic to be at least a hundred years old. They were to find out as the work progressed over the next few weeks that some of the trees were two hundred years old.

"I know in the Wheatbelt of Western Australia we have the Mallee [14] tree, and its root is a huge bole that penetrates into the earth. The roots spread out as far as possible to catch the limited amount of rain that falls in the area.

"The branches are crooked and reach some three yards or more just like these olive trees. The farmers have to dig these trees out and burn them before they can plough the paddocks.

"If we had the machinery, we could remove hundreds of olive trees using the ball and chain method. Two tractors or bulldozers drag a chain attached to a huge steel ball about two yards in diameter and all the trees are dragged out by the roots. It's a sight to see, I can tell you." [15]

Vic was in his expansive mood and was clearly a man of intelligence and great general knowledge.

Each day, the pairs were changed, so they got to know most of the men in the camp. This was also a clever ploy by the Germans, as you would not have time to plan an escape or some other escapade.

From the first day, there were many introductions as the men attempted to get to know one another.

The longer this went on, the more the group came to know each other, and bonding began. It intensified every time someone needed help or an explanation.

Ray Powell also found himself with an Englishman on his first day. He battled to follow the conversation.

The new man's accent was difficult to follow at first, and he had to ask for the name to be repeated.

"Edward Baker [16] is me name, but just go for Ted," said the young fellow standing in front of the older Australian. "First time away from my home. I'm from Battersea, just out of London. Miss me, mum, I do."

Ray looked at the rather white complexion and knew that London was a cold, snowbound place but a huge city well known worldwide. They shook hands and walked off with the guard, who would allocate them an olive tree to cut down.

By 1130 hours on that first day, all the men were complaining of blisters and sore backs. After four hours of slogging work, no one had their tree chopped down, and the branches cut into lengths that would be easy to drag. Even after a whole afternoon of chopping and grubbing, only a handful of men had dealt with their single tree. [17]

Once the trees were fully cut down and the roots grubbed out, each piece still needed to be dragged into the centre of the area being worked.

Over the months to come, they improved the rate of removing these trees, and a huge, flat, desolate surface emerged.

The sound of chopping echoed across the valley as the men diligently hacked into the olive trees that had been allocated to be removed.

It was a sad sight considering the trees were once owned by the local Cretan farmers and were the sole income for the family that helped work the groves. These families were losing everything. [18]

This revelation hit the prisoners hard as day by day each began to realise what was happening. There were many men lining up at Wally Holt's tent.

They were intending to protest long and loud at what they saw as criminal activity. They made demands they be excused from continuing work that saw the livelihood of the farmers smashed to pieces.

Wally was sympathetic but emphasised that he could do nothing to stop the work from progressing.

Arthur Hewett, a sapper from the Royal Engineers, had been co-opted into the German planning party because of his knowledge of surveying. Philip Manoy, Robert Chandler and John Magee had been trained by their armies to be engineers and had been selected to help with the project because of their experience in levelling large areas and making roads. [19]

These last three sat on one of the hills overlooking the area where the prisoners were working. Phil Manoy pointed his finger to the furthest denuded area and swept it in an arc until he pointed to the mountains. "You and I should tell the chief what he's going to have to deal with at the first flash flood [20] of winter."

John nodded his head in support but then said, "Just looking shows clearly what Arthur has been showing us each time he adds more contours to his map. The area that is being readied for an airstrip lies in the path of the flood plain of the creek that flows from the mountains. Tell the chief, and I'll guarantee you will be in a hell of a mess. Just get on with the work and say nothing," Phil said.

"Well, if there are German planes landing or sitting on the tarmac, they will end up in the Mediterranean unless the engineering group works out a solution to stop flash flooding from happening.

"He probably wouldn't listen anyway why do we need to point anything out?"

With that comment, the two stood up and wandered back towards camp.

—⚍—

In the meantime, the grubbing continued unabated. The guards were very heavy handed and often pushed, pulled, and shouted at the men to improve the speed of cutting down the trees.

After work and on days off there was plenty of time to be involved with the others. Whether playing games like poker, rummy, gin rummy or chess, there was always time to talk to your mates to find out about them and their lives before the war.

As each branch and limb was wrestled off the main tree it was dragged to a central point that was known as the bonfire. The thick trunks of the trees had to be cut into several pieces. As a single entity, they weighed several hundred kilograms and could not be carried or dragged. As the day progressed the pile from the attack on about 60 trees grew to cover a considerable area and height.

Each Saturday, around 1700 hours, the guards would call a halt, and a sidecar with a passenger and driver would arrive.

They would slowly circle the timber pile and use a small hose to pour petrol onto the heap from a jerry can.

This done, torches were lit and the guards walked around poking the flames into the heap at short intervals. In no time, the flames were billowing high, and the greyish, white smoke rose hundreds of yards into the sky. [21]

It never occurred to any of the prisoners that they were sending a cruel message [22] to the Cretans who lived in the nearby town of Tympaki. They were destroying the livelihood of hundreds of Tympaki farmers and their families. It also told them that the livelihood their ancestors had built up was being destroyed by the very men they had hoped would be Crete's saviours.

It became a ritual [23] for the Tympaki population to meet on the high ground above their town and wait for the huge plumes of smoke to leap into the sky just after 1700 hours every Saturday.

They would then turn their backs and wait for five minutes in silence before shuffling back home. Most had tears running down their cheeks and could only feel that the worst was still to come.

The area's history and olive trees go back centuries and involve many generations. Now, in almost one fell swoop, there was nothing. No trees, no greenery, no olives, no need for people to walk through the groves and admire the mature trees, no more picking the olives, no more pressing the oil from the ripening fruit.

Nothing!

While the fire was being lit the prisoners were hurried back to camp for a wash and dinner. The rations were meagre which would cause considerable unrest in the days to come.

Vic kept an eye on his diary for the important days in his life. It was brother Jack's birthday on Tuesday, September 16. [24]

The men all knew they were slave labour but to cover this, the Germans paid the men. A day's work was calculated to be 30 drachmas, but no one knew how much this was in English pounds. Added to this wage the men were given an issue of five cigarettes every two days or a cigar.

To make these payments even more laughable, there was no place to spend the money. The coins became worthless, and due to their weight, they were thrown away at the first opportunity. Later, when the prisoners began to befriend the Cretans, the money was handed to them, a small compensation for the destruction they were suffering.

Vic's first inkling of the local population attempting to help the prisoners came on the sixth day. He had been lined up with a New Zealander, Arthur Stubbs, Army number 4379 [25].

They introduced themselves as they set off with their tools swung over their shoulders. "Arthur Stubbs," Vic's partner said and presented his left hand.

As they walked, they filled each other in on their backgrounds. Arthur said he was a boy from Karori, a town on the North Island of New Zealand. He was married, but he had no kids. He was a qualified mechanic and was happy to tell Vic that there was no machine he couldn't mend.

Vic Petersen explained he was from Bridgetown, Western Australia, and knew how to drive a truck. He hoped to start up a delivery business.

The two soldiers reached the olive tree they had been allocated to grub out. As Vic stood looking at this century old olive tree, he couldn't stop tears from forming and trickling down his cheek. As he wiped the tears, he thought he saw a movement.

"You know," he said to Arthur, "the farmers around here have spent generations growing these magnificent olive trees.

"We come along and obliterate them in a matter of hours. It's just wrong."

He hefted the axe he had selected for the day's work and then swung it through the air. There was a tearing thud as the axe bit into the tree trunk. Vic attempted to pull the axe out of the timber ready for the next blow. The axe head remained embedded, and no amount of pulling and cursing caused the axe to break free. [26]

Arthur came to the rescue with his mattock, and using the grubber end, he chipped away at the timber surrounding the axe.

Vic managed to pull the axe free. He took the axe and readied for another blow when he thought he caught another glimpse of a movement some 50 yards ahead.

He fixed his sight on the exact position and waited to see what sort of animal was going to emerge.

"What's caused the hold up now?" asked Arthur.

"I'm not sure," said Vic. "I keep catching movement ahead of us but nothing comes out to get a good look at. I'm starting to think I'm imagining things." [27]

"What kind of movement are you seeing?" asked Arthur.

"Don't really know," Vic replied. "I've seen it twice, and it must be something that is small and lightning fast. I get a split second of movement and then nothing."

"Have you ever had migraines? [28] They play havoc with your vision. I get the ones where swirling patterns slowly develop across my vision. It goes on and on until my entire vision is covered. I feel that I am blind. At that stage, a headache develops, and my only option is to lie down."

"My goodness," said Vic looking rather shocked by the information from Arthur. "It must be very scary thinking you may remain blind?"

"It certainly was the first time I had an attack, but since then, I just accept the situation and sit it out. Anyway, that's not my point. Why I'm asking is that you may be having something similar."

There was an interval of some five minutes while Vic watched the place where he claimed he saw movement. Suddenly a young boy ran helter-skelter from behind a tree. [29]

"Did you see that?" asked Vic.

Arthur Stubbs was still in the large hole near the olive tree's bole, waist-deep. He stopped work and looked towards Vic's direction. He was mystified by the question, as the area beyond where they were grubbing was covered with olive trees and isolated. "No, what are you talking about?"

"I definitely saw a young Cretan boy about ten years old running for his life ahead of us." There was no time for further discussion as a guard was approaching and the look was one of 'work you lazy good for nothings!'

By midday, Vic and Arthur were ready to start on the roots. They were sweating profusely so they took a break, just enough for a sip of water and a handful of bread.

"What the hell is this?" asked Arthur standing over a small root and pointing towards the ground.

"Well, I'll be?" said Vic. "It looks like we are being offered some help from the very people whose olive trees we are smashing to bits."

Vic cautiously bent over, and there, neatly wrapped in red material, was a small cardboard box. It had been placed so the passerby would not see it but someone close would see the material.

"Oh boy look what's inside, yummy!" said Arthur, "Freshly baked bread and a small bottle of olive oil. There's also a couple of handfuls of sultanas."

The two men wolfed the food down as they were hungry. That was the one constant the prisoners of war found.

"So, I did see a small lad running through the olive trees. The Cretans are trying to help us even though we are destroying their livelihood. Keep a lookout while I take a look around. Tonight, we will need to alert everyone as to what the Cretans are up to. I would hate to see them caught because the trigger-happy Germans are likely to line them up, add a few friends and relations, and shoot them."

Vic wandered away towards the barbed wire fence where he had seen the Cretan youngster.

He covered about 50 yards of the fence and then noticed someone had interfered with the wire at one point.

He didn't have time to investigate fully so he took out a small piece of paper and a pencil these were always handy for writing up his diary and wrote, 'Thank you'. He stuck this on the barbs just above the area that had been disturbed.

That night Arthur and Vic caught up with Bert Chamberlain, Wally Holt, Ray Powell, Bernard Mitchell and Howard Holmes to tell them of their unusual experience while chopping their olive tree down. The team agreed to pass on the information to everyone.

They set out to catch up with everyone and whispered what they had discovered.

Everyone was sworn to secrecy and told to bring back all the food found so that it could be collected and shared fairly among all the men. The containers and material that came with the food were to be buried where the guards would not see them.

Vic was pleased that he and the others would get a little extra food over the miserable German ration they presently received. He had been very worried at losing a lot of weight since his encounter with the snake back in June. At that time, he weighed 11½ stone. Now his weight had plummeted to eight stone. His ribs stuck out and his energy was far less than at any other time in his life. [30]

On his scraps of paper that would constitute his diary, Vic added the entry, [31] "Greeks hiding food in holes by the side of trees ungrubbed overnight."[32] This entry was dated September 20, 1941.

—⚊—

The next day, Vic and another fellow prisoner, Raymond Day, from Gorey, Wessex, in Ireland, were placed together. They introduced themselves and Vic was taken by Ray's Irish lilt (accent).

Ray continued to talk while they both were working on their olive tree using an axe to cut the stem down. After listening to the Irishman chatting away Vic intervened and told Ray about his sighting of the young Cretan boy and the food he had found. He suggested to Ray that they go over to the fence where Vic had left a note to see if there was any evidence of anyone finding the note.

A few minutes later, the two men stood at the fence, and Vic pointed out the crude cutting of the wire near the ground. The bottom two strands parted and sagged, allowing enough room for a ten-year-old child could wriggle through. He was pleased to see that his note was missing.

Vic returned the fencing wire to its original look and turned to walk back to the olive tree they were working on when an orange hit the ground at his feet. "What the hell is going on?" he asked.

Ray looked dumbfounded and said, "An orange just landed at our feet, it must have been thrown from over the fence."

The two men looked up and down the fence line. A young lad of about 10 years of age stepped from behind an olive tree on the other side of the fence.

"You want oranges to eat?" queried the boy as he stepped towards the two men. In his left hand he held an orange which he pitched over the fence and Vic caught it with ease.

The boy had his pullover pulled up at the front and a heap more oranges nestled in the bowl shape made by the jumper.

The two men were quick to take up the offer so the boy began tossing oranges over the fence. While he threw the oranges, he was telling the two men that his family owned an orange orchard [33] further along the valley and there were heaps of the fruit ripening on the trees.

He offered to bring as many as he could carry every day and throw them to the men to share with their fellow prisoners. This idea was readily accepted. At this point the boy had offloaded all the oranges he had, turned and went back to a nearby olive tree. He returned carrying a large crate that was half full of oranges.

Vic was furiously digging a hole and dumping the oranges into it. Again, the boy began throwing oranges to the men.

There was a noise behind and both men jumped and ran off towards the tree they were chopping down. The boy ran for his hidey tree carrying the empty crate. He called out, "Tomorrow, yes?"

The 'Orange Boy' [34] was like manna from heaven, and the men were able to supplement the meagre German menu for days ahead. The number of oranges the youngster carried to the fence each morning was remarkable.

There were so many, in fact, that Vic and Ray had to co-opt two more helpers. Harry Barnes and Bill Cunningham soon learned to catch the oranges and hide them in the holes the men dug nearby. The oranges could be dug up daily at the needs of each prisoner. They seemed to keep for several days, but the hunger in camp was such that most were eaten within 48 hours.

Then, one day, the boy did not turn up. There were many theories as to what may have happened to this saviour, but none were ever proven. As Vic said, "I hope the boy is well, happy, and alive. He deserves a medal in appreciation. He put his life and that of his family on the line for all of us."

Two days after the oranges began being pitched over the fence, Vic added more to his diary related to the Cretans' livelihoods being destroyed. "Monday 22nd September 1941 camped at Tymbakion grubbing out old olive trees, some 100 years old.

"It is heartbreaking to see what it is doing to the local population, as this is their livelihood and the trees are loaded with olives." [35]

Around the same time at Souda Bay, Lieutenant Colonel Leslie Le Souef was making preparations to move the final group of wounded and ill onto a ship for transportation to Athens.

He was convinced that these men and the medics looking after them were the last of the Allies to remain on Crete. Once loaded, the ship would edge away from the wharf, severing all ties between the Allies and the Cretans. To Leslie, that final move would happen tomorrow morning at sunrise.

This final move was made on September 23, 1941, and as far as Le Souef was aware there were no more Allied POWs on Crete, Leslie was not aware of the 200 chaps who had sailed on the *Norburg* for Iraklion. The way they were dispersed at Iraklion was as though they had been spirited away.

Over 100km to the southeast, Vic Petersen woke up just as the medical rescue ship edged away from the Souda Bay wharf. He felt a cold shudder move along his spine. It felt like he was feeling abandoned, as though someone was leaving him behind. He threw the blankets off and went out to wash his hands and face to spruce himself up for breakfast and then the grubbing.

The medics and wounded who were sailing from Souda Bay at that very moment believed they had just gained the important historical trophy of being the last Allies on Crete.

However, a small group of prisoners of war at Tymbakion were the real champions and should have collected the trophy, a trophy neither group aspired to.

—m—

The Tymbakion crew had been spirited away and were lost to the Allies. These incarcerated men had a line in their records indicating they were missing around the time of the capitulation, June 1, 1941. Later another line would appear to indicate they had turned up at a stalag in Germany.

The dates in each individual's records are often not accurate. This is due to the 'catch-up' time needed.

Someone is involved with an activity worthy of note, but it can take several days or even months before the officer in charge finds out and records the date and activity.

A typical example for many of the men at Tymbakion is the date showing their arrival at Stalag VIII-B. Petersen's diary notes,

"Thursday 29th January 1942 Prisoner of war on the train enroute to camp in Germany and still plenty of snow about. Had hot soup about midday. Arrive destination camp Lamsdorf (which was Stalag VIII-B), about 1930 hrs. and had to march about ¾ hour from the station to the camp, which is a very large one."

In this instance, the Army's recorded date of arrival at VIII-B was March 19, 1942 a distinct difference.

Most have their German records marked as "Officially reported POW. Place of Detn (sic) STALAG VIIIB 19/2/42" which is also incorrect.

—⁂—

The Crete farmers' olive harvest season begins in October and lasts through the end of January. This means that they would have been organising the pickers while the POWs were travelling to Germany. These pickers would lay a sheet out under the branches of a tree they were going to pick olives from. Once organised, a long stick like bamboo would be used to thrash the trees, causing the blackish-purple olives to fall onto the sheet. The workers would collect the sheet and transfer the olives into a bin on a donkey drawn cart.

When the bin was full, the cart would be taken to the shed and the fruit offloaded.

The olives would be kept until it was olive oil making time, and then the oil press would be working continuously across each day until all the fruit was turned into olive oil. Another bin would be placed on the cart and taken back to the pickers.

The Cretans were very keen to celebrate the holy days and holidays and did not work on Sundays. Often, a small group would come to the commandant and ask if they could share food with the camp residents while celebrating. The monks and priests planned this strategy well, as it gave them the opportunity to keep the prisoners fed, reasonably healthy, and informed.

The sharing of information allowed the prisoners to catch the ears of the religious leaders so that they could work together to make it difficult for the Germans to get their project completed in a reasonable time.

One of these religious days was September 27, 1941. Vic's entry in his diary. [36] "They brought down plenty of food on the 27th from the hills. No work on the Sunday. Three Pecco planes landed on a new airfield. [37] This event caused quite an excitement amongst the men."

When they heard the first plane, they gathered in groups expecting a bombing raid. They certainly did not expect the planes to land. The fact that these planes could land and take off showed how much work the POWs had managed to put in.

The Cretan people were exceptionally clever in appearing to befriend the Germans when, in fact, they despised the invaders and what they had done, and continued to do, to their country and countrymen.

It was a type of Stockholm Syndrome [38] whereby the captives developed positive feelings towards their captors over time. This was more a pretence of developing positive feelings.

That way they were given more freedom. If the locals of Tympaki had any inkling of what the Germans had in mind for the near future they may have thought and acted differently.

The Germans were intent on starting to pave the airstrip with crushed rocks so that the surface would be able to take the heaviest of planes. The Cretans would be aghast at where this stone was coming from and how it was going to be moved.

There were more immediate matters to attend to before the crushing of rocks was to be ordered.

Grumblings started on the second day of high temperatures. The Australians nearly choked on their olive oil and one-sixth of a loaf of bread. These blokes were used to heat. The actual top temperature on the first day was 84° Fahrenheit, and on the second day, it was 90° Fahrenheit.

It wasn't just the heat but also the sweaty bodies that were caused by the toiling of chopping down the olive trees. By the third morning, men were complaining of the body odour of their sleeping mates.

It was Len Christmas who brought the issue to a head. He bravely put it to his mates, "You fellows stink to high heavens I can't handle another night squeezed next to any of you."

The comment started a full on argument with Jimmy Craig, Alex Hastie, Len McDonald and John Tatton joining in. This progressed rapidly to fists raised and then several punches thrown, some of which connected. Several men who were in the vicinity scattered so they couldn't be blamed for the melee. John Gorton, Rocky Lythgoe, Albert Matthews and Alf Buhagiar, ran for cover towards the dunny. Herb Hodson and Harold Brown took off in search of Wally Holt to get him to quell the fight.

The guards intervened and marched the five protagonists to the commandant. He was less than sympathetic and added to the fire that the smell emulating from each man was intolerable. He told them they needed to wash and to use soap. The men mumbled objections and excuses which ended with the commandant marching them to the creek. Here he was rather taken back by the dry stream.

He shrugged and told the five men to grow up and return to work.

On their way to catch up with the main work party, a plan was hatched. It had a modicum of danger, but at this stage, and feeling the day was headed for another high temperature, anything was better than continuing to smell and feel uncomfortably unhygienic.

The beach is about three miles from the work area. It is a light run for fit men in their 20s. No one was fit, but they considered they could make the run and enjoy a half hour in the water before returning to the work area. All they needed to do was distract the guards, set off, and encourage others to join in. The more, the better, as the numbers would confuse the guards.

Upon reaching the work area, the five in trouble began whispering the plan and trying to persuade others to join.

For most the idea of a swim in the cool Mediterranean Sea and having their clothes washed at the same time was blissful.

At the appointed time the men who weren't heading to the beach began walking back towards camp, complaining about the heat and their tiredness. Adrian Billings, Tom Bissett, George Bowen, Charles Brodie, George Brown, Fred Rice and Harold Brown led the retiring pack.

Another group, including Ray Day, Frank Dyson, Archie Forbes, Anthony Fraser, Edgar Goodwin, Stan Harrington, Frank Howie, Fred Hurren, Henry Johnson, Cyril Herbert, Andrew King, Anastosias Kollias, along with the five who worked out the plan, ran off towards the beach.

A third fellowship followed the organisers and ran off towards the next grove of olive trees. This group consisted of James Osborn, Syd Payne, Jack Prichard, Tom Wynn, Frank Walters, Eric Tregear, Herb Stratton, Les Stirling, Loris Smith, Stan Shirley and Harry Sherriff. They ran for the barbed wire fence where they would follow it to the sea. Having a third group confused the guards who didn't know which way to run.

The guards were caught out by the sudden movements and ran around shouting for everyone to return to work. The men walking towards camp pushed in tight with the guards which gave the other two groups a chance to disappear.

A fourth group formed when the men who weren't prepared to join in just sat down where they were and watched the running and yelling quickly dissipate.

The guards went with the men headed back to camp as they needed to get help from the commandant.

In the meantime, the prisoners who bolted for the sea were splashing happily in the delight of the water. A few minutes later group two arrived. Everyone was cavorting in the nude while they scrubbed their clothes.

A half an hour of fun and frolic was enough so they all dressed and made their way back to camp.

The commandant met them part way and he was furious, holding Wally Holt and Bernie Mitchell responsible for the out-of-control men.

While they walked back to camp, Wally explained the situation and brought the commandant around to see that a good swim would refresh everyone, and they would be appreciative of such a move.

The commandant worked this thinking into his own plan.

—⁂—

Upon arrival at camp, all the men were lined up and ordered to undress. They stood stark naked for the next six hours while being lectured about their unruly behaviour.

While dressing they did receive a positive message from the commandant. He told them he would allow them to wake an hour early every Sunday and be escorted to the beach for a swim and wash.

This was greeted with a whispered cheer but proved pointless as the dropping temperature meant that all the men preferred to stay in bed for an hour rather than freeze on the walk to the sea.

Vic wrote at the end of September, "Greeks brought us down plenty of food [39] and beans done in olive oil at dinner time. This food giving seemed to be on special occasions in their church." [40]

One particular evening, Bonnie Buirchell was returning to his hideout after checking his snares when he heard a German patrol near to where he was headed. He ducked down and began to back-pedal, staying as low as possible. As he moved downwards another patrol appeared coming up the hill. He was basically trapped between the two German groups.

The only opportunity he could see was a small abandoned village. He reached the houses, not knowing if the Germans had spotted him or not. Surefooted, he picked his way through the rocky terrain, all the while remaining doubled over. His clothing was patched so as to blend with the environment.

His heart was racing, and he was blowing hard. He began trying to open the locked doors. Each door disappointed him, as it was unable to be opened. He scrambled up a grapevine growing against a wall and tumbled onto the flat roof. Below where he was hiding, he could hear the German patrol searching the houses.

As he rolled away from the edge of the building, he felt a wet patch spreading across the sleeve of his khaki shirt. His first reaction was to grab at the area to stem the flow of blood.

He sat up and looked at the palm of his hand expecting to see the bright red of his blood weeping from a large wound along his upper right arm.

He started to chuckle, as the liquid on his arm was reddish-purple. It was definitely not the red of blood. A smashed, overripe bunch of red grapes lay on the flat roof.

The Germans were kicking at the doors and yelling, "*Nein*" as they found nothing at each residence.

The noise increased as the second patrol arrived. Bonnie didn't know whether they knew he was hiding in the village or whether the searchers were just curious about any signs of escaped prisoners.

Bonnie remained still and quiet until the noise abated and the sun had set. He clambered down and made a hasty retreat to his hideaway. These incidents were few and far between, but they had to be suffered. He had heard the trucks come and go a month ago in the lateness of the night and wondered what they were doing.

He later found out that there was a relationship between Tymbakion and Iraklion. [41] Quite often a truck or car would run between the two camps with messages and prisoners. Everything was done quietly, swiftly and after midnight.

The relationship between the two places did cause confusion with numbers at times, especially at census time. Some POWs were registered at one but not the other and some were at both that type of befuddlement.

Bonnie had gone for a walk one day and discovered the barbed wire fence that surrounded the Tymbakion Camp and was amazed at its extent. This was all new since he had been on the beach near this area back in June. He had no idea what the Germans were doing.

The relationship between Iraklion and Tymbakion made sense, especially when it came to medical needs. Even while he tried to think logically about the need for the two towns to operate as one, he did not for a moment consider that he, himself, would be trying out the medical hookup.

At the moment, he was healthy and happy, and until he found a way off the island, he would remain as such. He hoped beyond hope that the escape would come despite the unlikely end of the war. A victory by the Allies over the Axis countries would be the best outcome.

CHAPTER 19

A few weeks later, on October 1, Bonnie's curiosity got the better of him and he left his lair to venture down to the road he had found. He tracked tyre tread markings that were easy to see. He moved along the edge so that he was out of direct sight of anyone who was moving along the road.

Bonnie followed the treads for several miles until he saw a small house in the corner of a barbed wire fence enclosure. The house was typical of those seen in any Cretan village. It was made of stone with a flat roof. Around the outside were the obligatory grapevines and cactus plants. The grapevines climbed the walls and across the roof.

At the rear of the house were the remnants of an orchard containing an almond tree, oranges, lemon trees and a plum tree. These were well spread out so Bonnie guessed it had been much bigger until the Germans stripped the other trees.

The vegetable garden, or what was left of it, took up a substantial area of the plot. This was in keeping with the self-sufficiency that all Cretans practised. The farmers were particularly keen to grow their own due to the isolation of each farm, especially in the southern region of Crete.

It was overgrown with weeds, although the tomato bushes had a few bright red tomatoes hanging on the plants. As he watched and savoured the taste of ripe tomato in his mind, a small bird flittered down and landed on the furthest plant. It hurriedly pushed its long, sharp beak into the overripe tomato before flying away.

Bonnie turned his interest back to the 20 or more tents scattered around the area. He was intrigued by what this was all about, so he lay above the area and watched for any comings and goings.

Nothing seemed to be happening so he decided to veer around the fence and see if there was anything happening further towards the beach.

As he moved cautiously along, he began to hear chopping sounds and then voices. With every step he took the sounds got louder. The whole area inside the fence was abuzz with men cutting down olive trees whilst yelling back and forth to each other. He was especially concerned by the work of the inmates in cutting down the olive trees.

He understood immediately the mental damage this would be doing to the owners of these trees. [1] "Bastards," he thought aloud, "They don't care that those trees are a family's livelihood and prosperity. That action will kill the family unit as it will have to disperse and work on labouring jobs for other farmers."

Bonnie found a cosy position and lay in the warm sun watching the workers. His mind wandered back to his town in Western Australia. The memories were as strong as, or even stronger than they were when he first set foot on the ship taking him to the Middle East. As he waved to his wife, Clem, and their little girl he thought about all the cricket and Australian Rules Football he would miss.

He thought of his shearing mates who would wonder how he was faring. Everything in the shed was sharp and clear.

He had been in North Africa, Greece, and Crete, fighting against a foe that was, in military terms, brilliant. During the nine months of war, he had seen the most heinous things. The paratroopers' invasion of Crete was amazing but ended in so many deaths and the capitulation of the Allies.

He didn't accept his incarceration very well so escaped on two occasions. The last four months, living alone like a hermit, he had trouble conjuring up the face of the dark haired firebrand that he had married.

The world had become surreal in this faraway land, and all he wanted was to return to the peaceful life he had led in the small town of Kojonup. While his mind wandered, he was oblivious to a small insect that had landed on a bare patch on the back of his right hand. It was so tiny it was almost invisible. The mosquito jabbed its proboscis in through the skin and sucked out some of the warm blood. Being an Anopheles mosquito, it left behind microscopic malaria parasites. [2]

As the sun began to settle behind the distant hills Bonnie made haste back to his cave. On the way he visited his snares to see if he had caught a kri kri (or wild goat), hare or badger. He did not always catch one of these animals but did enough to eat meat each day. [3]

He used the chicken wire to fence in a pool of water. Around the wire, he would use more wire to make funnels. The animal coming to drink would circle the wire, and find the way in but not out. He used strands of fencing wire he had found near a house to make snares.

Finding all his traps empty of wildlife he continued to his base. He was still seething with disgust at what he had seen and the hurt the Cretan farmers would be suffering. The Cretan people were the most altruistic [4] he had ever met and knew that if he required help, he only had to approach them.

He also felt deep pity for the prisoners of war who were being forced to cut down the olive trees. This was slave labour pure and simple. [5]

He wondered what other sufferings the Germans were going to inflict on the Cretan people in the future.

Just ripping up all the olive trees seemed like a pathetic punishment. There must be more in mind than that. Maybe a huge prisoner of war camp? That was unlikely as he felt that most of the prisoners on Crete had already been shipped out.

There were still stragglers [6] wandering the hills and mountains awaiting a chance to find a way off Crete. Bonnie kept well clear of anyone in this category as he did not trust others. He could not bear to think about being back behind the wire. Unfortunately, his fate had already been sealed.

The next morning, Bonnie woke feeling hot all over, but he was also aware that he was shaking as though he was cold.

He pulled the blankets over himself and tried to go back to sleep. The shivering increased and he felt nauseous.

After a while, he was shivering so violently that he decided he needed to light a fire to keep warm. He was not thinking straight and he broke one of his golden rules: 'Never light a fire during the day'. Too many prying eyes would likely see the smoke on the faraway hills and send out a party to capture the firelighter.

He knew German patrols were wandering the hills and up into the mountains almost every day, sent out to find and capture the escapees from Crete's capitulation on June 1.

Bonnie would watch these men as they wandered around and he would hide deep in his cave until the coast was clear.

His mottos included 'safety by oneself', 'never trust others', and 'never use the same route'. So far, they had kept him safe and free.

With a small fire going, he felt a little better, but again, the shaking and cold sweats rushed across his entire body. He stacked more wood on the fire.

He slept off and on with strange dreams coming and going. After 24 hours he had run out of wood and was still suffering the symptoms of what he now guessed was malaria. [7]

Bonnie crawled out of the small hole at the entrance to his cave and stood up. He noted that the sun was high in the sky and estimated the time to be midday. The world seemed to spin and he felt as if he was plunging into a deep ravine.

He walked awkwardly, all the while feeling the swirling, and lost his balance, before he fell heavily and rolled down the slope. He lay still wondering if he had broken any bones.

His head was aching on the left side above his ear. Trembling, he reached up and ran his hand across the area that was painful. When he looked at his hand there was blood, a lot of blood. He must have hit his head on a sharp rock as he fell.

"Damn," he said aloud. "This was my worst-case scenario, falling and breaking bones or cutting some part of my body so badly that I would need help." He knew he had to move into a shadow as the sun was rather hot at this time of the year.

Crete enjoyed the Mediterranean climate, where summer ran from June to August. [8] With the sun beating down, it was a very hot autumn day, the type that is left over from those scorchers in summer.

He had lost track of time, relying only on the natural 24 hour rotation of each day to navigate around or lay on his blankets to have a rest.

He tried to clasp the rocks in front of his face and use his hands to pull himself along. After what seemed like an hour, he reached a rock overhang which gave a little shade. [9] He was now so thirsty he felt weak and his mouth was parched. [10]

At that time, he must have blacked out. When he awoke, he could hear strange noises from above his position. As he listened, they came closer and louder. It began to dawn on Bonnie that the noises were hooves on stone, moving slowly.

He heard a voice speaking in a foreign language. Through pain and fog he had lucid moments. He had glimpses of an elderly Cretan who was short and skinny, trying to lift him onto a donkey with big ears.

He heard English being spoken and the words, "Being sick, we'll take him from here." [11]

He woke every so often but didn't recall all that he saw or heard. In one of his lucid moments, which he thought was a dream, he was in a tent and a man in white was trying to give him water with a teaspoon.

Between Monday and Thursday, 6-9 October 1941, the system that the Cretans had devised to hide food for the prisoners went pear-shaped.

Some of the inmates caused a stir when they claimed others were eating the food left by the Cretans and not sharing it equally.

This made the guards suspicious that something was up and they went into each tent to investigate the situation.

To add to the problem some prisoners got overzealous and placed notes in the empty parcels that had contained food. Some of these were messages of 'thank you' whereas others were requests for food and personal needs. [12]

The most urgent request was for blankets. With the onset of autumn, bitter, freezing winds swept off the mountains. The men virtually froze all night. The winds also presaged winter with its cold, snowy conditions. To get hold of a blanket or two was imperative.

One of the German guards found a parcel and note and reported his find to the commandant. The Cretans were then forbidden to bring any more food in parcels and more guards were posted outside the wire with orders to shoot to kill anyone approaching the fence.

These guards patrolled along the outside of the fence where the prisoners were working. This seemed to be the obvious place the Cretans would come to leave parcels.

On October 9, Captain Holt was surprised when a visitor turned up at his tent. The stranger introduced himself and explained what he wanted to talk about. [13]

"Corporal Arthur Roland Richardson [14] 103829 out of London, sir. I'm one of the fly boys from the RAF tent over yonder. [15]

"I believe it is the right time for me to give you a rundown about what the Germans are doing at this site and why we all must hold up the works as much as possible." He had an educated English accent and looked very concerned.

Captain Wally Holt introduced himself and shook the RAF man's hand. The grasp was strong, warm, and welcoming. He had a friendly disposition and carried himself with an air of authority. His men saw him as a no nonsense leader who was resourceful.

Arthur Richardson suggested the two of them take a walk away from prying eyes and ears. Arthur looked over his shoulder and was satisfied there was enough space between them and the other men in their tents.

As they continued to walk Arthur told Wally things that made him realise that Tymbakion was not an ordinary prisoner of war camp, and the men working in it were handpicked because of their expertise and strength.

"Tomorrow the RAF boys will be moved out of Tymbakion to Germany," Arthur began. "Your team will continue to work until you have completely removed all the olive trees and flattened the area.

"You will also start to strengthen the tarmacs of the airfield using rocks concreted together to about a foot in depth. For this job, you will be helped by the men and boys from Tympaki and surrounding towns.

"That will mean a lot of men, donkeys, carts and rocks day in and day out. There will be a growing number of lorries if the Germans can get the machines, mechanics and fuel they will need.

I have heard talk about there being 7000 men available. It will be sheer slavery for these poor swine.

"The main runway must be able to land the heaviest bomber carrying the heaviest payload. This means a Junkers 88 water carrier. This runway is measured to six miles and runs north-south with enough room to land two planes at one time. [16]

"Down by the shore is an east west runway that was originally built by the British before the war. They used it as a staging centre to reach the Middle East quickly, requiring less fuel.

"The Germans have revitalised the area. It is now to be used for parking well over two hundred aeroplanes at one time, and a barracks to house all personnel. The Germans will place this on your list of to dos. What you will eventually see on this site is one gigantic German Luftwaffe camp."

Wally Holt stopped and stood looking at the ground. He slowly shook his head as if in denial of what he was hearing. Richardson thought for a second that the man would tell him he was spouting rubbish.

The seconds ticked away and then Wally lifted his head, made eye contact and said, "We have been complicit in so many ways to what could be the winning hand for the Germans.

"It's the Cretan people I have felt the most for. Poor buggers have been treated so appallingly with their farms confiscated, the olive groves grubbed out and their men shot under the pretext of reprisals. On top of all that they get their towns razed to the ground. They lose everything and have maintained a dignity and a friendliness like no other."

Richardson waited politely for Holt to finish before continuing his line of thought about the size of the airfield. "It will be the largest camp in the Balkans, covering six miles by four miles. The fence will be electrified to ensure no one can get inside.

"Inside and outside along the perimeter of the fence will be barracks with frescoes of the time, fixed artillery bases, trenches, underground shelters, barracks, command posts, and all the other facilities they need. There will be scattered fortifications built by the Germans to repel Allied landings.

"Although your men are prisoners of war, the Germans treat you in any manner they choose.

"You need to start protests and disagreements targeting your working conditions."

The major issue was doing work that was contrary to the Geneva Convention. This Geneva Convention was set up after World War One and was like the rules of war. [17]

One of the most contentious of these 'rules' was that prisoners should not work on projects that benefited the enemy. Prisoners should not help make weapons or machinery that would be used to wage hostilities against their enemy.

"The men have to be very vocal against the building of an airfield that could be used to bomb their fellow soldiers," Corporal Richardson added.

"In this case, the bombing will mainly target North Africa, Alexandria, the Suez Canal, and the Iranian oilfields. The commandant will be equally forceful and threaten to withdraw all food and handcuff the men. He will continuously deny that the area being cleared is for an airfield.

"You may not be aware but Goering [17] is in charge of the whole operation and has a Greek engineer overseeing every move. This airfield would give the Germans a huge advantage in hitting North African cities.

"They will especially target the Middle East countries. With that much under their control, it's almost 'the world's the limit'.

"Time wise, it will cut down the flying time to the Middle-East cities by half. The Luftwaffe will dominate the skies over the Mediterranean Sea. The navy will not be able to compete and the movement of German soldiers will be swift to any area required. Do you get the urgency in me telling you this Captain?

"For the security of the airfield, it will be built around, and inside the barbed wire fence, you can see ahead of us. Anti-aircraft bunkers will be on each corner of the runway.

"Much of the area from the airstrip to the fence will be mined, anti-tank traps will run along each runway. Hundreds of troops will live on-site and act as security."

"My goodness," remarked Wally "Why are you telling me this now when we should have had this talk days ago?"

"We had this place all planned to fall before Christmas but now we have been given our marching orders.

"We will be trucked out at 0630 hours to Iraklion, shipped to Salonika, and railed into Germany. They are going to keep us in isolation until the job here is done."

"And what can we do to stop or slow the plan down?" asked Wally.

"Very little," said Richardson shaking his head. "We were looking at an inside job. We were going to snatch some planes and sabotage others at the same time as the Royal Air Force in Alexandria would attack the runway, aeroplanes and barracks.

"We do know that the Germans are concerned that you are a group in the know. They don't want your men talking to anyone within the next six to twelve months and spilling the beans. So, it is highly likely you will also be trucked out fairly soon."

"There must be something we can do, surely," Wally implored. "I have 151 men under my command and they could do a fair amount of damage."

"The one thing that will slow them considerably is the Cretan question, which will shock you," Richardson continued.

"The Germans intend to use the Cretan men and boys from Tympaki and surrounding villages as slave labour, carting the stone for the main runway.

"Where will this stone come from? The obvious answer is the hills and mountains. They will need thousands of tons of rock broken into rubble and tons of concrete to smooth it over. The reason why this is not a viable proposition is that fuel to cart the heavy rock and to crush it to a usable size is not available.

"Hitler has stockpiled almost all his available oil, petrol and aviation fuel along the Polish border and is using it to keep his war machine operating against the Russians on the Eastern Front.[18] He is desperate to get North Africa and Iran under his control as these locations have plentiful oil.

"The simple answer is what you can see up on that hill to the west."

Wally turned and looked to the west and scratched his head. Arthur gave him time to think.

"Oh no you're kidding, they wouldn't?"

"Yes, they would, and in fact, they have already started," said Richardson. "You and your men must stir the Cretans as much as possible. You have to incite them so they run away or refuse to work, or they begin demonstrations or protests, whatever it takes to stop the work. The Tympaki houses are being blown up with dynamite and the stone salvaged. It will then be moved to the runway, broken down in a crusher and levelled out.

"The Cretans will not accept that without protest. We don't want just to protest they need to stop work, refuse to work, walk off the job and make claims that seem absurd. They need to act as one to disrupt, to use passive resistance, [19] that is, intentionally delay completion.

"The things the Germans have begun doing need to be pointed out and stirred up through the elders, leaders and the priests. The town of Tympaki will be smashed to the ground and even the cemetery will be dug up for the timber and rock.

"Stir these things up in every Cretan and stall the construction work. Hopefully, by then, the Royal Air Force and the Royal Navy will get their act together and take the airfield out."

Arthur Richardson turned and began to walk back to the camp. "Can't help you more than that. Best of luck and happy hunting."

—⚜—

Wally caught up to Arthur and asked matter of factually, "Do you mind telling me your story to this point?

"I would like to make sure you and your men are recognised for how you have acted so far."

Like most Air Force personnel, Arthur grinned and said, "Not much to tell, really, but if you don't mind walking the extra distance to my tent, I'll whip up a coffee and tell you, my story."

"Coffee!" said Wally a lot louder than he intended but he couldn't help himself.

"Yes, I have been trying to stay on the commandant's best side and ingratiate myself to him and that has worked.

"It has enabled me to learn so much about this covert project. In doing that he has been kind enough to give me a small jar of coffee."

Once seated and with a mug of steaming coffee in his hands Wally was ready to hear what this remarkable young man had been up to over the last two years.

"I'm a radio engineer having qualified before the war came along. I joined up on the 25th of February, 1940, and chose the RAF, and was put into Squadron A.M.E.S. 25 (Air Ministry Experimental Station and Section).

"We were flying out of Athens and assisting the Allies and Greeks to push the Germans back from the Greek border when we were shot down.

"Luckily, we all bailed out and landed in friendly territory. Next, I'm on Crete and in the hot spot of another war. After climbing over the mountains from Chania, I reached Sfakia and hoped to catch a ship back to Egypt. When the call came out to surrender, I joined a party and we took off into the hills. It concerned me to have such a large group trying to hide from the Germans so I took off by myself."Unfortunately, like many of the Allies, I was caught by a German patrol, and back to Chania, I was taken.

"I have always been keen on a challenge. The Germans sent me and a couple of other blokes, in a working party to a battery charging plant in June for a week or two. We filled up all the aircraft accumulators with commercial sulphuric acid and tap water. We so included some other cells.

"The other sabotage we happily got involved in was wasting petrol that was supposed to be for a plant.

"On 1st July I set off by myself into the hills. Again, I was caught, this time by German paratroopers five days later just north of Sfakia. My problem was that I was not physically fit.

"All the poor diet left me weak as hell. The Germans were not too happy with my attitude and decreed that I was to be taken to an isolated place in Crete along with a few others and be set to work. No matter how much I protested I found myself with 11 others here, at Tymbakion.

"We spent the days from early July until mid-September when you fellows all turned up digging post holes and mixing cement.

"This was used to erect the barbed wire fence around this so called vineyard. A total of 60 days."

Arthur stopped talking, so Wally stood up, shook his hand, and said goodbye. It was the last time they saw each other.

The next day, all 12 RAF personnel were taken out of the camp and moved by truck to Heraklion. From there, they were flown to Athens. The whispers went around the camp and were taken into the field. While the chopping of trees resounded throughout the Tymbakion area, the men heard all the news that came out of the discussion between Captain Walter Holt and Corporal Arthur Roland Richardson.

—⁂—

Captain Holt arrived at the commandant's office and knocked on the door but there was no immediate answer. He waited patiently and then the door swung open and a young German soldier ushered him in. "Sit at the table," was the brief demand. The lad disappeared through another door that opened into a passageway. He soon returned carrying a book and pushed this across the table towards Holt.

Holt politely accepted the book, sat and opened it. The names of POWs who had been captured in Crete were in the register. The Germans were sticklers for accountability and accuracy.

The book was set out with columns drawn down the two pages. Headings were at the top of each column. The first column began with a Number for the entry's number.

After this, the next column was Surname, then Christian name, POW number, Army number, Country and so on. [20]

The first entry Holt recognised was at number 1000. He thumbed through to find names he knew in the present group and soon noted they were bundled together from 4500. His own number was 4501.

—⁂—

He recalled the day he joined the long line of prisoners to be registered. It was one of those typical hot summer days when the temperature stayed above 86° Fahrenheit overnight and was over the century mark by midday.

"Just after lunch, the Germans began shouting for everyone to line up. At first, we thought we were getting another ration of food and water, which would have been welcome.

"The line formed rather quickly and there were few altercations as to who was pushing in or holding a place for a mate.

"The Germans had set up several tables out in the hot sun and dusty grounds at Galatas. We had all come from Sfakia and been escorted from the south where we had missed the ships that were going to evacuate us all to Alexandria. I was tired, weak, hungry and dehydrated."

For some odd reason, his name was shouted out first, even though he stood at least two hundred men further back. The shout came again, "Holt, Australian prisoner come forward."

Obediently he shuffled forward and went through an official registration as a prisoner of war.

He touched the dog tag [21] that had been around his neck since that day. The photographer was not the best amateur he had ever seen, but eventually, he had two pictures taken.

The first was a portrait, front on, holding a piece of wood with the prisoner's number, KR 4501, written in white chalk, and the other was a profile picture.

Holt never saw how these turned out. They were not in the Register Book he was looking at, so there must have been other official cards or books where the photographs would have been glued.

While being 'processed', the line of prisoners was channelled to four other tables. [22]

Information was written onto a profile card, which he surmised would later be transferred to the official book.

Holt recalled walking away along with the first wave of registered prisoners. Due to the huge number of men the process took all day and into the fading light before the Germans packed up. [23]

Several mates came over in the afternoon to share their experiences and tell Holt their prisoner of war number.

They came to the conclusion that Holt was first in the book out of the survivors because he was ranked captain. The Germans had unofficially made him the 'Man of Confidence'. [24]

There were others who visited Holt to tell him of their registration experience and their POW number.

Petersen, Buirchell, and Pedersen had numbers close to each other as they accepted Major Sandover's invitation to 'run for the hills' rather than make for Sfakia. They did not go to Sfakia, nor had they returned to Retimo by the time registration was first carried out.

Another column was added well after the original entries, headed T Camp. Running his finger down this column on each page, he soon realised it was T for Tymbakion.

These numbers were identifiers for men who had been sent to Tymbakion and each was numbered.

The Germans tended to want everything noted down so each man was given an identity letter and number. For example, Colin Murdoch was T-46, Leslie Pike was T-36 and Louis Dwen was T-116. To complicate matters some of the entries Wally saw at Tymbakion did not have a T.

Wally Holt wrote all this information down in his book, declaring to himself that he would ask the others for their opinions on how to identify who was at Tymbakion and who wasn't.

To add more mystery to the registration system there was a column headed 'I' which to Holt meant Iraklion. [25]

On the last page, there were the names of the 12 Englishmen who had been captured yesterday, [26] and at the very bottom of the list there was a 13th name, William Roy Buirchell, WX2280, Kojonup, Western Australia, POW number 4562, T-20.

The door opened from the corridor, and the young German soldier walked in and stood at attention opposite Holt. The wily captain deliberately took his time writing each name and then checking the spelling out loud. Holt looked at the names and nodded to the young German soldier.

—⟶—

Finally, he'd had enough fun and he closed the Register and slid it across the table. The soldier picked it up, turned and left the room. Wally looked at the page of his book where he had written the names of the Englishmen and smiled. He now had 151 men on site, made up of the 138 who were trucked in, Bonnie Buirchell and the dozen Englishmen who had only just arrived. He stood up and walked to the front door, turned the handle and pushed it open. The freezing wind hit him like a blast from the Arctic. He shivered and set off for his tent with a long, fast stride.

Although late, Bonnie and the British chaps were now a part of the Tymbakion group. [27]

Given a choice, Bonnie would have preferred to have remained in the hills, without malaria, until rescued.

For some time now, the men believed they were the final group and had been selected due to their skills and stamina to work on a project as large as building an airfield. A small amount of doubt was still there after they ran into Ray Blechynden at Iraklion in September. He wasn't part of the group, so what was his story, and where was he?

The other thought that left doubt about the way the Tymbakion team was made up centred on Alf Traub and Leslie Le Souef. These two Australians were ideal for this type of project and had shown time and again their credentials as skilled and professional men. Leslie as a doctor and Alf as an interpreter and fix-it man.

It was evident that the information Wally passed on to his leaders meant the 151 were a special group.

They had been selected by some process known only to the Germans. They knew now they needed to make the most of this situation for the good of themselves and the people of Crete. From all accounts, Alf Traub and Leslie

Le Souef had been put on a ship back a month or two and sent via Salonika to Germany.

Wally began to see what the Germans had been calculating for some time now. The evidence was stacking up for a covert project on the south coast of Crete. This planning must have begun just after the Allies capitulated on June 1, 1941.

The airfield at Tymbakion was the first planned project. The exact date would not be known but it had to be after June 6.

It was about this time that Major Sandover and his band of escapees were captured in the Tymbakion beach area. There was no evidence of activity by the Germans on the beach and surroundings.

The first part of the project was to fence the entire area. The Royal Air Force inmates completed this before the larger group was sent from Iraklion.

The Germans had to determine how many men were needed and what they could bring to the plan. For example, six engineers or sappers would be needed to survey the area and calculate the location of roads, bridges, and water courses.

—⚍—

One of the loneliest aspects of being a prisoner of war was the lack of communication with family and friends. Letters, cards and parcels seemed to take months before they were passed on.

Tymbakion was more isolated than most prisons, where the men could not get to a post office nor mix with other people.

Some letters and cards did get out, and some came in, but not as regularly as the POWs wished for. The exact movement of posts is not known, and clearly, those who sent or received messages either had secret means or political pull.

Vic Petersen wrote in his diary, "18th December 1941. Six English letters arrived at camp today."

Letters sent and received by Richard Lechmere [28] and his wife show this to be true. One of her letters was received a few days before December 21, 1941.

—⚎—

Further evidence of communication in and out of Tymbakion came from Private Norman Brown. [29] He posted a letter to his father who resided in Christmas Hills, Malvern, Victoria.

It was the first time the place of Tymbakion was mentioned to the public overseas.

In Norman's Red Cross records there was a line: "Vic. adv. N/K rec. letter dated 21/9/41 Camp Tymbakion Crete". The letter below was first published in the *Record* out of Emerald, Victoria, under the headline, "Took to the Hills Instead of Submitting to Enemy.".[30]

'First News of Local Digger Since Evacuation of Crete

Norman Brown believed to be enjoying freedom. Reassuring news of her husband's whereabouts after months of deep anxiety is contained in a letter received during the week by Mrs. N. Brown, of 382 Dorcas Street, South

Melbourne, wife of VX31518, Private Norman McLeod Brown, a former member of the South Melbourne City Council outdoor staff, from whom no word has been heard since the memorable battle of Crete.'

Some months ago, Mrs. Brown received an official message stating that her husband was listed as missing. Writing to the Commanding Officer of her husband's battalion in an endeavour to allay fears for his safety, Mrs Brown has since received the following letter: "I have made exhaustive enquiries concerning your husband, which reveal that he was last seen in the hills near Sfakia on June 2.

"It was reported that he was fit and well. An officer and an N.C.O. of the unit supplied this information to me. I regret the anxiety caused owing to the uncertainty of his fate, but you will realise that your husband is enjoying the freedom to a certain extent. Like others, there is still that hope of escaping and re-joining his unit."

From this message, it is believed that Brown is one of the many soldiers stranded on beaches [31] at the evacuation of Crete, who preferred to take to the hills, rather than submit to capture by the invading Germans. These men, with the assistance of friendly locals, have banded together and periodically descended from their hide-outs in the hills, raiding enemy outposts and confiscating rifles, ammunition, etc., with which they persistently harass the Nazis.

Since receiving this information, many friends have called the soldier's mother, Mrs Wells, of Dorcas Street, to express their delight at the heartening news.

A second letter followed indicating Norman was well. It was also published in the *Record* out of Emerald, Victoria, on January, 31, 1942, page 2.

"Long-Delayed Message from Missing Digger" [32]

Pte. N. Brown, a Prisoner of War in Crete

After many months of deep anxiety, during which she had heard no word to allay fears that had arisen following receipt of notification that her husband was 'missing,' Mrs Brown, of Dorcas

Street, South Melbourne, wife of Private Norman McLeod Brown, has received direct word from her husband informing her that he is in the war prison transit camp at Tymbakion, Crete, and enjoys very good health.

Until a month or so ago, Mrs. Brown, had almost despaired, but hopes for her husband's safety were revived when she heard from the Commanding Officer of her husband's unit that when last seen after the Battle of Crete, Pte. Brown was safe. Then in a more recent letter a South Melbourne Digger informed his mother that he had seen Pte. Brown some months previous. This good news was then capped off by a letter from the missing soldier himself.

As a result, his relatives, well-known residents of the district, are extremely happy. Before enlistment, Pte. Brown was attached to the South Melbourne Council's outdoor staff.

The lack of communication from the other prisoners suggests a deliberate policy of withholding such letters. Considering that the Tymbakion airfield construction was a covert plan, it is no wonder. The German censors would have removed any information from Norman's letter if they considered it would jeopardise the Tymbakion project.

Mrs Brown would have received the letter with blacked-out, redacted words and phrases or, worse, sections cut out, making it barely readable.

Vic continued to keep his diary up to date, mentioning grubbing out olive trees from October 12 to 14.

The expanse of vacant ground continued to grow day by day.

The Cretan families must have been crying buckets of tears.

There was a rumour that the men were sending their women and children to other places and relations.

—⚘—

Two days later Bonnie was wandering outside the field medic tent when he heard a cheery voice. "You're back from the dead old man. Good to have you looking well again".

Bonnie stopped and turned around. He didn't recognise the voice but it had to come from an officer. It had that authoritarian sound. He noted it was Captain Holt. "I'm afraid you won't be too happy to know where you are. Then again at least you are alive and hopefully ready to have a nice breakfast."

It was the captain, who was always so friendly and welcoming to anyone he had run into. Bonnie thought breakfast was a definite yes. He was famished after nearly five days without being able to keep any food down. [33]

The two headed for the mess ready to eat the ration of bread and olive oil. This was washed down with a herb mixed with water in a mug. As he slowly regained his health, he was keen to hear how he had arrived at Tymbakion.

Captain Holt, the unofficial officer or Man of Confidence in charge of the Tymbakion War Transit Camp prisoners, sat beside him and offered to fill in the gaps.

Wally had pieced the story together from a number of men who dealt with Bonnie from the time the Germans met the elderly Cretan man, who had initially found Bonnie, to the soldier's discharge from the medical tent at Tymbakion.

The very ill Australian was brought to the camp and nursed day and night until he responded to the treatment. Another day was left out in the elements, and he would have died from exposure.

At one stage in the treatment, there was talk of sending Bonnie by truck to Iraklion, where the medical facilities were far better. [34] He rallied enough for the decision to be rescinded and thereafter continued to improve. The malaria symptoms were the killers, but at least he could get immediate assistance from the medics rather than suffering in a cave in the mountains.

The medical staff nursed Bonnie back to fair health. They also diagnosed that he had malaria and found an eruption on the back of his hand where the mosquito had bitten him.

As the population of prisoners of war dropped to less than 300 throughout Crete, Iraklion had been set up to cope with their medical and mental requirements. If Bonnie's recovery had not been faster than expected, he would have been transferred to Iraklion. After a week, only the fits caused by the malaria hampered his wellness.

Now that he was on the mend, Captain Holt took Bonnie to breakfast and, after they had eaten, offered to take him for a walk around the camp.

As they walked, Wally explained what was going on. He also agreed to fill Bonnie in with the missing pieces of the past month.

He passed on a directive from the commandant that said he wanted the new bloke in the field tomorrow.

Bonnie had caught malaria and was on the verge of dying when an elderly Cretan found him near a track and got him on his donkey.

The kindly gentleman walked the donkey towards the Tymbakion Prisoner of War Transit Camp V when he, fortunately, met with a German patrol in a truck. They took over and transported Bonnie back to camp.

He was brought to the camp and nursed back to health. His first day was the worst as he had the terrors, [35] constantly yelling out and tossing around. The medical staff had to tie him down. Gradually, as each day passed Bonnie's health improved.

Two men were assigned to help him overcome his loss of language and conversation.

The latter occurred because he had no one else to converse with. Thomas Washer from New Zealand and John McInerney, an Australian, happily volunteered. It would give them a well-earned rest from chopping down olive trees.

—⚜—

Now he was on the mend, Captain Holt took Bonnie for a walk around the camp and explained what they were being used for. He also told him the commandant wanted the new bloke working in the field tomorrow. If he had time, Wally intended to watch Bonnie, the wood-chopping champion, cutting down a tree or two. Bonnie had shared his log-chopping prowess with Wally. He was the runner-up Champion of the Central Great Southern of West Australia in 1938,

One vital place pointed out was the latrine. [36] A single piece of wood about 3 yards long, foot wide, and an inch thick was set up across a pit. This was situated 50 yards to the west of the camp area. It was agreed to place it at that location as very few westerlies blew across the area. Most of the winds were channelled through the passes from the mountains to the north.

The distance was discussed and argued about between the men, but it was finally agreed to place the dunny 50 yards away. The trials indicated that the slowest and weakest bloke was thoroughly puffed from his dash, while any closer, and the smell would have been unbearable.

Bonnie was now a definite in the 151, he just had to take the long way around. He would have preferred to have stayed 'loose' in the hills.

Bert Chamberlain was deep in thought. He had been at Tymbakion Transit Camp V since September 12, 1941.

He felt exhausted and hungry [37] always hungry, and if this kept up, he would not be able to continue to work.

To idle the day away, he was making a pair of shorts. Whenever he got an opportunity, he would find some canvas and make a piece of clothing such as trousers, shorts, shirts, undies or garments by order. He was a master tailor and had to keep his skills and knowledge up to return to his former job when the war ended. He never knew who might need a new garment. [38]

As he stitched, an idea formed in his mind, and it took him back to his school days in Westport, New Zealand. Someone had brought a small, blank book to school in his second year of high school.

Bert handed the book to each student in the class and explained that, as the class members had formed a strong bond and had been so easy to get along with, he wanted to have a memento to remember each of them. Their year together would be forgotten once the group split up and went their individual ways. The autograph book would have their names to conjure up their faces and what they said and did in that final year.

Bert decided that an autograph style object with all the Tymbakion inmates' names inscribed on it would be just the thing. He wanted to look at the names and say, "I remember so and so, and they did this or that." With such a large number of inmates it would take up considerable room to write 151 signatures. Bert experimented writing name, number, and a message. He realised that this would take up too much room so he settled for the first three inscriptions per person.

The idea slowly became a pair of canvas shorts. They were neatly stitched with a hand-written heading across the belt area. [39]

Tymbakion was a covert [40] German camp and all these people would be the last to leave Crete. This should have made them all very proud that they would be remembered as the final Allies to be shipped out of Crete. The reality was quite different. They felt like failures, useless and incompetent. They had lost the wars, capitulated and surrendered. Their fore fathers would not have accepted such cowardness.

The pair of shorts might take away some of this negative thinking and offer the feeling of comradeship and camaraderie.

Add the fact that they were cutting down olive trees to make an enormous airstrip, and it must be something worth remembering, memories that would be triggered by this object with all the names on it.

It would also serve as a reminder of the terrible way the Allies were complicit in ruining the lives of thousands of Cretan people, their livelihoods, families, houses, communities and relationships.

After everything the Cretans had done for Bert and the other Allies, they could not simply be cast off and forgotten.

Bert had fond memories of the church leaders, especially the monks of Perivolia. These well known and well liked men showed real courage and leadership throughout the Crete invasion. [41]

During the Crete War, which raged from May 20, 1941, to May 31, 1941, some priests led their parishioners into battle. Evidence from field headquarters reported seeing, "several priests, keen duck shooters and therefore, 'pretty good' shots, who almost certainly took part in the fighting." They opened their churches as sanctuaries to any Ally who was escaping, they found clever ways to deliver food to those on the run and they stood at the front of the line when Germans were attacking communities.

Now, they were leading the Cretan population in a passive resistance movement to try to slow down the work on the Tympaki airfield and the wanton destruction of the township of Tympaki. Many lost their lives trying to comfort and help those in need.

It was through the strength of their religious beliefs, they offered the locals and the Allies hope.

Laying on the blanket that Bert had spread out was a partially completed pair of canvas shorts. He had started making these yesterday. It still needed the belt but everything else was ready.

Bert picked up the belt and began to write in thick, lead pencil. He licked the tip of the dark grey lead and wrote 'Prisoner of War Tymbakion Crete 1st June 1941'. [42]

He looked at the wording and thought, "It might be a bit confusing, particularly the date. Let's see what I have here. The only part that may be wrong is June 1 because, as a group, we only knew about Tymbakion from September 1941. Then again, we all became prisoners at the capitulation, which was June 1."

He poised, pencil in hand and was about to write his name and then had a charge of heart. He wanted the names of everyone else, he already knew his own story. He looked around the 10 man tent (the changing population had resulted in 14 tents of 10 and one of 11) and saw two people lying on their blankets so he asked, "Would you fellows be kind enough to sign my pair of shorts?"

Jim O'Grady lent over and took the pencil and shorts. He spread out the white shorts and began writing, 'J. O'Grady'. He said, "It needs something flat and solid underneath to stop the shorts slipping. And the pencil is rather light making it necessary to go over the signature several times. It is a lot clearer if you lick the lead. Maybe a 2B pencil would do the trick"

"To keep it still try stretching it across my knee or my back," suggested Eric Tyrer.

Jim pulled the shorts across his knee, and with Eric's help, they made them taut. Jim continued his writing. "There, that's much better," said Jim. "Your turn, Eric," Jim said, handing him the shorts.

Again, they helped each other, and the job was done. Bert held up the shorts and admired the two signatures on the front side, right.

J. O'Grady *106 R. H. A*
NX 30721 *E. Tyrer*
1ˢᵗ BATT, AIF *NX 8406*

"Thanks, fellows. Now I need to get around and pick up everyone's signature. My best approach, I think, is tent by tent after tea," [43] said Bert. "Wally Holt tells me there are 151 Allies here. It should keep me out of mischief for a while. Now where are the other seven of our lads from this tent?"

The signing of the shorts was big news around the prison the next day. Many men came to Bert and asked him when he would be visiting their tent. His answer was, "When I get there, boys when I get there."

There was no pattern in Bert's mind. He just showed up at a tent, and before he could explain what he wanted, the men in the tent lined up to sign the shorts. To make his visits to each tent easily coordinated, he used the black numbers they painted on when they had first arrived. Starting at his own tent, number one, and walking up and down the lines, he counted out the other 14.

CHAPTER 20

Vic Petersen's diary for Wednesday, October 15, to Saturday, October 18, 1941, indicated that the boss man was unhappy with the men's progress and considered them deliberately working slow. He introduced a new rule, 'get one tree per person cut down daily, or there would be no dinner for you or your mate'.

Parents of the 1940s were strict on their families staying together and always helping each other.

Writing this message in his diary gave Vic a good feeling. Clearly, the go-slow strategy was impacting work.

The inmates heard rumours of the Germans retreating as the Russians made a concerted effort to disperse the Nazis. Another rumour that resulted in the men wringing their hands was that the Italians had kicked Mussolini out. [1]

This was news that added positive thoughts to the men's morale. Hope was the only thing they could rely on, so they kept hoping that the gates would open one day and the guards would say, "You are free. You may now go home to your loved ones."

At the moment, Bert and everyone else had a more pressing concern. The weather was changing, making it difficult to sleep at night. Although the days were fine, the evenings were cool, especially as the men practically had nothing in the way of bedding to keep warm.

The men heard two news items, the first of Australian troops doing some mopping up in Libya and the second, British motorised divisions linking up with Soviet divisions. Most of these came from Greek sources and left a positive feeling among the inmates. [2]

Vic wondered whether there was such a thing as 'happy writing' because today he wrote happily in his diary, "The Greeks arrived en masse at the gate today. On a long pole carried by two strong-looking men was a cooked bullock." [3] All the men inside the wire cheered and called out their thanks.

This interaction of the Cretans with foreigners, such as the New Zealanders, Australians and British, is the continuation of a long tradition of *philoxenia*. This is defined as a 'love of strangers and an eagerness to show hospitality'. The Cretans have a long tradition of sharing and caring for visitors to their shores and beyond.

The commandant came to the gate and spoke to the two priests leading the procession of worshippers. He barked something to the guards, who promptly opened the gates and stepped aside. The priests walked in and flung their arms into the air as a thank you gesture to the commandant and their God.

Everyone had a delicious meal, and many slept well after filling their stomachs with beef.

Captain Holt caught the ear of the two priests and spent a considerable time telling them about the Germans' plans for the Tymbakion area.

Later, he told his fellow inmates who indicated they knew some parts but were shocked to hear about the demolition plan.

All Tympaki houses were to be blown up, and the stone removed for the airfield. All the Cretans were to be rounded up and forced to work as slaves blowing up their own homes and removing the stone and timber. The collected stone and wood were to be used in the airport project.

Holt explained the concept of passive resistance and the need to get the cooperation of all the Cretans. The priests assured Holt they would address everyone in the coming days in their church services.

Vic added a note to his diary, "Must mention all of our meals were midday and consisted of a bit of bread and salami sausage and night-time a bowl of lentils, like split peas. It is more likely that the loss of muscle and strength was mainly due to these meals which lacked in nutrition that caused the slowing of the work more than the protests."

On Monday, October 20, the German Government discussed conducting a census. The Commandant called Wally to his office to explain this census and suggest what the leadership group could do to make the experience efficient and easy.

—⁂—

That evening, an excited Bert Chamberlain got his tent buddies to sign the shorts. He showed them Jim and Eric's neat writing, explained why he did not sign the shorts, and then let them loose. He was rather surprised at how enthusiastic they all were and how neat they made their letters and numbers. There were no instructions for where the men could sign, so they happily chose a place and wrote away.

There was a lot of chatting about the canvas shorts and the idea of an autograph object. Some mentioned that it could become a mascot for a battalion specifically made up of the 151 men who served at Tymbakion. The talk was all positives making Bert feel proud.

Tent One
J, O'Grady, NX 30721, Australia, AIF.
E Tyrer, 905373, Liverpool, England, BEF.
J P McInerney, NX 8406, Australia, AIF.
I. Hardie, WX237, Australia, AIF.
J. J. Molloy, QX7772, Australia, AIF.
E. Pyatt, T/182533, England, BEF.
B. Mitchell, 4972574, England, BEF.
A. E. Chamberlain, 14242, New Zealand, NZEF.
L S Pike, PLX100950, Somerset, England, BEF.
Kollias, Anastasios Greek.

Tent One [4] was Chamberlain's own tent and so he felt there was no need to sign the shorts. As he already had two signatures from his earlier experiment, he only needed seven more for tent one to be complete. The full list of names from Tent One was displayed around the camp for all to see.

The next evening, he fronted up to Tent Two ready to have each man sign the shorts. Tent Two had two men absent and so a message was left for them to make contact if they wanted to sign the shorts. Bert was well aware that some men would not wish to be signatories.

Tent Two
G M Coombs, 22262, Hamilton, Waikato, New Zealand, NZEF.
T W Armitage, 33221, Manaia, Taranaki, New Zealand, NZEF.
J Rogers, 148797, Staffordshire, Britain, BEF.
D Rainford, NX1497, Redfern, Sydney, NSW, Australia, AIF.
C Aitken, 33221, Wanganui, New Zealand, NZEF.
J Magee, 32086, New Zealand. NZEF.
J Stuckey, NX11243, NSW, Australia, AIF.
LT Armstrong, 9996, Westown, New Plymouth, NZ, NZEF.
A Hewett, 2197321, London, England, BEF.
J T Tatton, 4973903, Cannock, England, BEF.

Vic was in contact with Bert and was ready if he needed any assistance.

Tent Three
L G West, VX5561, Lilydale, Victoria, AIF.
W Weatherall, 862968, Wimbledon, London, England, BEF.
J C Craig, 34623, Westport, New Zealand, NZEF.
C Giles, 3964606, Wellington, New Zealand, NZEF.
E J R Gaudion, 10356, Lumsden, New Zealand, NZEF.
L P Gusscott, 33096, Wellington, New Zealand, NZEF.
C M Herbert, S/154217, England, BEF.
H H Barnes, NX32898, Randwick, NSW, Australia, AIF.
R Day, 7633233, Gorey, Wexford, Ireland, BEF.
A A Fraser, 30024, Hawera, New Zealand, N Z E F.

Tent Four
C J Freeman, 148521, London, United Kingdom, BEF.
E East, 29292, Howick, New Zealand, NZEF.
A H Forbes, 6912, Auckland, New Zealand, NZEF.
C J G Grimsey, 148404, United Kingdom, BEF.

T Bissett, NX13592, Bexley, St George, NSW, AIF.
E G Goodwin, 1428576, BEF.
J Gorton, T/190420, England, BEF.
L W Dwen, 34554, Grafton, Auckland, NZ, NZEF.
H Warburton, 105895, Essex, England, BEF.
S Shirley, 9036, Dunedin, New Zealand, NZEF.

The enthusiasm coming from Tents Two, Three, and Four was encouraging. On Sunday, October 26, Bert was out and about getting signatures, which kicked off in earnest the next day.

Albert Chamberlain managed to get the occupants of the next two tents, all present and accounted for. It became quite an exciting game among the inmates to try to find a mate's name or read aloud someone's signature you didn't know. All the inmates of Tents Three and Four signed the canvas shorts.

Vic's diary indicated they had no work that Tuesday and the Germans searched the camp. They found nothing of interest.

That night Bert collected the shorts and a couple of 2B lead pencils and struck out for Tents Five, Six and Seven.

This appeared to be an ambitious night as he had to find 31 men and convince them to sign the pair of shorts. He was also aware that Tent Seven had the extra man.

At Tent Five, he was welcomed by the entire group of 10, all eager to see and feel the canvas that the shorts were made from. This tent's inhabitants contained three of the leadership group, Wally Holt, Ray Powell and Vic Petersen, who set the example and signed first. In Tent Six, Bert met the Ceylonese chap, Joseph Pullenayagam whom he had heard about but only saw from a distance. Again, all signed before Bert moved to Tent Seven. There was a shock when a guard called to him to return to his tent.

He reluctantly obeyed.

<u>Tent Five</u>
C A G (Vic) Petersen, WX571, Gosnells, WA, AIF.
R G Pestell, T/73338, Connington, England, BEF.
R E Powell, VX1114, Richmond, Victoria, Australia, AIF.
E Scanlon, 2197360, Pontypridd, Wales, UK, BEF.
F C C Jones, 34810, Porirua, New Zealand, NZEF.
W G Holt, NX12348, Manly, Sydney, NSW, AIF.
J Thompson, P/SSX20790, Barracks, Portsmouth, UK, BEF.
J A Rattenbury, NX 6877, Banks, NSW, Australia, AIF.
E Rees, 13237, Motupiku, New Zealand, NZEF.
L S Woods, WX 443, Perth, Western Australia, AIF.

Vic Petersen heard the challenge and popped his head out of the tent. "Problem Bert?" he called out.

"It's alright, we'll leave it be, but thanks," replied Bert.

<u>Tent Six</u>
F Dyson, VX5604, Horsham, Wimmera, Victoria, AIF.
A B Hastie, 33750, Waipukurau, New Zealand, NZEF.
J R Howes, NX 2918, Paddington, Sydney, NSW, AIF.
J P Pullenayagam, Motupikee, New Zealand, NZEF.
C Murdoch, 108113, New Zealand, NZEF.
P H Manoy, 7747, Wellington, New Zealand, NZEF.
A Matthews, T184386, Motvera, New Zealand, NZEF.
N J J Foley, 2996, Grey Lynn, Auckland, New Zealand, NZEF.

S R Harrington, 32257, Dunedin, New Zealand, NZEF.
H J Hodson, 20661, New Zealand, NZEF.

―⚏―

In the afternoon, Vic and his tent mates played Black Jack, and he managed to win, which pleased him, considering he was still a rank amateur at cards.

At lunchtime, Wednesday, October 29, there was time for a quick break, so while sitting under an old, gnarled olive tree, Bonnie began telling his partner Edward (Ted) Baker about the log chopping contests he entered in his hometown of Kojonup. [5]

"Sure adds plenty of muscle on your shoulders. I can cut a log in half that is a foot in diameter with less than twenty blows. You attack the log on one side with ten blows, switch to the other side and twenty more blows, or thereabouts, and you are through."

The men from nearby olive trees who were clearly having trouble cutting up their trees wandered across and invited Bonnie to 'show us how you do it'. Bonnie was in an obliging mood and held a trick or two. "Make the call, and you're on," Bonnie said. As the soldiers made for the nearest tree, they introduced themselves. "I'm John Moss from York in England. I'm in the York and Lancashire Regiment."

The next bloke said, "I'm John Skinner from Nottingham, a truly great city in central England."

The third seemed a little worried and said, "I'm Harry Christiansen from New Zealand and from a little town called Hawera, in the province of Taranaki. It's a beautiful part of the World and green all year round."[6]

The fourth chap added, "Roy Buchanan, Aussie through and through."

"James Nuttall, that's my name, to be sure," said the fellow who was lagging behind and seemed indifferent about the whole situation. "Bred and born in Liverpool and a proud member of the Royal Artillery."

The final member of the onlookers was an Australian, and he was wearing his slouch hat. "John Molloy," he said. "Banana Bender better known as a Queenslander from Australia. Former cane cutter, now a bloody olive tree hacker."

With that, he turned away from the group and spat on the ground.

Bonnie walked over to where the axe of one of the teams was lying in the grass. He lifted it and hefted it. "Bit blunt fellows," he said, "I should be able to shave with it. Here, I'll get my axe."

He wandered back to where he and Baker had been working and pulled the axe from the limb they had last cut. He returned on the double and said, "Stand aside and watch a master at work."

The tree that the men had pointed to was not one of great age. In fact, it was relatively young compared to many of the ones that had already been cut out and burnt to ashes.

Most of the older trees have lived for hundreds of years.[7] The oldest trees were huge at the base and gnarly. They produced hundreds of purple olives yearly and would have continued if left alone.

Bonnie lifted the axe and swung down, and a large slice of the trunk splintered away. Ten more hits and ten chunks flew in the same direction as the first. Bonnie moved around the bole until he was directly behind where the trunk had been sliced to the centre. "Twenty more, and it should keel over."

With that, he followed his own instructions, and the tree gave a long creak and fell. "Now, gentlemen," said Bonnie, "two drachmas each for the show, and you six get to drag all the chopped-up pieces from our three trees, and Baker and I leave early for a rest."

The other six were impressed and accepted their lesson.

It was a gruelling task, the ground beneath each tree a mix of unforgiving clay and rock. The olive roots, deeply entwined in the rocks, resisted every effort. German guards, offering their advice, often suggested the removal of the deep roots. Once the tree was felled and the roots painstakingly dug out, the timber had to be cut by axe or sawn and piled on the community bonfire, a testament to the sheer labour involved in wartime agricultural practices.

Other methods of removing the olive trees without using too many workers and labour began to be discussed around the camp. The ball and chain had been bandied around and forgotten. Wally Pedersen a Victorian offered a method he had seen used by the Australian farmers. "I have seen a way to clear hundreds of acres in a matter of days."

John Tatton, an Englishman from the Sherwood Foresters Battalion and only one of two from that battalion left on Crete, looked up and said, "Really, like what?

"We need to keep it hush hush and work slower and inefficiently then the Germans' plans for the airfield will stall. The slower we can go the less time they have to use the airstrip. "Are you telling me we could have had this job done with an easier method?"

"Correct," said Walter Pedersen, "It is as simple as burning out the roots and trees. The farmers in Australia have been doing this for years. Light a hot fire at the base of the tree and keep it stoked and within a week the tree and roots will all be gone. You can set fires to hundreds of trees and keep them burning. The whole groves we have taken weeks to remove could have been burnt out, roots and all, in a matter of a fortnight. Now keep that to yourself.[8]

"The other rather amusing thing about this burning method I found out as a youngster. I had been watching the fire lighters start the burning then left the area.

A week later my father drove through the area to ensure the trees were all burnt out, even the roots.

"In my eagerness to look around I saw a fire glowing hot from under the ground. The large area of the ash where the bole of the tree had been fired up was ten yards away. My father arrived and using a hoe, dug from one hot spot towards the other.

"He told me that the snake-like digging followed the root that had burned underground for ten yards. That meant the farmer could plough without the root systems of the mallee trees interfering."

Tents Seven, Eight, and Nine were next to receive a visit from Bert Chamberlain, who was bringing his pair of canvas shorts and 2B pencils. Bert could not believe how well the idea worked and how enthusiastic the men were. Their eyes shone brightly as they lifted the pencil and a grin from ear to ear told everyone how happy they felt. The constant boring life they had lived for five months and the likelihood that their incarceration could go on for years was the catalyst for the joy that shone in their beings.

Signing a pair of shorts gave the men a purpose and a feeling of belonging, both of which had been in short supply. After ten minutes he wrapped the shorts and set off for his own tent to get a rest.

<u>Tent Seven</u> [9]
F J Rice, T/117358, Kensington, England, BEF.
W R Buirchell, WX 2280, Kojonup, West Australia, AIF.
C S Bunyard, 865679, London, England, BEF.
A W Collins, Manawatu, Wanganui, New Zealand, NZEF.
J E Skinner, 218039, Nottingham, England, BEF.
D A Walker, T/111909, Gosforth, England, BEF.
C J Whatling, 902385, Cheshire, England, BEF.
G R W Brown, 2393, Auckland, New Zealand, NZEF.
P Busby, 25823, Pukepoto, Kaitaia, New Zealand, NZEF.
C J Ring, WX 2058, Woodanilling, West Australia, AIF.
W A Aldersey, 2075, Christchurch, New Zealand, NZEF.

<u>Tent Eight</u>
N M Brown, VX31518, Richmond, Victoria, Australia, AIF.
E S Carter, S/94334, Harrogate, England, BEF.

H A Christiansen, 2059, Norway, NZEF.
B Davenport, 7259305, Cobridge, Stoke-on-Trent, BEF.
J R Davis, 7347236, Woolwich, England, BEF.
R Chandler, 32271, Dunedin, New Zealand, NZEF.
W. F Daly, 8025, Riccarton, Christchurch, New Zealand, NZEF.
W Cunningham, Ch/X101130, Bathgate, Scotland, BEF.
L D Stirling, 9056, London, England, BEF.
T P Wynn, 898637, Liverpool, England, BEF.

Vic was showing his sadness at not receiving news from home. There were a number of concerns for prisoners of war, many psychological, which is why they needed to help each other. This is best done by talking about their sorrows but, more importantly, the better things in life.

Hope is a wonderful medicine.[10]

The following day the Greek population brought down quite a bit of food, being one of their church celebration days. It was clever of these people to use their connection with Christianity to win easier battles for the Allies as they also showed at times, they believed in a God.

The Germans were more than pleased to have extra food and particularly alcohol added to their basic diet. Bert was keen to get to Tent Nine. He set out and found everyone ready and willing to sign. He was impressed by Tent Nine's efficiency and left immediately after the signing was complete, believing Tent Ten would reflect a similar attitude.

<u>Tent Nine</u>
F H Hurren, S/94377, England, BEF.

H Brown, 34618, Hornby, Canterbury, New Zealand, NZEF.
H F Bolding, VX 7801, Wonthaggi, Victoria, AIF.
G B Harman, 4321, New Zealand, NZEF.
A McLean, 7902927, England, BEF.
C W Heenan, 8571, New Zealand, NZEF.
R Lechmere, T/203874, England, BEF.
H J Cooper, 7347238, England, BEF.
R J Chappell, 7347150, England, BEF.
F Walters, CH/X3473, England, BEF.

Bert moved quickly to Tent Ten to obtain autographs for his canvas shorts. Most people had been obliging but there were a stubborn few. He kept smiling and encouraging.

Tent Ten
G Burns, 10582, Fielding, New Zealand, NZEF.
C G Cooper, 5566, New Zealand, NZEF.
L R Smith, NX15308, Marrickville, Sydney, Australia, AIF.
J H Prichard, 6849702, Abergavenny, England, BEF.
J J Osborn, 6898510, Holborn, England, BEF.
A S Todd, 7272, New Zealand, NZEF.
W Topia, 22724, New Zealand, NZEF.
A E Pooley, 210653, Ilford, Essex, England, BEF.
J Moss, 4745238, England, BEF.
J W Miller, 7527, Ashburton, New Zealand, NZEF.

—m—

For three days from Wednesday, November 5, the whole camp worked on constructing a road that would pass over the river. Seven military engineers were in the camp, and the commandant had singled them out to plan and build the road and a bridge. [11] They were finally told that the area was being readied as an airfield.

One of the most important aspects that had to be considered was the flash floods that would send torrents of water from the mountains down the river, which was mostly barely trickling or bone dry.

To cope with these sudden and violent events, the engineers built breakwater walls upstream and ensured the bridge was well above the highest expected water level. Under the bridge they used huge brick drainage pipes to allow water to flow freely.

When completed, the bridge was an engineering masterpiece and the talk was all about watching how well it would work at the first flood. The men never got to see this.

The bridge would be strategically positioned to get fuel from the huge tanks buried in the sands on the second runway. As the planes landed and taxied to the northern end, they would be refueled and set off on their next mission. The process had to be completed in less than five minutes.

A broken bridge would stall plane movements for days which the German high command would not tolerate.

Two important dates were commemorated to maintain the men's morale and connect with home. First, Melbourne Cup Day, [12] was held on November 4, 1941; secondly, at 1100 hours on November 11, 1941, the team halted work to observe two minutes of silence to commemorate Armistice Day. [13] The latter was to remember the end of World War I and those who gave the supreme sacrifice. "It was a pity mankind didn't learn from these past wars," thought Vic.

A small group took charge of organizing the Melbourne Cup and was keen to run a day to remember. The main concern was the time zone between Melbourne, Australia, and Tymbakion, Crete. This difference would mean the race would be run early in the morning, Crete time, and the men would already know the result, thereby spoiling the excitement.

To overcome this, all radios were confiscated on the eve of the big race and placed in a secure spot. One person was in charge and would call the race at the appropriate time in Crete. The caller was up bright and early to listen and write a recording of the race.

He broadcast the race at 12:40 pm Crete time. The inmates bet according to their favourite horse. There would also be a Calcutta, a sweepstakes conducted prior to the race, with each horse raffled and then auctioned to the highest bidder.

Of course, there was to be plenty to do with two-up, the most exciting game. This was an Australian game based on tossing two coins in the air and onlookers betting on the result, which could be two heads, two tails, or odds.

The game was played by all the men involved and a spinner who stayed inside a circle. Everyone makes a bet with others in the crowd, and when all is ready, they shout, "Come in, spinner".

The coins are on a wooden paddle called a kip, and the man in charge is the boxer. When the coins are tossed above ten feet the game is live. The boxer or man in charge calls the results. All losers payout and get ready for the next game. Betting was in cigarettes as money was rare.

At the precise time of 12.40 pm, the race caller took his stand and began a broadcast, which he, in fact, read out with a fluent and dramatic voice. The real live broadcaster in Melbourne was Ken Howard, the best caller in Australia. Unfortunately for the Tymbakion camp population, they missed his call and had to be satisfied with their inmate's call.

With all the cheering and extra comments offered by the excitable crowd, the final results could not be announced until some 20 minutes after the barriers were released. Calling a two-minute race for more than 20 minutes was an amazing feat. All had good fun, and the winners received their prizes in cigarettes and food such as oranges and cherries.

The real winner of the 1941 Melbourne Cup was *Skipton*, and the winner of the camp raffle for selecting that horse was Alex Jackson, a New Zealander. Jack Singleton from England collected the second prize of the day by selecting the ticket with *Son of Auros* written on it. The third horse across the finishing line was *Beau Vite*, and Dave Walker, another British lad, collected on this horse.

—⁂—

By mid-November, Vic had succumbed to the hard work and lack of nutritious food. He was hungry and undernourished and had also seen the doctor about his injured hand. The doctor found a bed for him so he could keep an eye on what was a badly infected hand.

Vic spent four days in the first-aid post with the festering hand. He had accidentally been hit on the hand when his partner's axe head flew off.

Vic had been working with Edward (Ted) Carter from Harrogate, England.

When Ted swung his axe with gusto, the head had slipped off and flew towards his partner. Ted's cry of, "Watch out!" made Vic throw his hand to his face.

The axe head slammed into the back of Vic's hand slicing it below the knuckles. There was only a little blood so Vic soldiered on. But the cut was deep and over three inches long.

—⁂—

About an hour later Vic succumbed to the pain and nausea and was assisted to the first aid post by Ted. The medics cleaned the cut with an antiseptic wash, stitched the wound, and bandaged the area. While he was being attended to Vic started up a conversation with the three medics in the tent. They introduced themselves as Englishmen, Hans Cooper, Tom Palmer and John Davis. They were particularly keen to share the story of a Greek who had presented with food poisoning. They had to transfer him to Iraklion.

Vic was ordered to remain in bed and was released four days later. There had been talk of transferring him to Iraklion hospital but that did not eventuate. It was the first time Vic had heard of a relationship between Tymbakion and Iraklion. [14] It made sense because to have a fully equipped and manned hospital for an isolated place like Tymbakion was a waste of resources. Any medical emergency could be dealt with in Iraklion Hospital, which was 40 miles away and fully stocked. When Wally Holt came visiting, he mentioned what he had overheard. Wally dismissed the comments as he thought Vic may have been under anaesthetic and was mixed up.

—⁂—

The medics who looked after Vic while he was recuperating constantly brought up gossip about Iraklion.

Vic awoke one afternoon to hear Hans speaking to his two fellow medics: "Did you notice the 10 boxes that are in the far corner?"

"I saw them but kept my silence while hoping they contained medical supplies," said John.

"They arrived just after midnight by foot and placed in the tent. Not a word was said, and the Germans who carried them in disappeared like ghosts in the night; about half an hour later, two officers arrived and spoke in English to each other. I was lying down, pretending to be sleeping. They may have thought I was fast asleep. Anyway, they counted the boxes and became rather hot under the collar. Seemed they expected a dozen boxes from Iraklion but only six arrived."

At this stage, Vic dozed on and off again, resulting in a spasmodic conversation. He shared the parts of the conversation that had placed his mind on edge.

"One of the officers was angry and went into a long complaint about Iraklion officers and how they often have goods sent only to find something was always missing. He wanted an investigation but said every time he brought up the issue the Unteroffizier in charge of the warehouse silenced him. He told the soldier to do as he was ordered, no more, no less.

"I have seen several deliveries from Iraklion and always in the dead of night. I've never seen or heard any trucks, so I can only guess they stop well away and carry the deliveries into camp."

"That's really odd. What is in the deliveries?" asked Tom.

"The uncovered ones vary from medicines, medical equipment, food, clothing the sort of stuff used in the camp. Occasionally there is secrecy involved. The bundle is thoroughly packed and locked. It is placed away from prying eyes. I keep my nose clean. I haven't even mentioned this to Wally and the team, but after last night, I think I need to say something."

"So, what was different last night?" asked Tom.

"The conversation suggested that the type of goods being carried was getting dangerous and that the result may cause an uprising by the local Cretans."

"We needed to know what was in those boxes in the corner so we knew what we were dealing with. We also needed to tell Wally immediately about how the Germans were sending things from Iraklion to this location. I've always thought there was no significant relationship between Iraklion and Tymbakion. The goods you named are what I would have expected along with mail. Whatever the change, of course, we need to investigate. Maybe a change of German personnel has given a group a system of illegal movement of dangerous goods? Dangerous as in what?"

"The first thing was to put one of us outside the tent who could whistle if anyone approached in the next 15 minutes. The other two were going to determine what was in the boxes," said Hans. He had taken over the group as leader.

—⁂—

The next morning, Vic awoke feeling better and insisted he be released. After a quick examination by John, Vic was given the all-clear. He immediately dressed and set out to talk to Wally Holt again. The latter listened but decided Vic was hallucinating.

Two days later the medical trio sidled up to Wally, Ray and Bert while they were eating breakfast.

"We have discovered a secret smuggling operation and it might lead to a situation not of our liking, said Hans. He outlined the goings on by the Germans from Iraklion and waited to hear Wally's thoughts.

"Dynamite! Heaven help us all! If they intend to use this against us and the Cretans it will cause much devastation. The major question here is why they are filtering off part of the overall delivery. They are taking a small amount and sending the rest to the correct receiver. The amount going missing is small, so it's not worth worrying about."

"You know," said Ray, "This might explain the explosions in the vicinity of Tympaki."

Wally Holt was determined to short circuit it. Turning the whole underhanded business. "I'm not messing with this, for time appears to be of the essence. If these blokes mean nasty business, then we need to either put a stop to it or create mistrust between the men involved. I'll take a punt and go and tell the Commandant what we know. If he's mixed up in something dangerous, we are in trouble. If not, he will soon put a stop to the whole nasty business. What do you all think?"

All the heads nodded, so Wally set off for the Commandant's residence. He returned an hour later. The prisoners were chopping out the remaining olive trees when he found them. "The Commandant did know about the Iraklion and Tymbakion relationship and assured me that it was important due to the isolation of the South Coast prisoners. He was not happy to hear about the missing part of the deliveries and was furious when I told him about the dynamite."

"So, what happens now?" asked Hans.

"We keep the whole business quiet and wait for the Commandant to get back to me with a solution. He was aware that the relationship between Iraklion and Tymbakion was strong and pointed out that the need for his workers was critical as food, clothing, and medicines would be shipped in from Germany, and Iraklion was the obvious place to land these goods and then be trucked to us.

"The silence of the trucks he dismissed by admitting he ordered the delivery trucks to stop well away as he didn't want the noise waking the camp. The midnight deliveries were to ensure lorries were not ambushed by Special Operations Executive or SOE [15] or fighter aircraft."

Bert Chamberlain continued by displaying the pair of shorts and asking for an autograph from each man in each tent. [16]

He was always pleased to note the numbers growing and the shorts, front and back filling. It was quite amazing how so many men could find enough empty spots to sign their names and, in some cases, add their army number without encroaching on another's area.

Wally was summoned to the Commandant's office later to be informed about the outcome of the smuggling group. A new Unteroffizier at Iraklion saw an opportunity to make money by skimming from each order. As the operation seemed foolproof, he increased the stakes by offering ways for the Germans to retaliate against the Cretans for the deaths of their comrades during the Crete War. The stolen gelignite was used to blow up houses at Tympaki and to set booby traps along the roads regularly used by the locals.

There was also a plan to blow up the Tymbakion Prisoner of War Camp as the rumour indicated that the prisoners would be moving out after Christmas. To ensure they could kill every POW before they moved out, the smugglers were stockpiling gelignite to be buried inside every tent.

All who had been found to be involved had been rounded up and sent to the Russian Front.

The bridge and the road were finished on November 21, and again, the men went back to work on the runway under protest.

The whole camp rallied but the Germans asserted themselves and brought their rifles to their shoulders. They began threatening to shoot 10 men if the refusal to work continued, and rifles prevailed.

The tent visits continued with the members of numbers Eleven and Twelve were all waiting expectantly for Albert to arrive. When he arrived, there was an orderly signing although it was getting to be drawn out because everyone wanted to read out the names of those they recognized and add a few comments.

Tent Eleven

A Buhagiar, 6081, Mazarita, Egypt New Zealand, NZEF.

A Bunn, 33676, Waitara, New Zealand NZEF.

T V Foxon, 890183, Anfield, Liverpool, BEF.

A P Jackson, 1769, Christchurch, N.Z., NZEF.

T G W Palmer, 7347235, Essex, England, BEF.

S R Payne, WX612, Donnybrook, Western Australia, AIF.

S E Pearce, NX33248, Coogee, Watson, NSW, Aust, AIF.

J T Burne, 35322, Wellington, New Zealand, NZEF.

H Sherriff, Kilburn, London, BEF.

J Singleton, 1457787, BEF.

Tent Twelve

E J S Face, NX11441, Randwick, NSW, Australia, AIF.

H J Holmes, 37054, Gisborne, New Zealand, NZEF.

F J D McKain, 6488, Auckland, New Zealand, NZEF.

R D Buchanan, VX32961, Abbotsford, Melbourne, AIF.

T W Barrow, 14244, Reefton, New Zealand, NZEF.

K F Bowden, 30242, Wellington, New Zealand, NZEF.

C W Brodie, 13803, Linwood, Christchurch, NZ, NZEF.

F F Howie, WX 2348, Toodyay, Western Australia, AIF.

J Kirk, 30071, Hastings, New Zealand, NZEF.

J Nuttall, 902868, Lancashire, England, BEF.

The job changed with shifting earth [17] and the men using a spade to throw the soil into the back of a flat top truck. The Germans seem to have a never-ending number of these lorries. The men guessed the trucks belonged to the Cretans from Tympaki, while a number had been offloaded by the Allies when they arrived on the island. Every now and again a Cretan would be seen loading up his cart that was pulled by a donkey.

On many farms, the cart and donkey were traditional ways of moving loads from one place to another. The olives, after being knocked from the tree, were loaded into the cart, and the donkey walked the load to the processing shed.

The beauty of the donkey is its ability to traverse rocky terrain with sure footing and without complaint. They can confidently navigate the slopes of mountains and ravines. The Cretans used them as a form of transportation, sitting astride their backs and using a small switch stick to encourage a faster journey.

When it comes to calculating bodyweight for strength, the donkey is a very strong animal.

Albert set out to get signatures from Tents 13 and 14 and was pleased to see that the job was coming to an end. Once he finished with 14, he only had number 15 to go. So, he would be finished by next Tuesday.

Tent Thirteen
R A Johnstone, VX8887, Christmas Hills, Victoria, Australia, AIF
J R Ainsley, 195991, Ferryhill, Durham, England, BEF.
L Christmas, 32085, Yarmouth, England, BEF.
A King, NX 5424, Wellington, New South Wales, Australia, AIF.
A R Leviston, WX 6803, Ballarat, Victoria, Australia, AIF.
F Lythgoe, 4915533, England, BEF.
L E McDonald, 22289, Gisborne, New Zealand, NZEF.
R E Neale, 5736, New Zealand, NZEF.
R Veevers, 1441331, England, BEF.
W V Pedersen, VX 5571, Melbourne, Australia, AIF.

Tent Fourteen

J D Whitcombe, 22768, Ponsonby, Auckland, New Zealand, NZEF.
E Shaw, 8613, Denniston, New Zealand, NZEF.
J Crawford, 408857, Liverpool, England, BEF.
G A Roberts, 132569, London, England, BEF.
A G Stubbs, 4379, Karori, Wellington, New Zealand, NZEF.
E Tregear, VX 4658, Werrimull, Victoria, Australia, AIF.
R B Brownlie, 4446, New Zealand, NZEF.
G S Bowen, CH/X101376, Ilford, England, BEF.
R D Bristol, VX26839, Melbourne, Victoria, Australia, AIF.
H Johnson, 888099, England, BEF.

St Mary's Day was celebrated by the whole Cretan population. The gathering of hundreds of people was especially welcomed by the inmates who were given food. They ate an abundance of beef and were ever so thankful to the people of Tympaki and surrounding towns. These were the same people who were barely able to feed themselves yet managed to feed everyone at the prison transit camp.

To add to the party, the Germans offered an extra one-sixth of a loaf of bread for each man from the Greek engineer for working on the runway Although the engineer had been handpicked by Goering to plan the airfield and to use the POWs and Cretan population as slave labour, he was a decent chap to work under.

Tuesday, November 25 to Saturday, November 29, brought a taste of winter. The weather was turning with bitterly cold winds and snow falls on the mountains. The chills would soon hit the camp as winter in the Northern Hemisphere was December to February.

It was difficult for the Australians and New Zealanders to get used to this upside-down weather.

One of the happy days was, of course, Christmas, which they would be celebrating in a month's time. They all talked about looking forward to their very first white Christmas.

Tent 15 was next in line for signing the shorts, although several individuals sought out Bert during the days he was not visiting tents.

During the days following the tent visits, Bert was happy to see six more men enter his tent and sign the shorts.

These men were New Zealanders, Ernest Banner, Zamoni Foley, Roy Neale, Colin Murdoch, Ernie Shaw and John Miller. Each added their signature. A couple of Englishmen, James Nuttall and Cyril Grimsey, were the last to sign the shorts.

Vic noted in his diary that very heavy formation of German aircraft flew over the camp taking alpine troops to fight in Libya.

This sent shivers down everyone's spines as they watched what would soon happen at the Tymbakion Airfield. This airstrip would give the Germans a definite advantage in being able to move troops around quickly and easily. It would allow food and water to be airlifted to any of the North African countries and those of the Middle East.

The most concerning advantage was that Germany could keep a huge number of bombers that could fly out daily to any city in the region and bomb places with explosives. The final nail in the coffin was that the Luftwaffe would have control of all the Mediterranean and the countries bordering the sea. It was uncomfortable for the Tymbakion inmates to think about what they were forced to do.

Tent Fifteen
E A S Banner, 7502, High Street, Christchurch, N Z, NZEF.
W A Beacham, 23275, Auckland, New Zealand, NZEF.
M Beaton, 9724, Canterbury, New Zealand, NZEF.
A F Bennison, 5353, Allenton, New Zealand, NZEF.
R G A Bentley, 6488, Wellington, New Zealand, NZEF.
A Billings, 32174, Hauraki, New Zealand, NZEF.
H E Stratton, WX547, Belmont, Perth, Western Australia, AIF.
H H Arroll, 2086, Auckland, New Zealand, NZEF.
E Baker, 2065377, Battersea, London, England, BEF.
Petrou, Ionnis Greece.

Bert Chamberlain did not achieve a 100 per cent signing from those who were incarcerated in the Tymbakion Prisoner of War Camp. His effort resulted in four categories of men as shown in the table, he drew up, that can be seen below.

The total of men who were considered 'true' Tymbakionites, that word was made up by Tom Wynn in one of his happy moods, was found to be 151.

Wally and his team were concerned about the men who could be considered 'Fly by Nighters.' These people came and moved on quickly, so the issue became what rule to use in determining whether they were true Tymbakionite or not.

The RAF boys were the first to be sent to Tymbakion to erect the barbed wire strand fence. They were not counted as they left well before the short project came into Albert's mind. Then there were the 50 Englishmen who turned up one day and were gone the next.

The other dozen English and, of course, Bonnie Buirchell, who was found 'loose' on Crete, were at camp long enough to be considered.

With all of the comings and goings, Wally decided that they had covered the numbers fairly and truthfully.

The more important decision that anointed the men who were in the camp after Christmas and were on the list, 'Last Prisoners of War on Crete.'

CHAPTER 21

—⚞—

Overall count showed 151 inmates living at the POW camp.

The Germans appeared to be happy with this and did not pursue other statistics as expected by Wally and his team.

On the other hand, the Allied Team went further and looked at those registered through Tymbakion, Iraklion, Chania, and elsewhere. They were keen to see how the shorts' signing panned out. It was gratifying for Albert as it was his idea, and he did the follow-ups to each tent. He was extremely proud that he had 122 signatures out of a possible 151 people.

Below are the results of the Census of Australian, New Zealand and British soldiers who were at Tymbakion between September 12, 1941, and December 29, 1941.

(T) Registered in Tymbakion
(I) Registered in Iraklion
(C) Registered in Chania.

List of last Prisoners of War on Crete start on next page.
All soldiers' profiles are listed after Chapter 24.
✎ All prisoners of war who signed the shorts.

Note: Missing information is listed as MI.

Last Prisoners of War on Crete
December 29, 1941

✎	T-9	Ainsley John Robert
MI	T-93	Aitken Charles
MI	T-92	Aldersey William
✎	I-27	Armitage Thomas Washer
MI	T-95	Armstrong Leslie
MI	T-94	Arroll Herbert
✎	T-10	Baker Edward
✎	T-96	Banner Ernest Ambrose
✎	T-11	Barnes Harry Holcroft
✎	T-97	Barrow William
✎	T-98	Beacham William
MI	T-13	Beaton Malcolm
✎	T-99	Bennison Avery
✎	T-14	Bentley Reginald Guy Arthur
MI	T-100	Billings Adrian
✎	T-15	Bissett Thomas Alexander
MI	I-19	Bolding H F
✎	I-37	Bowden Kenneth Frank
MI	MI	Bowen George Stanley
✎	MI	Brodie Charles William
✎	T-16	Bristol Reginald David
✎	T-102	Brown George Robert William
✎	T-103	Brown Harold
MI	I-117	Brown Norman McLeod
✎	T-104	Brownlie Robert
✎	I-28	Buchanan Roy

284

✎	T-19	Buhagiar Alfred
✎	T-20	Buirchell William Roy
✎	T-105	Bunn Alan
✎	T-21	Bunyard Claud Stewart
MI	T-106	Burne Thomas
MI	T-107	Burns George
✎	T-108	Busby Ponaute
✎	T-23	Carter Edward
MI	T-22	Chamberlain Albert Edward
MI	T-109	Chandler Robert
✎	T-88	Chappell Ronald John
✎	T-110	Christiansen Harry Anthony
MI	T-111	Christmas Leonard
✎	MI	Collins Andrews Waltr
✎	T-112	Coombs Gordon
✎	T-113	Cooper Charles G
✎	T-87	Cooper Hans John
✎	I-29	Craig James Colvin
✎	T-84	Crawford John
MI	T-114	Cunningham William
✎	T-24	Davenport Joseph
✎	T-89	Davis John R
MI	T-25	Daly Wynn Francis
MI	T-115	Day Raymond
MI	T-116	Dwen Louis
MI	T-3	Dyson Frank
✎	T-117	East Edward
✎	T-26	Face Edward John Sydney
✎	I-54	Foley Zamoni James Joseph

✎	T-86	Forbes Archibald Henry
✎	T-28	Foxon Thomas V.
✎	I-53	Fraser Anthony Alexander
✎	T-6	Freemen Clifford James
✎	I-51	Gaudion Eric John Robertson
✎	T-30	Giles Charles
✎	T-31	Goodwin Edgar George
✎	T-32	Gorton John
✎	T-33	Grimsey Cyril James Gilders
✎	I-50	Gusscott Louis Patrick
✎	T-34	Hardie Ian Alexander
✎	T-118	Harman Geoffrey Bertrand
✎	I-49	Harrington Stanley Richard
✎	I-48	Hastie Alexander Brown
✎	I-47	Heenan Colin William
✎	T-35	Herbert Cyril M
✎	T-36	Hewett Arthur Albert
✎	I-45	Hodson Herbert Joseph
✎	C-182	Holmes Howard John
✎	T-1	Holt Walter Gerald
✎	T-37	Howes George Richard
MI	T-38	Howie Frank Freeman
✎	T-4	Hurren Frederick Henry
✎	I-43	Jackson Alexander Peter
✎	T-62	Johnson Henry
✎	T-40	Johnstone Robert Aitcheson
✎	I-40	Jones Frederick Cyril
MI	T-41	King Andrew
✎	I-32	Kirk James
✎	MI	Kollias Anastasios (Greek citizen)

🖊	T-91	Lechmere Richard James
🖊	T-42	Leviston Aubrey Reginald
🖊	I-35	Lythgoe Frederick (aka Rocky)
🖊	I-41	Magee John James
MI	T-5	Manoy Philip Herman
MI	T-43	Matthews Albert
🖊	T-18	McDonald Leonard Edwin
🖊	I-28	McInerney John Patrick
🖊	I-22	McKain Frederick James Dunmore
🖊	T-48	McLean Alexander
🖊	T-44	Miller John Walter
🖊	T-47	Mitchell Bernard
🖊	T-12	Molloy John Joseph
🖊	T-45	Moss John
MI	T-46	Murdoch Colin
🖊	I-39	Neale Roy Errol
🖊	T-49	Nuttall James
🖊	I-24	O'Grady James Clyde
🖊	T-50	Osborn James J
🖊	T-90	Palmer Thomas G W
MI	T-51	Payne Sydney Robert
🖊	T-53	Pearce Sydney Emden
🖊	T-52	Pedersen Walter Vernon
🖊	T-54	Pestell Roland G
🖊	T-55	Petersen Charles Amos Victor
🖊	MI	Petrou Ionnis (Greek citizen)
MI	T-56	Pike Leslie
🖊	T-57	Pooley Albert E
🖊	T-58	Powell Ray Edward

✎	T-59	Prichard Jack H
✎	MI	Pullenayagam Joseph Patrick (Ceylonese)
✎	T-60	Pyatt Ernest
✎	I-56	Rainford Douglas
✎	I-38	Rattenbury John Alfred
✎	T-61	Rees Edward
✎	T-63	Rice Frederick J
✎	T-64	Ring Cyril James
✎	I-34	Roberts G A
✎	T-65	Rogers John
MI	T-66	Scanlon Edward
✎	I-36	Shaw Ernest
✎	T-2	Sherriff Harold
✎	T-67	Shirley Stanley
✎	T-68	Singleton Jack
✎	T-69	Skinner John E
✎	T-70	Smith Loris Richard
✎	T-85	Stirling Leslie Douglas
!	T-71	Stratton Herbert Ernest
✎	T-119	Stubbs Arthur
✎	T-72	Stuckey John Edward
✎	T-39	Tatton John Thomas
✎	T-73	Thompson James
✎	MI	Todd Arthur Skuse
✎	T-74	Topia William
MI	I-30	Tregear Eric
✎	T-75	Veevers R
✎	T-27	Tyrer Eric
✎	T-77	Walker David A.
✎	T-78	Walters Frank

✏	T-76	Warburton Harold
MI	T-79	Weatherall William
✏	T-80	West Leonard
✏	T-81	Whatling Clive Joy
✏	T-29	Whitcombe John Douglas
✏	T-83	Woods Laurience Samuel
✏	T-82	Wynn Thomas Peter

CHAPTER 22

Tymbakion was an isolated place on the island of Crete, and as mentioned before, communication was difficult. It was a surprise when some of the men received a parcel from the National Greek War Relief Association late in December 1941,[1] including a pair of socks, a few cigarettes, a handkerchief, and a waistcoat jacket. How this organisation found the camp is anyone's guess, but it certainly was welcome.

Even with the start of December and the onset of winter, work continued on the airfield. The overall size of the operation meant there would never be an end to the work.

After a freezing night in the tents, the men welcomed the physical activity of chopping, shovelling and grubbing.

They especially loved Saturdays when the huge heap of olive tree branches, trunks, leaves, and roots was lit, and the heat penetrated their bodies. The oil in the leaves and fruit was particularly flammable and burned readily.

Across the month of December, the men worked like slaves cutting down the final lot of olive trees.

A lot is many hundreds of trees, so it wasn't that easy. It was made harder by the inadequate rations, which varied between watery soup and one-tenth of a loaf of bread. The occasional feast organised by the locals from Tympaki was always welcome.

One day they were so full that they ached because their shrunken stomachs couldn't take the huge helpings. Another day they were so hungry they could hardly lift the axe or shovel to cut down the trees.

Winter was in full swing, meaning snow-covered ground and piercing, freezing winds. The tent groups were packed closely together in an effort to maximise any warmth.

Vic continued to record some of the incidents around the camp. "Today, we were working on building the airfield. One Greek accidentally shot in the stomach during the morning." [2] He didn't tend to elaborate too much, keeping to the simple observation.

There was another set of calculations that Wally Holt wanted to work through and add to his diary. [3] He called the leadership group and put the problem to them. "In a few days time there is to be a count of everyone at this camp by the Germans. The Commandant tells me it is the German Census [4] and is considered important.

"I am of the opinion that this is all tied up with the work of the ICRC which is the International Committee of the Red Cross and another organisation working under the name of National Greek War Relief Association, NGWRA. Tymbakion Prisoner of War camp breaks all the Geneva Convention rules and that is why we are kept so isolated. Somehow, and it is my belief, the

SOE, short for Special Operations Executive has got word out about what is going on here.

"These organisations have the right to inspect the way we are being treated, and find out what is going on in regard to the civilian population. The Germans know that they will be in trouble if the truth be fully known. The Tymbakion area breaks so many of the Geneva Convention articles that it's loathsome.

"The census is an appeasement from the Germans to the ICRC and it will basically gloss over what is really happening. The Commandant is writing up his report which misses the major concerns such as the reprisal killings, the destruction of Tympaki, building of an airfield using slave labour and so on.

"He will have a minimum of points all positive in their conduct towards us and the local population.

"Our report and the activities need to be presented so if we are called up to give evidence the report becomes important. It will also contradict what the Germans are presenting. The written word becomes important if we are not around or been moved away from this location.

"They also will be checking on activities that the men have been involved in. What is anyone's guess? So, I need to know how many of our fellows are registered at Tymbakion and how many are not.

"Further, and this is where Bert will be able to help, I want the number of those who have signed the shorts and how many have not. This will be our 'Perfect Census' and the truthful one will be sent via the SOE and hopefully the Cretans and ourselves will get better treatment."

Bert quickly took out a piece of paper from his shirt pocket and started reading. He had a head count for those in each tent who had signed the shorts and a total for the camp.

Wally was busy drawing a rough table to record these results. When he got the other figures from Howard, he read the results aloud.

"So, we seemed to have covered everyone and the activities we have all been involved in. It also gives the impression we are all happy and getting along famously. The powers that be should be able to see through this."

	Tymbakion: December, 1941 Totals	151
✎	Registered as being at the Tymbakion camp and signed shorts	122
	Registered at Tymbakion and did not sign the shorts	29
	Not on Tymbakion Registry	19
✎	Total signatures on the shorts	122

Thursday, December 4, 1941, was an interesting day as the airfield was coming up to scratch, and German aircraft were using it. Vic wrote, "We are working on the airfield. Transport planes busy carting water and food to Libya."

Again, the men were disappointed to see the airstrip being used as it was intended. At full usage, they envisaged hundreds of bombers and fighter planes roaring in and taking their destructive munitions to be offloaded on the Allies in North Africa, Iran, and the Middle East.

December 4 became Census Day for Iraklion. The Tymbakion commandant called a parade and informed the prisoners of a special relationship between Iraklion and his camp.

He informed the parade that often, men would be swapped between the two, and any Tymbakion inmates who were injured or ill would be transferred to Iraklion. The odd part of this information was that no one had actually seen any proof of such a movement. In fact, most of the men who had needed to be treated for illness or injury always sought out Doctor Wally Holt. There was nothing in medicine that the doctor didn't know about or couldn't deal with.

The entire camp was paraded, and a roll call was made to ensure everyone who should have been there was present. The commandant informed the men that the census at Tymbakion would be held on December 14, 10 days time.

Later, at a meeting of the leaders' group, Wally Holt was flabbergasted by the timetable of the two censuses. He mused that it could be possible to have one person counted twice or, even worse, not to be counted at all. He added that he thought the Germans did not really hold much importance to the censuses even though they had suggested otherwise.

He was also mystified by the commandant's comment about the special relationship between Iraklion and Tymbakion, as he had not seen any swapping nor the ill being sent to the north.

A weather report issued for Friday, December 5, and Saturday, December 6, forecast snow and rain, with heavy snow expected on the mountains. There was plenty of shivering and huddling during those two nights.

One of the major concerns of the army engineers came to fruition on Sunday, December 7.

A plane crashed into the mountainside during a storm, all the crew were killed. As much as the prisoners were pleased to hear this, they kept their feelings to themselves. The urge to say loudly, "We told you so, but you wouldn't listen," sat on all the men's tongues.

The prisoners who were war engineers had many a meeting with Wally Holt to tell him what progress was like and what other activities were going to happen. One issue that they harped on was the location and direction of the airstrip. Coming in from the south the pilot had an easy entry over the Mediterranean Sea. Coming in from or leaving to the north faced pilots into the mountains. These mountains soared up to 4000 feet and were within a couple of miles of lift-off on the airstrip.

Consequently, the engineers believed that there would be many crashes into the mountains, whether from landing or taking off.

The first weeks of December saw Vic writing about world events. He was obtaining the news either from a radio or a German guard. The worst news came when Japan king-hit the United States at Pearl Harbor in Hawaii sinking most of its Pacific Fleet. [5]

The more encouraging news came on Friday, December 12 as the United States declared war on Germany.

This was welcome news as the United States was one of the most powerful countries in the world. Their added power would help immensely.

Sunday, December 14, 1941, became an official day for the Germans. They were ordered to carry out a full census of the camp and any areas associated with Tymbakion.

Captain Walter Holt was happy to oblige and even offered to help. He was interested in the area's population and the nationality of each person.

He sat at a small desk and began to work through all the movements that had come and gone through Tymbakion. He wrote the date Wednesday, September 10, 1941, and noted that there were 200 Allied troops on board the *Norburg* when it berthed in Iraklion. The group was split at this place, with 138 men sent in trucks to Tymbakion. There were 12 RAF personnel already camped at Tymbakion before the arrival of the main group.

On Monday, October 6, 1941, all the RAF men were sent to Athens.

On Saturday, October 11, thirteen men were caught in the hills and incarcerated at Tymbakion.

One of these men turned out to be Bonnie Buirchell, the Australian who had twice fled to the safety of the hills. He was unfortunate in contracting malaria and became so ill that he sought medical help. It did seem that there were medical personnel at Tymbakion, and even Arthur Lawrence references Jimmy Craig as a 'patient Tymbakion'. Vic Petersen, writing from Lamsdorf, says he ran into "one of the medical orderlies from Tymbakion".

On Sunday, October 19, 1941, another 50 men arrived to join the camp. At the beginning of December two Greeks were involved in leaving the camp. One needed medical help for a shooting wound in the stomach, and the other just escaped.

Having worked through the numbers Wally Holt added the comings and goings to calculate that there should now be 151 prisoners.

The guards were changed during the week, which was disappointing as the ones at the camp had been easy to get along with. It didn't take long before the commandant was unhappy with his new guards.

Wally Holt was insightful in calling the commandant's reaction displaced anger. This involved a superior taking their frustration out on a subordinate.

In this case, the Commandant was frustrated with his guards for not keeping watch carefully, so he placed them on double shift. They spent their guard duty time pushing, shoving, and kicking the prisoners who were doing nothing wrong.

There was still a dreaded feeling in the camp regarding the pillaging of houses in Tympaki for stone to be used on the base of the airstrip. Vic's note for December 15: "Working on the airfield and laying stones, and also digging drains."

The chief engineer, whom Goering had hired, tried to make the prisoners work until 1700 hours, reckoning that as there was a war on, everyone should pitch in and help get the project finished. He was very annoyed that the men continued to knock off at 1600 hours.

CHAPTER 23

—☡—

With Christmas approaching, the local Cretans anticipated organising a party and supplying oodles of food and that is exactly how things panned out.

On Wednesday, December 24, the men arrived at camp after a long slogging day removing the last of the olive trees, to find many crates of wine. Packed near the boxes were many packets of sultanas and various other items, given to the camp by the Crete population.

Each man also received 10 cigarettes in the evening.

An attempt was made to get Ron Pestell,[1] an English driver from Connington, England, into the kitchen to cook some special recipes. After clever enticement, Ron made fritters of rice, lemon sultanas, and parmesan fried in olive oil. He also showed his culinary expertise by making rice and raisins for dinner.

Christmas Day[2] came early with the whole camp up and moving. Thursday, December 25, 1941, was the first and only Christmas the Tymbakion POWs would have on the Island of Crete.

The Crete civilians began bringing food to the camp gate. One man handed in several small parcels during the day.[3] Another of the local Cretans arrived with crates of mandarins and each of the prisoners received a dozen all to themselves.

Added to the goodies was an overcoat each which was appreciated with the winter turning so cold.

To top off the Christmas lunch, the men were given a two gallon barrel of wine between seven.

The daytime meals left most too tired to stay awake. However, there was another line-up by mid-afternoon because the locals had come and left more goodies for everyone. Sultanas, oranges, bread, cherries, and rice were in abundance. It was a show of appreciation from the Cretans.

For dinner, the camp inmates received beef, cabbage, beans, gravy, and plum pudding. In the evening, a barrel of wine arrived, and they went on a bit of a drinking spree and everybody felt merry for a change. So, Christmas Day ended.

Boxing Day dawned, and due to the hangover from Christmas Day festivities, nobody was out of bed too early. The after effects of such a whopping Christmas Day slowed most down.

For those who did make an appearance there was tea and eggs for breakfast, tea and Greek bread for lunch.

For the evening meal, we had a stew with pork, cabbage, beans, and peas. A glass of wine during the day quenched many a dry mouth. The only miserable part of the day was the weather, which turned out to be cold and wet.

The next day, Vic added a comment to his diary: "I did not go to work today. Was this a precursor to what was about to happen to the camp?"

At 0800 on Sunday, December 28, everyone was told to pack up as they were shifting camp. Albert Edward Chamberlain made a beeline for his tent, found the pair of shorts with the 122 signatures. He carefully wrapped these and placed the package at the bottom of his knapsack.[4]

Other items were added until the total belongings that Bert had packed were things for transport. He flung the bag over his shoulder and set out for the trucks.

He stopped, turned back surveyed the area he knew as Tymbakion, took a long deep breath through his nose to get a smell of the air, stood to attention and saluted. He could never tell anyone why he did those final things but they seemed appropriate.

He climbed aboard the truck, and as he settled down the German guard said, "You are all off to Germany but the first stop will be Heraklion."[5]

The men would not get a chance to say goodbye to the people they had befriended over the past three months. Everyone had a heavy load on their shoulders.

The next morning, at Heraklion, the camp population was roused and the commandant called an assembly.

"I need to warn you all. You must not say anything about your time at Tymbakion and building an airstrip.[6] If one whispered word is heard, we will seek out each of you, and you will be shot.

"These are the words of General Goering so take them seriously. Captain Holt knows that we have all your personal information in a register so it will be very easy to find you and your colleagues. I repeat, do not whisper one word about Tymbakion from now until your remains are buried in the ground."

There was a low murmuring among the men before they were called to order.

Life was going to be brutal for the Tympaki population as they would be forced to labour on with the airfield construction.

To make matters unbearable they would be building one of the largest airstrips ever built using stones from their own homes and wood from the coffins of their deceased. The plan would see the houses blown up and the stone rubble transported to the airstrip site.

To cope with the trauma and the heart-breaking labour, they would send their women and children elsewhere to be looked after.[7]

The story of Tymbakion for the 151 men was at an end. They would now go through the same routines and routes as their comrades in arms went before them. They would suffer the same deprivations and loneliness as the others.

They would be taken by ship to Salonika, moved by train north to Germany and left in a stalag for the next three and a half years.

Even after the Germans opened the gates, these men and hundreds of thousands like them would continue to suffer. This time, it would be a Long March [8] where they would march aimlessly around southern Germany for up to four months until, thankfully, the American and British armies would find most of them and send them home.

Safe and free but no doubt damaged.

Others would find themselves in the hands of the Russians. Their freedom route would be through Odesa on the Black Sea, the Bosphorus, Mediterranean Sea before arriving back in England.

During the day Holt went from group to group in the camp to emphasise what the commandant had told them about staying silent regarding Tymbakion. He emphasised the register so that it was clear that they could all be located at any time in the future.

There was remorse for what they had done to the Cretan families was unforgivable, even with the understanding that they were under duress to carry out Germany's instructions. To walk into some stranger's property and decimate it, cause the break-up of the family and know that their earning power was reduced was criminal.

The Cretan population's reaction to the Allies' negative activities was amazingly gracious. They always clearly showed a deep understanding and genuine forgiveness.

The population of Crete as a whole, particularly the people of Tympaki, were so grateful for what the Allies did for them that they could not repay this kindness.

The Cretans had limited food but willingly and unselfishly shared it at every opportunity. They did not hold any malice towards the Allies, but that cannot be said for the Germans.

The tears that welled up in every man's eye as the trucks pulled out of Tymbakion were testimony to the relationship that had been established in such a short time. The tears were also for the future.

The first truck started to pull out and accelerated up the slight incline. It would travel over a mile before reaching the high point of the plain. The road then dipped into a valley, and after two miles, the mountains.

Lance Bombardier William Weatherall was alarmed that the group was being transported back to the north. Just as the truck in the lead reached the top of the road, William made a break for freedom. He jumped from the tray out the back. [9]

There was shouting and gunshots as the convoy came to a grinding halt. Men from every direction ran to the sixth truck ready to assist however they could.

CHAPTER 24

—︿〰︿—

They weren't needed as William Weatherall's daring escape ended where he landed, in a rather deep pothole. The nearest men helped him out and dusted him down. [1] He was looked over by the medics who had raced to the sixth lorry expecting to find at least one bullet lodged in someone's stomach. They were thankful it turned out to be a rather shaken Weatherall who limped around in agony due to his twisted ankle.

Captain Holt took charge and began to move the crowd back to the lorries. His persuasions started with a request that, "Everyone move back to where you came from."

This had little effect so he raised his voice and added that the guards may need to use the butts of their rifles. This had the desired effect, and men began to walk away.

Out of the crowd, a lonely voice called, "Look, look, you can see the Mediterranean Sea and the barren area where we grubbed out the olive trees for the past four months and..." The voice faltered and choked. Everyone turned to face the scene being described.

The men all stopped, and there was much pointing and commenting. Way in the distance, walking along the edge of the barbed wire fence, was a solitary figure leading a donkey.

He seemed to pause and wave, and everyone automatically waved back. The Cretan must have been visiting his former olive grove.

He undoubtedly would have been shocked by what he had seen, as the area was desolate. Every single tree had been cut down and all the roots grubbed out. The wood had been burnt to ash.

There was nothing he could do about his losses. Like his neighbours, the Cretan had to face an uncertain future. He was still looking towards the ridge where the convoy of lorries had come to a halt and wondered about the future of the prisoners of war who were being moved away from Crete and possibly into Germany.

The Cretan returned to the area he once saw as an olive grove where thousands of trees grew tall and strong. He looked towards the little township of Tympaki, or at least the remains of it, where the blowing up of houses, smashing the cemetery and crushing the rock for the airfield had been in full swing for the past fortnight. The Germans had already put him and his fellow neighbours to work.

The prisoners of war had toiled to remove all the olive trees and flatten the huge area in readiness for paving as an airfield. The Germans anxiously pushed for the job to be done, and then they would win the war with a fleet of bombers.

The Cretan would be left destitute and searching for his family, who had been dispersed across the island. How long their suffering would last could only be guessed at. The future of Crete might be based on the martyrs and the martyr villages, both of whom suffered. There will be stories to tell and read. Hopefully, they will offer a means of ensuring the population can finally and forever live as a free, peaceful and democratic island.[2]

The distance between the men on the rise and the man with the donkey was too far for anyone to notice that he had tears welling in his eyes.

PROFILES

Profiles of the 151 soldiers at the Tymbakion prisoner of war camp and elsewhere in Crete in December 1941, when the shorts were signed. Some of the profiles are incomplete. If you can help fill the gaps, don't hesitate to get in touch with email: jumper11@live.com your input would be appreciated.

After four months at Tymbakion, Crete, most of the men were sent to Stalag VIII-B, known as Lamsdorf.

Check out other profiles/stories of World War service person or if you would like to pay a tribute to a family member, go to the author's tribute website at www.prisonersofwarcrete.com

Ainsley, John Robert

Date of Birth:	January 23, 1915.
Place of Birth:	Ferryhill, Durham, England, UK.
Next of Kin:	MI.
Marital Status:	MI.
Rank:	Corporal.
Army number:	105991.
Date of Capture:	June 1, 1941.
Place of Capture:	Crete.
Internment:	Stalag VIIIB.
POW number:	4556.

Royal Army Service Corps. British Expeditionary Forces, BEF.
At Tymbakion was registered as T-9 in tent 13, and signed the shorts.

Aitken, Charles

Date of Birth:	July, 24, 1909.
Place of Birth:	MI.
Next of Kin:	A. Aitken, Seddon St, Aramoko, NZ.
Marital Status:	Single.
Residence:	Seddon St, Aramoko, NZ.
Employment:	Carpenter.
Rank:	Sapper.
Army number:	33229.
Date of Capture:	June 1, 1941.
Place of Capture:	Crete.
POW number:	5293.
Place of Internment:	Stalag VIIIB, Lamsdorf.

19th Army Troops Co. New Zealand Engineers. 2nd NZEF.
At Tymbakion was registered as T-93, in tent 2, did not sign shorts.

Aldersley, William Arthur

Date of Birth:	July 30, 1913.
Place of Birth:	Christchurch, New Zealand.
Next of Kin:	Mr F. Aldersley, Christchurch, N. Z.
Residence:	Hereford Street, Christchurch, New Zealand.
Marital Status:	Widowed pre-1940.
Employment:	Storeman.
Service number:	2075.
Rank:	Lance corporal (Sapper).
Date of Capture:	June 1, 1941.
Place of Capture:	Crete.
Place of Internment:	Stalag VIIIB, Lamsdorf.
POW number:	5261.

Headquarters, 2nd New Zealand Division Engineers.
At Tymbakion was registered as T-92, in tent 7, did not sign shorts.

Armitage, Thomas Washer

Date of Birth:	May 28, 1908.
Place of Birth:	Manaia, Taranaki, New Zealand.
Next of Kin:	C. H. Armitage, Manaia, Taranaki, NZ.
Marital Status:	Single.
Employment:	Draper.
Rank:	Sapper.
Army number:	33221.
Date of Capture:	June 1, 1941.
Place of Capture:	Sfakia, Crete.
POW number:	5252.
Place of Incarceration:	Stalag VIIIB, Lamsdorf.

19th New Zealand Army Troops Company, NZ Engineers, Second New Zealand Expeditionary Forces, Third Echelon.

At Tymbakion was registered as I-27, in tent 2, and signed shorts.

Armstrong, Leslie Thomas

Date of Birth:	June 3, 1900.
Place of Birth:	Westown, New Plymouth, New Zealand.
Next of Kin:	A. Armstrong, Takamatua, Timaru, NZ.
Residence:	Langdon's Road, Papanui, Christchurch, NZ
Employment:	Labourer.
Marital Status:	Single.
Army number:	9996.
Rank:	Private.
Date of Capture:	June 6, 1941.
Place of Capture:	Crete.
POW number:	5037.
Place of Incarceration:	Stalag VIIIB Lamsdorf.

2 Divisional Supply Column, 2nd NZEF.

At Tymbakion was registered as T-95, in tent 2, did not sign shorts.

Arroll, Roy Herbert

Date of Birth:	MI.
Place of Birth:	MI.
Next of Kin:	J.D.M. Arroll Kilmore St, Christchurch, NZ.
Residence:	Hotel Auckland, Auckland, New Zealand.
Marital Status:	Single.
Employment:	Clerk.
Rank:	Sapper.
Army number:	2086.
Date Captured:	June 1, 1941.
Place of Capture:	Crete.
POW number:	5289.
Place of Incarceration:	Oflag,79, Waggum,, Germany.

Second New Zealand Expeditionary Force, 1st Echelon.
Head Quarters, 2nd Division, New Zealand, Engineers.
At Tymbakion was registered as T-94, in tent 15, did not sign shorts.

Baker, Edward

Date of Birth:	January 17, 1905.
Place of Birth:	Battersea, London, England.
Next of Kin:	MI.
Residence:	MI.
Marital Status:	Single.
Rank:	Private.
Service number:	2065377.
Date Captured:	June 1, 1941.
Place of Capture:	Crete.

Royal Artillery Battalion, British Expeditionary Force.
POW number: 4596.
At Tymbakion was registered as T-10, in tent 15, and signed shorts.

Banner, Ernest Ambrose Smedley

Date of Birth:	April 2, 1915.
Place of Birth:	Fielding.
Next of Kin:	M. Banner, Evans Bay Rd. Wellington, N Z.
Residence:	High Street, Christchurch, New Zealand.
Marital Status:	Single.
Employment:	Radio Engineer.
Rank:	Lance Corporal (Driver).
Service Number:	7502.
Date of Capture:	June 1, 1941.
Place of Capture:	Sfakia, Crete.
Interned:	Stalag 383, Hohenfels, Bavaria.
POW number:	5012.

New Zealand Expeditionary Force 2 Division NZ Supply Co.
At Tymbakion, registered as T-96, and in tent 15, signed the shorts.

Barnes, Harry Holcroft

Date of Birth:	December 10, 1908.
Place of Birth:	Auckland, New Zealand.
Residence:	Bondi, New South Wales.
Marital Status:	Married.
Employment:	Bricklayer.
Service Number:	NX32898.
Rank:	Lance Corporal.
Date of Capture:	June 1, 1941.
Place of Capture:	Crete.
POW number:	4534.
Internment:	Stalag VIIIB, Lamsdorf.

Division 7, Australian Expeditionary Forces.
Tymbakion was registered as T-11, in tent 3, and signed the shorts.

Barrow, William

Date of Birth:	July 12, 1915.
Place of Birth:	New Zealand.
Next of Kin:	Mrs I. Barrow (mother) living in Reefton.
Residence:	Reefton, New Zealand.
Marital Status:	Single.
Employment:	Labourer.
Rank:	Private.
Army number:	14244.
Place of Capture:	Sfakia, Crete.
Date of Capture:	June 1, 1941.
Internment:	Stalag VIIIB, Lamsdorf.
POW number:	5458.

20th Infantry Reinforcements. Second New Zealand Expeditionary. At Tymbakion was registered as T-97, tent 12, and signed shorts.

Beacham, William Albert

Date of Birth:	September 19, 1918.
Place of Birth:	Auckland, New Zealand.
Next of Kin:	M. Beacham, Pt Chevalier, Auckland, NZ.
Residence:	Pt Chevalier, Auckland, NZ.
Marital Status:	Single.
Employment:	Labourer.
Service number:	23275.
Rank:	Gunner.
Date of Capture:	June 1, 1941.
Place of Capture:	Crete.
Internment:	Stalag XX-A Thorn.

5th New Zealand Field Regiment, NZEF.

POW number:	5227.

At Tymbakion, was registered as T-98, and in tent 15, signed shorts.

Beaton, Malcolm John

Date of Birth:	June 2, 1911.
Place of Birth:	New Zealand.
Next of Kin:	R, Beaton Waipounamu, Gore, NZ.
Residence:	C/- J. H. Pollock, Fairlie, Canterbury, NZ.
Employment:	Concrete worker.
Marital Status:	Single.
Service number:	9724.
Rank:	Driver.
Date Captured:	June 1, 1941.
Place Captured:	Crete.
POW number:	4584.
Internment:	Stalag VIIIB, Lamsdorf.

2 Divisional Supply Column, NZEF.

At Tymbakion registered T-13, and in tent 15, did not sign the shorts.

Bennison, Avery Francis

Date of Birth:	December 31, 1908.
Place of Birth:	Ashburton, New Zealand.
Next of Kin:	E B Bennison Creek Street, Allenton NZ.
Places of Residence:	Creek Street, Allenton, New Zealand.
Marital Status:	Single.
Employment:	Master Butcher.
Rank:	Private.
Service Number:	5353.
Date of Capture:	June 1, 1941.
Place of Capture:	Sfakia, Crete.
Internment:	Stalag VIIIB Lamsdorf.
POW number:	5350.

Headquarters, 2nd New Zealand Expeditionary Force Base.

At Tymbakion registered as T-99, in tent 15, and signed the shorts.

Bentley, Reginald Guy Arthur

Date of Birth:	May,12, 1918.
Place of Birth:	MI.
Next of Kin:	MI.
Marital Status:	Single.
Employment:	butcher.
Service number:	6488.
Rank:	Lance Corporal.
Date of Capture:	June 1, 1941.
Place of Capture:	Crete.
POW number:	4520.
Place of internment:	Stalag 383, Hohenfels.

22nd Wellington Battalion NZ Engineers. Second NZEF
At Tymbakion, registered as T-14, in tent 15, and signed the shorts.

Billings, Adrian Kinross

Date of Birth:	MI.
Place of Birth:	MI.
Next of Kin:	Mr G. Billings (father) Waitakaruru. NZ.
Residence:	Waitakaruru.
Marital Status:	Single.
Employment:	Worked in Hauraki District as a carpenter.
Service number:	32174.
Rank:	Sapper.
Date of Capture:	June 1, 1941.
Place of Capture:	Crete.
POW number:	5227.
Place of internment:	Stalag 383, Hohenfels.

19th Army Troops PS Company. NZ Engineers. Second NZEF,
At Tymbakion, registered T-100, in tent 15, did not sign shorts.

Bissett, Thomas Alexander

Date of Birth:	December 29, 1916.
Place of Birth:	Wollongong.
Next of Kin:	William Alexander Bissett (father).
Marital Status:	Single.
Employment:	Motor Mechanic.
Service number:	NX32898.
Rank:	Private.
Residence:	Bexley North, St George, New South Wales.
Army number:	PLX 100950.
Date of Capture:	June 1, 1941.
Place of Capture:	Crete.
POW number:	4546.

16th Brigade, 2nd/3 Infantry, Australian Imperial Forces.

At Tymbakion was registered as T-15, in tent 4, signed the shorts.

Bolding, Harold Frank

Date of Birth:	October 19, 1916.
Place of Birth:	Traralgon, Victoria.
Next of Kin:	John Bolding (father).
Places of Residence:	Wonthaggi North, Victoria, Aust.
Marital Status:	Single.
Employment:	Farmer.
Rank:	Private.
Service Number:	VX 7801.
Date of Capture:	June 3, 1941.
Place of Capture:	Sfakia, Crete.
POW number:	4531.
Place of Internment:	Stalag VIIIB, Lamsdorf.

Australian Imperial Force, AIF.

At Tymbakion was registered I-19, in tent 9, did not sign shorts.

Bowden, Kenneth Frank

Date of Birth:	August 15, 1908.
Place of Birth:	Auckland, New Zealand.
Next of Kin:	M. Bowden Brougham St, Wellington, NZ.
Place of Residence:	Brougham St, Wellington, NZ.
Marital Status:	Married.
Employment:	Baker in Wellington.
Rank:	Private.
Service Number:	30242.
Date of Capture:	May 22, 1941.
Place of Capture:	Crete.
POW number:	4598.
Place of Internment:	Stalag VIIIB, Lamsdorf.

Second NZ Expeditionary Force, Second Echelon.
At Tymbakion registered I-37, stayed in tent 12, signed the shorts.

Bowen, George Stanley

Date of Birth:	July 13, 1917.
Place of Birth:	Ilford, England.
Next of Kin:	NI.
Places of Residence:	England.
Marital Status:	NI.
Employment:	NI.
:	Private.
Service Number:	CH/X101376.
Date of Capture:	June 1, 1941.
Place of Capture:	Crete.
POW number:	4606.
Internment:	Stalag VIIIB, Lamsdorf.

Royal Marines British Expeditionary Force
At Tymbakion registered I-21 stayed in tent 14 and signed the shorts.

Bristol, Reginald David

Date of Birth:	June 4, 1920.
Place of Birth:	Melbourne, Australia.
Next of Kin:	Bristol R V Armadale, NSW.
Residence:	Sutherland Rd, Armadale, NSW.
Employment:	Storeman, motor accessories.
Rank:	Private.
Army number:	VX 26839.
Date of Capture:	June 1, 1941.
Place of Capture:	Crete.
POW number:	4512.
Internment:	Stalag VIIIB, Lamsdorf.

2/5 Battalion, Australian Imperial Forces.
At Tymbakion was registered T-16, in tent 14, and signed shorts.
Awarded British Empire Medal.

Brodie, Charles William

Date of Birth:	January 11, 1917.
Place of Birth:	Fielding, New Zealand.
Next of Kin:	R. Brodie, Hay Street, Linwood, Cch, NZ.
Residence:	Hay Street, Linwood, Christchurch, NZ.
Marital Status:	Single.
Employment:	Bushman.
Rank:	Private.
Army number:	13803.
Date of Capture:	June 1, 1941.
Place of Capture:	Crete.
Internment:	Stalag VIIIB.
POW number:	23552.

26th Canterbury and Otago Battalion. Second NZEF Third Echelon.
At Tymbakion was registered 1-29 and in tent signed the shorts.

Brown, George Robert William

Date of Birth:	August 31, 1912.
Place of Birth:	MI.
Next of Kin:	Mrs B Brown Howell's Lane, Dunedin, NZ.
Marital Status:	Married.
Residence:	Bradford Street, Parnell, Auckland, NZ.
Employment:	Welder.
Army number:	2393.
Rank:	Lance Corporal.
Place of Capture:	Sfakia, Crete.
Date of Capture:	June 1, 1941.
Interned:	Stalag VIIIB.
POW number:	5441.

5th Field Park, NZ Engineers. NZEF.
At Tymbakion was registered T-102, in tent 7 signed the shorts.

Brown, Harold Keith

Date of Birth:	September 7, 1919.
Place of Birth:	Christchurch, New Zealand.
Next of Kin:	Annie Brown, Junction Rd, Hornby.
Marital Status:	Single.
Residence:	Junction Rd, Hornby, Canterbury, N Z.
Employment:	Plasterer.
Army number:	34618.
Rank:	Sapper.
Place of Capture:	Crete.
Date of Capture:	June 1, 1941.
Internment:	Stalag VIIIB, Lamsdorf.
POW number:	5290.

19th NZ Army Troops, New land Engineers. 2nd NZEF 1st Echelon.
At Tymbakion T-103 was registered, in tent 14 not sign shorts.

Brown, Norman McLeod

Date of Birth:	August 27, 1900.
Place of Birth:	Richmond, Victoria.
Next of Kin:	Jean Brown.
Places of Residence:	Richmond, Victoria, Australia.
Marital Status:	Married.
Employment:	Labourer.
Army number:	VX31518.
Date of Capture:	June 1, 1941.
Place of Capture:	Crete.
Internment:	Stalag VIIIB.
POW number:	4559.

2/7th Infantry Battalion Australian Imperial Force.

At Tymbakion was registered I-117 in tent 8 and signed the shorts.

Brownlie, Robert Bould

Date of Birth:	August 14, 1920.
Place of Birth:	Johnsonville, New Zealand.
Next of Kin:	J. J. Brownlie, Campbell St, Karori. Wellington, New Zealand.
Residence:	Campbell Street, Karori, Wellington, NZ.
Marital Status:	Single.
Employment:	Farm hand.
Army number:	4446.
Date of Capture:	June 1, 1941.
Place of Capture:	Crete.
Interned:	Stalag VIIIB.
POW number:	5409.

4th New Zealand Res, MT Co Battalion, Second 1st Echelon.

At Tymbakion was registered T-104 in tent 14, signed the shorts.

Buhagiar, Alfred

Date of Birth:	December 10, 1914.
Place of Birth:	Alexandria.
Next of Kin:	MI.
Marital Status:	MI.
Residence:	17 Giacomo, Lumbroso, Mazarita, Egypt.
Employment:	MI.
Army number:	6081.
Rank:	Corporal.
Place Captured:	Crete.
Date Captured:	June 1, 1941.
Internment:	Stalag VIIIB, Teschen.
POW number:	4514.

Reserve 231 Mechanical Transport Co. R A S C. NZEF

At Tymbakion was registered T-19 in tent 11 did not sign shorts.

Buchanan, Roy Douglas

Date of Birth:	June 6, 1916.
Place of Birth:	Hamilton, Victoria, Australia.
Next of Kin:	D. J Buchanan, father.
Marital Status:	Single.
Residence:	Abbotsford, Melbourne, Victoria.
Employment:	Labourer.
Army number:	VX 32961.
Rank:	Gunner.
Place of Capture:	Crete.
Date of Capture:	May 29, 1941.
Internment:	Stalag VIIIB, Lamsdorf.
POW number:	4607.

3rd Light A. A. Regiment, Australian Imperial Force.

At Tymbakion was registered I-28, in tent 12, and signed the shorts.

Buirchell, William Roy

Birth Date:	September 11, 1912.
Place of Birth:	Kojonup, Australia.
Next of Kin:	Clemence Buirchell (wife).
Employment:	Shearer.
Rank:	Signalman.
Army number:	WX 2280.
Captured 1:	Massara Bay, Crete.
Date:	June 6, 1941.
Captured 2:	Tymbakion, Crete.
Date:	October, 1941 – hid in hills for 87 days.
POW number:	4562.
Internment:	Stalag VIIIB 1942 – mid 1945.

2nd/11 Battalion, Australian Imperial Forces.
At Tymbakion was registered T-20, in tent 7, and signed the shorts.

Bunn, Alan Harris

Birth Date:	May 4, 1919.
Place of Birth:	Eltham, New Zealand.
Next of Kin:	Mrs Rose Bunn, Anzac Parade, Wanganui.
Employment:	Transport driver.
Residence:	C/- L. Bunn and Sons, Waitara, NZ.
Marital Status:	Single.
Service Number:	33676.
Rank:	Sapper.
Date of Capture:	June 1, 1941.
Place of Capture:	Crete.
POW number:	5300.

19th Transport Company, New Zealand Engineers, Second NZEF.
At Tymbakion was registered T-105, in tent 11, did not sign shorts.

Bunyard, Claud Stewart

Birth Date:	April 21, 1910.
Place of Birth:	MI.
Employment:	Interior decorator.
Residence:	7 Mentos Court, 40 Abbey Road, London.
Service number:	865679.
Rank:	Corporal/Gunner.
Date of Capture:	May 30, 1941.
Place of Capture:	Crete.
POW number:	4609.

151 Battery, 59th HAA Reg, BEF.
At Tymbakion registered as T-21, in tent 7, did sign the shorts.

Burne, James Thomas

Date of Birth:	MI.
Place of Birth:	MI.
Next of Kin:	E. M. Burne Webb St, Wellington, N Z.
Marital Status:	Married.
Residence:	Webb Street, Wellington, New Zealand.
Employment:	Ship plumber.
Rank:	Private.
Service number:	35322.
Date of Capture:	June 1, 1941.
Place of Capture:	Crete.
POW number:	5264.
Internment:	Stalag VIIIB Lamsdorf.

Infantry Reinforcements, 2nd NZEF, 3rd Echelon.
At Tymbakion registered as T-106, in tent 11, did not sign the shorts.

Burns, George

Date of Birth:	November 4, 1913.
Place of Birth:	Fielding, New Zealand.
Residence:	MI.
Next of Kin:	MI.
Marital Status:	Married.
Employment:	MI.
Rank:	Private.
Service number:	33013.
Date of Capture:	June 1, 1941.
Place of Capture:	Crete.
POW number:	5266.

Infantry Reinforcements. Second NZEF, Third Echelon.
At Tymbakion registered as T-107, in tent 10, did not sign the shorts.

Busby, Ponaute

Date of Birth:	MI.
Place of Birth:	MI.
Next of Kin:	Mrs Busby (mother).
Residence:	Pukepoto, Kaitaia, New Zealand.
Employment:	Labourer Kaitaia, Northland.
Marital Status:	Single.
Service number:	25823.
Date of Capture:	June 1, 1941.
Place of Capture:	Sfakia, Crete.
Internment:	Stalag VIIIB.
POW number:	5443.

28th Maori Battalion, Second New Zealand Expeditionary Forces.
At Tymbakion was registered T-108, in tent 7, signed the shorts.

Carter, Edward S

Date of Birth:	September 22, 1915.
Place of Birth:	Harrogate, England.
Service number:	G4334.
Rank:	Private.
Date of Capture:	June 1, 1941.
Place of Capture:	Sfakia, Crete.
POW number:	4560.
Internment:	Stalag VIIIB Teschen.

E.F.I. Royal Army Service Corps, BEF.
At Tymbakion was registered T-23, in tent 8, signed the shorts.

Chamberlain, Albert Edward

Date of Birth:	May 6, 1907.
Place of Birth:	New Zealand.
Next of Kin:	Mrs R. M. Chamberlain (wife) Waimangaroa via Westport, New Zealand.
Residence:	Waimangaroa via Westport.
Employment:	General labourer post school.
Marital Status:	Married.
Rank:	Private (Driver).
Service Number:	14242.
Date of Capture:	June 1, 1941.
Place of Capture:	Crete.
Internment:	Stalag VIIIB.
POW number:	4532.

1st NZ Supply Co. Second New Zealand Expeditionary Forces
At Tymbakion registered as T-22, in tent 1, did not sign the shorts.

Chandler, Robert,

Date of Birth:	MI.
Place of Birth:	MI.
Next of Kin:	R. Chandler South Road, Dunedin.
Residence:	South Road, Dunedin.
Marital Status:	Single.
Employment:	Labourer.
Rank:	Sapper.
Service number:	32271.
Date of capture:	June 1, 1941.
Place of Capture:	Crete.
POW number:	5270.
Internment:	Stalag VIIIB, Lamsdorf.

19th Army Troops Company, NZ Engineers, 2nd NZEF, 3rd Echelon.
At Tymbakion registered as T-109, in tent 8, did not sign the shorts.

Chappell, Ronald John

Date of Birth:	October 31, 1920.
Place of Birth:	Devon, England.
Next of Kin:	MI.
Residence:	MI.
Marital Status:	MI.
Rank:	Private.
Service number:	7347150.
POW number:	4510.
Date Captured:	June 1, 1941.
Place Captured:	Sfakia, Crete.
Internment:	Stalag VIIIB.

Royal Army Medical Corps, British Expeditionary Forces.
At Tymbakion registered as T-109, in tent 8, signed the shorts.

Christiansen, Harold (Harry) Anthony

Date of Birth:	September 26, 1894.
Place of Birth:	Norway.
Next of Kin:	G. Christiansen (father).
Residence:	MI.
Employment:	Farm work.
Service number:	2059.
Place Captured:	Sfakia, Crete.
Date Captured:	June 1, 1941.
Interned:	Stalag VIIIB, Lamsdorf.
POW number:	5419.

Transport Co, New Zealand Petrol Co, NZEF.
At Tymbakion was registered as T-109, in tent, 8 signed the shorts.

Christmas, Leonard

Date of Birth:	October 1, 1902.
Place of Birth:	Great Yarmouth, England.
Next of Kin:	MI.
Residence:	MI.
Employment:	MI.
Rank:	Sapper.
Service number:	32085.
Date of Capture:	June 1, 1941.
Place of Capture:	Crete.
POW number:	5426.
Internment:	Stalag VIIIB, Teschen.

19th New Zealand A Transport Company, Engineers, NZEF
At Tymbakion registered as T-111, in tent 13, did not sign the shorts.

Collins, Andrews Walter

Date of Birth:	December 13, 1916.
Place of Birth:	Leeston, New Zealand.
Next of Kin:	J. Collins c/o Union Ship, Wellington, N Z.
Places of Residence:	Millers Road, Dannevirke, New Zealand.
Marital Status:	Single.
Employment:	Labour Dannevirke, Manawatu, Wanganui.
Rank:	Private.
Service Number:	5721.
Date of Capture:	June 1, 1941.
Place of Capture:	Crete.
POW number:	24196.
Internment:	Stalag VIIIB, Lamsdorf.

2nd Divisional Employment Platoon. Second NZEF, 1st Echelon.

At Tymbakion, I was registered in tent 7 but did not sign the shorts.

Coombs, Gordon

Date of Birth:	September 5, 1918.
Place of Birth:	MI.
Next of Kin:	Mrs E. Coombs Lara Lake, Victoria, Aust.
Residence:	Norton Road, Frankton Junction, NZ.
Marital Status:	Single.
Employment:	Labourer Hamilton, Waikato.
Rank:	Private.
Service Number:	22262.
Date Captured:	May 28, 1941.
Place Captured:	Crete.
Internment:	Stalag VIIIB Lamsdorf.
POW number:	5082.

Headquarters, 21st Battalion (Auckland). Second NZEF.

At Tymbakion was registered T-112, in tent 2, signed the shorts.

Cooper, Charles George

Date of Birth:	December 11, 1908.
Place of Birth:	MI.
Next of Kin:	K. Cooper Tama St, Lower Hutt, Well.
Marital Status:	Married.
Residence:	Tama Street, Lower Hutt, Wellington.
Employment:	Enameller.
Rank:	Private.
Service Number:	5566.
Date of Capture:	June 1, 1941.
Place of Capture:	Crete.
Left Crete Date:	January 1, 1942.
Internment:	Stalag VIIIB Lamsdorf.
POW number:	5164.

19th Infantry Battalion, Second NZEF, 1st Echelon
At Tymbakion was registered T-113, in tent 10, signed the shorts.

Cooper, Hans John

Date of Birth:	July 19, 1920.
Place of Birth:	London.
Next of Kin:	MI.
Employment:	MI.
Residence:	MI.
Rank:	Private.
Service Number:	7347238.
Date of Capture:	June 1, 1941.
Place of Capture:	Crete.
Internment:	Stalag VIIIB.
POW Number:	4509.

Royal Army Medical Corps, British Expeditionary Army.
At Tymbakion was registered T-87, in tent 9, and signed the shorts.

Craig, James Colvin

Date of Birth:	January 23, 1910.
Place of Birth:	Westport, New Zealand.
Next of Kin:	Mrs A. P. Craig (mother), Liverpool Street,
Residence:	C/- Newman Brothers, Westport.
Marital Status:	Single.
Employment:	Service car driver.
Rank:	Private.
Service Number:	34623.
Date of Capture:	December 13, 1941 (from Hills).
Place of Capture:	Hills at Tymbakion.
Internment:	Stalag VIIIB Lamsdorf.
POW Number:	4602.

Epsom, 20th Infantry Battalion, 1st Echelon, Second NZEF.
At Tymbakion was registered I-29, in tent 3, and signed the shorts.

Crawford, John

Date of Birth:	June 30, 1918.
Place of Birth:	MI.
Next of Kin:	MI.
Residence:	4 Crompton Street, Liverpool, England.
Employment:	Labourer.
Service Number:	408857.
Date of Capture:	June 1, 1941.
Place of Capture:	Crete.
Internment:	Stalag VIIIB, Lamsdorf.
POW Number:	4578.

106 Battalion Royal Horse Artillery, BEF.
At Tymbakion was registered T-84, in tent 14, signed the shorts.

Cunningham, William

Date of Birth:	August 28, 1904.
Place of Birth:	Bathgate, Scotland.
Next of Kin:	MI.
Residence:	MI.
Employment:	MI.
Rank:	Corporal.
Service Number:	Ch/X 101130.
Date of Capture:	1st June, 1941.
Place of Capture:	Crete.
Internment:	MI.
POW Number:	5269.

Black Watch, British Expeditionary Army.
At Tymbakion was registered T-114, in tent 8, not sign the shorts.

Daly, Wynn Francis

Date of Birth:	January 14, 1919.
Place of Birth:	Christchurch, Canterbury, New Zealand.
Next of Kin:	M. Daly Peverel St, Riccarton, CChurch NZ
Residence:	Ilam Road, Riccarton, Christchurch, NZ
Marital Status:	Single.
Employment:	Market Gardener.
Rank:	Private and Driver.
Service Number:	8025.
Date of Capture:	June 1, 1941.
Place of Capture:	Chania, Crete.
Internment:	Stalag XVIII – D Marburg.
POW Number:	4574.

4th New Zealand, Reserve Mechanical Transport Company. NZEF. At Tymbakion was registered T-25, in tent 8, did not sign the shorts.

Davenport, Joseph

Date of Birth:	January 23, 1907.
Place of Birth:	Porthill, England.
Next of Kin:	MI.
Residence:	53 North Road, Cobridge, Stoke-on-Trent.
Employment:	Miner.
Rank:	Sergeant.
Service Number:	7259305.
Place of Capture:	Sfakia, Crete.
Date of Capture:	June 1, 1941.
Internment:	Stalag VIIIB Lamsdorf.
POW number:	4555.

106 Battalion, Royal Horse Artillery, British Expeditionary Force. Tymbakion was registered T-24, in tent 8, and signed the shorts.

Davis, John R

Date of Birth:	December 14, 1917.
Place of Birth:	Woolwich, England.
Next of Kin:	MI.
Residence:	MI.
Employment:	MI.
Rank:	Private.
Service Number:	7347236
Place of Capture:	Sfakia.
Date of Capture:	June 1, 1941.
Internment:	Stalag VIIIB Lamsdorf.
POW number:	4592.

Royal Army Medical Corps. British Expeditionary Force. At Tymbakion was registered T-89, in tent 8, signed the shorts.

Day, Raymond

Date of Birth:	July 19, 1913.
Place of Birth:	Gorey, Wexford, Ireland.
Next of Kin:	MI.
Residence:	MI.
Marital Status:	MI.
Employment:	MI.
Rank:	Private.
Service Number:	7633233.
Date of Capture:	June 1, 1941.
Place of Capture:	Crete.
Internment:	Stalag VIIIB, Lamsdorf.
POW number:	5255.

British Expeditionary Force.

At Tymbakion was registered T-115 in tent 3 and did not sign shorts.

Dwen, Louis Willerton

Date of Birth:	June 9, 1908.
Place of Birth:	Hamilton, New Zealand.
Next of Kin:	O Dwen Bridge St, Grafton, Auckland, N Z
Residence:	Bridge Street, Grafton, Auckland, NZ.
Marital Status:	Single.
Employment:	Motor Mechanic.
Rank:	Sapper.
Service Number:	34554.
Place of Capture:	Crete.
Date of Capture:	June 1, 1941.
Internment:	Stalag VIIIB Lamsdorf.
POW number:	5299.

New Zealand Army Service Corps, NZEF.

At Tymbakion was registered T-116 in tent 4, did not sign the shorts.

Dyson, Frank

Date of Birth:	January 4, 1910.
Place of Birth:	Hull, England.
Next of Kin:	Mrs D. M. Dyson.
Residence:	Horsham, Wimmera, Victoria, Australia.
Employment:	MI.
Marital Status:	Married.
Service Number:	VX 5604.
Rank:	Staff Sergeant.
Date of Capture:	June 1, 1941.
Place of Capture:	Sfakia, Crete.
Internment:	Stalag VIIIB, Lamsdorf.
POW Number:	4503.

2/7th Infantry Battalion, Australian Imperial Force.
At Tymbakion was registered T-3, in tent 6, and signed the shorts.

East, Edward

Date of Birth:	September 18, 1918.
Place of Birth:	Parestone, New Zealand.
Next of Kin:	S. Parsons Halsey Drive, Avondale
Residence:	Cockle Bay Rd, Howick, New Zealand.
Marital Status:	MI.
Employment:	Labourer.
Rank:	Private.
Service Number:	29292.
Date Captured:	June 1, 1941.
Place Captured:	Crete.
Internment:	Stalag VIIIB, Lamsdorf.
POW number:	5201.

Second New Zealand Expeditionary Force 3rd Echelon.
At Tymbakion was registered T-117, in tent 4, signed the shorts.

Face, Edward John Sydney

Date of Birth:	October 13, 1921.
Place of Birth:	Randwick, New South Wales.
Next of Kin:	Mr E S Face (father) Randwick.
Residence:	Avoca Street, Randwick, Sydney, NSW, Au.
Employment:	Truck driver and mechanic.
Rank:	Corporal.
Service number:	NX11441.
Date of capture:	June 1, 1941.
Place of Capture:	Crete.
POW number:	4589.
Internment:	Stalag VIIIB, Lamsdorf.

2/1st Military Forces, Australian Imperial Force 6th Division,
At Tymbakion registered as T-26, in tent 12 and signed the shorts.

Foley, Zamoni James Joseph

Date of Birth:	1904.
Place of Birth:	New Zealand.
Next of Kin:	M. Foley Rose Rd, Grey Lynn, Auk, N Z.
Places of Residence:	Rose Road, Grey Lynn.
Marital Status:	Single.
Employment:	Clerk.
Engagement:	Miss J. E. Mayne (WRNS), January, 1945.
Rank:	Private.
Service Number:	MI.
Date of capture:	June 1, 1941.
Place of Capture:	Crete.
POW number:	MI.
Internment:	Stalag VIIIB, Lamsdorf.

18th Infantry Battalion, New Zealand Expeditionary Force.
Tymbakion was registered I-54, in tent 6, signed the shorts.

Forbes, Archibald Henry

Date of Birth:	December 10, 1910.
Place of Birth:	MI.
Next of Kin:	A. Forbes Faraday St, Napier, Hawkes Bay.
Place of Residence:	Bridge Street, Auckland, NZ.
Marriage:	Single.
Employment:	Butcher.
Rank:	Private.
Service Number:	6912.
Rank:	Corporal/Gunner.
Date of Capture:	June 2, 1941.
Place of Capture:	Crete.
POW number:	4511.
Internment:	Stalag VIIIB, Lamsdorf.

22nd Battalion, New Zealand. Second NZ Expeditionary Force.

At Tymbakion was registered T-86, in tent 4 and signed the shorts.

Foxon, Thomas Victor

Date of Birth:	September 7, 1919.
Place of Birth:	MI.
Next of Kin:	MI.
Place of Residence:	10 Westcott Rd, Anfield, Liverpool.
Employment:	Carpenter.
Service Number:	890183.
Rank:	Gunner.
Date of Capture:	May 26, 1941.
Place of Capture:	Crete.
Stalag of Internment:	Stalag VIIIB, Lamsdorf.
POW number:	4582.

106 Regiment Royal Horse Artillery RASC, BEF.

At Tymbakion was registered T-28, in tent 11, signed the shorts.

Fraser, Anthony Alexander

Date of Birth:	MI.
Place of Birth:	MI.
Next of Kin:	Mrs E. M. Fraser (wife) Collins St.
Place of Residence:	Collins St, Hawera, NZ.
Marital Status:	Married.
Employment:	Lorry Driver.
Service number:	30024.
Rank:	Private.
Date of Capture:	June 1, 1941.
Place of Capture:	Crete.
Internment:	Stalag VIIIB, Lamsdorf.
POW number:	5417.

2nd NZ Divisional Petrol Company, NZ Army Service Corps.
At Tymbakion was registered I-53, in tent 3, signed the shorts.

Freeman, Clifford James

Date of Birth:	March 1, 1904.
Place of Birth:	London.
Next of Kin:	MI.
Places of Residence:	MI.
Marital Status:	MI.
Employment:	MI.
Service Number:	148521.
Rank:	Sergeant.
Date of Capture:	June 1, 1941.
Place of Capture:	Crete.
Internment:	Stalag VIIIB Lamsdorf.
POW number:	4545.

Royal Army Service Corps, British Expeditionary Force.
At Tymbakion was registered T-6, in tent 4, signed the shorts.

Gaudion, Eric John Robertson

Date of Birth:	MI.
Place of Birth:	MI.
Next of Kin:	Mrs F. Ferris (sister), Waikaia, NZ.
Place of Residence:	Lumsden, New Zealand.
Marital Status:	Single.
Employment:	Lorry driver.
Rank:	Corporal.
Service Number:	10356.
Date of Capture:	June 1, 1941.
Place of Capture:	Crete.
Internment:	Stalag VIIIB Lamsdorf.
POW number:	5203.

23rd Canterbury & Otago Battalion, 2nd NZFE.

Tymbakion was registered I-51, in tent 3, signed the pair of shorts.

Giles, Charles

Date of Birth:	MI.
Place of Birth:	MI.
Next of Kin:	Mrs C. Greig (mother), Wellington., NZ
Places of Residence:	MI.
Marital Status:	MI.
Employment:	Motor Truck Driver.
Rank:	Sapper.
Service Number:	3964606.
Date of Capture:	June 1, 1941.
Place of Capture:	Crete.
Internment:	Stalag VIIIB Lamsdorf.
POW number:	4530.

9th Reinforcements New Zealand Engineers, NZEF.

At Tymbakion was registered T-30, in tent 3, and signed the shorts.

Goodwin, Edgar George

Date of Birth:	March 16, 1907.
Place of Birth:	Kingston.
Next of Kin:	MI.
Residence:	MI.
Marital Status:	MI.
Employment:	MI.
Rank:	Gunner.
Service Number:	1428576.
Place of Capture:	Sfakia, Crete.
Date of Capture:	June 1, 1941.
Internment:	Stalag VIIIB Lamsdorf.
POW number:	4565.

Regiment Royal Artillery, British Expeditionary Force.
At Tymbakion was registered T-31, in tent 4, signed the shorts.

Gorton, John

Date of Birth:	April 14, 1916.
Place of Birth:	Hollywood, Derbyshire.
Next of Kin:	MI.
Residence:	MI.
Marital:	MI.
Employment:	MI.
Rank:	Private.
Service Number:	190420.
Place of Capture:	Sfakia, Crete.
Date of Capture:	June 1, 1941.
Internment:	Stalag VIIIB Lamsdorf.
POW number:	4544.

Regiment Royal Army Services Corp, British Expeditionary Force.
At Tymbakion was registered T-32, in tent 4, signed the shorts.

Grimsey, Cyril James Gilders

Date of Birth:	April 27, 1910.
Place of Birth:	Poplar.
Next of Kin:	MI.
Residence:	MI.
Marital Status:	MI.
Employment:	MI.
Rank:	Private.
Service Number:	148404.
Place of Capture:	Sfakia, Crete.
Date of Capture:	June 1, 1941.
Internment:	Stalag VIIIB Lamsdorf.
POW number:	4516.

Regiment Royal Army Service Corps, British Expeditionary Force.
At Tymbakion was registered T-33, in tent 4, and signed the shorts.

Gusscott, Louis Patrick

Date of Birth:	March 13, 1918.
Place of Birth:	MI.
Next of Kin:	Mr T. B. Gusscott, Kelburn, Wellington.
Residence:	Rimu Road, Kelburn, Wellington, NZ.
Marital Status:	Single.
Employment:	Warehouse man.
Rank:	Gunner.
Service Number:	33096.
Date of Capture:	June 1, 1941.
Place of Capture:	Crete.
Internment:	Stalag VIIIB, Lamsdorf.
POW number:	5017.

1st Supply Company, New Zealand Expeditionary Force.
At Tymbakion registered I-50, in tent 3, and signed the shorts.

Hardie, Ian Alexander

Date of Birth:	March 11, 1918.
Place of Birth:	Peak Hill, Western Australia.
Next of Kin:	Adrian Hardie.
Marital Status:	Single.
Residence:	Wooroloo, Western Australia.
Employment:	Gold miner.
Service Number:	WX2371.
Rank:	Private.
Date of Capture:	June 1, 1941.
Place of Capture:	Crete.
Internment:	Stalag VIIIB Lamsdorf.
POW number:	4507.

2/11th Battalion, Australian Imperial Force.

At Tymbakion was registered T-34, in tent 1, signed the shorts.

Harman, Geoffrey Bertrand

Date of Birth:	December 28, 1913.
Place of Birth:	Nelson, New Zealand.
Next of Kin:	C Harman Kaiwai Street, Nelson, N Z.
Residence:	Maida Vale Rd, Roseneath, Wellington, NZ.
Marital Status:	Single.
Employment:	Clerk.
Rank:	Private.
Service Number:	4321.
Date of Capture:	June 1, 1941.
Place of Capture:	Crete.
Internment:	Stalag VIIIB, Lamsdorf.
POW number:	5396.

2nd Div Petrol Company, New Zealand Expeditionary Force.

At Tymbakion was registered T-118, in tent 9, signed the shorts.

Harrington, Stanley Richard

Date of Birth:	MI.
Place of Birth:	MI.
Next of Kin:	Mr John Harrington (father).
Residence:	Andersons Bay Road, Dunedin.
Marriage:	Single.
Employment:	Salesman.
Rank:	Sapper.
Service Number:	32257.
Date of Capture:	June 1, 1941.
Place of Capture:	Crete.
Stalag of Internment:	Stalag VIIIB Lamsdorf.
POW number:	5412.

19th Army Troops Company, New Zealand Expeditionary Force.

At Tymbakion was registered I-49, in tent 6 and signed the shorts.

Hastie, Alexander Brown

Date of Birth:	April 18, 1914.
Place of Birth:	Dunedin, New Zealand.
Next of Kin:	Mr A J Hastie, Waipukurau (father).
Residence:	Waipukurau.
Employment:	Lorry driver.
Marital Status:	Single.
Rank:	Sapper.
Service number:	33750.
Place of Capture:	Crete.
Date of Capture:	MI.
Interned:	Stalag VIIIB.
POW number:	5257.

19th NZ Army Troops Co, Engineers, 2nd New NZEF, 3rd Echelon.

At Tymbakion was registered I-48 in tent 6 signed the shorts.

Heenan, Colin William

Date of Birth:	February 9, 1911.
Place of Birth:	New Zealand.
Next of Kin:	Mr W Heenan, Kaikorai, NZ Dunedin, New Zealand.
Residence:	Greenock Street, Kaikorai, Dunedin, NZ.
Employment:	Farm hand truck driver.
Marital Status:	Single.
Service number:	8571.
Rank:	Driver.
Place Captured:	Sfakia, Crete.
Date Captured:	June 1, 1941.
Internment:	Stalag VIIIB, Lamsdorf.
POW number:	5411.

New Zealand Petrol Co, 2 Division Supply Column, NZEF.
At Tymbakion was registered I-47, in tent 9 signed the shorts.

Herbert, Cyril M

Date of Birth:	October 4, 1916.
Place of Birth:	Coventry, England.
Next of Kin:	MI.
Residence:	MI.
Employment:	MI.
Service number:	S/14217.
POW number:	4539.
Rank:	Lance Corporal.
Place of Capture:	Sfakia, Crete.
Date of Capture:	June 1, 1941.

Royal Army Service Corp, BEF.
At Tymbakion was registered T-35, in tent 3, signed the shorts.

Hewett, Arthur Albert

Date of Birth:	May 31, 1914.
Place of Birth:	London, England.
Next of Kin:	MI.
Residence:	MI.
Employment:	MI.
Service number:	2197321.
Rank:	Sapper.
POW number:	4576.
Place of Capture:	Sfakia, Crete.
Date of Capture:	June 1, 1941.
Internment:	Stalag VIIIB, Lamsdorf.

Royal Army Engineer, BEF.
At Tymbakion was registered T-36, in tent 2, and signed shorts.

Hodson, Herbert Joseph

Date of Birth:	February 9, 1911.
Place of Birth:	New Zealand.
Next of Kin:	L. Hodson Stevenson Street, Blenheim.
Residence:	Stevenson Street, Blenheim.
Employment:	Lorry driver.
Marital Status:	Single.
Army number:	20661.
Rank:	Bombardier.
Date of Capture:	June 1, 1941.
Place of Capture:	Sfakia, Crete.
Internment:	Stalag VIIIB, Lamsdorf.
POW number:	5437.

28th Artillery, New Zealand Expeditionary Force, Second Echelon.
At Tymbakion was registered I-45 in tent 6, signed the shorts.

Holmes, Howard John

Date of Birth:	August 28, 1917.
Place of Birth:	Gisborne, New Zealand.
Next of Kin:	G A Holmes (father).
Nick-name:	"Slim".
Residence:	McLean Street, Gisborne, New Zealand.
Marital Status:	Single.
Employment:	Tailor.
Rank:	Private.
Service Number:	37054.
Date of Capture:	June 1, 1941.
Place of Capture:	Sfakia, Crete.
Internment:	Stalag VIIIB, Lamsdorf.
POW number:	5119.

19th Infantry Battalion, Second New Zealand Expeditionary Force.
At Tymbakion was registered C-182, in tent 12, signed the shorts.

Holt, Walter Gerald

Date of Birth:	June 13, 1899.
Place of Birth:	Manly, NSW.
Marital Status:	Married Anthea Mack, December 12, 1939.
Employment:	General practitioner in Darlinghurst.
Residence:	Post war Darlinghurst shifted to Wentworth.
Service Number:	NX12348.
Rank:	Captain.
Date of Capture:	June 1, 1941.
Place of Capture:	Sfakia, Crete.
Internment:	Stalag VIIIB Lamsdorf.
POW number:	4601.

2/7th Field Ambulance, Australian Imperial Force.
At Tymbakion was registered T-1, in tent 5, signed the shorts.

Howes, George Richard

Date of Birth:	November 22, 1913.
Place of Birth:	Chatham, England.
Next of Kin:	Mrs Thomas Henry Howes, (mother).
Residence:	Glenview Street, Paddington, Sydney, NSW.
Employment:	Driver.
Marital Status:	Married.
Service Number:	NX2918.
Rank:	Private.
POW number:	4580.
Date of Capture:	May 28, 1941.
Place of Capture:	In hills of Crete.
Internment:	Stalag VIIIB Lamsdorf.

Australian Imperial Forces. 6 Division, A. A. S. C.

At Tymbakion was registered T-37, in tent 6 signed the shorts.

Howie, Frank Freeman

Date of Birth:	September 17, 1906.
Place of Birth:	Perth, Western Australia.
Next of Kin:	Gertrude Howie Paddington, NSW.
Residence:	Adelaide Terrace, Perth, West Australia.
Marital Status:	Single.
Employment:	Truck driver.
Rank:	Private.
Service Number:	WX 2348.
Date of Capture:	June 4, 1941.
Place of Capture:	Rethymno, Crete.
Internment:	Stalag VIIIB Lamsdorf.
POW number:	4523.

2/11, Infantry Battalion. 4th Reinforcements, Aust Imperial Forces.

At Tymbakion was registered T-38, in tent 12 did not sign the shorts.

Hurren, Frederick Henry

Date of Birth:	June 15, 1913.
Place of Birth:	Essex.
Next of Kin:	MI.
Marital Status:	Single.
Employment:	Carpenter.
Rank:	Sergeant.
Service Number:	S/94377.
Date of Capture:	June 1, 1941.
Place of Capture:	Crete.
Internment:	Stalag VIIIB Lamsdorf.
POW number:	4504.

Royal Army Service Corps, BEF.
Tymbakion was registered T-4, in a tent, 9 did sign the shorts.

Jackson, Alexander Peter

Date of Birth:	January 28, 1908.
Place of Birth:	New Zealand.
Next of Kin:	E. Harrison, Wordsworth St, CChurch, NZ.
Residence:	Wordsworth Street, Christchurch, NZ.
Marital status:	Single.
Employment:	Carpenter.
Service Number:	1769.
Rank:	Private.
Date of Capture:	June 1, 1941.
Place of Capture:	Crete.
Internment:	Stalag IVB Muhlberg.
POW number:	5424.

18th New Zealand Battalion. NZEF.
At Tymbakion was registered I-43, in tent 11, signed the shorts.

Johnson, Henry

Date of Birth:	June 15, 1910.
Place of Birth:	Liverpool.
Next of Kin:	MI.
Place of Residence:	MI.
Marital Status:	MI.
Employment:	MI.
Rank:	Gunner.
Service Number:	888099.
Date of Capture:	June 1, 1941.
Place of Capture:	Sfakia, Crete.
Place of Internment:	Stalag VIIIB Lamsdorf.
POW number:	4563.

The Royal Horse Artillery 106 Battalion, 3rd Echelon. 2nd NZEF. Tymbakion was registered T-62, in tent 14, signed the shorts.

Johnstone, Robert Aitcheson

Date of Birth:	February 4, 1918.
Place of Birth:	Malvern, Victoria.
Next of Kin:	Johnstone Robert (father).
Residence:	Christmas: Hills.
Marital Status:	Married.
Employment:	Motor Driver.
Service Number:	VX8887.
Rank:	Private, signalman.
Place Captured:	Crete.
Date Captured:	June 1, 1941.
Internment:	Stalag VIIIB.
POW number:	4550.

2/7th Battalion, AASC, AIF

At Tymbakion was registered T- 40, in tent 13, signed the shorts.

Jones, Frederick Cyril Charles

Date of Birth:	September 6, 1919.
Place of Birth:	London, England.
Next of Kin:	Mrs M. Jones Eastwood's Avenue, Porirua.
Residence:	Eastwood's Avenue, Porirua.
Marital Status:	Single.
Employment:	Concrete worker.
Rank:	Sapper.
Army Service Number:	34810.
Date of Capture:	June 1, 1941.
Place of Capture:	Crete.
Internment:	Stalag VIIIB Lamsdorf.
POW number:	5302.

19th Army Troops Co, Second NZEF, 3rd Echelon, NZ Engineers.
At Tymbakion was registered I-40, in tent 5 did not sign shorts.

King, Andrew

Date of Birth:	February 11, 1901.
Place of Birth:	Mudgee, New South Wales.
Next of Kin:	Charles King, Lee St, Wellington, NSW.
Residence:	Lee Street, Wellington, NSW.
Marital Status:	Single.
Employment:	Labourer.
Service Number:	NX5424.
Rank:	Gunner.
Date of Capture:	June 1, 1941.
Place of Capture:	Sfakia, Crete.
Internment:	Stalag VIIIB, Lamsdorf.
POW number:	4590.

2/3 Australian Infantry Battalion, AIF.
At Tymbakion registered T-4, in tent 13, but didn't sign the shorts.

Kirk, James

Date of Birth:	February 25, 1904.
Place of Birth:	London, England.
Next of Kin:	M. Walling, 29 Darnley Rd, More St, Hackney, London, UK (sister).
Residence:	Pacific Hotel, Hastings, N. Zealand.
Marriage:	Single.
Employment:	Farmer's Labourer.
Rank:	Private.
Battalion:	2 Battalion (Wellington).
Service Number:	30071.
Date of Capture:	June 1, 1941.
Place of Capture:	Crete.
Place of Internment:	Stalag VIIIB Lamsdorf.
POW number:	4593.

22nd Wellington Battalion, 2nd NZEF.

At Tymbakion was registered I-32, was in tent 12, signed the shorts.

Kollias, Anastasios

A Greek citizen who befriended some of the Allies as a prisoner of war on Crete. At Tymbakion was not registered but was in tent 1 and signed the shorts.

Lechmere, Richard James

Date of Birth:	November 17, 1914.
Place of Birth:	MI.
Residence:	The Fleet, Fittleworth, Sussex, England.
Next of Kin:	MI.
Employment:	MI.
Rank:	Driver.
Date of Capture:	June 1, 1941.
Place of Capture:	Crete.
Place of Incarceration:	Stalag VIIIB Lamsdorf.
Service Number:	T/203874.
POW number:	4616.

No. 1 Reserve MT Coy, Royal Army Service Corps, BEF.
At Tymbakion was registered T-91, in tent 9, signed the shorts.

Leviston, Aubrey Reginald

Date of Birth:	October 13, 1918.
Place of Birth:	Ballarat, Victoria.
Next of Kin:	Mrs D. Leviston (mother).
Residence:	Anderson Street, Ballarat Victoria, Aust.
Marital Status:	Single.
Employment:	Timber worker.
Service Number:	VX7803.
Place of enlistment:	Wonthaggi, Victoria.
Date of Capture:	June 1, 1941.
Place of Capture:	Sfakia, Crete.
POW number:	4568.
Place of Incarceration:	Stalag VIIIB Lamsdorf.

2/7th Battalion, Australian Imperial Force.
At Tymbakion was registered T-42, in tent 13, signed the shorts.

Lythgoe, James Frederick 'AKA Rocky'

Date of Birth:	September 27, 1922.
Place of Birth:	Salford, England.
Next of Kin:	Frederick Lythgoe, father, labourer.
Places of Residence:	MI.
Marital Status:	Single.
Employment:	MI.
Rank:	Private.
Date of Capture:	June 1, 1941.
Place of Capture:	Crete.
Service Number:	4915533.
Internment:	Stalag VIIIB Lamsdorf.
POW number:	4547.

South Staffordshire Regiment, BEF.

At Tymbakion, I was registered I-35 in tent 13 and signed the shorts.

Magee, John James

Date of Birth:	MI.
Place of Birth:	MI.
Next of Kin:	E. Magee, Day St, Newton, Auckland NZ.
Residence:	Day Street, Newton, Auckland, NZ.
Marital Status:	Single.
Employment:	Storeman.
Rank:	Sapper.
Service Number:	32086.
Date of Capture:	June 1, 1941.
Place of Capture:	Crete.
Place of Internment:	Stalag VIIIB Lamsdorf.
POW number:	5496.

19th Army Troops Company, Second NZEF.

At Tymbakion was registered I-41, in tent 2 sign the shorts.

Manoy, Phillipp Herman

Date of Birth:	January 25, 1910.
Place of Birth:	Motvera, New Zealand.
Next of Kin:	A. I. Manoy, The Terrace, Wellington, NZ.
Residence:	MI.
Marital Status:	Single.
Employment:	Warehouseman.
Service Number:	7747.
Rank:	Staff Sergeant.
Place of Capture:	Crete.
Date of Capture:	June 1, 1941.
Place of Internment:	Stalag IIIC Lubben.
POW Number:	4541.

19th Army Troops Company Engineers, 1st Echelon, Second NZEF.
At Tymbakion was registered T-5, in tent 6, signed the shorts.

Matthews, Albert

Date of Birth:	September 22, 1916.
Place of Birth:	Wolverhampton, England.
Next of Kin:	MI.
Residence:	MI.
Marital Status:	MI.
Employment:	Morce.
Service number:	8895.
Rank:	Fusilier.
Place of Internment:	Stalag VIIIB Lamsdorf.
POW number:	4581.

British Expeditionary Force.
At Tymbakion was registered T-43, in tent 6, did not sign the shorts.

McDonald, Leonard Edwin

Date of Birth:	MI.
Place of Birth:	MI.
Next of Kin:	Mrs M. F. McDonald (wife), Belmont Road,
Places of Residence:	Paeroa, Aberdeen Road, Gisborne, NZ.
Marital Status:	Married.
Employment:	Hairdresser.
Rank:	Sapper.
Service Number:	22289.
Date of Capture:	June 1, 1941.
Place of Capture:	Crete.
Place of Internment:	Stalag VIIIB, Lamsdorf.
POW number:	4566.

21st (Auckland) Infantry Battalion, 2nd Echelon, 2nd NZEF.

At Tymbakion was registered T-18, in tent 13 signed the shorts.

McInerney, John Patrick

Date of Birth:	October 26, 1910.
Place of Birth:	Wingen, New South Wales, Australia.
Next of Kin:	C. McInerney, Aberdeen St, Scone, Aust.
Residence:	MI.
Marital Status:	Married.
Employment:	Labourer.
Rank:	Private.
Service Number:	NX 8406.
Date of Capture:	June 1, 1941.
Place of Capture:	Tymbakion, Crete.
Place of Internment:	Stalag VIIIB, Lamsdorf.
POW number:	4519.

22nd N Z Division Signals, NZEF.

At Tymbakion was registered I-28 in tent 1, signed the shorts.

McKain, Frederick James Dunmore

Date of Birth:	August 28, 1902.
Place of Birth:	New Zealand.
Next of Kin:	M. E. McKain, Newton Road, Auckland.
Residence:	Newton Road, Auckland, New Zealand.
Marital Status:	Married but separated.
Rank:	Signalman.
Service Number:	6488.
Date of Capture:	June 1, 1941.
Place of Capture:	Crete.
Place of Internment:	Stalag VIIIB, Lamsdorf.
POW number:	4520.

2nd N Z Division Signals, Battalion, Army, NZEF.
At Tymbakion was registered I-22, in tent 12 signed the shorts.

McLean, Alexander

Date of Birth:	June 25, 1914.
Place of Birth:	Ayr, Scotland.
Next of Kin:	Miller, Suffolk Street, Ashburton, NZ.
Residence:	Suffolk Street, Ashburton, NZ.
Marital Status:	Married.
Employment:	Truck Driver.
Rank:	Driver.
Service Number:	7902927.
Date of Capture:	May 26, 1941.
Place of Capture:	Maleme, Crete.
Internment:	Stalag VIIIB, Lamsdorf.
POW number:	4506.

Royal Armoured Corps, NZEF.
At Tymbakion was registered T-48, in tent 9, signed the shorts.

Miller, John Walter

Date of Birth:	October 12, 1913.
Place of Birth:	Christchurch, New Zealand.
Next of Kin:	M. Miller, Suffolk Street, Ashburton, NZ.
Residence:	Suffolk Street, Ashburton, NZ.
Marital Status:	Married.
Employment:	Truck Driver.
Employment:	Driver.
Service Number:	7527.
Date of Capture:	June 1, 1941.
Place of Capture:	Crete.
POW number:	4608.
Internment:	Stalag VIIIB. Lamsdorf.

1st New Zealand Supply Company, NZEF.
At Tymbakion was registered T-44, in tent 10 signed the shorts.

Mitchell, Bernard

Date of Birth:	October 11, 1914.
Place of Birth:	Grimsby, England.
Next of Kin:	MI.
Residence:	MI.
Marital Status.	MI.
Employment:	MI.
Service Number:	4973574.
Rank:	Private.
Date of Capture:	June 1, 1941.
Place of Capture:	Sfakia, Crete.
Internment:	Stalag VIIIB, Lamsdorf.
POW number:	4573.

1st Sherwood Foresters. Nottinghamshire & Derbyshire Regs, BEF.
At Tymbakion was registered T-47, in tent 1, signed the shorts.

Molloy, John Joseph

Date of Birth:	May 5, 1916.
Place of Birth:	Arvnine Bank, England.
Next of Kin:	MI.
Residence:	MI.
Marital Status:	Single.
Employment:	MI.
Service Number:	4745238.
Rank:	Private.
Date of Capture:	June 1, 1941.
Place of Capture:	Sfakia, Crete.
Internment:	Stalag VIIIB Lamsdorf.
POW number:	4603.

The York and Lancaster Regiment. BEF.
At Tymbakion T-12 was registered, in tent 1, signed the shorts.

Moss, John

Date of Birth:	February 5, 1916.
Place of Birth:	York, England.
Next of Kin:	MI.
Places of Residence:	MI.
Marital Status:	Single.
Employment:	MI.
Service Number:	4745238.
Rank:	Private.
Date of Capture:	June 1, 1941.
Place of Capture:	Sfakia, Crete.
Internment:	Stalag VIIIB, Lamsdorf.
POW number:	4536.

The York and Lancaster Regiment, 2nd Battalion, BEF.
At Tymbakion was registered T-45, in tent 10, signed the shorts.

Murdoch, Colin

Date of Birth:	October 29, 1912.
Place of Birth:	Stirling.
Next of Kin:	M. Murdoch, Balclutha, New Zealand.
Marital status:	Single.
Employment:	Cook.
Rank:	Driver.
Service Number:	9619.
Date of Capture:	June 1, 1941.
Place of Capture:	Crete.
Internment:	Stalag VIIIB, Lamsdorf.
POW number:	4524.

2nd New Zealand, Expeditionary Force, Echelon 1.
At Tymbakion was registered T-46, in tent 6, did not sign the shorts.

Neale, Ray Errol

Date of Birth:	February 22, 1916.
Place of Birth:	Whanganui, New Zealand.
Next of Kin:	E. S. Neale mother, Matai St, Lower Hutt.
Marital Status:	Single.
Employment:	Labourer.
Service number:	5736.
Rank:	Private promoted to Corporal.
POW number:	5240.
Place of Capture:	Crete.
Date of Capture:	June 1, 1941.
Place of Internment:	Stalag VIIIB, Lamsdorf.

22nd Wellington Batt, New Zealand Second Expeditionary Force.
At Tymbakion was registered I-39, in tent 13, signed the shorts.

Nuttall, James William

Date of Birth:	November 14, 1914.
Place of Birth:	Liverpool, England.
Next of Kin:	MI.
Marital Status:	MI.
Residence:	MI.
Employment:	MI.
Service number:	902868.
Rank:	Gunner.
POW number:	4522.
Place of Capture:	Sfakia, Crete.
Date of Capture:	June 1, 1941.
Place of Internment:	Stalag VIIIB, Lamsdorf.

Royal Artillery, British Expeditionary Force.
At Tymbakion was registered T-49, in tent 12, signed the shorts.

O'Grady, James Clyde

Date of Birth:	April 4, 1914.
Place of Birth:	Walgett, NSW.
Next of Kin:	Mrs Kathleen Shaw.
Marital status:	Single.
Residence:	1949 Alexandria, Cook, N.S.W, Australia.
Employment:	Labourer.
Rank:	Private.
Service Number:	NX 30721.
Place of Capture:	Sfakia, Crete.
Date of Capture:	June 1, 1941.
Internment:	Stalag VIIIB Lamsdorf.
POW number:	4597.

Australian Imperial Force, 2/1st Battalion, AIF.
At Tymbakion was registered as I-24, in tent 1, signed shorts.

Osborn, James J

Date of Birth:	February 17, 1920.
Place of Birth:	Holborn, United Kingdom.
Next of Kin:	MI.
Marital status:	MI.
Employment:	MI.
Rank:	Rifleman.
Service Number:	689851.
Place of Capture:	Crete.
Date of Capture:	June 1, 1941.
Internment:	Stalag VIIIB Lamsdorf.
POW number:	4595.

King's Royal Rifle Corps, British Expeditionary Force.
At Tymbakion was registered T-50 in tent 10 signed the shorts.

Palmer, Thomas George W

Date of Birth:	May 24, 1916.
Place of Birth:	Finsbury, England.
Next of Kin:	MI.
Residence:	Wanstead Park Rd, Ilford, Essex, England.
Marital Status:	MI.
Employment:	Silver and metal spinner.
Rank:	Private.
Service Number:	7347235.
Place of Capture:	Crete.
Date of Capture:	May 24, 1941 (recorded by soldier).
Internment:	Stalag VIIIB Lamsdorf.
POW number:	4526.

Royal Army Medical Corps, British Expeditionary Force.
At Tymbakion was registered T-90, in tent 11 signed the shorts.

Payne, Sydney Robert
Date of Birth:	January 29, 1917.
Place of Birth:	Donnybrook, Western Australia.
Next of Kin:	C. Payne Coro Street, Donnybrook.
Residence:	Donnybrook, Western Australia.
Marital Status:	Single.
Employment:	Labourer.
Rank:	Private.
Service Number:	WX612.
POW number:	4588.
Place of Capture:	Crete.
Date of Capture:	June 1, 1941.
Place of Internment:	Stalag VIIIB.

2/11th Battalion, Australian Imperial Force.
At Tymbakion was registered T-51, in tent 11 did not sign the shorts.

Pearce, Sydney Emden
Date of Birth:	November 13, 1914.
Place of Birth:	Barraba, NSW.
Next of Kin:	Pearce, Joseph (father).
Residence:	1937 Coogee, Watson, NSW, Aust.
Employment:	1937 labourer (wool classer).
Service Number:	NX33248.
Rank:	Corporal.
POW number:	4518.
Place of Capture:	Crete.
Date of Capture:	June 1, 1941.
Internment:	Stalag VIIIB.
POW number:	4518.

Australian Imperial Forces.
At Tymbakion was registered T-53 in tent 11 signed the shorts.

Pedersen, Walter Vernon

Date of Birth:	July 20, 1907.
Place of Birth:	Melbourne, Victoria, Australia.
Next of Kin:	Mrs Christina Pedersen (mother).
Marital Status:	Married.
Employment:	Labourer.
Rank:	Private.
Service Number:	VX 5571.
POW number:	4515.
Place of Capture:	Crete.
Date of Capture:	June 1, 1941.
Internment:	Stalag VIIIB in Germany 1942 – 1945.

2nd/7 Australian Infantry Battalion, AIF, 6th Division,
At Tymbakion was registered T-52, in tent 13, signed the shorts.

Petersen, Charles Amos George Victor

Date of Birth:	August 27, 1913.
Place of Birth:	Bridgetown, Western Australia.
Next of Kin:	Alice Petersen.
Residence:	1936 Manjimup, Western Australia, (Aust Electoral Roll 1903-1980 abode).
Employment:	Farm hand.
Rank:	Private.
Service Number:	WX 571.
POW number:	4538.
Place of Capture:	Massara Bay, Crete.
Date of Capture:	June 1, 1941.
Internment:	Stalag VIIIB, Lamsdorf.

2/11th, City of Perth Battalion, AIF, 6th Division, 1939 – 1945.
At Tymbakion Vic was registered T-55, in tent 5 signed the shorts.

Pestell, Ronald G

Date of Birth:	March, 16th 1915.
Place of Birth:	Connington, England.
Next of Kin:	MI.
Employment:	Driver.
Service Number:	T/73338.
POW number:	4528.
Place of Capture:	Crete.
Date of Capture:	June 1, 1941.
Place of Internment:	Stalag XVIIID, Marburg.

Royal Army Service Corps, BEF.
At Tymbakion was registered T-54, in tent 5, signed the shorts.

Petrou, Ionnis

Greek citizen who befriended some of the Allies while a prisoner of war on Crete.
At Tymbakion in tent 15 signed the shorts.

Pike, Leslie Samuel

Date of Birth:	March 16, 1913.
Place of Birth:	Wellington, England.
Next of Kin:	MI.
Residence:	Sunnyside, Langford, Budville Tauton, Somerset, England.
Marital Status:	Single.
Employment:	Packer.
Rank:	Marine.
Service Number:	PLX 100950.
Date of Capture:	May 25, 1941 (from record).
Place of Capture:	Crete.
Internment:	Stalag VIIIB, Lamsdorf.
POW number:	4553.

British Royal Marine, BEF.

At Tymbakion was registered T-56, in tent 1, did not sign the shorts.

Pooley, Albert E

Date of Birth:	September 17, 1912.
Place of Birth:	Islington, England.
Next of Kin:	MI.
Residence:	44 Ripley Road 7 Kings, Ilford, Essex.
Employment:	Farmer.
Rank:	Driver.
Service Number:	210653.
Date of Capture:	June 1, 1941.
Place of Capture:	Crete.
Internment:	Stalag VIIIB, Crete.
POW number:	4583.

Royal Army Service Corps, no. 2 Reserve, BEF.

At Tymbakion was registered T-57, in tent 10, signed the shorts.

Powell, Ray Edward

Date of Birth:	May 17, 1919.
Place of birth:	Devonport, Tasmania.
Next of Kin:	Noumea Powell.
Places of Residence:	34 Freeman Street, Richmond, Victoria.
Marital Status:	Married Lorraine Mary Burns 1948.
Employment:	Boiler attendant.
Private:	Signalman.
Service Number:	VX1114.
Place of Capture:	Crete.
Date of Capture:	June 17, 1941, reported missing.
Place Internment:	Stalag VIIIB, Lamsdorf.
POW number:	4569.

2/7th Infantry Battalion, Australian Imperial Force.
At Tymbakion was registered T-58, in tent 5, signed the shorts.

Prichard, Jack H

Date of Birth:	September 29, 1916.
Place of Birth:	Abergavenny, England.
Next of Kin:	MI.
Residence:	MI.
Marriage:	MI.
Employment:	MI.
Service Number:	6849702.
Rank:	Rifleman.
Place of Capture:	Crete.
Date of Capture:	June 1, 1941.
Place of Internment:	Stalag VIIIB, Lamsdorf.
POW number:	4600.

The King's Royal Rifle Corps, British Expeditionary Force.
At Tymbakion was registered T-59, in tent 10 signed the shorts.

Pullenayagam, Joseph Patrick (Sri Lankan Citizen)
Date of Birth: April 19, 1911.
Place of Birth: Katahane.
Next of Kin: D. Rees, Junction Hotel, Takata Motupiku.
Marital Status: Single.
Employment: General servant.
Rank: Private.
Service Number: 13237.
POW number: 4522.
Name of Last Ship: *Goalpara*.
Ship's Official Number: 141914.
Date of loss of ship: April 26, 1941.
Place of Internment: Marlag und Milag Nord.
POW number: 7297.
22nd Wellington Battalion. New Zealand Expeditionary Force.
At Tymbakion was registered in tent 6 signed the shorts.

Pyatt, Ernest
Date of Birth: December 31, 1919.
Place of Birth: MI.
Next of Kin: MI.
Place of Residence: MI.
Employment: MI.
Rank: MI.
Service Number: T/182533.
Place of Capture: Crete.
Date of Capture: June 17, 1941 reported missing.
Place Interned: Stalag VIIIB, Lamsdorf.
POW number: 4558.
4th Light Field Ambulance, R.A.S.C., BEF.
At Tymbakion was registered T-60, in tent 1, signed the shorts.

Rainford, Douglas Clyde

Date of Birth:	December 19, 1917.
Place of Birth:	Coff's Harbour, New South Wales.
Next of Kin:	C. Rainford, Baptist Street, Redfern, NSW.
Marital Status:	Single.
Employment:	Labourer.
Place of Capture:	Crete.
Date of Capture:	June 29, 1941.
POW number:	4601.
Interned:	Stalag VIIIB, Lamsdorf.
Rank:	Private.
Service Number:	NX1497.

2/1st Battalion, Australian Imperial Force.
At Tymbakion was registered I-56, was in tent 2, signed the shorts.

Rattenbury, John Albert

Date of Birth:	October 17, 1913.
Place of Birth:	Leichardt, NSW.
Next of Kin:	Mr. Rattenbury, Stoney Creek Rd, behind the wire.
Marital Status:	Single.
Place of Residence:	Hurstville West, Banks, NSW, Australia.
Employment:	Welder/ M-T driver.
Service Number:	NX 6877.
Place of Capture:	Crete.
Date of Capture:	June 1, 1941.
POW number:	5331.
Internment:	Stalag VIIIB, Lamsdorf.

2/1 Battalion, Australian Imperial Force.
At Tymbakion was registered I-38, was in tent 5, signed the shorts.

Rees, Edward

Date of Birth:	May 25, 1910.
Place of Birth:	New Zealand.
Next of Kin:	Mr D. Rees (father), Junction Hotel, Takata.
Residence	Motupiku.
Marital Status:	Single.
Employment:	Grocer's Assistant.
Rank:	Private.
Service Number:	13237.
Date of Capture:	Galatas, Crete.
Date of Capture:	May 27, 1941.
Internment:	Stalag VIIIB, Lamsdorf.
POW number:	4591.

26th Canterbury and Otago Battalion, NZEF

Tymbakion was registered T-61, in tent 5 and signed the shorts.

Rice, Frederick J

Date of Birth:	December 10, 1916.
Place of Birth:	Kensington.
Next of Kin:	MI.
Places of Residence:	MI.
Marriage:	MI.
Employment:	MI.
Service number:	117358.
Rank:	Driver.
Date of Capture:	June 1, 1941.
Place of Capture:	Sfakia, Crete.
Internment:	Stalag VIIIB, Lamsdorf.
POW number:	4594.

Royal Army Service Corps, British Expeditionary Forces.

Tymbakion was registered T-63, in tent 7, and signed the shorts.

Ring, Cyril

Date Born:	July 25, 1910.
Date of Birth:	Perth, Western Australia.
Next of Kin:	Father James H (Jas).
Employment:	Farm hand Woodanilling, WA.
Residence:	Woodanilling, WA.
Rank:	Private.
Service Number:	WX 2058.
Date Captured:	June 24, 1941.
Place Captured:	Rethmynon, Crete.
Internment:	VIIIB Lamsdorf.
POW number:	4540.

2/11th Australian Imperial Force, 3 Reinforcements.
At Tymbakion was registered T-64, in tent 7, and signed the shorts.

Roberts, Geoffrey A

Date of Birth:	December 1, 1915.
Place of Birth:	London, England.
Next of Kin:	MI.
Residence:	MI.
Marriage:	Single.
Employment:	MI.
Rank:	Private.
Service Number:	132569.
Date Captured:	June 1, 1941.
Place Captured:	Crete.
Internment:	Stalag VIIIB, Lamsdorf.
POW number:	4615.

Royal Services Army Corps, British Expeditionary Force.
At Tymbakion was registered I-34, in tent 14, and signed the shorts.

Rogers, John

Date of Birth:	July 31, 1915.
Place of Birth:	South Shields.
Next of Kin:	MI.
Place of Residence:	MI.
Marital Status:	MI.
Employment:	MI.
Rank:	Private.
Service Number:	48797.
Internment:	Stalag VIIIB, Lamsdorf.
Date Captured:	June 1, 1941.
Place Captured:	Crete.
POW number:	4557.

British Expeditionary Force.

At Tymbakion was registered T-65, in tent 2, and signed the shorts.

Scanlon, Edward

Date of Birth:	February 24, 1914.
Place of Birth:	Pontypridd, Wales.
Next of Kin:	MI.
Residence:	MI.
Marital Status:	MI.
Employment:	MI.
Rank:	Sapper.
Service Number:	2197360.
Date of Capture:	June 1, 1941.
Place of Capture:	Crete.
Internment:	Stalag V, Crete then Stalag VIIIB.
POW number:	4587.

Royal Engineers, British Expeditionary Force.

At Tymbakion was registered T-66, in tent 5, did not sign the shorts.

Shaw, Ernest

Date of Birth:	September 14, 1911.
Place of Birth:	Lancashire, England.
Next of Kin:	Mr C. Shaw (Father), Blackball, NZ.
Place of Residence:	Denniston, New Zealand.
Marital Status:	Single.
Employment:	MI.
Rank:	Private.
Service Number:	8613.
Date of Capture:	June 1, 1941.
Place of Capture:	Crete.
Internment:	Stalag VIIIB, Lamsdorf.
POW number:	4525.

4 NZ Res MT Co, New Zealand Expeditionary Forces.
At Tymbakion was registered I-36, in tent 14, and signed the shorts.

Sherriff, Harold

Date of Birth:	March 29, 1897.
Place of Birth:	England.
Next of Kin:	MI
Place of Residence:	Tennyson Road, Kilburn, London.
Marriage:	MI
Employment:	MI
Rank:	Squadron Quarter Master, Sergeant.
Service Number:	10670180.
Date of Capture:	June 1, 1941.
Place of Capture:	Crete.
Internment:	Stalag VIIIB, Lamsdorf.
POW number:	4502.

Royal Army Service Corps. British Expeditionary Force.
Tymbakion was registered T-2 in tent 11 and signed the shorts.

Shirley, Stanley

Date of Birth:	February 3, 1912.
Place of Birth:	New Zealand.
Next of Kin:	MI.
Places of Residence:	Earl Road, Dunedin, New Zealand.
Marital Status:	MI.
Employment:	Baker.
Date of Capture:	June 1, 1941.
Place of Capture:	Crete.
Internment:	Stalag VIIIB, Lamsdorf.
POW number:	4533.
Rank:	Driver.
Service Number:	9036.

49 R.M.T., Second NZ Expeditionary Force, Third Echelon.
Tymbakion was registered T-67, in tent ,4 and signed the shorts.

Singleton, Jack

Date of Birth:	MI.
Place of Birth:	MI.
Next of Kin:	MI.
Places of Residence:	MI.
Employment:	MI.

Royal Artillery, British Expeditionary Force, Royal Artillery.

Date of Capture:	June 1, 1941.
Place of Capture:	Crete.
Internment:	Stalag VIIIB, Lamsdorf.
POW number:	4537.
Rank:	Gunner.
Service Number:	145778

Royal Artillery, British Expeditionary Force, Royal Artillery.
Tymbakion was registered T-68, in tent 11 and signed the shorts.

Skinner, John E

Date of Birth:	June 30, 1914.
Place of Birth:	Nottingham, England.
Next of Kin:	MI.
Place of Residence:	MI.
Marital Status:	Single.
Employment:	MI.
Rank:	Driver.
Service Number:	218039.
Date of Capture	June 1, 1941.
Place of Capture:	Crete.
Internment:	Stalag VIIIB Lamsdorf.
POW number:	4537.

British Expeditionary Force.

Tymbakion was registered T-69, in tent 7, and signed the shorts.

Smith, Loris Richard

Date of Birth:	February 10, 1903.
Place of Birth:	Wellington, NZ.
Next of Kin:	Laura Smith.
Places of Residence:	Blaxland Street, Marrickville, Sydney A.
Marital Status:	Single.
Employment:	Labourer.
Service Number:	NX15308.
Rank:	Private.
POW number:	5530.
Date of Capture:	April 28, 1941 (as recorded by soldier).
Place of Capture:	Sphakia, Crete.
Internment:	Stalag VIIIB, Lamsdorf.

2nd/1 Australian Battalion, Australian Imperial Forces.

At Tymbakion was registered T-70, in tent 10 and signed the shorts.

Stirling, Leslie Douglas

Date of Birth:	January 4, 1919.
Place of Birth:	London, England.
Next of Kin:	MI.
Place of Residence:	18 Bentinck House, Westway, London.
Marital Status:	Married.
Employment:	MI.
Rank:	Private, (Driver), RFN D/Mechanic.
Service Number:	6846877.
Date of Capture:	May 27, 1941.
Place of Capture:	Crete.
Internment:	Stalag VIIIB, Lamsdorf.
POW number:	4517.

1st Battalion Rangers, King's Royal Rifle Corp, 2 Armoured Division, BEF.
At Tymbakion was registered T-85, in tent 8, and signed the shorts.

Stratton, Herbert Ernest

Date of Birth:	April 5, 1918.
Place of Birth:	Manjimup, Western Australia.
Next of Kin:	S. Somers, Belmont, WA.
Marital Status:	MI.
Employment:	Butcher.
Service Number:	WX 547.
Rank:	Private.
Date of Capture:	June 1, 1941.
Place of Capture:	Crete.
Internment:	Stalag VIIIB, Lamsdorf.
POW number:	4561.

2/11th Battalion, Australian Imperial Force.
At Tymbakion was registered T-71 in tent 15 and signed the shorts.

Stubbs, Arthur Gordon

Date of Birth:	May 18, 1902.
Place of Birth:	Oamaru, New Zealand.
Next of Kin:	E. Stubbs Allington Road, Karori, Wellington, NZ.
Places of Residence:	Cornford Street, Karori, Wellington, NZ.
Marital Status:	Married.
Employment:	Mechanic.
Rank:	Lance Corporal.
Service Number	4379.
Date of Capture:	June 1, 1941.
Place of Capture:	Crete.
Place of Internment:	Stalag VIIIB Lamsdorf.
POW number:	5508.

Army New Zealand, Expeditionary Force. Driver, Petrol Co.
At Tymbakion was registered T-119, in tent 14, signed the shorts.

Stuckey, John Edward

Date of Birth:	December, 30, 1915.
Place of Birth:	North Sydney, NSW.
Employment:	Carrier.
Next of Kin:	Mr Edward Stuckey King St, Tempe.
Marital Status:	Single.
Service Number:	NX 11243.
Place of Capture:	Crete.
Date of Capture:	June 1, 1941.
Place of Internment:	Stalag VIIIB, Lamsdorf.
POW number:	4567.

2nd/11 Battalion, Australian Imperial Force.
Tymbakion was registered T-72, in tent 2, signed the shorts

Tatton, John Thomas

Date of Birth:	September 28, 1914.
Place of Birth:	Cannock, England.
Next of Kin:	MI.
Residence:	Well Street, Tunstall, Stoke-on-Trent, Staffordshire.
Marital Status:	Single.
Rank:	Private.
Service Number:	4973903.
Place of Capture:	Sfakia, Crete.
Date of Capture:	June 1, 1941.
Place Interned:	Stalag VIIIB, Lamsdorf.
POW number:	4571.

Sherwood Foresters. 50th D Battalion, Commandos, B E F. Tymbakion was registered T-39, in tent 2, and signed the shorts.

Thompson, James

Date of Birth:	December 23, 1914.
Place of Birth:	Hesleden, England.
Next of Kin:	MI.
Marital Status:	MI.
Rank:	Able seaman.
Service Number:	20790.
Place of Capture:	Maleme, Crete.
Date of Capture:	May 23, 1941.
POW number:	4551.
Internment:	Stalag VIIIB.

Royal Airforce, British Expeditionary Force.
At Tymbakion was registered T-73, in tent 5 and signed the shorts.

Todd, Arthur Skuse

Date of Birth:	May 18, 1910.
Place of Birth:	MI.
Next of Kin:	Mrs A. E. Todd, C/o Post Office, Tomahawk, Dunedin.
Marital Status:	Married.
Employment:	Publican.
Residence:	Brighton, Dunedin, New Zealand.
Service number:	7272.
Rank:	Lance Corporal.
POW number:	4585.
Place of Capture:	Crete.
Date of Capture:	June 1, 1941.
Place of Internment:	Stalag VIIIB, Lamsdorf.

2nd New Zealand Expeditionary Force, 1st Echelon.
At Tymbakion was registered in tent 10 and signed the shorts.

Topia, William

Date of Birth:	February 5, 1917.
Place of Birth:	Hokianga, New Zealand.
Next of Kin:	Mrs Agnes Topia (mother), Hokianga, NZ.
Places of Residence:	Maungaturoto, North Auckland, N.Z.
Employment:	Labourer (Whangarei).
Rank:	Private.
Service Number:	22724.
Place of Internment:	Stalag VIIIB, Lamsdorf.
POW number:	4585.
Place of Capture:	Crete.
Date of Capture:	June 1, 1941.

21st Auckland Infantry, Second New Zealand Expeditionary Force.
At Tymbakion was registered T-74, in tent 10 and signed the shorts.

Tregear, Eric

Date of Birth:	October 13, 1912.
Place of Birth:	Melbourne, Victoria.
Next of Kin:	David McMichael, Foley Street, Kew, Vic.
Places of Residence:	Werrimull, Victoria.
Marital Status:	Single.
Employment:	Labourer.
Rank:	Private.
Service number:	VX 4658.
Stalag of Internment:	Stalag VIII, Lamsdorf.
POW number:	4548.
Date Captured:	May 29, 1941.
Place Captured:	Chania.

2/7th Infantry Battalion, Australian Imperial Force.

At Tymbakion was registered I-30, in tent 14 and signed the shorts.

Tyrer, Eric

Date of Birth:	October 27, 1920.
Place of Birth:	Liverpool, England.
Next of Kin:	MI.
Places of Residence:	MI.
Marital Status:	MI.
Employment:	MI.
Rank:	Gunner.
Service number:	905373.
Stalag of Internment,	Stalag VIIIB, Lamsdorf.
POW number:	4579.
Date Captured:	June 1, 1941.
Place Captured:	Crete.

Royal Artillery, British Expeditionary Force.

At Tymbakion was registered T-27 in tent 1 and signed the shorts.

Veevers, Ralph

Date of Birth:	April 22, 1901.
Place of Birth:	Clitheroe, England.
Next of Kin:	MI.
Places of Residence:	Pendle Road, Clitheroe, Lancashire.
Marital Status:	MI.
Employment:	Plasterer.
Rank:	Gunner.
Service Number:	1441331.
Date of Capture:	May 22, 1942.
Place of Capture:	Crete.
Place of Internment:	Stalag VIIIB, Lamsdorf.
POW number:	4552.

52 Light Anti-aircraft, Royal Artillery Regiment, BEF.
At Tymbakion was registered T-75, in tent 13 and signed the shorts.

Walker, David Alexander

Date of Birth:	July 1, 1916.
Place of Birth:	Gosforth, England.
Next of Kin:	MI.
Places of Residence:	MI.
Marital Status:	MI.
Employment:	MI.
Rank:	Driver.
Service number :	T/111909.
Date of Capture:	June 1, 1941.
Place of Capture:	Crete.
Incarceration:	Stalag VIIIB, Lamsdorf.
POW number:	4572.

Royal Army Services Corps, British Expeditionary Force.
At Tymbakion was registered T-77, in tent 7 and signed the shorts.

Walters, Frank

Date of Birth:	December 15, 1921.
Place of Birth:	Pontefract.
Next of Kin:	MI.
Place of Residence:	Willow Park, Baghill, Pontefract, Yorkshire, England.
Marital Status:	MI.
Employment:	Plumber.
Service Number:	CH/X3473.
Rank:	Marine.
Date of Capture:	May 26, 1941.
Place of Capture:	Maleme, Crete.
POW number:	4543.
Internment:	Stalag VIIIB, Lamsdorf.

Royal Marines. 1st M.N.B.D.O., British Expeditionary Force.
At Tymbakion was registered T-78, in tent 9 and signed the shorts.

Warburton, Harold

Date of Birth:	July 6, 1906.
Place of Birth:	Leeds, England.
Next of Kin:	MI.
Residence:	Andrews Road, Shoeburyness, Essex.
Rank:	Bombardier.
Service Number:	1058195.
Date of Capture:	June 1, 1941.
Place of Capture:	Sfakia, Crete.
Internment:	Stalag VIIIB, Lamsdorf.
POW Number:	4554.

102nd Royal Horse Artillery Battalion, British Expeditionary Army. Tymbakion was registered T-76, in tent 4 and signed the shorts.

Weatherall, William

Date of Birth:	August 4, 1918.
Place of Birth:	West Hartlepool.
Next of Kin:	MI.
Residence:	Hartfield Road, Wimbledon, London, UK.
Employment:	Storekeeper.
Marital Status:	MI.
Service Number:	862968.
Rank:	Gunner.
Date of Capture:	May 29, 1941.
Place of Capture:	Crete.
Internment:	Stalag VIIIB, Lamsdorf.
POW Number:	4535.

Battalion Royal Horse Artillery, British Expeditionary Army.
At Tymbakion was registered T-79, in tent 3 and signed the shorts.

West, Leonard Gordon

Date of Birth:	November 13, 1914.
Place of Birth:	Lilydale, Victoria, Australia.
Next of Kin:	Ada West St Leonard's Rd, Healesville, Vic
Residence:	St Leonard's Rd, Healesville, Victoria, Aust.
Employment:	Labourer.
Marital Status:	Single.
Service Number:	VX 5561.
Date of Capture:	June 1, 1941.
Place of Capture:	Crete.
Internment:	Stalag VIIIB, Lamsdorf.
POW Number:	4586.

2nd/7 Battalion, Australian Imperial Force.
At Tymbakion was registered T-80, in tent 3 and signed the shorts.

Whatling, Clive Joy

Date of Birth:	September 17, 1919.
Place of Birth:	Moreton.
Next of Kin:	MI
Residence:	Knutsford Rd, Moreton, Cheshire, UK.
Service Number:	902385.
Marital Status:	MI.
Rank:	Gunner.
Date of Capture:	June 1, 1941.
Place of Capture:	Sfakia, Crete.
Internment:	Stalag VIIIB, Lamsdorf.
POW Number:	4599.

2nd Armoured Division. Battalion Royal Horse Artillery, BEF.
At Tymbakion was registered T-81, in tent 7 and signed the shorts.

Whitcombe, John Douglas

Date of Birth:	February 12, 1911.
Place of Birth:	Fiji.
Next of Kin:	MI.
Residence:	Emmett St, Herne Bay, Ponsonby, Auckland, NZ.
Marital Status:	MI.
Employment:	Mechanic.
Service number:	227682.
Date of Capture:	June 1, 1941.
Place of Capture:	Sfakia, Crete.
Internment:	Stalag VIIIB, Lamsdorf.
POW Number:	4605.

H. Q. 21st (Auckland), New Zealand Expeditionary Force.
At Tymbakion was registered T-29, in tent 14 and signed the shorts.

Woods, Laurience Samuel

Date of Birth:	January 12, 1917.
Place of Birth:	Perth, Western Australia.
Next of Kin:	William Henry Woods (father).
Residence:	Golding Street, West Perth, WA.
Marital Status:	Single.
Employment:	Truck driver then an engineer.
Service Number:	WX443.
Rank:	Private.
Date of Capture:	June 1, 1941.
Place of Capture:	Retimo, Crete.
Internment:	Stalag VIIIB, Lamsdorf.
POW Number:	4564

2/11th Battalion, Australian Imperial Force, 6th Division.
At Tymbakion was registered T-83, in tent 5 and signed the shorts.

Wynn, Thomas Peter

Date of Birth:	January 4, 1919.
Place of Birth:	Liverpool, England.
Next of Kin:	MI.
Residence:	11 Clarence Street, Liverpool, England.
Employment:	Cook.
Marital Status:	MI.
Service Number:	89637.
Rank:	Gunner.
Date of Capture:	June 1, 1941.
Place of Capture:	Sfakia, Crete.
Internment:	Stalag VIIIB, Lamsdorf.
POW Number:	4577.

106th Royal Horse Artillery, 7th Armoured Division
At Tymbakion was registered T-82, in tent 8 and signed the shorts.

NOTES

Acknowledgements

1. There were 138 prisoners of war taken to Tymbakion, an area on the south coast of Crete in autumn 1941 (Northern Hemisphere time). This number grew to 151 by December 29, 1941. By following these men from May 20, 1941 it was possible to know why they were spirited away to this desolate place.

2. Lustre Force was the name of the Allied troops who were sent to the aid of Greece. Fierce fighting around Mount Olympus resulted in Germany overwhelming the Force. The Australians, British and New Zealanders were ordered to retreat to Athens where an armada of battle ships from the Royal Navy whisked them to Crete.

3. Petersen, C.A.G.V *Diary*. The book describes his amazing methodology. The Petersen Diary is the only reference the researchers found related to Tymbakion.

4. Secrecy of the activities at Tymbakion was evident from the speech by the German commandant at Iraklion as he farewelled the prisoners. There is a similar warning given by the Allies in each soldier's form, *The UK and Allied Countries, World War II Liberated Prisoner of War Questionnaires, 1945-1946*.

5. Other mentions of Tymbakion, post WWII can be found in records such as *Medical Records and The UK and Allied Countries, World War II Liberated Prisoner of War Questionnaires, 1945-1946*. These were invaluable but did not have the details of Vic Petersen's diary.

6. The author numbered all the tents to collect signatures easily. This enabled each man to be part of the story at least three times in the book.

7. The count of 125 who signed the shorts while incarcerated on Crete was agreed upon, although it is possible that more were signed due to fading.

8. Ian Hardie wrote a number of letters home from the Middle East that filled the gaps in the overall story. Another soldier was wearing Hardie's great coat containing a diary in a pocket. This soldier was unfortunately shot and died. The German soldier who fired the fatal bullet found the diary and wrote in it, "This brave man died instantly. He did not suffer." He returned the diary to Ian Hardie's family after the war.

9. Mementos are so valuable in researching historical events.

10. Private William George Henry (Bill) Taylor WX 2061 1945 C Company 2/11th Battalion. *Diary* covers the years 1941 –1945.

11. Wes Olson is the author of *Battalion into Battle*. Wes was astute in starting his research while many Crete veterans were still living and remembering.

12. *Trove* is part of the National Archives of Australia. It is the search engine for newspapers throughout Australia. During the war years, the newspapers kept those at home informed of what was happening to their loved ones. The individual stories can be found in dozens of newspapers. Letters from the front are also published. For online searching for Newspapers, go to www.trove.nla.gov.au

13. Molly Watt, author of *The Stunned and the Stymied,* Westralian Publishers, *1996.*

14. Search engines on the internet are numerous but worth their weight in gold for authors and researchers. The one's listed in this book are reliable and true. Find every serving soldier from Australia online at www.pow-memorialballarat.com.au

Introduction
1. Albert Chamberlain certainly was the keeper of the shorts but finding definitive proof he made the shorts is difficult. Vic Petersen's diary mentions two times he saw men making shorts out of canvas. Albert was a tailor with skill and ability to make the shorts, and he was the one who took them back to New Zealand

2. A thorough search found 125 signatures on the shorts. There may be more, as the shorts were carried through many unusual places before settling in Christchurch, New Zealand. The courier was Albert Chamberlain, who carried the shorts through Salonika, Stalag VIII-B, and the Long March across Poland, Germany, England, and New Zealand.

3. Andrew is a university researcher. He found the shorts and spent hundreds of hours on the project.

4. Tent canvas was often used to make clothing during the Second World War. Vic Petersen mentions the POWs making clothes from discarded canvas in his diary.

5. Evidence agreed with the idea that they were processed together, e.g. at Skines after returning from Sfakia. However, there are men who were never at Skines, so they were processed as POWs elsewhere.

6. Lamsdorf or Stalag VIIIB was a German prison for war captives in Poland. Many of the Crete captives were incarcerated.

7. From January 1945 to May 1945, Hitler opened all stalags and wanted the men to march to Berlin. With the Russians closing in from the east and the Americans and British from the west, he wanted the Allies to be massed in Berlin, the reason being that they would not bomb their own men. The POWs marched here and there without any real idea where they were going. Many died of exposure, cold and lack of food. See en.wikipedia.org "The March 1945" and lamsdorflongmarch.com, *Taking the Long Way Home* by Dave Lovell and Ian Bowley.

8. RSA stands for Royal New Zealand Returned and Services Association. It offers help to all service personnel and their families.

9. Kreta is the Germanic name for Crete. All POWs had the letters KR chalked with their prisoner number on a wooden board then a photograph was taken for recognition.

10. One of the major problems in this research was finding those still alive. Most of our subjects had passed on. Books where authors did make contact back in the 1990s were invaluable, diaries kept by participants, especially the one by Vic Petersen, gave direct descriptions of life at Tymbakion.

11. Unfortunately, most original signing persons were deceased, so the next generation was contacted. Many interesting and successful contacts were made. You would be most welcome to find more. Use the contact addresses if you are interested.

12. The scars were not only due to their experiences of discipline and deprivation by the Germans but also the training they were forced to undergo. Training a civilian into a fighting and killing machine can only happen by breaking down that person's humanness.

13. The Profile section lists all who were proven to be at Tymbakion. The author has divulged as much information about each man as he could. The total number of POWs on the *Norburg* who were offloaded at Iraklion was 200. Some 62 were maintained at Iraklion, and the others went to Tymbakion in September 1941, but every POW was moved to Germany at the end of 1941.

14. Abel Tasman was a Dutch explorer who sighted Tasmania in 1642-1643 and called it Van Diemen's Land. He sailed on to New Zealand.

15. Haka is a traditional Maori war cry, and the yelling and bodily gestures send fear into the enemy. Words to the Haka can be found at www.nzhistory.govt.nz. A Maori soldier roused the Maori Battalion into battle against the Germans on 42nd Street during the Crete War.

16. The Crete people have had continuous wars with surrounding countries. They were pleased to have the Allies arrive to help them keep the Germans off their island.

Chapter 1

1. Adolph Hitler had already decided to attack Russia under the code name Barbarossa. To do this, he needed as many of his troops as possible. By using the POWs to carry out jobs to keep the German economy going and produce money, he could achieve his goal of defeating Russia.

2. What was the question on everyone's lips? Does the truth lie somewhere between planning a selection process and random selection? The Germans would have seen the group as general labourers.

3. Albert Chamberlain, a New Zealander, thought up the idea of making a pair of shorts and having POWs at Tymbakion sign them. The shorts may

have been made later, in December, after the 50 extras were sent to the camp.

4. New Zealand money pre-1967, used pounds, shillings, and pence denoted by the symbols £ / p. A pound was worth 20/-.

5. Joining the army to leave your home and venture thousands of miles away was heart-rending. The question became, 'Stay at home and be safe around your loved ones or venture out for king and country and be paid.' Many men chose the second as a way of securing a solid future.

6. Non-combatant means not carrying arms, including roles such as medics, signalmen and cooks. Many men wanted to support their King and country, and taking a non-combatant role meant not shooting at other humans.

Chapter 2
1. Dorothea MacKellar, (1885, - 1968) was an Australian poet and fiction writer. She penned the poem My Country, which depicts the wildness and beauty of the country.

2. Joseph Banks, a botanist on board the *Endeavour* explored many places and collected specimens of plants and drew the fauna. This information helped the British Government select Sydney Cove as a settlement site 1788.

3. The First World War, 1914-1918, was fought on two fronts over four years. Initially, the diggers were sent to Gallipoli to fight the Turks at Anzac Cove. The steep hills beyond the beach were called Gallipoli. The second place was in Europe, in places like Belgium and France.

4. The Southern Cross is a constellation seen only from the Southern Hemisphere. The larger star on the Australian flag, the Commonwealth Star, has seven points representing the states and territories of Australia.

5. Many types of ball games are played in Australia, with Australian Rules Football the most popular. It is unique to Australia because, unlike soccer, players can use their hands to mark and handball the oddly shaped ball.

6. Binder twine is a natural sisal twine or string and was used for a multitude of purposes on farms.

7. Australia's vegetation is unique and varied. One plant, spinifex is spiny, hardy and found in desert areas.

8. A gun shearer is the best, who can shear more sheep per day than any other shearer. Most sheds have friendly competitions to name their 'gun'.

9. Cuppa is Australian slang for cup of tea. Australia is renowned for its slang and idioms.

10. Bales are filled with the same classed fleece, and a tin stencil with the farm's name is inked on each bale, ready to be sent to the wool stores for sale.

11. Dags are faeces stuck in heavy wool around the anus of the sheep.

12. A pedal radio was invented to communicate between isolated areas in Australia. It generates the power needed to operate, and it can be used by anyone.

13. Swig, a schooner of ale, means to drink a glass of beer.

Chapter 3
1. General Erwin Rommel (1891-1944) was known as the Desert Fox because of his cunning and as a brilliant strategist. He was a German Generalfeldmarschall during World War II. He was the commander of the 7th Panza Division during the successful invasion of France in 1940. This prompted Hitler to send him into North Africa to command the Afrika Korps using Panza tanks to secure victories there. He also served in the Wehrmacht of Nazi Germany, Reichswehr of the Weimar Republic and the army of the Imperial Germany. He was injured multiple times in both wars.

2. Many of the recruits saw the chance to sail away on an adventure and enjoy the opportunity to explore foreign countries they had heard about but were never likely to see or visit.

3. The constant swaying caused many to have seasickness and lay in their bunks for days on end. The sickness is caused by conflict in the inner ear, which confuses the brain as to whether the person is stationary or moving.

4. The Italians joined Germany as partners in the Axis. The Italians were not willing foot soldiers and were poorly trained. In North Africa, they surrendered in their thousands. Many became prisoners of war and were sent to Australia and New Zealand until the end of the war.

5. Leslie Le Souef and Alf Traub were professional in all their dealings with the Germans and respected them, which gained the trust of the German officers. When difficulties arose, these two were able to sort them out.

Chapter 4

1. The Axis powers included several countries, including Japan (which joined in 1940), Italy, Hungary, Romania, Bulgaria, Finland, and Thailand.

2. Lustre Force was the Allied movement of British, Australian, and New Zealand troops from Egypt to Greece in 1941. This was in response to Italy's failed invasion and the high likelihood of a German invasion. The threat was uncovered through the Ultra Intelligence decrypted from March to April 1941.

3. "To War Without a Gun" by Leslie Le Souef. Artlook, 1980 Perth, WA. The book is out of print but can be located through second-hand booksellers.

4. The 2/11th Battalion A I F was the Western Australian Battalion, also known as the City of Perth Regiment.1939 to 1945 Middle East, Greece, Crete, New Guinea.

5. Most of the Allies had not fired a gun in anger at this time and, therefore, still found it like an overseas trip.

6. Desert training was essential as the Allies were not used to such conditions.

7. Corporal J.J. Donovan, *Benalla Ensign*, December 4, 1941, *Trove*.

8. These rocks jutting out of the water were the famed Greek Isles.

9. Athens is built across the Seven Hills, well known in ancient history. These hills are the Acropolis, Areopagus, Philopappou, Hill of the Nymphs, Pnyx, Lycabettus, and Tourkovounia.

10. Mount Olympus is the highest mountain in Greece, at 9000 feet. Much of Greek Mythology is centred around Mount Olympus, where the first Olympic Games were held in 1898.

Chapter 5

1. The location of the Hawke's Bay Regiment in Napier, New Zealand, is idyllic and attractive to young recruits. It was founded in 1863 and was the Napier Volunteer Rifles. Amalgamated with other volunteer corps to form the 9th Regiment in 1911. The Duke of Edinburgh is the Colonel in Chief of the Regiment.

2. Hospital ships were vital to the war effort. The faster the wounded could be placed with specialists, the better their chance of survival. Female nurses manned these surgeries and were a great comfort to the patients.

3. At this time, Hitler was busy planning the invasion of Russia using the code name Barbarossa. He believed Greece's capitulation to his storm-troopers was a matter of days and wouldn't hold up his more important capture. He was proved right in taking Greece, but the Russians were far more difficult.

4. The Germans were too well-armed, and their planning was immaculate. They swept through the Monastir Pass with little resistance. The village of Vevi is 16 miles south of the Yugoslav border and stands at the narrow end of the Monastir Valley. The Germans won the Battle of Vevi in 1941.

5. Brollas Pass is in Greece, and the Germans were far too strong and mobile than the Allied troops. A withdrawal south was ordered. The New Zealand and Australian troops were commanded to hold the pass until the rest of the Allies had escaped from Greece.

6. The German Stukas were designed with special parts attached to the aeroplane to make a screeching noise. The parts were called the Jericho Sirens. These gave out a noise that was designed to confuse and disorientate psychologically those in the vicinity.

Chapter 6

1. The 2/7th Field Ambulance was an Australian Army Medical Corps (AAMC) unit. It was raised at Puckapunyal, Victoria. It had representatives in Palestine, Egypt, Libya, Greece, Crete, Syria, New Guinea and Darwin.

2. The reputation of the New Zealanders and Australians was such that they were called upon to be the rearguard in several engagements. They would hold out for as long as possible and then retreat before defending again. This hopping allowed the rest of the army to get to the rescue ships and sail safely away.

3. The order to spoil and destroy was to lessen the weight of what they carried, making it quicker to move. Secondly, it ensured that the Germans did not get to use that which was discarded.

4. A military strategy of burning or destroying crops or other resources that might be useful to an invading enemy force. Definition from Oxford Reference online oxfordreference.com.

5. A Bren gun can fire 120 bullets per minute sustained and up to 500 practical. With a 303 calibre and good velocity, they could bring a plane down, even more so with their sights trained on an enemy plane.

6. The SS *Costa Rica* was a Dutch passenger steamship built in 1910. She was an Allied troop ship in both World Wars. The sinking of the SS *Costa Rica* off Souda Bay was a story for Private Ray Powell to tell.

7. The SS *Costa Rica* sank after near miss bombs stretched the plates. The *Hereward* and *Defender* went to the crew and passenger assistance. All 2600 on board were saved.

8. The 2/11th Battalion reached the shores of Athens and was rowed out to the Thurland Castle. They were all exhausted but managed to be assisted onto the deck before the ship moved away. The next day the men on the *Thurland Castle* disembarked on Crete.

9. The rumour that did the rounds daily was that Crete would be invaded from the sky.

Chapter 7

1. The New Zealand 28th Battalion was a frontline infantry unit comprised of volunteers. It developed a reputation for bravery and never took a backward step after the action against the Germans at 42nd Street and Maleme.

2. Ian Hardie was an Australian in the 2/11th Battalion. He was a writer and often sent news or ditties to the papers that serviced the Mid-West of Western Australia. He also swapped his name twice with fellow prisoners allowing them to escape.

3. Papers that Ian Hardie had items published; *Meekatharra Chronicle* and *Yalgoo Observer* found in *Trove*. These papers were from businesses in small goldfield towns of West Australia.

4. Quote from a letter Ian Hardie wrote to his fiancée and published in, *The Yalgoo Observer* and *Murchison Chronicle* 1940. He mentions receiving parcels and funds; the soldiers would have all been grateful for these. Army life would have been tough in foreign countries.

5. Most 2/11th soldiers escaping from Greece did so by catching the *Thurland Castle*.

6. Lists of soldiers who fought in World War II were originally kept by the Australian Red Cross before being transferred to the University of Melbourne. Now available online and is a historical list for researchers.

7. Tymbakion was an isolated secret transit camp on the south side of Crete. Communication between inmates and the outside world was pretty much nonexistent. Miss D. Wakefield, the fiancée of Ian Hardie, managed to have a letter delivered to Ian on December 29, 1941.

Chapter 8

1. Oil was the most essential resource for Germany's mechanised army. In the late 1930s, the main source was found in Iran. Hitler wanted to capture Iran so Germany could control the oil output.

2. Women were not used in combat, but many volunteered to be nurses. Injured or ill troops most welcomed their presence in surgeries and hospital wards.

3. Before moving to the battlefield of northern Greece, the officers gave every man a one day furlough. This recreational day was welcomed to settle the nerves and build camaraderie before the battle.

4. The agricultural areas of Greece were blossoming as it was spring. The Northern Hemisphere has a different sequence of seasons than the Southern Hemisphere. This confused the soldiers from the antipodean countries like Australia and New Zealand.

5. Airmail was in its infancy and would have been rare. To get a letter or card from New Zealand to London and then onto the battlefield would have taken many aircraft hops across many countries in small fixed-wing planes.

6. The Mackay Force at Klidi Pass was a battle between the Allies and Germans. The Allies were under the command of Iven Mackay.

7. Bralos is a small town in northern Greece. This was a battlefield that went against the Allies with many casualties. It was also the place where the Allies saw the full thrust of the German Army.

8. The Thermopylae Line was a defence line set up by the Allies. It was here that the Allies realised that the German Army was too strong and organised for them so they withdrew. The Australian and New Zealand battalions were left to be rearguards, leapfrogging as they moved down the Greek Archipelago. This gave time for the rest of the Allies to reach Athens and find a warship to take them to the safety of Crete.

Chapter 9

1. Sir Winston Churchill was the Prime Minister of Great Britain and insisted that help be sent to northern Greece to stop the flow of Germans into Greece.

2. The acronym ANZAC was popularised during the Gallipoli Campaign when the Australians and the New Zealanders fought side by side against

the Turkish forces. Anzac stands for Australian and New Zealand Army Corps.

3. Tobruk was a small coastal North African town that played an important part in the history of the Second World War. Between April and August 1941, the garrison was besieged by the Afrika Korps under the command of General Rommel. While the Allies, who became known as the Rats of Tobruk, fought to stay alive, members of Lustre Force were sailing from Alexandria to Greece.

4. Private Alf Traub WX858, who was Jewish, was a soldier for all seasons. He trained in Northam, West Australia, and joined the 2/11th Battalion. He was fluent in both English and Yiddish, having learned the latter from his parents. Yiddish is historically a West Germanic language. He became an interpreter for officers and his fellow soldiers.

After the war, Alf Traub applied to have his promotion recognised due to his acting as an interpreter. The army refused this. He was never recognized as having the rank of sergeant he deserved.

5. Peter Ewer, *Forgotten Anzacs: The Campaign in Greece 1941*, Scribe Publications, London, UK, 2016.

6. Alan Clark, *The Fall of Crete*, Cox and Wyman Ltd, London, UK, 1962, considered the Stuka cumbersome and slow. Due to their noise as they dived, the Allies considered them terrifying.

7 Warships to the rescue in moving the Allies from Greece to Crete. The ship's personnel were amazing to be able to operate in the dark, offshore and with a war raging all around.

8. The Germans were at a distinct advantage because they would have seen the supplies that were left behind when the Allies left Greece. A simple calculation would have put them well to the fore in strength.

9. The loss of his favourite weapon, a Boys anti-tank rifle, left Alf Traub feeling unarmed (which he was).

10. Although most of the 2/11th battalion were taken on board the *Thurland Castle* to leave Greece, there were some, like Alf Traub, who found themselves on the HMS *Hasty*.

11 Rumour kept the Allies guessing in the field. General Freyberg was in the know because he had the decryption to the German's ULTRA code.

Chapter 10

1. They get their name, White Mountains, from the water laden limestone terrain that gleams silvery white in bright sunshine.

2. The British had the good fortune to capture the German communication code ULTRA, which allowed them to know exactly what the Germans were planning.

3. The Argyll and Sutherland Highlanders were attacked on their way back to the south side of Crete. This action saw the loss of hundreds and the abandonment of some MLCs (motorised landing crafts).

4. In their haste to leave Greece, the soldiers were ordered to dispose of their arms. They landed on Crete with few guns and low calibre rifles. The Allies on Crete were poorly equipped to fight the Germans who invaded Crete.

5. General Freyberg's brilliant tactic was to set up sectors on the island's north side. Each sector was to defend its area and keep the Germans from capturing the airfield and the port.

Chapter 11

1. Peter Brune, in his book We Brand of Brothers, pointed out that the Australian, New Zealand and British forces on Crete were short on men and weapons. For instance, Brigadier Puttick, in command of the New Zealand contingent, was short of soldiers but did have all his divisional personnel.

2. The British contingent was far more war ready than the others, wrote Peter Brune in his book *We Brand of Brothers*.

3. Continuing with numbers, Peter Brune, *We Brand of Brothers,* noted that the Greeks consisted of eight recruit battalions that were poorly equipped and had little in the way of weapons and ammunition. In addition, there was a large number of Greeks in three garrison battalions.

4. General Freyberg worked his defence of the four sector system. This covered the northern area of Crete, where the German invasion was assumed to be coming from.

5. The Australian defence was oddly divided into two parts. One group was in Heraklion, and the other was in Georgioupoli to Rethymno.

6. The northern beaches were divided into four sectors.

7. The leader's address to the troops at Neo Chorio made them believe that Freyberg was a great leader. This changed as the invasion raged.

8. Generally referred to as the battle on the Eastern Front. The freezing winters and determination of the Russians eventually beat the Germans.

9. The German invasion plan was the idea of General Kurt Student, who seized on the success of former blitzes in the Lowlands. Properly trained and well-orchestrated, the plan may have worked. It turned into chaos and unnecessary deaths caused by their own. These paratroopers were a branch of the Luftwaffe.

10. Even though the Allies had the Ultra code from the Germans and knew the invasion was to be on May 20, many gave up believing this. They became frazzled with the numerous rumours rather than the factual information in the Ultra messages. If they had listened, they would not have been wandering to the beach and ending up in the midst of the first wave of the German invasion. If you hear something repeatedly but nothing happens, you eventually decide it won't happen.

11. When men lose their battalion due to hospitalisation or movement, they are placed in an X Battalion and operate under an officer until they can be reunited with their original battalion.

12. Every morning, the Germans sent a reconnaissance aeroplane over Crete to take photographs. This was called the Shufti plane, which is Arabic and means, "Have you seen?"

13. The German word gebirgs means mountains. The 5th Gebirgs Division, or 5th Mountain Division, was an elite formation of the German Wehrmacht.

14. General Student was the architect of the airborne invasion. He trained the crack German *Fallschirmjagers*. *Crete The Battle and the Resistance,* Antony Beevor, John Murray (Publisher), 1991.

Chapter 12

1. The morning of the invasion is described in Wes Olson's *Battalion into Battle*. Quality Press, 2011, Welshpool, West Australia.

2. Under the direction of the German Major General Kurt Student, the plan to invade Crete was established around an airborne attack. The plan was to capture strategic positions using Fallschirmjager (to capture the three airfields) and then bring in more troops. In the meantime, an armada of ships and troops would sail from the north to assist.

3. Wes Olson's *Battalion into Battle*. Quality Press, 2011, Welshpool, WA, p155.

4. During the airborne blitz, the Germans faced a lot of problems, which caused the death toll to rise well above expectation. The Allies watched the parachutists float in waves before firing in defence.

5. The coloured parachutes marking the canister's load took the Allies time to digest. They were not totally aware that they needed to reach these before the Germans and thus cut off the vitals the Germans needed.

6. Edgar Randolph in WX908, Wes Olson: *Battalion into Battle,* page 157.

7. The key to German success in parachuting onto Crete was getting to the bigger canisters where the larger weapons were packed.

Chapter 13

1. One of the most important needs for the Australian and New Zealander troops was to become acclimatized to desert conditions. The New Zealanders and the mostly city bred Australians had never been in an environment of sand, sand storms, sandflies and days on end of hot weather. It was easy to become lost in the continuous and identical scenery.

2. 'The danger that lurked' was a reference to the German Navy and Army.

3. *HMS Hasty* was a British warship that came to the rescue of troops who were trapped in Greece. Many of the troops were Australians from the 2/11th Battalion. The Hasty ferried the soldiers to Crete.

4. The Royal Navy not only moved 40,000 troops from Greece but also tons of equipment and medical supplies.

5. The Australian 2/11th Battalion was to defend Hill 107 and Maleme Airfield. It was critical to defend Maleme Airfield. In the days after Maleme was secured, the Germans, in desperate action, sent a group of commandos to take the airfield in the dead of night.

6. 42nd Street was a main track in Crete running along the northern coast. It became famous during the Crete War when a German patrol was confronted by the New Zealand Maori 28th Battalion, the Australian 2/11th and some of the local Cretans. The Maoris, screaming the Haka led an attack followed by the Australians and the Cretans, put the Germans to the sword.

7. The Haka is a traditional Maori war cry used to frighten the enemy. The noise and words are backed up with facial expressions and poking out of

the tongue. *The Sun* (UK) September 29, 2013, published a story about the Haka and included the lyrics. See www.thesun.co.uk

8. Ponuate Busby was a Maori in the New Zealand 28th Battalion. He was the only Maori left in Crete at the beginning of September 1941 and became one of the last ones left in Crete.

Chapter 14

1. Interview with Alf Traub early in the 1990s by Wes Olson: *Battalion into Battle* pp 366–369. The interview covered a lot of the May 20 to June 6 period.

2. The Cretans did not have many weapons, so they had virtually no defence. Their only means of fighting off an aggressor lay within their houses and barns.

3. The local population of Perivolia attacked the German parachutists who landed near their township. They used non-military weapons which was to have dire implications later on. Wes Olson: *Battalion into Battle*.

4. Spontaneous mobilisation is the formation of a fighting group by the local population when they find themselves being overrun by an enemy.

5. Father Stylianos Frantzeskakis was a leader and was not going to tolerate the German invasion of his country and countrymen. His willingness to take up arms and march to the front of his flock was truly inspiring. Beevor, A., *Crete*, John Murray, London 2005.

6. Many of the Allies were aware of the reprisal executions and would verbally protest given the chance. There was little else they could do.

7. General Ringel commander of the 5th Mountain Division of Parachutists was adamant that reprisals must be carried out as an example to stop further killings by civilians.

8. The top Nazi who agreed with the reprisal system was General Goering. He ordered the killings and razing of towns. After the war, he was placed before the War Crimes Committee, and the reprisals were one of the issues he was charged with.

9. On June 1, 1941, General Freyberg decided that too many of his men were being gunned down, so he decided to capitulate. He told all field officers to surrender on June 1, 1941, at dawn. The soldiers took the news badly, and many were disgusted with having to fly the white flag. Further anger arose because Freyberg and his officer entourage escaped Crete, leaving thousands behind who would now go behind the wire.

Chapter 15

1. This is a typical action by Alf Traub, who put his fellow humans ahead of himself. He was selfless.

2. A rearguard action by the Australians and New Zealanders to buy time for those escaping by sea.

3. The effort by the Allies to move thousands of troops from the north side to the south side of Crete in less than three days was an amazing feat.

4. The expression 'rage fluttering' was used by Le Souef, Leslie., *To War Without a Gun,* Artlook, Perth, 1980, means extreme anger.

5   The withdrawal by the officers on Crete caused a great deal of angst among the foot soldiers. General Freyberg was considered to have snuck

away with his entourage leaving the soldiers leaderless. Certainly, Alf Traub was not impressed, nor were the thousands of others forced to surrender.

Chapter 16

1. Leslie Le Souef was not one of the 151 group, however, his heroics in field medicine meant many of that group had survived.

2. Surrender was a word no Allied soldier believed he would hear, never mind say aloud. Le Souef, Leslie, *To War Without a Gun*, Artlook, Perth, 1980 awoke to hear the men murmuring about surrender. The order had come from General Freyberg, much to the chagrin of the men. General Freyberg left a dismayed force that believed he should have shown leadership and fought longer.

3. The last ships to sail from Sfakia on June 1, 1941, were the cruiser *Phoebe*, destroyers *Kimberley*, *Hotspur* and *Jackal* and minelayer *Abdiel*. 3710 troops landed at Alexandria and 54 senior officers by Sunderland flying boat.

4. Molly Watt, author of the book *The Stunned and The Stymied*, described the morning of the surrender and the anticipation of the arrival of the Germans.

5. William (Bill) Gunther brought the message of surrender to Le Souef. His reaction was one of disbelief and disgust. Like most of the Australians, he could not fathom the idea of 'surrender'.

6. The final chapters describe some of the men's changes since leaving home and their experiences fighting before being incarcerated in prisoner-of-war camps.

7. Rare as it was, suicide was an outcome for some who were living on the edge at a time of great stress.

8. The soldier who voided had no control over his bodily functions and the intensity of the stress he felt must have been extreme.

9. Described by Le Souef in *To War Without a Gun*, Artlook, Perth, 1980, page 145.

10. Le Souef, *To War Without a Gun*, Artlook, Perth, 1980.

11. The expression "run for the hills" was added to the Australian vernacular on June 1, 1941.

12. Le Souef, *To War Without a Gun*, p146. Upon observing every man's facial expression Leslie saw, "resignation, consternation and incredulity."

13. Le Souef, *To War Without a Gun*, p147.

14. Maleme Airfield was badly messed up, so taking off was not for the faint-hearted or the wounded. There were so many wounded and ill that the exodus of these patients to Greece took most of June and July.

15. Le Souef, *To War Without a Gun*,

16. The Cretans' friendliness and concern for the Allies shone through at Kalyves. Despite German disapproval, the locals brought food for the prisoners.

17. The disaster of the evacuation from Sfakia would forever be etched in the men's lives.

18. Another officer of the 2/11th Battalion was Major Raymond Sandover.

19. C.A.G.V. (Vic) Petersen kept a diary from the June 6, 1941. It was in the form of pieces of paper that amounted to a considerable number by the time of his liberation.

20. The Sandover group were all from the 2/11th Battalion.

21. Greek coin is called drachma.

22. The bravery of such a young child to be out at night looking to help the Allies is amazing. There was a war going on and German patrols everywhere, yet here he was helping the Sandover group.

23. Another example of the helpful Cretans and the way they all pitched in to assist the Allies.

24. The Cretan men were volunteering to go many miles out of their way to assist the Sandover and Honner groups.

25. The escapers were trying to locate a boat of sorts that would be seaworthy enough to get to Egypt. The MLCs were left over from the Argyll Black Watch expedition.

26. To deny another human being food and water was related to punishment and sapped energy from the captive thus making escape impossible.

27. Idecca, a small township in the hills of Crete. There were many such small towns dotted throughout Crete. C.A.G.V Petersen, *Diary 1941*.

28. First entry by Vic Petersen in his diary 1941.

Chapter 17

1. An interesting read. Petersen, C.A.G.V *Diary*.

2. There are over 100 poisonous snakes in Australia and four in Crete.

3. All names used throughout the book are real but the activities and discussions are fictitious.

4. See note 3.

5. See note 3.

6. Transit camp conditions were poor, so the men tried to get improvements by whatever means was possible.

7. They were referred to as transit camps because the men stayed only a short time before moving through Salonika and into Germany to more permanent camps in poor and brutal conditions. Often, the men challenged the authority of the Germans. As observed in Petersen's diary, C.A.G.V. German discipline was extremely harsh. There appear to be about five transit camps on Crete referred to as I to V.

8. Hopelessness was a major issue for prisoners of war, especially after the humiliation of surrender. They felt they had nothing to lose by trying to escape.

9. Quote from Petersen, C.A.G.V *Diary*.

10. Hygiene was not a priority but when it was possible to wash, the men delighted in the cleanliness.

11. See note 3.

12. A metal dish with a handle that can be used for cooking and eating out of. Usually compact, it is easy to carry in their pack.

13. Use of such cruel punishment was seen as important to keep others in line.

14. Ray Blechynden WX 619 from 2/11th Battalion showed up in many places during the latter half of 1941. Identified by Vic.

15. Quote from Petersen, C.A.G.V *Diary*. Tongue in cheek comment re weight and poor nutrition. Poor diet saw men lose condition resulting in weakness and fatigue.

16. Very serious illness resulting in paralysis below the neck. The lungs don't pump oxygen around the body so doctors placed patients in iron lungs to assist this process.

17. Vic thought the German food was sub-standard and not to his liking and said as such.

18. Was this where the canvas shorts were made? The signatures indicate the shorts were definitely handed around at Tymbakion. Therefore, the canvas shorts could have been made before Vic got to Tymbakion or, at the latest, at Tymbakion.

19. A random selection of the 151. They were real men but they may not have been in this exercise.

20. Vic continued to hear names and record them feeling that these men were being specially selected.

21. 'Bite the dust' is an Australian idiom meaning to crash or fall heavily and to die doing so.

22 Amazing how rumours and news circulated through the prison camps.

23. The *Norburg* was an old coastal freighter used to move POWs from Crete to Salonika.

24. This was the start of the mystery, 200 men packed in the hold of the *Norburg* awaiting their disembarkment.

25. The decision to sail was withheld for four days. The men were used to do odd jobs on the wharf while awaiting the *Norburg* sailing.

26. Vic Petersen was not able to swim and feared drowning while on a boat. Swimming was not part of the syllabus at schools, the army or at home.

27. The news that the torpedo had missed was well received, especially by those terrified on their first journey.

28. The *Norburg* was torpedoed while tied to the wharf. It was damaged and was in need of repair.

29. The truck convoy transferred 138 men over the mountains. No one knew they were headed for Tymbakion.

30. Ian Hardie WX2371 was a West Australian in the 2/11th battalion. At one stage in Stalag VIII-B, he swapped identities with another prisoner,

Sergeant T. E. Allanson, Royal Air Force. He repeats this again, becoming Sergeant C. J. Woodroffe of the Royal Air Force. He was considered a hero for his willingness to assist others to escape.

31   There were 62 men left at Iraklion who were most likely to be used to clean up Heraklion Airfield.

32   Cain killed his brother Abel. God then cursed Cain, sentencing him to a nomadic life. Cain lived in the land of Nod (Arabic for wandering), where he built a city and fathered a line of descendants beginning with Enoch. This story is from the Old Testament of the Bible.

33. The fence surrounded the entire area and was very isolated. It was 6 to 8 feet high and made of barbed wire strands.

34. A Horticulturist is an educated person in agriculture who knows about growing and managing plants.

Chapter 18

1.   A comprehensive, day-by-day blow of the life of a prisoner of war during the Second World War. Vic was able to name the place, Tymbakion.

2.   Victor Petersen did not have a diary per se. He wrote daily comments on small pieces of paper. He began on June 6, 1941 and wrote a comment almost every day. He would have returned to Australia in May 1945 which would have amounted to nearly 1400 pieces of paper. Vic's brother's daughter-in-law offered to type these into a chronological diary.

3. When first on the beach in early June, the escapers saw a signpost indicating the location of Tymbakion. Some men standing on the beach in September also saw the signpost in June.

4. The term ute is an Australian shortened form of utility.

5. The word Khyber is Australian slang for backside.

6. Tymbakion Prisoner of War Camp was a transit camp meant for a short period before the prisoners were moved to the mainland and Germany. Inmates of Tymbakion were registered as Kreta Camp V and then their POW number.

7. There were 12 Royal Air Force personnel at Tymbakion. The narrative assumes they arrived before the main bulk of prisoners, who arrived on September 12, 1941. Richardson was a real person. He was randomly selected for the position in the story but may not have been the real officer in charge.

8. The RAF boys worked in the area. The history records place 12 RAF men at Tymbakion from September 1941 to October 1941 before being moved to Athens. They were not available to sign the shorts according to the timeline. Petersen, C.A.G.V *Diary*. According to wartime protocol, airmen of rank were exempt from working parties and held in their own stalag, called a luft.

9. The area, the Germans had the Prisoners of War working in, was a large one and was fenced off.

10. The RAF is the Royal Air Force, which, prior to the war, ruled the skies above the Mediterranean. Since the arrival of the Luftwaffe, it has been decimated to less than half a dozen planes.

11. All names used throughout the book are real but the activities and discussions are fictitious.

12. The olive trees have been growing on Crete for centuries and have thick, twisted trunks. They each produce about six litres of oil depending on seasonal conditions. Oil production is the main pursuit of Crete's farmers across the island. The project to plant grapevines, was to be modelled on the Champagne area of France. It was a sham to throw any inquisitive enemy off the track. Basically, it was a covert scheme to cover the building of an airfield.

13. Gaudion profile is found later in this book.

14. Mallee trees are found in the agricultural areas of Australia. They have adapted to the light rainfall and have massive roots that spread out to catch whatever water is available. They must be removed permanently before a crop can be planted.

15. Ball and chain clearing opened vast areas of farmland in Australia.

16. Baker's profile is in a later chapter.

17. Olive trees are very hardy and thick at the bole. The root system is serpentine and spreads for many yards due to the low rainfall where they are planted.

18. The POWs slowly realised that they were complicit in wrecking the livelihood of every Tymbakion olive oil farmer and family. This, in turn, split families and left people scattered throughout Crete.

19. Chandler, Manoy and Magee were sappers and their profiles can be found later in the book. Although there was no proof of their being in the planning group with the chief Greek engineer, it is highly likely that this happened. The project was too big and covered a wide area for one man to supervise.

20. The removal of vegetation leaves an area vulnerable to erosion of all types. At Tymbakion, it was the sudden rushing of water from the mountains that washed down as flash floods.

21. The bonfire was built of the tree pieces cut down over the week and fired up on Saturday. It was a sense of achievement for the POWs as they first missed what they were doing to the local population.

22. Slowly, the POWs came to the realisation and guilt that they were wrecking the Cretan's livelihood.

23. The Tympaki people created a ritual to show their disgust at what was happening to their farms and town.

24. Vic Petersen kept a close watch on important dates in the barracks' calendar.

25. Arthur Stubbs worked with Vic Petersen on the day. A profile is found later in the book.

26. Another peaceful idea to hold up the workings. Jam the axe in tight and spend time trying to extricate it.

27. The imagination can play tricks, especially under stress.

28. Migraines, for those suffering from them, can be quite debilitating.

29. Vic believes there is a boy passing food through the wire to the POWs.

30. Hunger was a constant and the little food offered was not nutritious.

31. Petersen, C.A.G.V *Diary* noted that the Cretans were hiding food in holes. This was a clever and lifesaving idea.

32. The food parcels were placed in holes near the ungrubbed olive trees. This ensured that the prisoners found the package left by the Cretans.

33. A ten-year-old Cretan boy understood the situation the Allied prisoners of war were facing in terms of starvation and friendship. He also knew the consequences of assisting the enemy of the Germans, yet he stood tall to help.

34. The Orange Boy is a true story. The youngster did exist, and he did throw oranges over the fence. The title 'Orange Boy' came from the author's imagination. It is based on a true story related by the Cretan boy to friends in 2011. The gentleman was 95 in 2011.

35. Cutting down and burning the tree parts was not just physical. The Allies realised they were killing the soul of every Cretan. They were taking away their farms, families, livelihood and products and leaving them with nothing.

36. Petersen, C.A.G.V *Diary*. The priests brought food to the prisoners as part of a celebration of a religious day.

37. Petersen, C.A.G.V *Diary*.

38. Stockholm syndrome, whereby the captives develop positive feelings towards their prisoners over time.

39. Any excuse was offered by the Cretan priests to bring food to the prisoners. Vic Petersen Diary September 29, 1941.

40. Priests brought lots of food to the POW camp related to special church celebrations.

41. It wasn't evident to the prisoners but the Germans knew there was a relationship between Tymbakion and Iraklion. Iraklion was the main headquarters for the two areas, as Tymbakion was more of an outpost. Vital supplies and medical facilities were maintained at Iraklion and sent on at request. Communication with an isolated camp and Berlin would need an efficient system, and only Iraklion would have this available. Iraklion would have a garrison for troops to move to Tymbakion upon call.

Chapter 19

1. The mental damage to the Cretans who were disenfranchised from their farms and thus the damage to their way of life, was inestimable.

2. Malaria is a debilitating disease caused by the bite of an Anopheles mosquito. Once bitten, the victim will have malaria symptoms for the rest of their lives.

3. Meat is valuable source of protein which is vital for humans to grow and develop. It also contains nutrients the body needs, such as, iodine, iron, zinc and vitamin B12.

4. Altruistic describes the Cretan people aptly. It means showing a selfless concern for the well-being of others, unselfish.

5. Slave labour was the first thought of Bonnie Buirchell as he lay watching the men at work grubbing out the olive groves.

6. Stragglers were few and far between on Crete by September 1941. There were several rescues that moved dozens of POWs off the island. See ergo.slv.viv.gov.au *Australians Who Escaped from Crete, Trove, The Advertiser, Adelaide,* June 18, 1941, *"Daring Rescue from Crete".*

7. Malaria was rife through the Middle East Greece and Crete. It was finally eradicated from Greece in 1974 through an intensive control program (1946 to 1960). It was highly likely all soldiers would get this disease.

8. September to November is autumn in the Northern Hemisphere and the start of the cold days.

9. Without a shadow to keep the searing sun from causing dehydration and heat stroke, Bonnie would most certainly have died. Autumn in Mediterranean climates can still produce extremely hot days that may be dangerous.

10. Bonnie was dry-mouthed, which placed him in danger of dehydration. It was a hot autumn's day, concussed and dehydrated. He was in danger of dying.

11. English was well known and used in Crete. The British were part of Crete before the Second World War and, in fact, built the Tymbakion Airfield in 1938.

12. The unthinking and jealous can do much harm. In a POW camp, there is too much at stake to be envious.

13. The leader of the RAF prisoners visits Captain Holt and must pass on important information. This in turn will help the POWs and the Cretans to cope with future problems.

14. Corporal Arthur Roland Richardson, 916557, from England, was one of the 12 Royal Air Force men who was at Tymbakion Transit Camp in September and October 1941. To enable the narrative to continue he has been given the position of team leader. He was a real member in the RAF.

15. The Royal Air Force POWs were already at the Tymbakion Transit Camp when the bulk of the others arrived. They were given the job of building the barbed wire fence.

16. The airfield was planned to be the biggest in the Balkans and was to dominate the entire region.

17. Reichsmarschall Hermann Goering was the planner of the Tymbakion airfield. He hired a Greek engineer and set in motion the work of having the POWs and Cretans clear the site, construct the runways, and secure it.

18. Hitler was too busy working on Barbarossa and defeating the Russians on the Eastern Front.

19. Using passive resistance, the Cretans hoped to stall the work on the Tymbakion Airfield. These protests did not contravene the Geneva Convention but did frustrate the Germans.

20. The prisoner of war numbers allocated to Tymbakion POWs on Kreta (Crete) were from 4501 (Captain Walter Holt) to 4607 (Roy Buchanan).

21. A dog tag had the name and number stamped on a metal tag. It was colloquially referred to as a "dog tag".

22. The amount of equipment needed to carry out a registration must have been brought in earlier than the June 1, 1941, capitulation.

23. The efficiency of the Germans would have ensured they could register thousands of POWs in a day.

24. The 'Man of Confidence' was a name given to the inmate of a camp who displayed leadership qualities and communication skills with their captors.

25. T for Tymbakion, I for Iraklion. Was an indicator of their place of registration.

26. The 12 Englishmen who had recently arrived had already been added to the register showing the efficiency of the Germans.

27. The number of prisoners who had been at Tymbakion from September 12, 1941, to this day was difficult to be accurately ascertained. The count that was accepted by the leadership team was 151.

28. Richard Lechmere was a UK soldier whose wife was able to communicate with him in Tymbakion during the latter part of 1941.

29. Private Norman Brown wrote a letter from Tymbakion, and somehow, without a postal system in place, it was delivered. The headline indicates that the evacuation of Crete was complete, meaning no POW was left. However, the group at Tymbakion was clearly still on Crete.

30. Trove, "Took to the Hills Instead of Submitting to the Enemy" letter from Private Norman Brown VX 31518, to parents, September 21, 1941.

31. Private Brown's letter suggested that the men still on Crete were stragglers. According to the letter, the men who should have capitulated were "stranded on the beaches preferring to take to the hills".

32. A second letter was received by Private Brown's wife. Trove, *"Long Delayed Letter from Missing Digger", Record, Emerald,* Victoria, December 31, 1941.

33. After his illness, William Buirchell, was taken under the wing of Captain Walter Holt. This shows Holt's compassion and kindness and why he was chosen as the 'Man of Confidence".

34. The link between Tymbakion and Iraklion was thought to be strong, but little evidence supports this assumption.

35. Bonnie Buirchell had a further legacy due to malaria he contracted in Crete. He would have dreams that were described by doctors as the 'terrors'. To stop him thrashing about, his wife would hold him down with all her strength. These lasted for many years.

36. The latrine was mentioned so that others knew its location, but also because it was a pit of disease, the men had to ensure they maintained a high level of hygiene after a visit.

37. Albert Chamberlain was a typical POW at Tymbakion. He was always hungry and exhausted, lacked nutritious food, and was losing weight.

38. The tailors were making clothes out of tent canvas. This happened at any spare time and when canvas was available. This was to give the former tailors something to cover their boredom and to have spare clothes for whoever might need them.

39. Albert's idea of making a pair of shorts and having the inmates sign it was a winning move and well-received.

40. Tymbakion was an isolated place, and except locals, very few visitors came near. It was a covert project that the Germans wanted to keep quiet until it was fully operational.

41. The priests were amazing in supporting the Allied POWs, finding ways to get into the camp, to bring food and to engage the men. All the while they looked after their local congregation.

42. The message on the belt of the pair of shorts was thoughtfully considered by Albert Chamberlain.

43. The system to obtain all the POW signatures was pure Albert Chamberlain. He was well organised and a problem solver. To visit tent after tent was efficient and inclusive.

Chapter 20

1. The current news from Vic Petersen was that Hitler had attacked the Russians on the Eastern Front and was winning. His problem began when the winters were extreme with temperatures plummeting well below zero, snow feet thick, which meant getting supplies through was extremely difficult. Mussolini lost his popularity in Italy and his own people turned on him. He was arrested and removed as Prime Minister before being executed.

2. Hope is the ingredient to keep those lost and incarcerated alive.

3. The priests and monks had led their parishioners from the front throughout the Crete War and on the side of the Allies. The supply of cooked bullock showed their belief in their God and in humanitarianism. Feeding the masses kept these people alive and strong.

4. The tent numbering is fictitious but was used to introduce all the men at Tymbakion.

5. Wood chopping was very popular, especially at country shows and drew big crowds. Bonnie Buirchell was one of the top four in Kojonup.

6. All men named are real and did serve as POWs at Tymbakion. As an example: Harry Christiansen was a New Zealand soldier. His Army number was 2059 and he was from Harewa, New Zealand.

7. The olive trees were old but nowhere near the oldest in the world. The Ano Vouves tree in Crete is the oldest on Earth being 2000 - 4000 years old. (approachguides.com).

8. When burning trees, the roots will smoulder underground for many days.

9. Fifteen tents, with 10 in each, equal 150 men. The extra man was in Tent 7.

10. With soldiers under such stress and worry a counsellor would have been required. This never happened so it is no wonder that these men arrived home in the mental state they did. Many were totally different men to the ones that loved ones said goodbye to as they sailed for the war zone.

11. The bridge constructed over the river was a team effort, with everyone joining in. The river was more like a stream, although it could be quite wide during heavy rain. The major issue the Germans seemed to ignore was the possibility of flash floods.

12. Fun time was always sought so when it was Melbourne Cup Day, the soldiers all joined in.

13. On November 11th the group had a shorter but more solemn ceremony to remember Armistice Day. This occurs on the eleventh hour of the eleventh month when the Treaty of Versailles was signed.

14. One would have expected many accidents because of the nature of the job and the tools used. This doesn't seem to have eventuated. Vic received a bad cut on his hand, which then festered and required hospitalisation. Although Tymbakion was in many ways tied to Iraklion, Vic was not transferred there for more treatment.

15. A volunteer force named the SOE, short for Special Operations Executive, was set up in Crete to wage a secret war. The SOE was started in June

1940 with agents such as Patrick Leigh Fermor, Chris Woodhouse and John Pendlebury tasked with activities against the Germans, such as sabotage and subversion behind enemy lines.

16. A reminder that all men in the story are real and the tents were not numbered in any physical way.

17. In November 1941, the work changed from grubbing out olive trees to moving earth and rocks. This was the start of the runway base, which was to be one foot deep.

Chapter 21 (No Notes needed for this chapter)

Chapter 22
1. The National Greek War Relief Association was founded by prominent Greek-American businessmen. In October 1940, the Greek Orthodox Church became involved in raising money to buy food and medicine for the population of Greece.

2. Petersen, C.A.G.V *Diary*. Wednesday, 3rd December 1941, Vic Petersen kept up with news on the site.

3. Captain Holt, like most officers, took the opportunity to keep any records that might come in handy once the war finished. The Nuremberg Trials proved that these records were essential.

4. The forthcoming census would allow the Germans to decide where to place the Tymbakion prisoners when they had to move them. This census is possibly a hint of the camp being shut down.

5. The news of the bombing of Hawaii came as a shock to the POWs. It showed the strength of the Japanese and their strategies, which were superior to those of the Americans at this time.

Chapter 23

1. Christmas was approaching, and there seemed to be an atmosphere of joviality. The priests and locals delivered food for a feast; Ron Pestell was keen to show his culinary expertise. The Christmas lunch was a one off feast that was appreciated by the prisoners. Coats were presented to each man, and alcohol flowed freely. It gave the impression that someone knew what the future held.

2. Christmas Day came, and everyone in the camp joined in. It was the only Christmas Day they had on Crete. The early start to festivities gave the impression that the group future was headed in a different direction.

3. Christmas was special for the Cretan people and they wanted to repay the kindness and sacrifices of the Allies. Petersen, C.A.G.V *Diary* describes the items the locals delivered to the camp. The religion in Crete was Greek Orthodox. As a show of solidarity with the Allies, the Greeks celebrated Christmas a week earlier than their Greek Orthodox Christmas. The Greek Orthodox Christmas Day is January 7th because the church uses the Julian Calendar, which is 13 days different from the modern Gregorian Calendar.

4. Albert Chamberlain certainly collected the shorts and packed them. What ritual, if any, he carried out is unknown.

5. There is an air of disappointment when the men are told to pack. They had been at Tymbakion for 104 days under the appalling working conditions, in isolation from the rest of the world. They had been unwittingly

destroying the lives of the Cretans, who were poorly fed and working like slaves. Now they were reluctant to pack and move.

6. The secrecy warning was issued twice to the men once by the enemy and again after the war was over by the Allies. Why was it considered so hush-hush?

7. The Cretans were warned that their families would be punished if they disregard the Secrecy Message.

8. What is the Long March? R J Burbidge *Long March* January 18, 1942, Straubing 11th May, 1945.

9. Lance Bombardier William Weatherall injured his ankle in an escape attempt. The attempted escape by Weatherall was told to his family.

Chapter 24

1. Petersen, C.A.G.V *Diary*. Private Weatherall had a badly sprained ankle and could not walk for the rest of the journey to Salonika.

2. Crete was finally liberated in 1945, but the damage done by the Germans, especially around Tympaki and the reprisal towns, left the population scattered and disoriented for many years.

BIBLIOGRAPHY

Beevor, Antony. *Crete The Battle and the Resistance*, John Murray Ltd, 1991. Penguin Books 1992.

Brune, Peter. *We Band of Brothers*, Allen and Unwin, 9 Atchison Street, St Leonards, NSW, 2000.

Burbidge, R J. *Long March January 18, 1942+ Straubing 11th May, 1945*

Chalkiadakis, Emmanuel III. *Tympaki*.

Clark, Alan. *The Fall of Crete*, Efstathiadis Group, Athens, 1981.

discovery.nationalarchives.gov.uk The National Archives, Kew, Richmond, online.

Donovan Corporal J. J. Donovan VX10677 2/2 Field Ambulance Ref. article in *Trove*

Ewer, Peter. *Forgotten Anzacs, the Campaign in Greece*, 1941. Scribe Publications, 18-20 Edward Street, Brunswick, Victoria, 3056, Australia.

Hill, Maria. *Diggers and Greeks*, A UNSW Press Book, 2010.

Jager, Charles. *Escape from Crete*, Floradale Productions Pty Ltd. Gary Allen Pty Ltd, 2004.

Johnson K.T. *The History of the 2/11th (City of Perth)*. John Burridge, Military Antiques, 91 Shenton Road, Swanbourne, 2000.

Le Souef, Leslie. *To War Without a Gun*, Artlook, the Western Australian arts magazine, Frank Daniels Pty Ltd, 1980

interactives.stuff.co.nz. In Honour of New Zealand's Surviving WWII Veterans, New Zealand Institute of professional photography.

(ref: Map 6: March-April 1941, showing existing and proposed lines of defence: Olson, Wes "Battalion into Battle" p100).

Monteath, Peter. *P.O.W., Australian Prisoners of War in Hitler's Reich*, Pan Macmillan, Australia, 2011.

Olson, Wes. *Battalion into Battle The History of the 2/11th Australian Infantry Battalion. 1939 – 1945*. Quality Press, 2011.

Olson, Wes "Battalion into Battle, ref: *Map 6: March-April 1941*, showing existing and proposed lines of defence p100.

Petersen, Charles Victor *Vic Petersen Diary 1941 – 1945*

Poppel Martin. *Heaven and Hell, The Diary of a German Paratrooper*. Spell Mount Publisher 2008.

Schubert, Fritz.

Taafe, Brian. *The Gatekeepers of Galatas*. Sabicas, Suite 2/171 Fitzroy Street, St Kilda, Australia.

Taylor, Bill. *Taylor Diary*. The Battle of Crete Memorial Committee of Western Australia, 2023.

Watt, M. R. (1996). *The Stunned and the Stymied: the P.O.W. experience in the history of the 2/11th Infantry Battalion*, 1939-1945 https://ro.edu.au/theses/966

Woods, Don (with Ken Scott). *Soldier, Prisoner, Hunter, Gatherer*, Fortis Publishing, 2021.

Interviews go to prisonersofwarcrete.com. Profiles of the following service people researched through relations:

- William Roy Buirchell (Anthony Buirchell, son), Dianella, Perth, West Australia.

- Ray E Powell (Greg Sampson and Ray's daughters)

- Alfred Traub (Sue Wilson, daughter and Peter Wilson), Perth, West Australia.

- Bernard Mitchell (Kristal Mallon, step-granddaughter)

- Vic Petersen (Sue Petersen, daughter-in-law and grandson Grant)

Internet Articles and Direct Interviews

Ancestors.familysearch.org Howard John Holmes (will need to create an account).

gallery.its.unimelb/edu.au. Search online for servicemen medical records.

historyguild.org The Battle of Greece – Australia's Textbook Rear-Guard Action.

prisonersofwarmuseum.com. Stalag VIIIB Lamsdorf.

uk.forceswarrecords.com.

discovery.national archives.gov.uk. The National Archives (United Kingdom). Search engine for service people in World War II

madeincrete.com. Crete During World War II: Battle of Crete.

nzetc.victoria.ac.nz. Prisoners of war Part II: The Crete Campaign.

Baker, Ralph. List of 2NZEF Prisoners of War. media.api.auckland museum.com.

25 Years Online Cenotaphauckland museum.com.

POWmemorialballarat.com.au. Ex-Prisoners of War Memorial. Online search engine

    awm.gov.au. Battle for Retimo.
    awm.gov.au. Captain Walter Gerald Holt.
    en.wikipedia.org, Massacre of Kondomari
    Commons.wikimedia.org/wiki/Category
    www.nzhistory.govt.nz
    vwma.org.au Virtual War Memorial Australia

Newspapers
Record Emerald, Victoria, December 31, 1941 https://trove.nla.gov.au/newspaper/article/164983007?search

    Term=Norman%20mcLeod%20Brown.

Trove.nla.gov.au

Donovan, Corporal J. J., Young Soldier's Vivid Description. *Benalla Ensign*. Friday December 5, 1941.

10 000 Armed Germans Still on Crete. *Townsville Daily Bulletin*, Thursday December 21, 1941.

Troops Rescued from Crete is Cleared of All Men in Hiding, *Adelaide Advertiser*, December 22, 1941.

Last Days in Crete, *Sunday Times*, Perth, August 3, 1941. (Description of paratroopers' fighting).

Allies Could have Won Battle of Crete, *Townsville Daily Bulletin*, May 9, 1946.

nzge.com. Operation Mercury: The Battle of Crete.

stuff.co.nz, A gunner's diary: Jim Quinn's battle on Crete,

General Questionnaire for British/American Ex-Prisoner of war

Red Cross Casualty section held in Melbourne University. awm.gov.au

German records for Allied prisoner of war. (2 pages)

Register of Prisoners of War from Kreta, February 26, 1942

INDEX

1642	28	25th April	84	
1788	38	18th May	56	
1854	37	**1941**	2 13 21 61	
1913			145	
27th August	113	February	47	
1914	38	March	50 82	
11th October	74	**April**	3 56 62 145	
1917		1st April	55 56 72 75	
28th August	60	6th April	63 78	
1918		10th April	63 83 121	
11th March	71	11th April	79	
1919		12th April	62	
17th May	56	14th April	79	
28th June	26	19th April	56 64	
1929-1935	27	21st April	64	
1936	43	25th April	84	
1937	31	26th April	68 117	
1938	247	30th April	88	
1939	2 75	**May**	89	
September	47	6th May	95	
November	113	15th May	98	
24th November	56	17th May	94 95 100	
December	47	19th May	94	
1940	49	20th May	100 102 105	
25th February	234		112 117 123	
March	114		126 250	
15th April	56	24th May	125	
20th April	114	27th May	118	

432

1941 cont.

29th May	127 128 131	10th August	170
31st May	131 141 250	20th August	73
June		25th August	170
1st June	7 16 23 52 125	27th August	170 171
	129 133 210	30th August	172
	241 251	31st August	172
2nd June	243	**September**	4 21 30 71
3rd June	129		119 251
4th June	121	3rd September	173
6th June	4 7 145 153	5th September	173
7th June	154	6th September	174
8th June	121 155	10th September	296
9th June	155	12th September	5 8 13 16 20 73
10th June	157 159		182 248 283
12th June	162	13th September	187
20th June	73	16th September	202
24th June	163	20th September	30 207
28th June	165	21st September	73 242
July		22nd September	209
12th July	73	23rd September	210
19th July	165	27th September	212
20th July	73 165	**October**	
21st July	165	1st October	220
22nd July	166	6th October	226 296
23rd July	166	9th October	226 227
24th July	167	11th October	296
26th July	168	12th October	245
27th July	168	14th October	245
August		15th October	254
1st August	169	18th October	254
3rd August	169	19th October	296
4th August	170	20th October	256
		26th October	259

1941 cont.			19th March	211
29th October	261		**1945**	
November			May	7 19 145
4th November	268		**1973**	19
5th November	267		**2018**	4
11th November	268		**2019**	5
15th November	16		**2020**	19
21st November	276			
25th November	279			
29th November	279			
December	23 290			
4th December	293			
5th December	294			
6th December	294			
7th December	294			
12th December	295			
14th December	294 295			
15th December	121 297			
18th December	242			
21st December	242			
24th December	298			
25th December	268			
28th December	300			
29th December	5 8 13 20 73 283			
31st December	4 73			
1942	3			
29th January	211			
30th January	73			
31st January	243			
15th February	4			

Australia

2/1st Field
Ambulance — 55

2/1st Infantry
Battalion — 64 69 76 97
106

2/1st Machine
Gun Battalion — 69

2/3rd Battalion,
16th Brigade — 100 113

2/4th Australian
Battalion — 97

2/5th General
Hospital — 139

2/7th Australian
Infantry Battalion — 56 68 69 79
100 118 130

2/7th Field
Ambulance — 55 66 67 111

2/8th Infantry
Battalion — 69 118

2/11th Battalion — 9 10 51 55 64
67 69 72 82-86
94 97 106 113
114-117 128
130 147 157
163 169 177

2/28th Battalion — 63
6th Division
Australian — 55 57

23rd Australian
Battalion — 118

City of Perth
Battalion — 113 114 157

Britain

1st Sherwood
Foresters,
Nottinghamshire
& Derbyshire — 10 74 185 264

7th Medium
Regiment — 96 97

14th Brigade
British — 96 97

106th Royal
Horse Artillery — 96

British Armoured
Brigade — 55

Northumberland
Hussars — 96

Argyll and
Sutherland
Highlanders — 94

1st Sherwood
Foresters,
Battalion — 185

Germany

1st Air Landing
Assault Regiment — 123

3rd German
Parachute
Regiment — 108

Germany cont.
3rd German Parachute Regiment 108 123 124
5th Mountain/ Gebirgs Division 103 126
7th Engineer Battalion 124
German Motorcycle Reg/ Detachment 125 152
Leibstandarte Hitler Division 116

Greece
4th Greek Battalion 97
5th Greek Battalions 97
8th Greek Regiment 124

New Zealand
1st N Z Supply Company 55 101
2nd Echelon 73
2nd N Z Expeditionary Force 14 35 47 61 101
5th N Z Infantry Battalion 130
18th N Z Battalion 101
19th Hawke's Bay Battalion 60 108
19th Infantry Battalion 61 92
21st N Z Battalion 101
26th N Z Battalion 126
28th Maori Battalion 28 71 118 126
28th N Z Battalion 118 126
29th N Z Battalion 101

U.S.A.
Pacific Fleet 295

42nd Street 71 118-120 122
Abbotsford,
Melbourne 277
Abergavenny,
England 267
Acropolis 58 78 115
Aircraft 295
Airfield 16 103 106 112
 118 228-231
 268 279 293
 297 301 305

Agia, Crete 129
AIF Casualty
Cards 11
Ainsley, John R 171 278 284
 307
Air Mail 77 273
Airborne Blitz 126 134
Airborne Invasion 22 94 96-98
 100 105 108 109
 124 222
Aitken, Charles 89 258 284 **308**
Albania 63 78
Albanians 50 54 83
Aldersey,
William 89 265 284 **308**
Alexandria,
Egypt 5 6 10 50 51
 55-57 61-63
 72-75 82 83 88
 91 94 115 121
 128 131 142

Alexandria,
Egypt cont. 151 186 230
 231 237
Aliakmon Line 63 64 78 92
Alikianos, Crete 124-125
Allen,
Brig Arthur 113
Allenton, NZ 281
Alliance 74
Allied
Forces/Troops 9 10 13 21 22
 26 50-52 56 62
 64-66 69 70 71
 74 78-82 87 88
 91-93 96 100
 105-112 116
 117 120 122
 125 128-129
 130-133 135
 137 139 140-
 143 150 153
 157 163 164
 176 209 222
 234 241 249-
 252 266 283
 293 296 302
Allied Troop
Ship 128 140-142
Alpine Troops 280
American Army 295 302
Andrew 1 5 7-9 17-23
Anopheles
Mosquito 222 246

437

Anti-aircraft Bunkers	231	**Australians** cont.	119 127 131 134 165 170 189 213 247 254-255 262 280 296
Anti-aircraft Weapons	96	**Australian** Army	101
ANZACs/Day	18 26 56 82 84 130 131	**Australian** Commandos	141 142
Anzac Line	79	**Australian** Farmer	265
Arcadia (ship)	141	**Australian** Flag	38
Armistice Day	268	**Australian** Football League (**AFL**)	27 38 44 221
Armitage, Thomas Washer	166 258 284 **309**	**Australian** Imperial/ Infantry Force (AIF)	51 56
Armstrong, Leslie	89 90 258 284 **309**	**Australian** War Memorial	11
Army Engineers	294	**Austrian** Elite Paratroopers	103 137
Arroll, Herbert	195 281 284 **310**	**Austrian** Trained Commandos	112 113
Athens, Greece	10 51 52 55 58 62 66-68 71 72 76-78 81-85 92-93 115 140 209 234 296	Axis	50 74 219
		Baker, Edward	198 261 262 263 281 284 **310**
Auckland, NZ	195 265 277 281	Balkans	229
Australia	4 6 11 26 27 38 55 74 159 166 173 257 269	**Ballarat**, Victoria	276
Australians	8 9 17 18 20 54 57 63 64 66 72 79 84 5 94 96 108 116 118	**Banks**, Joseph	38
		Banks, NSW	260

438

Banner, Ernest A	280 281 284 **311**	**Bentley,** Reginald	195 281 284 **314**
Barbarossa	55		
Barb Wire Fence	15 21 181 186 191 215 220 231 281 305	**Berlin,** Germany	126 93
		Bessell-Browne, Major Ian J	122
Bardia, Libya	50 82	**Bexley,** NSW	259
Barnes, Harry H	166 208 258 **284 311**	**Billings,** Adrian	215 281 284 **315**
Barrow, William	164 277 284 **312**	**Bissett,** Thomas A	215 259 284 **315**
Basic Training	56 74 113	**Black** Sea	302
Bathgate, Scotland	266	**Black** Watch	144
		Blamey, Lt Gen. Sir Thomas	113
"Battalion into Battle" by W Olson (book)	10 106 111 121	**Blechynden,** Ray	169 178 240
		Blitz	103 107 144
Battalion Records	83	Blitzkrieg/Day	54 117
Battersea, Eng	198 281	**Bolding,** Harold F	267 284 **315**
Battle of Crete	157 243 244		
Bayonet	71 88 119 136	Bomb/ Bombardier	104 144 303
Beacham, William	195 281 284 **312**	Bosphorus Strait	302
		Bowden, Kenneth Frank	164 277 284 **316**
Beaton, Malcolm	89 90 281 284 **313**	**Bowen,** George	215 279 284 **316**
Beau Vite	270	**Boxing Day**	299
Behind the Wire	2 10 142 143 153 223	Brallos Pass/ Bralos (Village)	64 79 84
Belgium	26 54	Bren Gun	68 81 107 109 189
Belmont, WA	281		
Bennison, Avery	171 281 284 **313**	**Bridgetown,** WA	113 202

Bristol, Reg D	195 279 284 317	**Buirchell**, Anthony	9 19 20
Britain	47 55 61 118	**Buirchell**, Bonnie (W R)	6 8 9 19-21 27 37-46 50 51 55 84 86 110 146 149 159-163 217-218 220-225 238-240 245-248 261-263 265 282 285 296 321
British Empire	26 38		
British Government	38 47 55 75		
British Navy	67 91 109 133		
British Ships	82 117 128 130		
British Soldiers	10 17 47 54 64 74 82 83 89 94 96-98 116 118 134 144 165 240 255 302		
Brodie, Charles William	215 277 284 317	**Buirchell**, Clem (nee Penny)	42-46 221
Brown, George R W	215 265 284 318	**Buirchell**, George	37
		Buirchell, Mick	38
Brown, Harold	214 215 267 284 **318**	Bully Beef	76 100 153 174
		Bunn, Alan H	90 277 285 **321**
Brown, Norman McLeod	242-244 265 284 **319**	**Bunyard**, Claud S	265 285 **322**
		Burne, J Thomas	195 277 285 **322**
Brownlie, Robert Bould	195 279 284 **319**	**Burns**, George	267 285 **323**
		Busby, Ponaute	28 71 119 265 285 **323**
Buchanan, Roy Douglas	262 277 284 **320**	**Campbell**, Col. Ian R	122
Buhagiar, Alf	214 277 285 **320**	Canisters	107 108 109 111 112

440

Cannock, Eng	258	**Chania**, Crete	88 97 107 110
Canowindra,			119 124 139
NSW	195		140 141 166
Canterbury, NZ	281		167 169 174
Capitulate/			234 283
Capitulation	52 129 133 138		
	157 210 222	**Chappell**,	
	241 250 251	Ronald John	164 267 285
			325
Ceylon/		**Cheshire**, Eng	265
Ceylonese	8 17 259	**Christchurch**,	
Carter, Edward	168 265 270	NZ	1 5 14 265 277
	271 285 **324**	**Christiansen**,	
Casualties	66 79 109	Harold A	262 266 285
	139		**326**
Casualty List	73	Christmas Day	282 298
Census	218 256 283	**Christmas Hills**,	
	291-295	Victoria	242 278
		Christmas,	
		Leonard	213 262 278
Chamberlain,			285 **326**
Pte A E (Bert)	7 14 17-21 24		
	27 28 30-36 50	**Churchill**, W	
	62 174 182	(British PM)	3 50 82 89 98
	192 206	Coastal Freighter	173
	248-252	**Cobridge**,	
	254-260	Stoke-on-Trent	266
	265-267	**Cochrane**,	
	274-276	Captain Archie	137
	278 280-282	**Collins**,	
	283 285 292	Andrew Walter	166 265 285
	293 300 **324**		**327**
Chandler, R	199 266 285	**Commonwealth**	
	325	Troops	55 64 79 84
			94 117

Connington, Eng 260 298
Constellations 156
Convict 37 38
Convoy 57 59 61 62 68
99 108
Coogee, NSW 277
Cook,
Captain James 28 38
Coombs,
Gordon Maxwell 195 258 285
327
Cooper,
Charles George 267 285 **328**
Cooper,
Hans John 164 267
271-274
285 **328**
Covid Lockdown 19
Craig,
James C (Jimmy) 15 18 213 258
285 296 **329**
Crawford, John 89 90 279 285
329
Creforce 88 107
Cretan 119 123-129
135 141 146
147 149 150
155 163-164
182 201 202
205-207 209
212 213 223
225-229
232-233

Cretan cont. 245-247 250
255-256
273-279
292 298 302
305
Cretan Farmers 198 201 203
211 220 223
Crete War 21 250 276
Cricket 27 38 44 170
173 221
Cunningham,
William 208 266 285
330
Daly,
Wynn Francis 266 285 **330**
Davenport,
Joseph 168 266 285
331
Davis, John R 266 271-273
285 **331**
Day, Raymond 207 208 215
258 285 **332**
Denniston, NZ 279
Depression 27 31
Deputy German
Chancellor 4 54
Desert
Exercise/Warfare **49 56** 74
Devonport,
Tasmania 56
Diarrhea 165

Diary	4 7-8 10 18 23	Endeavour	28 38
	28 109 145 147	Engineers	267 279 295
	155-157 166	**England**	37 85 185 302
	170 178 182	**English** Soldiers	18 63 75 165
	202 206-212		170
	242 245 254	Equator	50 156
	280 291 300	**Escape**/Escapers	145 163 304
Dikti Range	88	**Europe**	26 30 34 47 51
Doctor	9		58 75 94 99
Dog Tag	237	**Face**, Edward J S	165 277 285
Donkey	146 187 211		**334**
	225 228 247	**Ferryhill,**	
	278 305 306	Durham, Eng.	278
Donnybrook,		Field	
WA	277	Headquarters	51 65 127 250
Donovan,		**Fielding**, NZ	267
Corporal J. J.	10 57 58 75 76	**Firing** Squad	125 127 129
Dornier,			175
"Flying Pencil"	102 104 105	**Flannagan,**	
Dunedin, NZ	259 261 266	Sgt George	100 101
Dwen, Louis	239 259 285	Flash Flood	199 200
	332	**Floria**, Crete	129
Dysentery	140	**Flying** Boat	57 63 131
Dyson, Frank	215 260	**Foley,**	
	285 **333**	Zamoni J J	168 260 280
East, Edward	168 258 285		285 **334**
	333	**Forbes,**	
Eastern Front	55 232 276	Archibald Henry	215 258 286
Egypt	72 115 234		**335**
El Alamein,		**Forces War**	
Egypt	50	Records	11
Emerald,		**Fournes**, Crete	124
Victoria	242 243		

443

Foxon,		**German** Aircraft	99 106 200 280
Thomas V	168 277 286 **335**	**German** Army	64 65 76 116
		German Censors	244
France	19 38	**German** Codes	70 89 98
Frantzeskakis,		**German** Codes (other)	
Father Stylianos	125	**ULTRA** Codes	98 109
Fraser,		ULTRA	
Anthony A	215 258 286 **336**	Intelligence	89 105
		ULTRA Sources	105
Freeman,		**German**	
Clifford James	171 258 286 **336**	Commandant	10 159 167 192-95 214-216 230 247 255 267 274-276 291-297 300 302
Fremantle, WA	37		
French Warships	57		
Freyberg,			
General Bernard	70 88 89 94-95 96-98 110 117 120 127 129 131 133 135	**German** Commanders	96 112
Furlough	76	**German** Doctor	51 158 166
Galatas, Crete	237	**German** Fighters	152 172
Gallipoli		**German** Forces	63 75 92 112
Campaign	38	**German** Government	256
Gaudion,		**German**	
Eric J R	196 258 286 **337**	Headquarters	102 122 137
Gaza, Palestine	115	**German** High Command	63 193 268
General Questionnaire British/American Ex-POW	11	**German** Navy	108
		German Patrol	125 151 163 186 188 190 217 218 224 227 234 247
Georgioupoli,	97		

German
Reconnaissance
Aeroplane 91 102
German
Spotter Plane 100
German Tanks 69 145
German
War Machine 2 65 135
German-Italian
Axis 51
Germans 9 15-17 30 49
52-55 61-65
66-68 70 71
74-76 78-82
85 86 89 91
92-95 96
98-100 102 103
105-108 110-113
115-120 121-129
130 131 134-139
143 152-156
157 161 165
167 169 174
175 177-179
181 186-189
192 195-197
202 205 212
213-218 220
223 227-241
243 246 249
250 254-264
266 272-277

Germans cont. 279 280 283
291-295 301
302 305
Germany 2 15 26 51 52
58 61 75 82 95
97 123 135 173
175 210 211
231 241 275
280 300-305
Giles, Charles 166 258 286
337
Gisborne, NZ 60 277 278
Glenlossie 44
Gliders 52 99 103 104
106 107 109
Goering,
Gen Herman 127 230 279
297 301
Goodwin,
Edgar G 215 259 286
338
Gorey, Wessex,
Ireland 207 258
Gorton, John 214 259 286
338
Gosnells, WA 260
Grafton,
Auckland, NZ 259
Grapes/Vineyard 16 91 143 145
148 157 179
180 183 187
188 193 196
220

445

Great Britain	4 11	**Greta**, NSW	114
Greece	2-5 22 50-52	**Grey Lynn**,	
	54-58 61-63 68	Auckland, NZ	258 260
	72 74 75 78 81	**Greymouth**, NZ	164
	82-85 88 89-99	**Grimsby**, Eng	74
	102 103 117	**Grimsey**,	
	121 130 134	Cyril J G	168 258 280
	137 140 141		286 **339**
	222 257 281	Guards	141 154-162
Greece, Northern	3 21 54 56 62		167 171-179
	75 92 116		181 182 194
Greece, Southern	84 108 116		195-198 200
Greek			214-215 226
Archipelago	81		227 263 295-
Greek Army	54 92 116 117		297 300 304
Greek		**Gunther**,	
Government	50 55 56	W. W. (Bill)	133 134 135
Greek Isles	58 115	**Gusscott**,	
Greek Money		Louis Patrick	168 258 286
(Drachma)	146 202 263		**339**
Greek Relief		Haka	28 119
(National Greek		**Hamilton**, NZ	195 258
War Relief		**Hardie**,	
Association)	290 291	Pte Ian A (Jock)	8 71-73
Greek War	6 21 80 94		180-182
Greeks/Soldiers	8 17 54 76 79		185 189 257
	82 83 96 115		286 **340**
	122 163 164	**Hargest**,	
	168 207 216	Brig James	61 64
	234 255	**Harman**,	
	296	Geoffrey B	168 267 286
Grenades	90 112		**340**

Harrington,		**Hitler,** Adolph	35 47 50 54 55
Stanley R	215 261 286		63 99 193 232
	341	HMAS **Defender**	68 69
Harrogate, Eng	265 270	HMAS **Perth**	83
Hastie,		HMAS **Vendetta**	84
Alexander B	213 260 286	HMAS	
	341	**Waterhen**	84
Hastings, NZ	277	HMHS **Nevasa**	114
Hauraki, NZ	281	HMS **Ajax**	84
Hawera,		HMS **Coventry**	84
Taranaki, NZ	258 262	HMS **Glengyle**	71 84 94
Hawke Bay's,		HMS **Hasty**	84 85
New Zealand	60	HMS **Hereward**	68 69
Heenan,		HMS **Kimberley**	84 93
Colin William	164 267 286	HMS **Ramilies**	114
	342	Royal **Sovereign**	
Heinkels	104 105	Class **Battleship**	
Hemispheres	156 279	HMS **Wryneck**	84
Heraklion, Crete	15 89 91 94 95	**Hodson,**	
	96 99 100 112	Herbert Joseph	214 261 86
	118 144 153		**343**
	155 234 300	**Holborn,** Eng	267
Herbert,		Holidays/	
Cyril M	215 258 286	Holy Days	212 279
	342	**Holland**	38
Hewett,		**Holmes,**	
Arthur Albert	171 199 258	Pte Howard J	
	286 **343**	(Slim)	18 28 60-62
Hill 107	108 117		91-93 206 277
Hill A	95 110		286 293 **344**
Hill B	95 105		
Hill C	95		
Hill D	95		

Holt,
Capt Walter G   9 139 174-178
                   180-182 184
                   185 187-195
                   199 206 214
                   216 227 229-
                   240 245-248
                   256 259 260
                   271-275 276
                   281 282 283
                   286 291-297
                   301 302 304
                   344
Honner,
Major Ralph   143 145
Hornby,
Canterbury, NZ   267
Horsham,
Wimmera, Vic   260
Hospital   66 **88**
Hospital Ships   63
Hosti, Chania 124
Howard, Ken   270
Howes, George
Richard   195 260 **286**
                   345
Howick, NZ   258
Howie, Frank F 214 277 286
                   345
Hurren,
Frederick Henry   215 266 286
                   346
Ida Range, Crete 88

Idecca, Crete   154
Ilford,
Essex, Eng   259 267 279
Imballion, Crete   146 148
India   74
Infantile
Paralysis   159 170
Interpreter   123
Invasion Day   123
**Invasion of
Crete**   6 71 105 250
Iraklion, Crete   15 157 172-179
                           180 210 218
                           219 231
                           239-241 246
                           271-275 283
                           293 294 296
Iran   75 230 232 293
Italian Army   54 116
Italians   51 54 63 74 82
                           83 116 117 254
Jackson,
Alexander Peter   270 277 286
                           346
Japan   295
Johnson,
Deborah   20
Johnson, Henry   215 279 286
                           347
Johnstone,
Robert A   165 278 286
                           347

448

Jones, Frederick	260 286 **348**	**Kozani**, Greece	79
Junkers	99 104 105 107	**Kreta** POW Dog	
	108 109 111	Tags	20 237
	140 141 228	**Kyrtomados**,	
Kakopetria,		Crete	129
Crete	129	**Lake Ayi**	124
Kalamata,		**Lakkoi**, Crete	124
Greece	117	**Lamia**	79
Kalyves, Crete	141	**Lamsdorf**	
Kandanos, Crete	125 129	POW List	18 211 296
Kantara,		**Lancashire**, Eng	277
Palestine	56	**Larissa**, Greece	79
Karanos, Crete	124	**Lassithi**, Crete	88
Karori,		Latrine	247
Wellington, NZ	202 279	**Lawrence**,	
Katanning, WA	44 45	Arthur	15 18 296
Kensington, Eng	265	**Le Souef**,	
Keritis River	124	Lt Col Leslie	9 10 53 55 66
King, Andrew	215 278 286		67 98 133-141
	348		192 209 210
Kirk, James	164 277 286		240 241
	349	**Lechmere**,	
Klidi Pass	79	Richard James	15 171 242 267
Kojonup, WA	8 37 42-46 163		287 **350**
	222 239 261	**Leichhart**, NSW	173
Kollias		**Leviston**,	
Anastasios	164 215 257	Aubrey Reginald	171 278 287
	284 **349**		**350**
Komitades, Crete	137	**Libya**	254 280 293
Kondomari,		**Lilydale**,	
Crete	123 129	Victoria	258
Konledes,	139	**Linwood**, NZ	277

Livadero, Greece	64	**Maleme** Airfield Cont.	117-119 123 124 140 160 169
Log Chopping	6 248 261		
London, England	198 257 258		
Long March	19 301	Mallee	196 265
Luftwaffe	79 86 94 97 102 105 128 138 142 144 172 228 230	**Mallon**, Kristal	10
		Man of Confidence	9 238 245
		Manaia, NZ	258
Lumsden, NZ	258	**Manawatu**, NZ	265
Lustre Force	2 3 5 51 54 55 61 63 64 70 72 82 84 118	**Manly**, NSW	260
		Manoy, Philip H	199 260 287 **352**
Luxembourg	54	**Philoxenia**	255
Lythgoe, Frederick	214 278 287 **351**	**Maori**	28 118 119 136
		Marble Bar, WA	43
M(MacKay) Force	79	**Marrickville**, NSW	267
		Marsa Mutruh, Egypt	50
Macedonia	63		
Machine Guns	81 137 109 150	**Massara Bay**	144
Magee, John J	164 199 258 287 **351**	**Matthews**, Albert	214 260 287 **352**
Mail	77 273		
Malaria	222 224 240 246-247	**Maxwell**, Lt Col Duncan	113
Malaxa Escarpment	118	**McDonald**, Leonard E	213 278 287 **353**
Maleme, Crete	99 107 108 110 112 131 139	**McInerney**, John P	247 257 287 **353**
Maleme Airfield	89 91 93 95 97 100 108 112 113		

McKain, Frederick J D	171 277 287 **354**	**Middle East**	47 49 51 55 56 72 114 221 228 230 280 293
McLean, Alexander	164 267 287 **354**	Migraine	204
		Miller, John W	267 280 287 **355**
McNab, Major	146 150 151 153 159 186	**Mitchell**, Pte Bernard	10 74-76 178 185 191 192 194 206 216 257 287 **355**
McRobbie, Lt Art	146		
Mediterranean Sea	11 21 51 56-58 68 75 86 87 91 94 102 103 115 124 134 135 142 148 173 185 200 214 230 280 295 302 304	**Molloy**, John Joseph	257 262 287 **356**
		Monastir Pass/Gap	64 74 79
		Morshead, Brig Lesley	113
		Morse Code	51
Meekatharra (Meeka), WA	72	Mortar Bombs	108 109
		Mosquito	222 246
Megara Beach, Greece	84 293	**Moss**, John	172 261 267 287 **356**
Melbourne Cup	268-270	Motorcycle	125 152
Melbourne University Lists	11 73	**Motorised** Landing Craft (**MLC**)	94 144 151 186
Melbourne, Victoria	195 269 279		
		Motupikee, NZ	260
Menzies, Robert; Australian Prime Minister	56	**Motupiku**, NZ	260
		Motvera, NZ	260
Messerschmitts	105		

Mount Olympus	59 66 69 76 79 83 84 91 115 116	**New Zealand** Commandos	128 141 142
Mrs Brown	242-245	**New Zealander**	7 8 17 28 47-50 54 61-64 66 71
Murchison Chronicle	72		79-81 84-86 91-93 94 96 97 101 108
Murderers' Bay, New Zealand	28		116 118 119 127 130 134 136 161
Murdoch, Colin	239 260 280 287 **357**		187 196 202 255 280
Mussolini, Benito, Prime Minister of Italy	74 254	**Non-Military** Weapons **Norburg** (Ship)	10 124 126 173-178 210 296
Nauflion, Greece	117		
Nazi High Command	127	**North Africa**	30 47-51 56 61 74 82 83 115 222 230 232
Nazis/Nazism	30 47 69 254		280 293
Nea Roumata, Crete	124	**North Island,** NZ **Northam**	27 28 202
Neale, Roy Errol	278 280 287 **357**	Training Camp **Norway**	51 71 83 113 266
Neo Chorio, Crete	97	**Nottingham,** Eng **Nuttall,** James	261 265 262 277 280 287 **358**
New South Wales	9 165 258	**O'Grady,**	
New Zealand	1-8 14-21 26-28 195 247 257-260	James Clyde Odesa, USSR	251 252 256- 257 287 **358** 302
New Zealand Battalion	71	**Olive** Oil	95 147 164 184 213 298

Olive Trees 2-6 16 71 91
 182 184-189
 193-198
 201 203-209
 215 221 223
 228 229 245
 261 263 275
 290 298 304
 305
Operation
Barbarossa 98
Operation Lustre 82
Mercury
(Plan Merkur) 99
Orange Boy 208
Oranges 208 209
 220 270 299
Orthouni,
Chania 124
Osborn, James J 215 267 287
 359
POW
Repatriation
Forms 11
Paddington,
Sydney, NSW 9 180 195 260
Paleokhoria,
Crete 125
Palestine 49 56 74 115
Palmer,
Thomas G W 271 273 277
 287 **359**

Panzer Tanks 116
Parachutes/
Parachutists 104-112 125
Paratroopers/
Fallschirmjager 52 71 73 87 99
 103 104
 107-112
 122-124 126
 222 235
Pauley, William 86 146 147 152
 159
Payne
Sydney R (Syd) 215 277 287
 360
Peak Hill, WA 71 180
Pearce,
Sydney Emden 171 277 287
 360
Pearl Harbor,
Hawaii 295
Pecco Planes 212
Pedersen,
Walter Vernon
(Wally) 159 188-193
 238 263-264
 278 287 **361**
Perivolia, Crete 95 111 123 126
Perivolia River 95 250
Perth, WA 19 20 72 113
 114 164 260
Pestell Roland G 260 287 298
 362

Petersen,
C A G Victor
(Vic) 4 7 10 15 16 18
55 86 110 113
114 115-117
143 145-148
153-156
157-158 159
163 164-170
172-175
176-178 181
182 185-190
193 196 197
202-205
207-211 212
217 238 242
245 254-256
258-261 266
269-273 280
287 291 293
295 296 297
300 **361**

Petrou, Ioannis 164 281 287
362

Phillip,
Capt Arthur 38
Pike, Leslie 239 257 287
363
Piraeus, Greece 55 58 62 75-76
92

Platanias, Crete 123
Pooley, Albert E 267 287 **363**
Port Pireaus,
Greece 58 62 66
Powell, Noumea 56
Powell, Pte Ray
Edward 9 56-58 62 66
68 69 76 77
189 197 198
206 258 260
274 287 **364**
Prases, Chania 124
Prichard, Jack 215 267 288
364
Prison Camp 161 216 223
Prison
Valley/Road 110 124
Prisoner Of War
(POW) 2-8 15 18 22 30
52 53 73 121
133 140 142
155 164 167
168 170 172
176-181 187
190 194 199
201 202 205
208-212 216
218 226 230
236 242 243
249 266 276
279 283 294
295 297 298

Protein
Deficiency 141
Puckapunyal,
Victoria 56
Pukepoto,
Kaitaia, NZ 265
Pullenayagam,
Joseph P 259 260 288 **365**
Puttick,
Brig Edward 96
Pyatt, Ernest 90 257 288 **365**
Queensland 262
Rabbit Trapper 38
Rainford,
Douglas 165 258 288 **366**
Randolph, Edgar 111
Randwick, NSW 258 275
Rattenbury,
John Alfred 173 174 178 260 288 **366**
Rearguard 66 67 81 84 127 128 131 136 141
Record
(Newspaper) 242 243
Recruitment
Office/Officer 47 75
Red Cross/Cards 11 73 242 291
Redfern, NSW 258

Reefton, NZ 277
Rees,
Edward (Ted) 89 90 187 188 260 288 **367**
Register Book 236-239 301
Reich 52 53 99
Reprisals 22 125-129 141 150 174 229
Researcher 1 4 6 10 14 20 73
Rethymno 96 97 99 107 112 131
Rethymno
Airfield 89 91 97 100
Retimo, Crete 95 105 118 154 157 159-161 163 168 238
Retimo Hospital 158 159 163
Retimo Sector 95 112 122
Riccarton, NZ 266
Rice, Frederick J 215 265 288 **367**
Richardson,
Cpl Arthur R 227-234 236
Richmond, Vic 260 264
Rifle, 3.03mm 48 119 125 190
Ring, Cyril J 265 288 **368**
Ringel,
General Julius 126
Roberts, G A 166 279 288 **368**
Rogers, John 258 288 **369**

Rommel,		Sandflies,	49
General Erwin	47 49	**Sandover,**	
Rouseabout	42	Major Raymond	106 107 111
Rowing Boat	90 93 151 152		143-150 238
Royal Airforce			241
(RAF)	97 172 191	**Savige,** Brig S	113
	193 227 228	**Scanlon,** Edward	260 288 **369**
	231 233 235	Schooner	43 44
	241 281 296	**Scramble** Nets	67 117
Royal Artillery	262	Seaward	
Royal Engineers	101 199	Invasion	70 87 91
Royal Marines	93	**Sectors**	95 97
Royal Navy	52 62 80 108	**Servia,** Crete	64 80
	109 117 127	**Seven Hills**	58
	144 233	**Sfakia,** Crete	10 21 125 127
			127-131
Royal Navy			133-135
Vessels	80 81 85 130		137-139 141
RSL			142 143 234
(Return Soldiers			237 238 243
League)	26	**Shaw,** Ernest	279 280 288
Run for the Hills	137 145 238		**370**
Russia/Russian	55 99 232 254	**Shear**er, Gun/	27 38 39-43 45
	255 276 302	Shearing	39 45 222
Rutherford,		**Sherriff,** Harold	215 277 288
NSW	114		**370**
Ryan, Capt		**Shirley,** Stanley	215 259 288
James J (Doctor)	146		**371**
Sahara Desert	50	**Shorts**	4-10 13-25
Salonika, Greece	6 52 175 192		30-31 53 74
	231 241 301		145 248-253
Salonika Prison	135		256-259 265-
Salonika, Gulf of	92		267 275 280
			293 300

Shufti Plane	102	SS **Costa Rica**	9 68 69 84
Signals/man	8 51 84 131	SS **Thurland**	
Signatures	7 14-23 249	**Castle**	69 84 86
	257-260 265-	**SS** Troops	116
	267 275-282	**Staffordshire**,	
	293 300	Britain	258
Singleton, Jack	172 270 277	**Stalag**	6 22 52 135
	288 **371**		175 210 301
Skines, Crete	124 139	**Stalag** VIIIB	7 14 18-19 121
Skinner, John E	166 261 265		145 211 307
	288 **372**	**Stavromenos**,	
Skipton (horse)	270	Crete	95 105
Skirt the Dags	42	**Stirling**,	
Smith, Loris R	215 267 288	Leslie Douglas	215 266 288
	372		**373**
Snake	158 159 163	**Stockholm**	
Somerset, Eng	257	**Syndrome**	213
Son Of Auros	270	Stragglers	59 153 223
Souda (Suda)		**Stratton**,	
Bay	9 15 18 69 73	Pte Herbert E	55 110 149 159
	89 93 95 99		215 281
	100 108 118		288 **373**
	119 141 157	**Stubbs**, Arthur	202-206 279
	168 173-175		288 **374**
	191 209 210	**Stuckey**,	
South Island, NZ	27 28 61	John Edward	165 258 288
South			**374**
Melbourne, Vic	188 243-244	**Student**,	
Southern Cross	38 156	General Kurt	99 103-104 126
Soviet Divisions	255		127
Squadron		**Stukas**	64 65 68 79 84
A M E S 25	234		86 92 104 105
			116

Stunned and the Stymied (The), **by** Molly Watt	10 134	Tents/Canvas	7 13 16-20 76 170 181 184 248 251
Sturm, German Force Commander, Colonel Alfred	110	**Thermopylae,** Greece **Thermopylae** Passes	80 64
Submarine	57 176 177	**Thompson,**	
Submarine Chaser	176	James	165 260 288 **375**
Suez Canal	74 115 230	**To War Without**	
Surrender	2 21 109 133 134-138 143 153 154 234	**a Gun** by Leslie Le Souef	10 55 98 133
Sydney, NSW	38	**Tobruk**, Libya	50 82
Tailor	14 17 19 20 27 31 74 249	**Todd**, Arthur S	166 267 288 **376**
Taranaki Company	108	Tommy Guns **Toodyay**, WA	189 277
Tasman, Abel	28	**Topia**, William	166 267 288
Tatton, John Thomas	213 258 264 288 **375**	**Train** **Trans** Australia-	**376** 210
Taylor, Pte William (Bill)	10 86 109 110 145 146-148 159-161 162	Crete-England- New Zealand Research Project **Transit** Camp **Traub**, Alfred	18 166 167 193
Tents (1-15)	257 258 259 260 264-267 277 278 279 281	(Alf)	9 10 53 55 82 83 85 86 110 121-123 130-132 192 240

458

Treaty of
Versailles 26
Tregear, Eric 215 279 288
 377
Trenches 78 83 229
Trove 10 73
Truce 137
Truck Convoy 76-79 15 305
Turkey 26
Turkish Army 38
Two-up 269
Tymbakion 2 4-10 15-18 20
 30 53 71 73
 145 159 187-
 190 192 209-
 211 218 219
 238-242 244
 245 249 251
 256-257 269
 271 273 275
 280 281 283
 290-296 300
 301 302 303

Tymbakion
Airfield 16 241 244 280
 290 291 301

Tymbakion
Transit Camp V 2 4 7 9 15-17
 187 191 193
 218 227 235
 242-249 251
 270 276 283
 291 307

Tymbakionites 281
Tympaki, Crete 2 3 4 22 94 201
 213 228 232
 233 251 255
 274 277 279
 291 292 297
 301 302 305

Tympaki
Airfield 250
Tympaki Martyr
Villages 4 306
Tyrer, Eric 172 251 256-
 257 288 **377**

U.S.A.R. 380-5 5
UK National
Archives, Kew 11
Ultra Codes 109
Ultra Intelligence 70 89
Ultra Sources 89 98
United Kingdom 51 56 75 258
University of
Melbourne 11 73
USA 295
Vasey,
Major General
George Alan 96 97
Vatolakos, Crete 124
Veevers, Ralph 172 278 288
 378
Vermion-
Olympus Line 64
Vevi, Greece 63 79

459

Victoria, Australia	165 265	**Wellington,** NZ	164 195 258 260 277 279
Virtual War Memorial	11	**Werrimull,** Vic	279
Vitamins	141	**West,** Leonard G	172 258 289 **380**
Volunteer Defence Corps	100	**Western Australia** (WA)	7 19 39 196
Waipukurau, NZ	260	**Western Australian Weston,**	37 110 113
Waitara, NZ	275		
Wakefield, Miss D	73	Major General E	94 133
Walker, David	172 265 270 288 **378**	**Westown,** NZ	258
		Westport, NZ	19 249 258
Walker, Lt Col Theodore G	136 137	**Whatling,** Clive Joy	166 265 289 **381**
Walters, Frank	215 267 288 **379**	**Whitcombe,** John Douglas	172 279 289 **381**
Warburton, Harold	166 259 289 **379**	**White Mountains**	88 128 162
Warships	67 93 116 127 128	**Wild,** Lt Gerry	106
Washer, Thomas	247	**Williams,** Lou	85
Watt, Molly	10 134	**Wilson,** Gen Henry M	94
Wavell, Gen Archibald	54	**Wimbledon,** Eng	258
Weatherall, William	258 289 303 304 **380**	**Wine**	147 148 177 182 298 299
Wellington, NSW	278	**Wonthaggi,** Vic	267

Woodanilling, WA	265
Woods, Laurence S	164 260 289 **382**
Wool Classer	41
Woolwich, Eng	266
Work Party	159 167
World War I	26 230 268
World War II	2 13 17 19 26 38 47 113 117
World War II Liberated POW Questionnaires	6
Wynn, Thomas	215 266 281 289 **382**
X Battalion	101
Yalgoo Observer	72
Yarmouth, Eng	278
York, Eng	261
Yugoslavia	63 78 92 116

ABBREVIATIONS

AAMC	Australian Army Medical Centre	HQ	Head Quarters
		I	Iraklion
AGH	Australian General Hospital	ISBN	International Standard Book Number
AIF	Australian Imperial Force		
		Lancs	Lancashire
AKA	Also Known As	LCM	Landing Craft, Mechanised
ANZAC	Australian and New Zealand Army Corps		
		MT	Motor Transport
Aust	Australia	NAA	National Archives of Australia
AWM	Australian War Memorial		
		NCO	Non commissioned officer
BEF	British Expeditionary Force		
		NI	No Information
Brig	Brigadier	NX	Soldier's state eg VX Victoria
Aust	Australia		
C	Chania	NZEF	New Zealand Expeditionary Force
Capt	Captain		
CCh	Christchurch (New Zealand)	Pte	Private
		RAF	Royal Air Force
CO	Commanding Officer	RASC	Royal Army Service Corps
Cpl	Corporal		
Detn	Detention	Res	Reserve
Div	Division	RMO	Regimental Medical Officer
Fd	Field		
For.	Force	Spr	Sapper
HAA	Heavy Anti-Aircraft	T	Tymbakion
HMAS	His Majesty's Aust Ship	Vic	Victoria
		WO	Warrant Officer

NB: Bralos is a village in Greece and Brallos is a mountain pass in Greece.

462

ABOUT THE AUTHOR

Anthony William Buirchell has always had a passion for writing and researching. He has been a teacher and a School Principal for 45 years. It was three years teaching in a Pre-Primary Unit that he began making up rhymes and emphasise phonics in teaching reading. He went on to write several children's books based on his character Cric Croc.

His partner, Deb Johnson offered him a challenge to find out about her father's background and her family's ancestry. This led to trips to Victoria, New South Wales and Queensland. The latter became the main target area.

Anthony maintained an ever expanding Johnson family tree, and wrote a book about the family ancestors (*The Restless Danish Immigrants*) who came to Australia in 1856 to settle in Daylesford before trekking north to Queensland. He wrote three books in the trilogy *Destiny in Disguise*:

(*Destination Daintree,
Daintree Reflections and
Daintree and Beyond*)

which covered the three generations from 1856 to 1959.

Anthony knew his father was a signaller in the 2/11th Battalion and served three and a half years in Stalag VIIIB. When he was out of the blue contacted by a New Zealand researcher he was shocked to discover his father was a hero. He had been in the Greece War, Crete War and spent over three months alone but free on Crete while the Germans hunted him. The research that resulted helped Anthony to find out about the last 151 POWs to be on Crete. From the research he wrote *Spirited Away* his latest historical fiction novel. It has been five years in the writing and researching.